I0846610

The Corpse War
of 1793

A Soldier's Account

Published by The Native Oak, LLC. 2025.

www.nativeoak.org

ISBNs

Paperback: 979-8-9910130-4-8

eBook: 979-8-9910130-6-2

Copyright ©2025 The Native Oak, LLC

Text by Brandon Fisichella.

Original artwork by Kyle Dunn, commissioned for this book.

All rights in the text and artwork owned by The Native Oak, LLC.

All rights reserved. No part of this publication may be reproduced, stored in a retrieval system, or transmitted, in any form, or by any means, electronic, mechanical, photocopying, recording, or otherwise, without the express written consent of The Native Oak, LLC, except for brief quotations in critical review and certain other noncommercial uses permitted by copyright law. For such permissions please contact us by visiting www.nativeoak.org.

This is a work of fiction. Any similarity to real persons, living or dead, is coincidental and not intended by the author.

About *The Native Oak*

The Native Oak promotes the study and appreciation of history by publishing accessible and engaging historical content. We believe that history both defines our past, and drives our future.

In furtherance of our educational mission, we donate ten percent of all our profits to museums, historic properties, reenactment societies, veterans' causes, and other charitable organisations.

For more information, and to learn how you can get involved, visit us at www.nativeoak.org.

For Sarah

Ever loving,
and ever patient
of all my silly schemes.

While *The Corpse War* is thankfully a work of fiction, its characters and events draw inspiration from the recorded experiences of real historical soldiers.

If you wish to learn more about the era in which this story is set, the following real memoirs of British soldiers are excellent starting points:

Adventures of a Soldier
by Edward Costello

A Journal of Occurrences during the Late American War
by Roger Lamb

Journal of a Soldier of the 71st Regiment of Foot
by John Howell

Journal of the Waterloo Campaign
by Cavalie' Mercer

The Recollections of Rifleman Harris
by Benjamin Harris

The Life and Travels of John Robert Shaw
by John Robert Shaw

The Subaltern
by George Robert Gleig

These and many other historical texts are available free of charge via the digital library at www.nativeoak.org.

Contents

Title - 1

Part the...   ...wherein

The Great Battle of Stowlham.

The Melancholic

WAR *of* CORPSES

containing a

COMPLEAT & AUTHENTICK account

of the

Defolation of Stowlham

and the

GREAT BATTLE

between the

LIVING *and the* DEAD

mors et fugacem

perfequitur virum

LONDON:
S. KLEMMER, 24 MARCH STREET, STRATFORD.
MDCCXCIV.

An Explanation of the Several Parts of the
Short Land Pattern Mufket

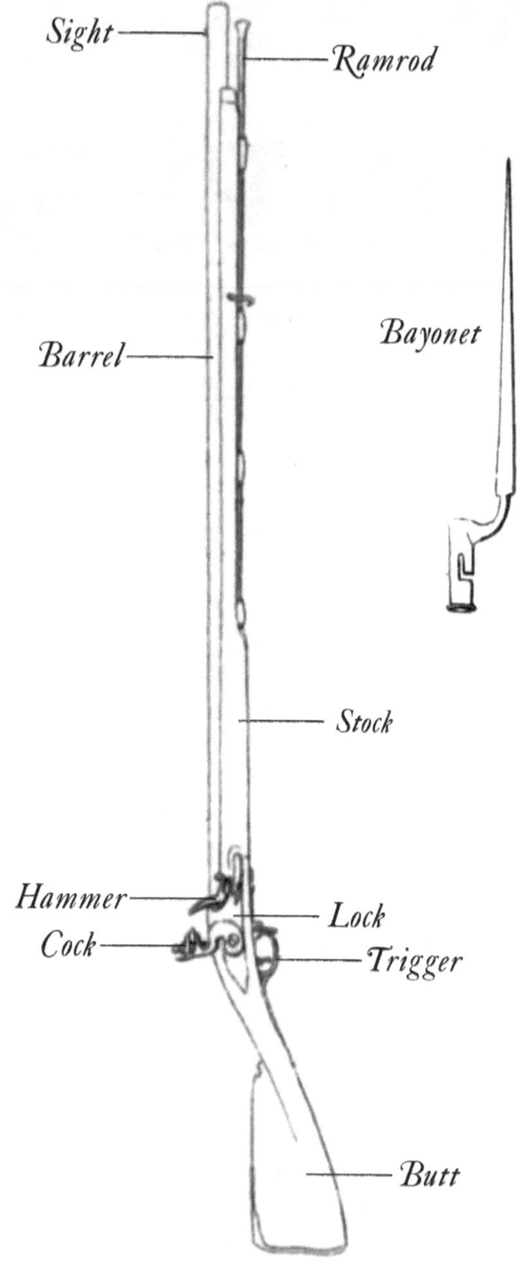

An Explanation of the
Uniform & Accoutrements
of a Britiſh Soldier

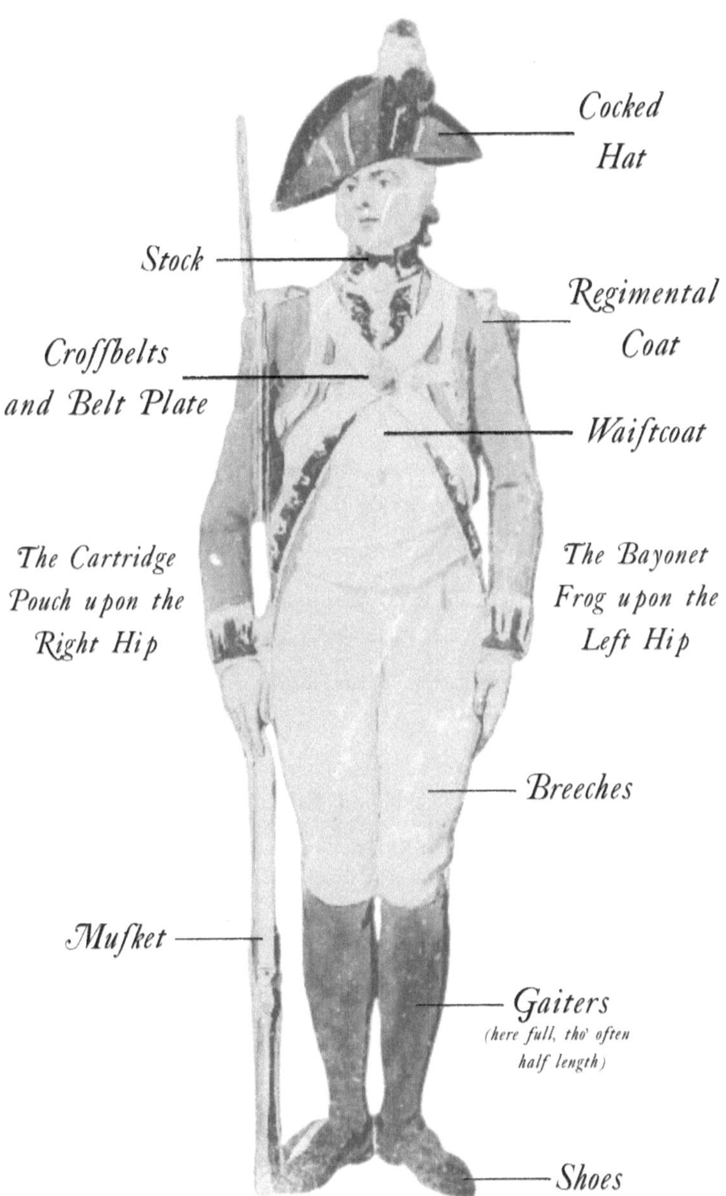

A Brief Dictionary

Deſcribing Certain Terms of a Military Nature uſed within this Publication.

Abatis. A work of tree branches and other natural entanglements, worked together as to form a great barrier when turned towards the enemy.

Aide de Camp. An officer aſſigned to aſſiſt a ſenior officer in taſks of adminiſtration and oeconomy.

Batman. A private ſoldier who acts alſo as a ſervant to an officer.

Battalion. A body of foot, commonly conſiſting of near five-hundred men. Moſt regiments in our ſervice conſiſt of but one battalion, and the flank companies.

Battalion Company, or Hat Men. The greater number of companies within a regiment, conſiſting of common ſoldiery.

Black Ball. The means for a ſoldier to blacken his gaiters and ſhoes, ſtiffen them, and ward them againſt water.

Black Hole. A cell, tent, or other place reſerved to keep ſoldiers condemned to ſome puniſhment.

Boatſwain. In the naval ſervice, a warrant officer reſponſible for the good management and behaviour of a ſhip and her crew. Spoken as "boſun".

Brick Duſt. The means for a ſoldier to poliſh the braſs of his equippage.

Brigade. An amalgam of battalions or other ſoldiers, commanded by a brigadier. Brigades are not fixed, but are formed for ſervice as required.

Brown Beſs. A colloquial term among ſoldiers for their muſketry.

Captain. The commander-in-chief of a company. He is to march and fight at the head of his men, and has the power of making corporals and ſergeants within his company. He ought to be vigilant, and acquainted with the diſpoſitions of all his men.

Chevaux de Friſe. A ſpar of wood with holes cut along every ſide, through which pickets are run. Thus the points ſtand out every way, to act as a barrier to the enemy.

Colours. The banners carried by regiments into battle, for their identification and greater ſpirit. Regiments typically carry two Colours: the King's, and the Regiment's.

Company. A ſmall body of foot, generally from fifty to eighty, commanded by a captain who has under him a lieutenant and enſign. A company uſually has three ſergeants and three corporals.

Corporal. A non-commiſſioned officer, under a ſergeant. He relieves the ſentinels and keeps good order in the ranks, being armed as a private ſoldier.

Diviſions, Sub and Grand. The leſſer parcels into which a battalion iſ divided in marching and in battle. Each wing of the battalion to be divided into two Grand Diviſions, each Grand Diviſion to be divided into two Sub-Diviſions.

Enfilade. The ſituation of a poſt, which can diſcover and ſcour all the length of a ſtraight line, which, by that means is rendered almoſt defenceleſs. To enfilade is to ſweep the whole of a line with ſhot.

Enſign. The moſt junior commiſſioned officer, being ſubordinate to the lieutenant and captain in the company. It is an honourable poſt for a young gentleman, at his firſt coming into the army. He may take charge of the Colours, and is to die rather than loſe them.

Flank Companies. The grenadier and light companies. They are often detached from their regiments for independent ſervice, or combined to form their own brigades.

Followers, or Camp Followers. They who follow the regiments by permiſſion of its officers, being chiefly the wives and children, and alſo the ſutlery.

Forlorn Hope, or Enfans Perdus. Men appointed to give the firſt onſet in battle, or the breach of a place beſieged; ſo called for the imminent danger they are expoſed to.

Fugleman. A ſoldier detached from the ranks in drilling, to ſerve as an example to hiſ fellows in performing the Exerciſe.

Gabions. Great baſkets, 5 or 6 feet high, being filled with earth to make a cover or parapet againſt the enemy. They are commonly uſed in batteries, to ſcreen engineers, and in other ſiegeworks.

Grenadiers. A foot ſoldier of great courage and ſtrength. Grenadiers are typically veterans of long ſervice, and march in the van of their battalion. In former years, grenadiers wielded grenadoes to ſtorm works.

Huzza. A common exclamation of joy or courage, and mark of a corps' good ſpirit in face of the enemy. Spoken as 'huzzay' in moſt parts.

Inveſtment, or to Inveſt. To lay ſiegeworks about a ſettlement or fortification.

Knock-Chops. A common game among the ſoldiery, wherein two men ſit againſt one another's backs, each attempting to knock aſide the hat of the other.

Lieutenant. The ſecond commiſſioned officer of the company. He inſpects the actions of the ſergeants and corporals, and may direct a ſub-diviſion in battle.

Light Infantry, or Light Bobs. A foot ſoldier of independence and virility. Light infantrymen are typically veterans of long ſervice, acting as ſkirmiſhers and markſmen. They train at extended orders and frequently utiliſe obſtacles in the firings, and are of great uſe in broken terrain.

Manual Exerciſe, The. The baſic inſtruction for a ſoldier in ſtanding and marching, and in his firings. It is the principle part of a ſoldierly air, in which every recruit muſt become perfectly expert.

Militia, or the Embodied Militia. The trained bands of a town or country, who arm themselves, upon a fhort warning for their own defence, often being chofen for fervice among all able-bodied men by lots. When embodied, regiments or independent companies of militia march under difcipline, in uniform and under Colours as if regulars.

Oeconomy. Here referring to the interior management, financial and otherwife, of a battalion, and alfo to the good hufbanding of a foldier's pay.

Pioniers, or Pioneers. Men employed in mending ways for the army by clearing roads, erecting bridges, etc. and alfo working on intrenchments with the aid of the foldiery.

Platoon. The leffer part of a fub-divifion. There are two platoons per fub-divifion, and are typically commanded, as required, by fubalterns.

Private Man, or Private Soldier. The loweft rank of common foldiery. The private man is elifted, and receives pay, in fervice to his King in war.

Regiment. A body of feveral companies or troops of foot or horfe. Among the foot, typically being ten companies, one of which is of grenadiers and another of light infantry, the whole being commanded by a colonel, lieutenant colonel, and major.

Regimental Wives. The wives of foldiers, on the regimental eftablifhment and fanctioned by its officers. They are held to equal ftandards of good character and fobriety as the men, being often employed for nurfes and laundreffes.

Sergeant. A non-commiffioned officer, above a corporal. Sometimes he commands fmall detachments, and, among other things, it is his particular duty to fee the men difciplined, fober, clean, and keeping good ranks.

Sergeant Major. The feniormoft fergeant in a regiment, of preeminence over them, with charge over the good conduct and fobriety of the non-commiffioned officers.

Squad of Infpection. A fmall collection of private foldiers under the purview of a corporal or fergeant, who minds their wellbeing, fobriety, difcipline, and overall readinefs.

Subaltern. A lieutenant or enfign.

Sutler. One who follows the camp, and fells all forts of provifions to the foldiers.

Taptoo, or Tattoo. The concluding order of a day, for all foldiers to return to billets and to feal the barrack gate.

Troop of Horfe or Dragoons. A fmall body of about 50 or 60, commanded by a captain who has under him a lieutenant and cornet. Akin to a company of the foot.

Wheel, as in marching. A motion that brings a battalion to front on the fide where its flank was, in like manner to a fwinging door. In this motion, the ranks muft take care not to bend, but every one keeps his due diftance; and there muft be very able fergeants at the angles, to fee the files do not break and fall into confufion.

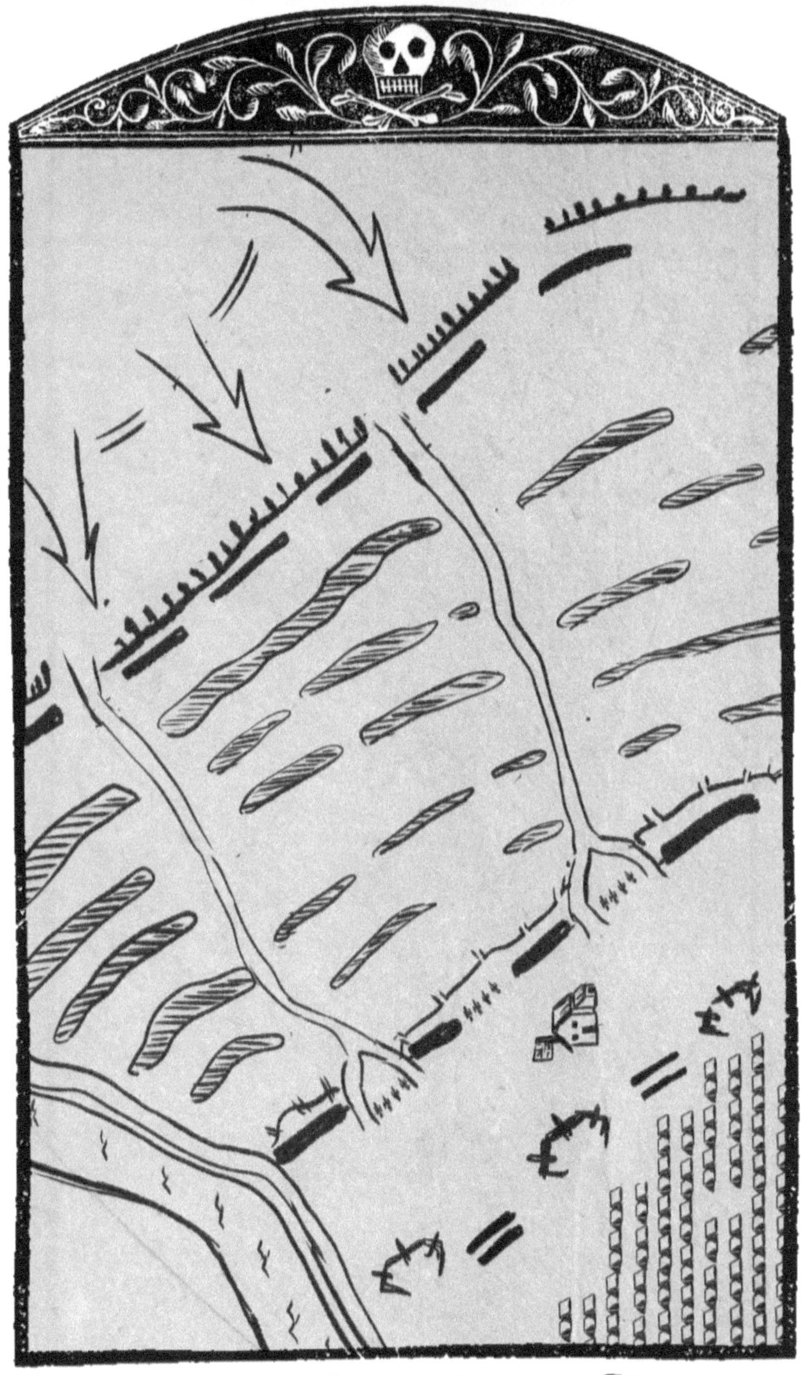

A Plan of the Great Battle of Stowlham.

The Author, upon the Start of the Vile Campaign.

Part the
FIRST

wherein the author learns

of the Choleric Dead.

It had been said that corpses were walking in Norfolk; that some devilry had roused them from the grave with a hatred for the living, and that the bowels of Hell had been loosed upon the earth.

Of course, there was little reason to question the madness of any who might bandy such tales in earnest. The occasional tale of a flying Jack-o'-lantern, or banshee in the mist, held far greater credibility and commonality than such new-fangled faerie tales. They seemed, at the time, of comparatively little imagination in the great pantheon of ghost stories. Still, such ravings had a representative around every fire and across every table. Within my own company, it was a young soldier named John who first thrust it upon us. He hung crookedly over the bar, speaking in a low whisper as if he had a great secret to tell. We had joked about how he fancied himself an Eastern mystic. He seemed to us more of a fool.

"They're without minds, they say. Nary a thought besides the fastest way to your throat! I heard tell of a farmer being roused in the night when he heard a crash, only to rush out and see it, lying headfirst in his chicken coop! It was thrashing all about and tearing the poor things to bits, biting their heads off!"

There was a moment of silence in our party, then. It was not the sort of disquiet which John intended, so much as our coming to understand that he might have been *serious*. Yet before any might try and talk some sense into the lad, our attentions were pulled away by some more importantly amusing racket.

Loud and skilful swearing was heard from across the dingy little pub in which we, and some dozen or more other soldiers, then caroused. One of our new recruits had picked a fight with a local, and Corporal White was in the process of shouting him down. Upon every cruel remark, the men saw fit to raise great cheers. They cared not who won the verbal struggle; only that it was being had, and presented some entertainment. Before long, the recruit had been thrown from the premises and most of the crowd followed after him, that the affair might be continued, as White allowed, in a more *regulated* fashion. Only the older souls, for whom the fun in wrestling had long since passed in favour of a good bottle, remained inside, besides those of us sitting with John.

"Gnawing on the chickens, you said?" Bennett, an awkwardly tall and toothy soldier, reopened the board. He was always in good spirits, and a dear friend of mine. "Oh, that weren't no devil! I'm sorry. You know how I get when I'm hungry!" The self-sacrificing joke was met with uproarious laughter, its humour aided by a most inappropriate degree of libations.

"'Twasn't a drunken soldier!" Replied a dismayed John. "It assuredly was a devil, of some sort or another, and you'd do well to pay the report heed!" Again our commotion died down as our storyteller pressed the severity of his case. "From what I was told, after the farmer went and shot it, it just kept.. .*flailing about.* Then he shot it again, and still it carried on. So he and his sons took their tools to the thing and stabbed and beat it 'til their arms went sore. Didn't change a thing. Hell, it seemed like it wanted to do *them* as it did the bloody chickens, were it not held fast by the coop!" The talk was met with more incredulous glances and shy smiles.

"So, then," I broke my own silence, "what did our intrepid heroes do?" The question felt, at the time, of little consequence. I had been enjoying the drink, and John's nonsense, right alongside the others. I hardly believed he could take his own tales for truth. Now I fancy that it was something of a marked point upon my life, for I shall never forget the desperation in John's gaze, nor the madness in his voice, as he quietly uttered his next words.

"They set it alight. As the fire spread, and it charred the thing black, the creature didn't so much as squeal. It just lay there, carrying on as it had been. Soon enough the whole coop just collapsed in on itself, but even then, they had to hold the thing against the flames with their pitchforks. It made to *attack* them. Fixed its dead eyes upon them, and never looked away. Didn't seem to care a bit about the heat, even as its limbs began to crack and curl up like a dead spider. And the worst of it? Through it all, the only noise it made, besides the popping of fat beneath its skin, was the chattering of its teeth. Like it was *freezing* while it *cooked.* Took hours, as I heard it told, and the farmer's sons had to keep piling up firewood to keep it going. The thing just...refused to die. The bonfire is what drew in the night watchman, who arrested the lot."

John didn't even seem pleased with his tale. His eyes never lost their intensity, nor broke from my gaze. Something about his countenance had rather changed my attitude and, while I did not believe a word the man had said, I found myself deeply troubled by them all the same. The others, however, did not consider themselves taken in by the tale, and soon recommenced their japery.

"Hang on now!" Exclaimed Bennett, slamming his cup comically hard upon the table. "Why arrest the old codger? That's a poor way to end your story! Why not, I don't know, give it a chase of sorts?"

The advice clearly irked the storyteller, whose brow furrowed.

"I can't well change what happened, now can I? I was told the man was arrested, so that's what I told you!"

As he attempted to relay the seriousness of the situation, poor John's efforts were again undermined, this time by the group outside returning. The local man was at their centre, having won his cause. An eye shone black, but he brandished a wide grin as my fellow soldiers competed for the chance to buy him a drink; some even implored him to enlist with the regiment!

"But what was he arrested for? Roasting his own fowl?" Bennett's attention was never drawn from John. He seemed annoyed at the young soldier's insistence upon the story's veracity. "Can't well be illegal to kill a monster, now can it?"

The crowd had once more become merry and forced John to lean closer. Still he was committed to keeping quiet, as if he told a great secret.

"That's the point, you woolhead!" Hissed he. "By all appearances, it *weren't* a monster. It was a *man*...just, different somehow. Unkillable, and thrown into a senseless rage. By the time the watchman showed up, it was just a blackened corpse being hacked to bits by the farmer and his kin. Of course they were all arrested!"

Now it came time for another in our party, old Richards, who had seen many years of soldiering, to speak up.

"But what sense does it make?" Asked he, with his usual judgemental glare. "Why carve the monster...or, man, or whatever have you...why carve it up like a goose? Now I don't question your good intentions, son, but it sounds more like your farmer was already well mad, and concocted a story to match. Assuming there ever was a farmer to start with, tha-"

"You're not understanding!" Interrupted John. "They cut it up because they *didn't believe* it was *dead*. Why should they, after all it had already survived? Even by the time it was cut to ribbons and burnt nearly to dust, they say its fingers were still twitching. Its mouth, all detached, still biting at the air..."

The words set me to shivering, despite a roaring fire in the narrow little pub. Nonsensical though it sounded, the account was a dark and discomfiting one, and set my mind ablaze with thoughts of necrotic villains in the night.

My compatriots were less disturbed by the nightmare, however, and continued to interrogate the young soldier and make a mockery of his tale. After some time, John surrendered his hopes of convincing them, and left with a huff.

Our conversation then drifted to other, more *pressing* matters of soldiering. Chief among them, naturally, was our excitement at the prospect of sailing for the Continent! The French had been behaving quite poorly, all agreed, and the murder of their King seemed to us a far greater disruption of the natural order than any 'walking corpse'. The Continental powers had been fighting for some time, by then, and all suspected that we would soon abandon our sleepy garrison duties to rejoin our regiment, march south, and be shipped at last to the Low Countries where the Duke of York had already met the French in open field. Fancies of glory and treasure filled our minds; nor were even Richards' more sobering tales, from his service in the American War, enough to deter us. So we drank and made merry for many an hour, paying tribute to Bacchus until Mars might again rear his ugly head.

That night, as with every night in those long and dull days, Mars' call came in the form of a drummer marching through the village sounding *Taptoo*. Some lads would always make a show of insisting they did not hear the distant order, and protested the keener-eared barkeep cutting them off. Before long, even an artilleryman could not deny the summons, and the usual threats by a corporal were always convincing enough. Thus our revelry came to an end, with all thoughts of devilry well cast from our minds. Save, of course, those ones more *familiar* to the soldiery.

As I ambled steadily on with the others to our company's small encampment, then upon the outskirts of the small Wiltshire village where we had long harassed the locals, I allowed myself to lag somewhat behind, that I might enjoy some quiet. I recall, now, with sadness how the brisk chill had danced across my flushed cheeks, and the beautiful colour the setting sun lent to the clouds. It was my last feeling of true *contentedness*. There was a bucolic stillness about my little world, and I envisioned it to be soon filled with adventure. I fancied myself a hero in the making, and pictured the fine cut I'd make marching *over the hills and far away* with my friends.

After all, I had abandoned my former life, a one of little

interest to any discerning readership, for far more than drinking, drilling, and stories of ghouls in the night.

With that thought came the reminder of John's stories. How deeply his gaze bore, and the genuine feeling behind his conveyance of what, to any *sensible* man, would appear as nonsense. Yet as the air about me grew colder and darker, and my cronies gained some pace ahead, I found my mind drifting to visions of burnt, biting corpses. Try as I might to cease such thoughts, I soon found myself imagining every dark corner to host some vile horror or other.

Having jumped at the sudden creaking of a tree branch and cursing myself for a fool, I made to rejoin my compatriots whilst praying they would not suspect me of dwelling upon John's silly story. In those happier days, few things concerned me more than the approbation of my brother soldiers.

Soon we came upon our little block of tents and, making ourselves known to the sentry, made to complete our final duties before sleep. The others were all still in high spirits, and more enthusiastic than usual for the morning to come, as it was suspected we might finally be marched off. For my part, I spent the time attempting to expunge a dull speck from my belt plate, rubbing away at the brass with brick dust until my fingers had grown more raw than the metal had shiny. Keeping one's musket and cartridge pouch in good order, while on peacetime duty, was a simple enough matter, but a soldier must *always* wear his bayonet and frog while outside of camp, and its belt plate always needed polishing before the morning's inspection. As I sat thus hunched over my work, forcing my mind to dream of the day my equipment might actually see some *use*, rather than of devils skulking in the brush about our camp, I jumped with a shameful fright when a dark figure appeared behind me. It was John, just going into the little tent we shared with the other men from our squad of inspection.

"Damn your eyes, you shouldn't do that." I muttered to him, again praying none of the others saw my reaction.

John seemed little amused by my fear, but had evidently not snuck up with any ill intent. Instead, as I met his eyes, reflecting the embers of a distant dying campfire, his countenance was deadly serious. It was as if he were expecting to receive grievous news.

"I know you take me for a fool. You needn't mock me so." Said he.

To my eternal shame, I recall feeling a queer sort of relief that he thought my genuine surprise had been another cruelty towards him and his stories. I tried to play the whole thing off with an awkward laugh, but the poor man wouldn't have it. To his mind the stories were a portent unheeded by any but himself. I now understand how maddening his position must have been; the sort all too common in our military world.

"You know," he continued quietly, "I pray you're all right. I pray that I *am* a fool. But mark me, by the end we'll all be praying for a Frenchman's bullet. We aren't going anywhere near the Continent."

The man had a flair for the dramatic, and I told him so. "There's already plenty of fighting to be had." Said I. "Even Sergeant Percy has been saying the orders should come any day now. Where would you have us go? To sit and guard the graveyards?"

The young soldier, the only one among us to see the world clearly, was dejected. He would not meet my gaze, but only ducked into the tent. On finishing my work, I soon followed.

My rebuke of him, besides further crushing his own spirit, seemed to have worked wonders for my own. Any thoughts of devilry had been supplanted by those of John being a mere peddler of nonsense. As I drifted off to sleep in the crowded little quarter, amidst all the men's snoring and jostling for room, I could hear him yet awake.

His weeping was scarce perceptible.

Captain Lawrence issues our fateful orders.

Part the
SECOND

wherein the author

difcovers his fate.

𝕿𝖍𝖊 𝖓𝖊𝖝𝖙 𝖒𝖔𝖗𝖓𝖎𝖓𝖌 proceeded as usual. We were awoken by the duty drummer far earlier than necessary, donned our smallclothes amidst crowding elbows, and jostled outside our little tents to relieve ourselves. There was just time enough for a shave and brush, and to give some final attention to our arms, invariably infested with flecks of rust from the night air's moisture, before the arrival of our superiors. It was nearly a full hour before sunrise, then, when Sergeant Percy came to snap us into order. Our squad had the *'honour'* of his direct attention.

With my musket at the shoulder, and done up snugly in my stock, I felt through the grogginess of an early morning that I must have looked a very fine soldier, among a very fine band. How appropriate it was, then, that the good sergeant took near immediate note of some imperceptible infraction to dash my hopes. With a swift motion, he had snapped off the offending button, which was apparently too loose, and hurled it some way across the ground with a promise that, should I not find and reaffix it properly before he next saw me, I should be given extra duty. Ultimately, it was a threat made good.

Percy was a hard man, and the exigencies of peacetime

service allowed him little opportunity to demonstrate such. The greater part of his scorn was always reserved, however, for Bennett. That morning it seemed the brass furniture of his firelock had gone without sufficient polishing, and he was at once made to hoist it high above his head and run laps about the camp, religiously chanting "I love my musket" as he went. It was a struggle to hide my smile, lest I should join his exercise.

Adorations aside, we were then paraded as custom to the centre of camp with all the other squads, and thence redistributed to our usual places, according to height, to form the full company. Again we were inspected, with Percy making great use of his old halbert to push us into a *'proper'* line.

Most of the army's sergeants had cast aside their halberts, by then, and taken up the new pikes in accordance with recent uniform changes. Even Sergeants Dawe and Greene, who sat by the side and observed Percy's shoving with some amusement, had done so without complaint. Yet Percy was a stubborn man, a veteran of Gibraltar, and less trusting of change than his compatriots who had served in America. Having been forced to put his halbert into stores for the siege, and take up a firelock like a *'damned private man'*, he swore he would only surrender it again when the colonel himself came to seize it. Such was his only trait contrary to the regimental standard, and Captain Lawrence had little cause to push the issue further. Whether by halbert or by pike, that we men were aligned to our proper dressing was the pertinent issue of the day.

As our assembly was concluded, we stood in eager silence for some time. How excitable we were for a time of action; the end to our drudgery at last!

"Officers in camp!" The sharp cry of Sergeant Dawe was accompanied by our snap to attention. The trio of finely decorated gentlemen who sauntered towards our little parade were adorned with gold lace and silver gorgets that winked in the faint morning glow from behind thick blue cloaks. Each of them was every inch an officer and gentleman of quality; and each of them seemed in some distress.

Our captain always bore an intentionally placid visage. He held in much regard the proper emotional distance between himself and his men, and to know what he was thinking was normally an impossibility. Yet on that morning, all could see his disquiet. As he passed between the ranks on his inspection, his eyes seemed hollow, as if detached from the uniforms and equipment usually so keenly surveilled. He did not even blink at my missing button. He was troubled, and lost in thought.

James Lawrence was a good officer. A disciplinarian, to be sure, but fair. He did well by his men, and we trusted him to lead us nobly on the day we first met the enemy. I believe he was a distant relation to some minor nobility in the north, and so of little personal means, having only advanced beyond his ensigncy by the patronage of our colonel. It had always been clear that he was eager to make good on that investment and prove his worth in the coming struggle. He had been attentive to our needs and encouraged all of Percy's severity in drilling, that we might show ourselves the best of the regiment when the time came for action. Nor was his zeal ever derided by the private men, for we all shared in it. Indeed prior to the captain's appearance that morning, only John had demonstrated anything *near* a lack of enthusiasm, and even he, I had thought, must surely be shaken back into tolerable spirits with the escape of idle garrison duty.

So, I could only wonder, what had changed? What foul news did he bear?

"Good morning, men." Spoke the captain as he concluded his ceremony and took a place before us. "As you all know, I am returned from Salisbury last night."

The cathedral city had housed our colonel for some time, alongside nearly half the battalion. The remainder, ourselves included, were scattered amongst the various towns and villages surrounding to better maintain our oeconomy and reputation amongst the locals. That the captain had been summoned to the Regimental Headquarters directly, we all suspected, *surely* meant orders from the Secretary at War himself.

"I understand that much has been said of our prospect to march for the coast. I admit, I have partaken in such excitement myself. Perhaps I have not done well by you, in allowing such idle conjecture."

At this, the company was immediately roused. It was clear what Captain Lawrence was building up to. Some harsh whispers even arose from the ranks, before Sergeant Percy soon barked them down.

"Steady on, lads." Continued the captain as we grew silent again. There was a palpable disappointment in his voice. "Know that while I share your desire for glory on the Continent, I relate to you my orders in trust that you shall enact them with the faith and good spirit becoming of British soldiers, and with which you have so long held yourselves. Men, we are to break down this camp and rejoin with our regiment to march for further garrison duties. In Norfolk."

The disquiet rose; a stifled groan, some shuffled feet, and more whispers harshly silenced.

Norfolk? How could such a posting make *any* sense, I wondered?

Immediately my mind went to John's foolish rumours, and I found myself breaking attention to glance his way. His eyes were wide, frozen in overwhelmed terror. What must have been going through his mind? For my part, I desperately attempted to determine any answer beyond corpses rising to gnaw on chicken bones.

"The regiment is to take post in Downham, and we, alongside the Major's Company, shall take our billets in the nearby town of Stowlham."

Yes, there was a *definitive* anxiety in Lawrence's voice, then, and *all* of us knew it.

"I do not expect," said he, "that our duty there shall be a long one. I have been assured that His Grace, the Duke of York, is eager to receive us into his army the moment we might be had. But in the meantime, the King demands our services elsewhere. There have been reports of certain riotous behaviours in the countryside, and we shall be there to put an end to them! To secure the King's peace, and ensure the good flow of commerce. Lads, I understand your disappointment.

That is why I tell you these things, as no other officer might. Yet our duty is clear, and we shall meet it, unflinching, *wherever* it may call us! God Save the King!"

"God Save the King!" Our cheer was hardly enthusiastic. No hats were thrown, no huzza'ing was to be had. After the chant came a deadly silence, more of confusion than of fear.

Why *Norfolk?*

The thought prevailed above all others even as the sergeants dispersed the formation and began their expected abuse towards those men who had embarrassed them by muttering in ranks. Indeed, we had behaved childishly, but the reader must understand the deep woe which might affect so devil-may-care a body of troops as our own, at having the anticipated end of our idleness thus ripped away. We were exchanging the promise of booty and advancement for yet further monotony in drill and fatigue, endlessly preparing for an occasion which seemed never to come; and above all else, there rose the fear of uncertainty. Although none would show it, the likes of John's rumours surely rang through many a mind with greater credence than ever.

It is curious how a story, first appearing nonsensical, might take on new air the moment it becomes of consequence to the listener.

'Riotous behaviours'? In Norfolk, of all places, where nothing of note had occurred since Boudicca's revolt!

It was difficult for any man to believe that such public disturbances were sufficient to warrant anything beyond some local yeomanry. Especially when all of Europe was alight with war! There had been nary a hint of trouble from those parts. Save for John's story.

From whom had he heard it, again? Where did he say that infernal chicken coop was? The details of it all danced through my mind with a new, terrible vigour. Packing away the encampment was a hectic enough task, yet through all the tearing down of tentage and stuffing of carts, my thoughts were seized by images of charred, grasping hands and burnt lips peeled away from chattering teeth.

John's story had firmly entrenched within my mind, yet I found myself without the courage to interrogate him upon it further. For what shame might demonstrating my fears bring, when the others' spoke only of continued boredom? From the few glances I caught of John throughout the day, he seemed more anxious than ever. Whenever some duty would normally have pulled him closer to me, there always seemed some excuse for him to be elsewhere. I would find some opportunity to interrogate him on the march, I told myself, and finally dash aside such nonsensical thoughts.

So we all did our duties and before long were ready for our departure. We had our small breakfast, and those men with cronies or working obligations in the village took some time to bid farewell and offer apologies for tasks incomplete. Before long we were all formed up and parading beyond the outskirts to rolling drums and the well wishes of those we had befriended - and the pointed neglect of those we had not!

Captain Lawrence and the other officers went at our head, and our civilian followers came up at the rear with our baggage. We carried on with the pretence of parading for a few hundred yards beyond the settlement, ultimately breaking into a route step along the narrow country lanes. This provided some opportunities for conversation, although the topics thereof were strictly regulated by our non-commissioned officers. Any faerie-tales of devilry were soon suppressed in favour of more pleasant topics less damaging to morale.

Still, some accounts were to be had. During those few days of marching I heard tell of many falsities. From a rampant plague in Lynn, to swarming rats in Norwich, it seemed every *sneeze* in those parts was soon reported upon as utter *cataclysm*. There came even variations of the coop story, ranging from laying blame upon a mad farmer who murdered his neighbour, to mad tales of pagan cults conducting their evil magick in the woods.

As our ultimate destination drew nigh, the rumour mill

churned ever more quickly, turning out tales increasingly ridiculous and varied. Though ironically, these came to have a *comforting* effect upon us, for it became all the easier to treat them as they must have been; silly stories told by shepherds to entertain themselves in their long, dull hours. Consequently, as our tales grew all the darker, so too were we assured of our imminent *lack* of adventure!

Save, of course, for one of our number.

John's anxiety was not stemmed by the tide of tales. Rather, with every fresh iteration of his original story, shared around campfires or over bumpers, his frustration and intensity seemed only to grow. I no longer desired to question him as he became all the more insistent on declaring the '*truth*' to any who might listen. His tale, unchanging, became dull and was taken with ever less gravity. John was purely in earnest, and among soldiers seeking entertainment, it was the worst thing a man could be.

Eventually, his rhetoric of doom even reached the ear of our impressionable young Ensign Tell, who had through his innocence been ignorant of such foulness for the longest time. In his naivety he offered John his ear, and was put into a terrible fright. The poor boy awoke that night in a fit, only consoled upon insistence that the devil he saw grasping at him was, in fact, but a nightmare. Though he tried to avoid it, Captain Lawrence forced a name from the little gentleman, and the next morning our company was called out for punishment. John was flogged most severely for blasphemy, dishonesty, disrespecting his officers, and spreading 'disquieting lies' among the men. From then on, he became less keen on repeating himself. He became distant and fearful of the world, and I often heard him weeping when he thought himself alone. Still, I did nothing for him.

By the time we arrived at Stowlham, then, any fears borne of John's tales seemed utterly ridiculous to me. Had any of our company harboured similar anxieties, they surely came to feel the same. I recall the shame with which I compared myself to the childish boy so taken in by stories, and desired only to put the whole affair behind me. After all, what power could imaginary devils have when the very real prospect of a far worse fate, *idle boredom,* hung so dark over us?

Now upon my recollections, however, I see more clearly than ever the foolishness of my resolve. Had I known then even a *quarter* of what would transpire, though the admission brings me no cheer, I would no doubt have abandoned my comrades, sold off my coat, and forever cursed His Majesty's service. I would have embarked upon a ship for America to live the remainder of my days digging ditches. Should I have been caught, the worst they might have done would be to whip the skin from my back and hang me.

It would have been a fate preferable to what awaited me in that cursed town.

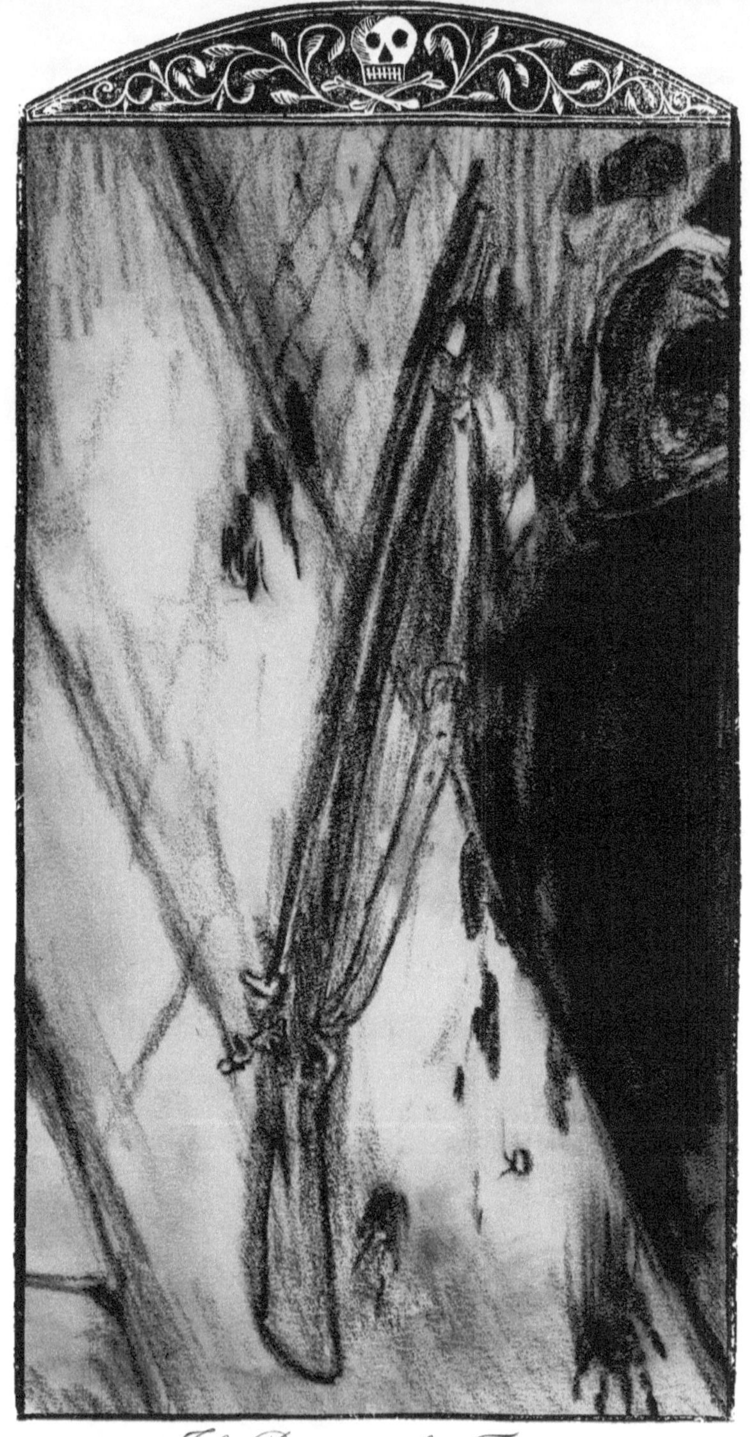

The Remains of a Friend.

Part the

THIRD

wherein Hell breaks

upon Stowlham.

Our arrival in Stowlham was quiet. It felt as if the townspeople had not been expecting us, and awoke that morning to the surprise of soldiers marching through their streets under arms and, more pressing for them, expectant of billets and supplies.

We played no drums. Major Bray, whose company we had earlier joined with, sought not to emphasise our presence on what seemed an *unenthusiastic* populace. Thus our only herald was the steady cracking of shoes along cobblestones, the creaking of leather accoutrements, some groaning supply wagons, one crying child, and the usual medley from the major's horse. The result being that, far from inconspicuous, our march felt all the more oppressive.

The morning was unnaturally warm and dry for its season, and the air was thick with a shroud of dust we kicked up. It soon coated every inch of our clothing, ensuring that again the laundresses would be called up in force upon our halt. I felt as though my very lungs were being buried from within; it was a foul omen, had I but recognised it at the time.

At least, however, we common soldiers could comfort ourselves with the knowledge that being in a proper town, rather than a village of fewer people than even our company's

~ 27 ~

women, would mean better accommodation than mere tentage! Captain Lawrence had secured billets in a disused warehouse along the town's little quayside before our arrival, while the major's men would lodge in homes on the other side of town.

As we passed through the streets, I recall what might only be described as a general uneasiness. Normally the arrival of troops would see excited crowds jostling to meet the newcomers. In previous parading we had well learned to anticipate the dazzled gazes of young maids, and the envious glares of their dullard husbands, alongside the enthusiasm of children who would run along our column and tug at our coats. They always delighted in asking how many Frenchmen we had shot - to which we would naturally lie in boastful good humour.

Yet as we passed through the tiny pockets of humanity in that stagnant place, there were no pretty girls, no shouting merchants, nor old veterans to greet us. There were not even children in the streets, as if they had all been shuttered away. Instead the few eyes we saw peered out from within poorly-kept homes or behind dark corners. They were filled with distrust, and perhaps even fear; but of *what?*

Invariably my mind fell, for the first time in some while, to John's old stories. I began to notice every sign of sickness amongst the population; every distant cough or pox-marked face became symbols, to me, of some horrible decay about the wretched place.

Why was it so *quiet?* If we had heard the stories so far as Wiltshire, then surely here, at their heart, the locals had as well. What did they think? Were the tales mocked as drunken ravings, or heeded as warnings to bar their doors and keep their children inside? How could *mere stories* prove sufficient for the cobbler, the tailor, and the draper we had passed to *all* be shuttered up?

And *why*, I continually wondered, were *so many* soldiers posted to such a remote place? In what felt foolish at the time, I began to suspect that corpses might rush at any moment from every alley, ripping away at us while those dreadful locals stood by and watched with half-dead stares.

Would that such terrors were, indeed, foolish.

Before long, though it felt a great time, our column was halted before the Customs House, near the river on which the town relied for its little commerce. There, after some seemingly terse conversation between the local magistrate and our officers, which I could not discern from within the ranks, our good captain ultimately returned to us and issued our arrangements.

No soldier is ever saddened by the order to disperse, though I was *exceptionally* grateful in that moment to be away from the street and its visions of so many grabbing monsters in dark alleyways.

Damn that John, for having put such ridiculous notions in my mind, thought I with a grimace! Nor was I the only one disquieted by the place's air, for while none dared speak of their fears, there seemed a generalised anxiety all through the ranks. Since John's punishment, none had dared speak of hearsay; yet even the officers were uneasy, as if they suspected some darkness but were unable to address it.

Regardless of any fears, our first days in Norfolk passed much the same as in any other peacetime service. We had our regular fatigue, and patrols, and stood sentry; we aided the sour-faced customs officials, and otherwise sought local employment to supplement our wages and waste on merriment...although wretched Stowlham seemed devoid of such opportunities.

Indeed, whenever the garrison engaged with the locals upon *any* matter, commercial or otherwise, we found only general disinterest, or outright hostility. They seemed suspicious of any souls from without their little town, even beyond the usual attitudes of such rural environs. Those of us capable of finding employment were only paid but begrudgingly, while most taverns outright refused to treat with the soldiery unless we drank our fill outside, away from the exceedingly few usual patrons.

In the early days, I suspected, as surely others had, that

such prudishness *must* relate to the horrors of which we had heard tell. Try as I might to secretly inquire amongst the locals for the truth of such, however, not a man would offer me a meaningful word in reply. It seemed the inhabitants felt that to speak the very words might bring some great calamity upon them. Yet far from driving my suspicions of the supernatural, it rather made me imagine the locals as so many children playing at make-believe. For how might a community, faced with any *genuine* threat, behave in so childish a manner?

Thus, as we fell into the usual routines of garrison, and day after day faced no horrors save *idleness*, I, like my compatriots, became resolved to believe the tales nothing more than utter nonsense; the droll efforts of a melancholic peoples to find some excitement in their drab lives, as is so often the case amongst common peasantry. *I* was a *soldier,* and even in idleness, assured myself that I was a cut above their ragged sort.

Truly, I had begun to hold a great disdain for the local people, much as I pitied them their miserable existence.

The locals' continued queerness notwithstanding, we in the garrison had grown quite comfortable. Our anxieties had totally shrunk from the unnatural, and were replaced with more usual grumblings. I recall with a most dour fondness how poor Bennett joked that he had come to fear his boredom more than anything, and almost wished to sight some devil or other, if only to give him some *action!*

"Mark me well!" Laughed he, before heading to post sentry one night. "If I'm not eaten alive by the time you relieve me, I'll have skewered myself on my own bayonet instead! God, I hate how quiet it all is here."

Yet that cruel joke, spoken on our tenth night in that foul place, was the last my old friend ever spoke to me. For it was during that same night when Stowlham's corruption finally bore its rotting putrescence.

I had been turned out by Corporal White for my own sentry duty, along with my old crony Richards and two other fellows, DeRosa and Pratt. In the little moonlight that pierced the warehouse's old walls, and cursing the lateness of the hour, we donned our coats and our belts. We took little care to avoid waking our sleeping comrades all about us. The warehouse was a great luxury compared with mere tentage, and we had grown rather lax in our comfort and regularity, despite the sergeants' best efforts to impose upon us otherwise.

Meeting the corporal outside, we of the relief began to march down the quayside. I recall how our clacking shoes echoed loudly along the moonlit river. It was indeed terribly quiet, almost unnaturally so, but I rather enjoyed that which so bored Bennett. The air felt tranquil, as I fancied it a perfectly pleasant night; not quite chilly enough for a watch coat, nor so unseasonably warm as the days had been. Thoughts of necrotic, grasping monsters in the dark had all but faded from my mind. Their prospect was then an idle cause of good humour, rather than any honest fear. For the first time in our short-lived occupation, I did not dread the prospect of lone sentry duty in the dark, but rather looked forward to admiring the river before the Customs House, whence my duty was to be had.

Assuming, I recall thinking with a grin, that poor Bennett wouldn't spoil my mood by having skewered himself on my post!

Yet as we passed along the gentle river to where the Customs House loomed, dark and impressive on the quayside, and rounded the corner of the great structure whence our sentry post stood, my last smile was stolen away from me.

Bennett was not there at all. Instead, there sat only a discarded hat and a musket at full cock. They glistened in a silvery, moonlit crimson.

The blood was everywhere.

It splattered the stone wall in thick globs, and had settled into little rivers between the cobbles. Chunks of gore were flecked across the scene, as if flesh had been wrested from bone and thrown to the wind. Immediately my heart leapt and my bowels turned to water. For but a second there was only our shock, and a hearty swear from Pratt, before Corporal

White leapt into action. Porting his firelock, he turned to survey the streets around us.

"Hell!" Growled he while cocking his piece. "You're all loaded? Good. DeRosa! Pratt! Both of you run, hard, back to the others. You wake Sergeant Percy, and tell him to rouse the garrison. Now!"

The corporal's tone bore a ferocity I had never heard even at the worst infraction; they were the first words of *true action* I had heard, and they struck at my soul.

The two men nodded vigorously and ran off without a word, while the rest of us darted our eyes from shadow to shadow. I found my hands growing wet about my firelock. I had never been so frightened before.

"Listen here, you whoresons." The corporal's tone had sunk quiet. "Some bastard has attacked our own, and it looks like it wasn't long ago. I don't care about any damnable faerie tales. Our man might need help, and I don't mean to wait around for the company to muster. So keep your wits and follow me."

Without a second glance, the corporal rushed on where he had caught sight of a blood trail. It looked as if the body of my old friend had been dragged away.

But *why?*

My ears were ringing and my head felt as though it were stuffed with wool, so that I could hardly comprehend the others' words as we ran on and passed into a narrow alleyway. It felt as though my legs were moved by some unseen force, for I could hardly feel them.

"Corporal..." said Richards with an experienced sternness as we slowed down, checking every corner with a raised musket. "Even the Indians weren't so brutal at their worst. *What the Hell is this?*"

"Would that I knew." Replied the other veteran. "I don't trust it any more than you. Now keep quiet. Whatever blackguard did this can't have gone far."

The irregular trail of red we followed still glistened fresh.

I struggled to manoeuvre my musket around the narrow alley, unsure even of what I was looking for. I was expecting some fiend to be tucked within every shadow.

Had Bess *always* been so heavy? Why did my hands tremble so?

I could hardly see through the darkness, for in those narrow passes the moon penetrated little. The night was not so still for long, however, as suddenly the distant peal of a bell began to pierce the air. Nor was it a counting of the hour, but the continual sounding of an alarm!

Soon thereafter, from the direction of the garrison's billets, we heard also a drum call faint on the wind. It was impossible to tell the signal, but it must have been the assembly.

It was impossible for the others to have reached the company in so short a time...and why the bells? For one soon became many, pealing in panic right across the town.

"What the Hell..." Richards' swear trailed off. He was unnerved as he cast his eyes upwards to the sound, searching along the rooftops for answers.

"Whatever it is, it's beyond our sights right now." Corporal White was harsh in his own slow panic. "Keep on the task at hand. We've got a man ou-" He was cut off as we rounded a corner and stumbled across our quarry in the dark, but a few yards distant.

Bennett, it appeared, had *not* been killed.

He stood still, and gazed with tilted head out to the distant bells as if confused by their very nature. From the side of him, I saw his shoulders were oddly slumped, and his legs seemed to wobble erratically, like a babe first learning to stand. His fingers were all grasping at nothing, as if they were desperate to seize the air at his side.

They ran red with blood.

In the little light, which cast all in shadow, I could see his mouth working senselessly. It was not in an effort to speak. Rather, it opened and shut, over and over again in a slow-burning fit, his large teeth sounding a dreadful *clack …clack…clack*, over and over again.

We were silent only a moment, beholding our friend in shock, before Corporal White took his final step forward.

"My God, man. Are you alr-" His whispered inquiry was cut off sharply.

In that pained moment my world collapsed.

What remained of poor Bennett turned jaggedly about, as if the body fought against its own limbs, to reveal an unnaturally pale face. His eyes were bloodshot and stared wide and unblinking at us, while the side of his nose had become a pulp of flesh, as if crushed between grinding stones. His cheek was torn asunder into little ribbons, while his every violent bite at the air seemed to tear it further. Where the poor man's neck had been lay only a great hole, which leaked in a steady trickle, as if well drained.

The chattering of his teeth reached the intensity of a drummer's call. I did not know it at the time, but my friend was long dead.

There was no time for thought as he, *it*, approached us. Slowly at first, in an unsteady shuffle with arms outstretched and snapping fingers that offered an almost pitiable sight. It was as if the wretch were no more than a frightened child attempting to glean some comfort from its mother's skirts. Yet every stumbling pace fell into the next, gaining in rhythm to progress at a remarkable speed despite itself.

Richards was the first to break from our collective trance. With a curse of fear and confusion and anger, he rushed forward and levelled his piece. The musket fired with a hiss and a crack, flooding the little alley with smoke. Squinting through it, we saw his shot had rung true, as the heavy ball met Bennett's shoulder to carry off a great heap of skin and muscle.

Still on it came at the same terrible speed, seemingly unaware of the grievous wound. The shock of this strange development was sufficient to delay my own action, as my trembling hands refused to take aim.

How could I even *think* to do so? This was Bennett! What had happened to him?

A foul warmth had flooded my breeches, and my vision went practically black. Within a second, before Corporal White could react either, our once-friend set upon poor Richards.

He initially kept the thing at bay with a ported musket. Yet his attacker seemed mindless, not seeking to grapple in any way, but instead throwing itself bodily against him with as much force as it could muster. Its torn neck craned as biting teeth struggled to meet any piece of living flesh they might, whilst uncaring, flailing limbs reached out to grasp and carve at whatever came to hand.

Richards screamed terribly as they reached his face and neck. It was only a moment before he stumbled back and fell to the ground. Teeth connected with his face.

Even in the dark, I could see the blood spurting as a hunk of flesh was stringily ripped away.

By then, Corporal White had already rushed in, and having dropped his musket, he took hold of the thing's shoulders in an effort to heave it off. Yet the devil was wholly determined to continue tearing at Richards.

On a second heave, White managed to gain some advantage, and soon the creature was dislodged as they both fell back. The men's screaming bled into one another with a piercing discordance, as much in confusion as in horror.

What had happened to poor Bennett?

By the time I regained any sense of myself, only a breath's time having passed, the devil had already turned about, and was forcing itself on the corporal.

I had *no choice.* Though I wept, and could hardly lift my firelock, I rushed on and pushed my bayonet into its side. The long steel cut at once through my old crony's coat and flesh. I felt every scratch of the blade against his bones.

Yet despite a surely fatal blow, Bennett did not seem to mind in the least. Still *it* forced itself onto White, its teeth sinking deep within his neck, just above his stock.

I wrenched my bayonet free, nearly dropping the musket as I did so, for how fiercely I trembled, and with a great cry made to stab hard into Bennett's back. I struck again, and again, and again. My eyes stung with tears and sweat as I wailed and thrust, all to no avail.

The corporal's screaming soon turned to a gurgled choking. Then the gurgling ceased.

His limbs lost their strength and fell to the ground as he died. Yet such was only the terror's advent; for no sooner had White been so horrifically slaughtered, when my bedevilled *friend* made to spin about and grasp at me!

Try as I might to force my attacker away with another thrust, I found myself without the strength. It did not try to parry my blow, but leapt for my legs, as if driven by mindless impulse. With a cry, I made to evade the biting teeth and stumbled backwards, falling hard upon the cobbles. Then, I did drop my musket.

I kicked at the devil with all of my strength, but found myself little able to deter it. I still recall the sensation of my heel cracking through those big teeth. Nothing dissuaded him.

As I thus fought to keep the corpse at bay, it frantically scratched and clawed at my gaiters, carrying off a few poor-kept buttons as it did so. My legs thus exposed, so too did they suffer beneath the assault, as the white of my stockings began to turn red.

It was then, through my panic, that I noticed a sign I first took for a blessing. Corporal White was *rising to his feet!*

"Corporal!" I cried to him in folly. "Help me! Please!"

I was panicking as Bennett gained a better hold with my every breath. My leg was red raw with shallow scratches, and I feared at any moment the devil might finally bite flesh with its remaining, bloodied teeth.

My little hope then transformed into abject horror, as I saw the corporal's jagged movement. The *irregularity* of it, and his deathly silence...save the working of his teeth.

Then, as if by some unseen signal, the same commenced with old Richards. As he succumbed to his wounds, I saw his body begin to violently twitch. It was first slow, and then, in a rising furor, I heard his own jaw begin to clatter.

His dead, *utterly uncomprehending* eyes fixed wide on me. It was only by the capricious will of the Fates, then, that my life was preserved. I discerned the pounding of many shoes and the shouting of men from behind me.

"What's happening here?" Came a heavy, authoritative voice. I knew it immediately as Sergeant Percy. "Get back, damn you!"

Suddenly I felt two pairs of hands set upon my shoulders, hauling me back as I continued to kick away my assailant. Another man, his musket slung, tried to take hold of Bennett. The last two then came on with ported arms to either side, making to aid my former colleagues who seemed, to them, injured and unsteady.

"No! They're n-" I had not time to finish my shout before the horrific scene recommenced.

The men who came on to Richards and White found themselves set upon immediately by the fresh corpses.

The other, who had made to haul Bennett away, found the devil soon turned about and biting hard at his hand.

The alley again became a scene of blood-soaked chaos. The two who pulled me away, in their terror, dropped me to the ground and fumbled to level their bayonets. I saw Sergeant Percy then appear at their side, his old halbert in hand as he surveyed the alley in bewilderment.

The sound of tearing flesh and rushing gore had already silenced one of the men's screaming.

"It isn't them, sergeant! It isn't them!" I choked my warning through wracking gasps and tears.

Yet it mattered not, for the sergeant spared no thought for me, but immediately advanced. Bellowing an awful war-cry, Percy brought the blade of his halbert through Bennett's carcass. It did nothing save spray further gore.

The two men who had saved me likewise ran to aid their comrades who had been set upon by Richards and White. As I struggled to regain my footing, feeling warm blood trickling down my leg, another man was already pulling back from the struggle with a hand held fast to his neck. He staggered, and I saw the terror in his eyes glaze over as blood spat from between loosening fingers. He fell to the ground and was still for but a moment, before his limbs began to twitch.

I knew then that he was soon to rise, also.

I was frozen then, beholding it all in utter *incomprehension*. The alley seemed to pulse with rent flesh, both dead and dying. The whole world seemed to spin. Everything became intermixed in my failing, clouded vision. I was losing all sense, and felt faint.

Sergeant Percy held one of the devils in place while others stabbed it repeatedly with bayonets. It cared not.

Another soldier wrested himself away from a grapple, and with great vitriol hoisted his bayonet high, thrusting it through the cheekbone of his attacker! He pulled his trigger, and again a shot echoed down the alley. The ball ripped through the devil, whilst smoke poured from a great hole of jagged flesh and broken bone. Yet even then, the shot did *nothing* to deter the corpse, which set itself firm upon its wretched victim and cut ferociously with the half of its jaw that remained.

The man whose hand had been caught by Bennett then managed to slink away, clutching his wound in the corner, while another soldier slipped on the cobblestones, so coated were they with gore.

Another face was bitten. A flailing hand caught upon and burst open an eye. The three creatures were then four, and then five, and still multiplying.

I heard screaming; someone calling out to me for aid. Was it Sergeant Percy? I saw him crashing his halbert into flesh, and the sound of cracking bone came to me through the pounding of blood in my ears. I could taste blood, and knew not whether it was from myself, or the spray which covered the alley.

In three quick blinks, the soldiers' fate was assured. What so many men had failed to achieve against three, I was soon to face alone against a mob of nine.

The stench of gore and urine and sulphurous powder filled my nose. I knew not how much of the blood that covered me was my own, or belonging to my compatriots. I could neither think, nor speak, nor see any path beyond the one behind me. I was in a panic.

So with tears stinging my clouded eyes, I turned and I fled as quickly as my uncertain legs might carry me, nearly stumbling to the ground with every step. Even now, my final vision of Sergeant Percy, whose eyes revealed a fear I could never before imagine in such a man, presses heavily on my soul.

I have since learned that the ghosts of the dead care not for the *excuses* of cowards.

As I ran, I ducked this way and that through the myriad alleys and side-streets in an effort to throw off any would-be pursuers. I soon cleared the density of ramshackle houses to appear again by the quayside whence I had first arrived. In my addled state, I found myself staring upon the pool of gore where once Bennett had idled on sentry. It then reflected a new light, brighter and fiercer than that of the placid moon above.

Again I noticed the tolling bells, which had risen to a great cacophony over the distant shouting of so many men. Looking across the town, I saw in the crisp night air a black smoke rising with a harsh red glow at its heart. A fire had risen in the town's market square!

Glancing all about me, and fearing pursuit by the devils, I dashed forward and took up Bennett's old firelock, flecked as ever with little pieces of rust. It was sticky with blood, but still loaded.

I then rushed on towards the flames, for there was no question in my mind that the company would have been formed to combat the blaze alongside the townsmen. While I had already proven myself a coward against an insurmountable foe, I was not utterly lost to the gravity of my duty. The garrison would need to be alarmed to the greater threat, I knew, if there was to be any hope of our survival.

The town had become a pandemonium by that point, with cries of "Fire! Fire!" echoing on the lips of men who ran every which way, leather buckets in hand, aiming to do their part. They paid no mind to a blood-caked, half-crazed soldier rushing about with loaded arms and calling out for his officers. Theirs, they thought, was a greater duty: to save their town.

Such zealous commitment would ultimately end in their slaughter.

As I rounded a corner, I saw precisely what I had expected. The fire, now a great conflagration that rained thick ash upon the streets, had started in one of the homes around a large market square and quickly spread to the other terraces alongside some of the stalls.

The nearby pump was being worked continuously to fuel a bucket brigade, which had been formed by a long line of soldiers in myriad states of undress.

Immediately I saw, to much horror, that only a small collection of them had their muskets slung over their backs. I may only presume that, by the time Pratt and DeRosa had arrived at the garrison, the men were already being turned out to fight the fires. Upon their explaining there had been a murder, some of the men had been ordered to take up their muskets to meet us in pursuit, but the majority of that section was soon countermanded to move for the fires instead. Thus was sent out the small, condemned contingent under Sergeant Percy.

At the centre of the bucket brigade I saw Lieutenant Farwell, a good and independently minded officer, directing the men's efforts. He was moving up and down the line, shouting encouragement to the men and guiding the water-throwers to attack those portions of the flame where it seemed weakest. Likewise, he was attempting to coordinate the civilian men's efforts, yet many seemed oblivious to his orders as they tossed water vainly into the heat.

Breaking all forms of military decorum, I rushed on to the lieutenant and grasped hard upon his arm, spinning him about to meet my mad gaze. He looked down at me in shock, his jaw agape below a face crusted over with sweat and ash.

"Sir!" I struggled to claim my breath through the choking smoke.

"What's the matter with you?" The Lieutenant interjected. "Go and join Corporal Marshalls in running the empty buckets to the pumps! Quickly now!"

"Sir, you don't understand, yo-"

"By God, man." The officer at last fathomed my vile state. "What's happened? Where has Sergeant Percy gone?"

"Sir, I-I regr...Sergeant Percy is dead, sir." I gulped and blinked my stinging eyes. "Bennett is dead. He, he set upon us, he killed Richards, they aren- I mean, he didn-"

I was babbling incoherently. How might I even begin to describe the terror I had witnessed? The horrors of which poor John's stories had spoken were made manifest! The dead were setting themselves upon the living whilst Stowlham burned, and I could not find the words to explain myself.

So it soon became the lieutenant's turn to grab hold of me. He slapped my face hard to try and restore me to some sense, but it was of no help.

"Damn your eyes, man, spit it out! What's happened? Where is-" He was soon interrupted by an awful scream, which pierced through the din. It was borne of the most wretched *pain* and *horror*, and I had heard its like before.

The devils had found us.

Lieutenant Farwell's Heroic Stand.

Part the
FOURTH

wherein

the garriſon falls.

𝕬 **creature had burſt** into the square and latched on to
some poor boy, probably not yet fifteen, tearing into his guts
with a savage frenzy. Yet significantly more troubling than
the general horror of the scene, was that this devil was not one
of my former comrades, but the brutalised remains of a once
young woman.

She wore only a woefully torn shift, once white but now a
dripping red, as if she had been set upon while abed. Who
knew, then, how many corpses stalked that fiery night?

The victim was already well strewn across the street before
aid finally reached him. A man rushed on and tackled the
corpse, striking it hard with his bucket. Yet even with this
hasty rescue, it was clear there was no hope for the boy, as his
bowels had been spilled.

Soon a crowd, emboldened by the first man's courage,
gathered around the scene while he wrestled with the she-
devil. Yet the creature gained an upper hand in the struggle,
biting hard upon the man's ear and ripping it away. As he
screamed, others went into the fray attempting to separate
them.

Already the boy's body was twitching in its post-mortem

throes, and I could do naught but look on in abject horror alongside the lieutenant.

It was happening again.

All efforts to combat the fire had collapsed as the square turned to chaos. The disembowelled child had been taken up in the arms of a panicked older man, perhaps a father or grandfather, who wept and shook and called to his boy. Suddenly and silently his sire replied, lunging forward to gorge upon the mourner's exposed neck. Weeping then gave way to screaming, and was soon silenced.

The others, still attempting to stave off the first devil, quickly found themselves set upon by *yet another* creature, which stumbled in from the same alleyway. This one was once a young man, likewise wearing only his shirt. Perhaps he had been taken alongside the woman? The devil joined in her efforts and latched soundly upon the nearest civilian to bite hard upon his face.

All at once, then, it seemed as though a great flood had been unleashed. All about us countless bodies began swarming into the square. Some of them were calling for help, while others silently bit and grasped at the air, stumbling and falling after would-be victims.

The mob all ran this way and that, as every man sought sanctuary, only to collide with a fresh oncoming corpse. After a quick, brutal struggle, the victims too found themselves joining in the orgy of flowing viscera, which pooled with the water of so many dropped buckets.

In but a moment, the square was wholly overwhelmed.

The Army, however, was not idle during this time. In those initial moments, many of our bravest soldiers, armed with muskets, water buckets, or merely scraps of wood pulled from smouldering buildings, rushed at once to strike at the foes and rescue some person or another.

It was young Ensign Tell who first leapt eagerly into action. I saw him from across the square as he drew his sword and waved it about in a great show, calling on those soldiers closest to him.

"Arm yourselves, men!" His squeaky voice carried terror and zeal alike. "Some devilry is afoot! Give not an inch! Drive them off!"

Thus, with a gaggle of troops, the young officer hurried off with a dream to bring salvation to the devils' first victims, and prove the hero of the day. He was, perhaps, the best of us; for despite his fears and inexperience, still he did not shirk from the very gates of Hell.

For our own part, straight upon the first assault, I forced away the lieutenant's grip in a bout of impertinence which under any other circumstance might have seen me flogged. Suddenly Farwell had a fresh perspective on my appearance, and understanding washed atop his face.

"John's story, sir!" I cried. "The dead attacking the living!"

Yet before I could conclude the thought, the lieutenant's cooler head prevailed. He left me at once, and likewise drawing his sword, set about a more tactical course of action.

"Form the company!" Cried he. "Form ranks! Form th- damn it, where is my drummer? Form the company! Hurry!"

Soon the young drummer was at his side, pounding away at his instrument as best he could while running with the lieutenant, opposite the flames to the edge of the square. Behind them, soldiers streamed from the bucket-brigade line and all about the square, dodging corpses and victims alike as they made to form up down a central lane, away from the chaos.

The crowd had by then lost any semblance of order. Half its number had become women and children, flying into the square in futile search of security against the mutilated attackers at their heels. They crashed into the original fire-fighters in confusion, then, as the latter tried desperately to flee *without* the square, and the attackers inside it!

Many others, hearing our drummer's call, rushed on with the soldiers to take refuge behind our rapidly growing line. All the while, the devils augmented their numbers, from six to twelve to twenty and more; once a person was caught out, be they a soldier or a child, there was no escape. In the chaos, the only way to distinguish the dead from the living became the unnaturally erratic and rapidly jagged motions of their stiffening limbs, or, more morbid still, their gore-soaked faces as victims were claimed. Their scarlet masks glistened in the light of open flames beneath wide, uncomprehending eyes.

Somehow during the struggle, a sufficient quantity of soldiers managed to extricate from the crowd to form a semblance of a line. We were not assembled by size or armament, but by the chance of whatever place a man found himself in. Thus I stood at the fore, bayonet before me, with petrified and disoriented men on either side.

They seemed oblivious to my ghastly state, but shook and jostled in the line as if to push it backwards.

"Stand fast, men! Firelocks to the front! *Prime and load!*" The lieutenant had been bellowing his commands ere half of us were in position; nor did any man need to be told twice.

With a trembling hand I retrieved a cartridge from the pouch at my side, and, biting off its end, made to sprinkle some powder into the musket pan before I saw it was shut, and remembered the piece was already loaded.

Bennett hadn't even fired off a shot before he was set upon by whatever devil had taken him.

So I cast the torn cartridge aside and raised my musket to the ready position, desperately surveying the scene. It was impossible to focus on any one object, as my vision blurred in the chaos. I could breathe only with great difficulty as black smoke swirled with ever-increasing intensity about us. Even through the drumming and those appalling, unrelenting screams, I could make out the *chattering* of so many teeth, ravenous at the prospect of slaughter.

I saw Lieutenant Farwell then rush along the line before us, eyes fixed ahead in a frightful state. As more and more of our men straggled into formation alongside the refugees, he would stop them at swordpoint, to look them up and down and confirm their comradeship with the living, before urging them behind.

Still, not every soldier had heeded his word to retire from the chaos; some fought on amidst the mob, being overtaken one by one as the enemy's numbers grew. Aimless shots were ringing out amidst the discordant choir.

"Tell!" Cried Farwell above the din. "Mr Tell! Retire to the line! Tell!"

The young ensign was nowhere to be seen, lost amidst the sea of tearing bodies. The cry for him was shortly taken up by others in the line, as were the names of many other comrades.

Our cries served less to bring out friends, however, and more to attract the attentions of the dead! For not long after we formed ranks did I spy the first of their stumbling limbs flailing towards us, soon followed by many more.

As the quantity of *living* bodies in the town square, upon which the devils might bite and tear, declined, so too did our formation become all the more tantalising a prospect for them.

"Damn it all!" I heard the lieutenant swear as he ran to our right, clearing the way before our muzzles.

"Make ready! Present!"

At the commands we cocked and levelled our muskets, as many called still for their cronies lost in the throng.

"Bugger all, I can't tell who to shoot!" Cried the man to my left. The one behind me, armed only with a heavy stone, was muttering a prayer.

"F-fire!"

The desperate call was met with a ragged volley, muskets firing in their own time against so many oncoming corpses. Every round carried off with itself great splatters of flesh, yet the rushing corpses took no care of such paltry injury. It would not be long, we all saw, before the first of them would collide with our bayonets.

Yet through the crowd, not every figure was so *stoic* for the balls they took. Three or four bodies instead collapsed, as if their every muscle abruptly gave way. With cries and groans they clutched at their guts and their shoulders, yet these were only little pains compared with what followed upon their heels.

They, our *living* victims, were at once set upon by the horde all about them, and their cries sounded all the more wretched for our part in them. Many men, blinking away sooty tears which burned our eyes, could not look on as they were ripped asunder.

"What are we doing?" The man to my left now openly wept, and it was all he could do not to drop his musket.

"Recover! Prime and load!" The lieutenant ordered atop all the pitiable sounds, while the drummer beat furiously, and uselessly, away. Yet as I brought down my firelock and made again to prime the pan, my limbs flowing through the *Exercise* as if by an unseen force, I realised the piece had misfired. With all the madness, I hadn't noticed, and might have gone right on with double-loading were it not for the cock still resting, impotent, against the hammer!

Damn that Bennett for his obstinance, thought I!

With so dull a flint, and a poorly kept mainspring, it wouldn't have even mattered if he *had* fired upon his assailant! Percy had not been half too hard on my old friend before his demise, it seemed.

That thought, a fleeting recollection of happier times, was near enough to make me gag in sorrow. I had no choice but to pull back the cock anew, and wipe so hard as I could at the flint with my sleeve, praying my next shot would take better hold.

Whilst thus engaged in maddening minutiae, cursing and mourning poor Bennett's memory all at once, the chaos about us continued to build. About me, men cursed as trembling fingers dropped cartridges and ramrods fenced unceremoniously in the air. All were in a panic, and the enemy would hardly wait for our inexperienced hands.

Lieutenant Farwell continued his attempts to reassure us, his voice shaking most pitifully at the realisation of his order upon the innocents.

It was then that Ensign Tell reappeared at last.

Through the smoke and bodies, cast against the flames, I glimpsed him running along with another soldier and some refugees, two men and a woman, making a mad dash for our line. He held his sword no longer, but his arm was mangled and coated in blood as he clutched it hard. Notwithstanding, there was a *determination* in his eyes, and he managed to outright dodge one devil which leapt for him.

"Come on, sir!" All our line took up the cry together. "You can make it! Come on!" Yet all our hopes for salvation, both of ourselves and our colleagues, soon proved for naught.

While the young gentleman was deft in evading the corpses' awkward stumbling, one of his party proved less so, and was soon tripped up by a fresh-turned devil on the ground. It was one of our own, no less, who had lost his intestines in the struggle.

The civilian man yelped in fear as the dead hand grasped hard upon his ankle, and he tumbled to the ground. The other refugees, even the living soldier, merely trampled over and past him in their panic.

Yet brave Ensign Tell, who might have made such a wonderful officer in kinder times, refused to leave the man behind. Instead, realising what had occurred, he stopped on his heel and went back, heedless of his injury and the devils which swarmed all about.

"Leave him! Come on!" Called our line, yet whether the gentleman could comprehend our words was unknowable, for he at once made a swift kick to the attacking devil's skull. Still its grip was inescapable, as the victim tried to crawl away and regain some footing to no avail. Another kick of Tell's heavy shoe burst apart some additional wound on the devil, but still it held fast. Meanwhile, in the struggle to liberate his charge, the officer did not notice a second corpse coming up from his rear.

Our cries of warning were fruitless, nor could our attention be laid upon the boy for long. Already some other creatures had begun to push towards us, and Farwell yelled to commence an independent *firing by files,* so that our line again erupted in peppering whatever devils were closest at hand. They were only a few yards away, then, yet I found I could pay them no heed. My eyes were instead fixed upon the ensign's terrible fate.

He was upon the ground like so many others, wrestling to keep the burnt carcass away from himself, and soon he wailed in terror as teeth bore down upon his shoulder. The devil could not quite pierce the thick wool of his coat, but kept him pinned firm upon the ground as a second husk, and then a third, each came bowling over them.

The ensign was quickly buried beneath a copious weight of bleeding flesh, and despite the gunsmoke and heat haze, I swore I could discern the abject panic in his eyes.

He looked to us, to *me,* pleading for salvation. I could no more help him than if he were a world away. Already the devil nearest our firing line, shrugging aside three well aimed balls, was soon to stumble into our bayonets.

I was yet to even fire when one of the creatures above Tell gained, at last, a firm grasp upon him. First with deep cutting fingernails, and then its desperate, clacking jaws, which bit down hard upon the boy and spread thin the sinew of his neck.

His cries then pierced the cacophony of Hell in such a way as shall never leave my soul. In that brief moment, I saw with clarity what I needed to do. With trembling fingers, I brought up my piece, took careful aim, and fired.

My first and only shot, outside of drill, was thus to kill my own officer.

The ball whizzed past a devil that was only an arm's-length from falling upon me, and crashed messily into the top of Tell's skull. His screaming halted instantly as the devil atop him was pelted with brains. The biting upon Tell's neck ceased as his assailants found his body stiff; nor could I comprehend the *horror* of my *mercy* before I, likewise, was set upon.

It was half from the memory of my muscles that I had brought down my firelock after taking the tragic shot, and a stroke of pure fortune that this put my bayonet on a level with the oncoming devil's sternum. In my daze, I was no more cognizant of it than the moon. Yet when I felt the jolt of the devil's full weight against my arms, I was hauled back immediately to the present.

My cry then was one of sorrow, as much as fear, as stiff fingers clambered along the length of my musket to grip upon me. The rabid, cracking teeth seemed a hair's breadth away from me. It was all I could do to push against my vile assailant, which heaved on in dreadful abandon, my bayonet poking out of its back.

I heard a shout behind me, and suddenly there appeared my rear-rank man with a large spar of burnt wood! He plunged it over my shoulder and into the devil's eye. The man to my left, then, after struggling to pivot his firelock in the melee, made to shoot the devil's neck, further coated us all in rotting fluids. Regardless of all injury, it pressed, and bit, and seemed ever to near.

I heard my colleagues exclaiming something, but could not discern a word - my whole world was nothing save those dreaded teeth, and the cold, desperate, wide stare of the devil's one remaining eye.

Nor could any of the others provide us aid, for all down the line similar scenes transpired, as one by one the creatures plunged into our ranks. The men tried to keep them at bay, but before long they were piled against us in putrefactory push.

Heavy stones were thrown, wooden debris was jabbed, musketry cracked, and bayonets pierced continually from our rear ranks. Nor did the men of Stowlham bring dishonour upon their kin, as they fought with even greater ferocity than us soldiers. They stood not in defence of themselves, but of their *homes* and *property*, of their *wives* and *children*. To both our left and right, they struck at the oncoming corpses with fists and buckets alongside their makeshift weaponry. For every one to slip and fall in the deepening mess of spilled offal, another civilian would rush on from somewhere to take his place, and prayerfully allow his escape. The surviving women and children had come to huddle behind the lot of us, uncertain of where they might flee, while many even joined in the fight beside their men. Yet even the strongest of wills could not long withstand the physical crush of so many unthinking killers.

There arose then a general commotion upon my left, betraying what had long been inevitable. One of the front-rank men had lost his footing, and fell backwards into his fellows. The devils pushed through the gap, and thus commenced their slaughter anew.

The remainder of our ranks were not long to stand. The weeping man to my side lost himself for only a moment. He stumbled, and a gap appeared between us, into which a smaller corpse fell and bit upon his hand at the musket's swell. Instinctively, he dropped the piece to push his attacker away, and so a second floodgate opened. The line all about me began to collapse as devils poured inwards, falling upon themselves, with the poor man crushed beneath them. His file partner, dropping the spear of wood he held as a weapon, had already turned and fled, forcing himself past so many others. Soldiers soon joined with women and children, flying into the night with screams upon their lips.

"Hold fast! Hold, you blackguards!" Farwell was shouting from somewhere to the right, yet it would not do. Those few men remaining were soon to be crushed beneath the weight of corpses, while the rest were scattering into the harsh winds, which had become a fierce and continual rush dragging towards the growing flames.

Had I a *hero's* courage, I could not have held.

In some horrible compulsion, I found myself looking away from my piled attackers to my comrade underfoot. In vain he struggled to keep the creatures from his body, yet they bit hard at every part of him, and blood spluttered from between his teeth.

Collins. That was his name, I then recalled.

He was a quiet man in the company, but a good and honest soldier. His wife had followed us on the establishment. She would have been back at the warehouse just then, wondering about her husband's fate, alongside so many others.

I could offer Collins nothing more than my sorrow.

Another devil had quickly crawled through the heap before us, and made for my leg. It was only with a risky backstep that I could avoid it. The man at my rear had fled. Thus, with a final great heave, I too released my hold. The devils before me immediately fell inwards, grasping for my back as I stumbled away and ran.

With a glance over my shoulder, I saw the few, most steadfast among us, then fully overwhelmed by the foe, which clambered one over another in a frenzy to reach the living. I heard men screaming terribly as guts were strewn about the cobblestone street. Collins was totally buried beneath the devils, as was soon the man who had stood upon my right, and was thus abandoned in my flight.

I saw Sergeant Dawe holding back three devils alone with his pike, being forced back against the wall of a shop as they clawed across his face. Lieutenant Farwell was also soon overwhelmed by the horde. He cut and sliced ferociously with his sword, but was unable to weaken the hands which snatched at his once-glittering uniform. He fell back under yet another bloody, ashen pile.

My retreat alongside so many others was desperate and disordered. One man forced his way past me viciously, as I in turn jostled others, in the mad dash to abandon our brother soldiers and the civilians we were duty-bound to defend.

Gradually, then, the screaming behind us died down and subsided into a wider clamour all across the city. The violence evidently was fast becoming general. It was a sick kind of consolation, then, that as the devils concluded their slaughter in the square, their desire was not fixed solely upon ourselves.

The bells began, one by one, to cease their tolling, and all the air ran thick with falling ash as pillars of smoke blotted out the moon's little glimmering light. By then, there was only the flickering red of distant flames to illuminate our path.

It seemed we had truly entered Hell itself.

As we shirkers fled through the streets, I knew there was neither hope nor function to reforming our company. The whole of our command had gone, with our only remaining corporal now long lost in the mess of retreat. We were hopelessly scattered as every man abandoned his comrades to try and save his skin, deciding on some fancy of flight or other.

No doubt many would make their way back to the billets and their families, and for a time I thought to retire there as well, before realising that I knew not how to find my way in the dark, nor had I the courage to risk stumbling across the foe on my own.

As I ran from street to street alongside a handful of others, our way determined only by where the chaos seemed least near, one of the men at our head came to a sudden halt. The motion frightened us all to equal stillness. Holding up a hand, he tilted his head as if listening for something. My recollection, then, of Bennett's similar pose set me to shiver.

"Do you hear that?" Wheezed the man through haggard breaths. In the distance, I fancied I could discern the tapping of drums through all the wretched noise.

"It must be the Major's Company!" Said he, stunned by his realisation. "They're still standing!"

"Maybe they just haven't been hit yet!" Another of our number replied in a trembling voice. "We should make for th-"

"Like Hell I will!" Then interrupted a third. "I didn't 'list for whatever *this* is, and I'm not sticking around for it!" Without another word, the blasphemer took up running again, pointedly *away* from the drums. Most of the others in our little crowd soon trailed after him in their bid to flee the town. Nor do I believe they deserve a bit of blame for their attempted desertion. The fate of Stowlham had long been decided. The town was a corpse yet living, the same as its assailants.

Still, I was indecisive in my fear, and had I desired to follow after them, I quickly lost my chance. Ultimately, it was the chaos to chart my course.

"Come on then." Said the first man. "Captain Lawrence was with the major. He'll be helping form a new defence.

That'll be our best shot."

We half-dozen or so remaining soldiers thus carried on, through the bloody night, towards the distant drums. First we heard a continual call of assembly, and then only scattered tones, difficult to discern; likely of loading and marching. Our progress was slow, with our self-assigned leader checking around every corner and we moved as through the shadows.

As we did, the carnage's quick spread became more apparent, as we passed helplessly by numerous scenes of degradation. In the depths of one alley, I saw one of the devils trailing organs as it went. It snapped its head to-and-fro in a horrible fit, as it sought out some fresh victim. Blessedly, it did not catch sight of us. Nor did another pack of creatures, which we saw rushing from the road to crash through a ground floor window, whence they had discovered some little girls peering out and screeching in fear. Not a man of us rose a prospect of attempting their rescue, but we slinked past the home, noisy with screams.

All down the street we witnessed men, women, and children, some together and some alone, all being caught in their efforts to escape the town. Each was subsequently torn, limb from limb, by the roving packs of corpses which discovered them. Whether it was wisdom or cowardice that spurred us away from each scene, we sought to help not a single soul, nor to investigate the many homes with their doors flung open and windows shattered.

At length, despite not having heard the drums for some time, we ultimately discovered the Major's Company.

It was as we rounded a corner that we found them standing, bold and straight in well-drawn ranks, four abreast in a column at the end of a narrow street. Immediately we made ourselves known, running towards our comrades and frantically waving our arms while crying out for aid.

After but a moment, however, the column halted its march. Even from such a dark distance we could tell that the men were jostled and frightened, uncertain of their footing.

It seemed they were untrusting of our intentions - and who

might have blamed them? All the town had completely turned upon itself.

"*Make ready!*" I heard a shout from the column's head, surely their sergeant. Still, the intention of our friends did not first register to us, and we pushed ourselves on in desperate flight. We were nearly upon the column, and the greater safety we thought it might provide.

"*Present!*" Eight muzzles in two ranks came parallel to the road.

"Get down!" I was already flat upon my belly by the time I heard the shout of a comrade.

"*Fire!*" The alleyway exploded with sudden light as the muskets spat fire and lead. I thought, in the moment, although it may have been pure fancy, that I heard a shot sing just over my head.

Not all were carried so far, however; nor were all of our little number so lucky as myself. Directly before me, one man had only thought to kneel and plead with his comrades. I hardly heard him declare his living status ere a ball pierced his scalp, scattering cranial fragments all about me as I lay. He collapsed slowly, straight down upon the ground. His expression, undisturbed, still bore a queer tincture of fear and hope.

Another soldier, further to my side, sat even less fortunate. He clutched at his bloody stomach in disbelief, looking slowly from his wound to the column, as if he did not even feel the pain.

"*Retire!*" The sergeant ahead barked as the next rank of men strode forward in their well-rehearsed street firings. Another round would soon follow. As some of our number then leapt back up to run, damning the firers as they went, I made to try and aid the wounded man. I took him by the shoulder, and he looked at me perplexed. He seemed more distraught by the *injustice* of it all, than any pain.

"Come on, Dunn!" I recognised him in that moment, through the little light of distant fires, as the fresh recruit whom Sergeant Dawe had coerced with the promise of a fine uniform in Ely.

He had finally got his coat from the tailor but a few nights prior.

With an almost drunken nod, he made to follow with me, yet on his attempt to clamber to his feet, the pain of his wound seemed all at once to flood his senses. The man half collapsed as all the air in his lungs rushed out with a horrible shudder.

"Christ's blood, leave him! Come on!" A voice bellowed from ahead. Whether from one of my comrades, or the column itself, I knew not. The lingering smoke sat heavy in the air and obscured the lot of them.

"*Make ready!*" Again came the clicking of so many locks. But, thought I, if they knew us to be living allies, why would they fire?

The revelation prompted me to glance over my shoulder, where faintly illumined in the red glow I discerned the silhouettes of a vertiable *wall* of shambling corpses. They rushed towards us as fast as their legs could carry them, stumbling atop one another in the process, and taking on the appearance of a great *wave*. Their greatest hindrance was ironically their superior number, for in their fit they clogged the narrow road, and easily slipped on their own flowing gore as musket balls smashed into earlier wounds.

Yet still, on they came, their jaws all clicking in mad anticipation. Those former workers and craftsmen, their wives, even some children, all compelled only to tear at us.

"Come on, man, we have to go!" I pleaded with my charge. He had fallen to his knees and his face glistened with sweat.

"*Present!*" Again the muzzles dropped.

"*I...can't...*" The man could scarcely whisper. Again I had no choice. I could only weep, and curse, and plead my regret as I dropped him, ducking to the side of the road just before the volley.

"*Fire!*"

In that awful memory, still I pray that a ball silenced the recruit's pain before he was set upon by the creatures, for I could not spare another moment to look upon him. I ran as quickly as I could to reach the column while their front ranks were retiring to the rear, the next men stepping up and preparing to fire. They moved with ever greater alarm then, and I saw the fear in their eyes. They had seen enough, by then, to understand the nature of their strange foe.

"Damn you for a fool, get behind the line!" Bade their sergeant, before his attention returned to the men.

"*Ready! 'Sent! Fire!*" His commands came quickly then, and the front rank men retired close on my heels as we slid through the narrow gap between the column and the wall alongside.

Eight muskets per volley, even fired at so clockwork a pace, would never be sufficient; and the sergeant seemed to know it. The creatures were close at hand then, and while every shot would force many to stumble, they were soon overtaken by the others behind them.

A great *tide of flesh* was flowing through the streets of Stowlham.

I came to the column's end with the soldiers as they rushed to their rear rank, and immediately began to load on the orders of another sergeant. I saw the major himself then, sitting resplendent and thoroughly agitated atop his horse, over which he barely kept rein. Catching the scent of such foul, unnatural decay had put the beast nearly to frenzy, and the officer could but with difficulty keep his control.

At the major's feet, with a firmer grasp upon the horse's bridle, Captain Lawrence was furious.

"This position is untenable, sir!" He shouted over the bellowing of the horse and another volley being fired. "They gain ground with our every shot!"

"I'll not abandon my position, captain! We must advance to the square, and throw the enemy back!" Spat the major, his wrinkled eyes never looking away from the front. His seemed the sort of determined hatred more appropriate for an old adversary than whatever novel horrors we then faced.

"I shall not have it!" He reiterated as another volley rang out, more ragged than the last. The men were rushing through their motions; the desperation was rising.

"We must rejoin with my company." Argued Captain Lawrence. "Thence we may form a united defence, about th-" He was cut off as I appeared alongside the other refugees from our company. An old lieutenant attempted to stop us, but Captain Lawrence bade us forward with haste. He could hardly conceal his shock at our depredated state.

"What's happened?" Demanded he. "Where's Farwell?"

"Gone, sir." I replied, hardly able to believe the words as I spoke them. I had never spoken directly to my captain, before then. "He...the company was set upon, sir. While fighting the fires. We couldn't stop them!" The final words came out in a broken choke. Every regular musketry blast set my heart to skip, as I envisioned the encroaching *Fleshtide*. The tale was thus taken up by one of my comrades.

"The other officers are dead, sir." He reported more matter-of-factly. "Sergeant Dawe, too."

A horrible cry then issued from the front. The whole of the column shuddered backwards as men recoiled at some terrible sight. Their non-commissioned officers and the lieutenant kept the men in their ranks, some with bodily force, and shouted encouragement to keep the foe at bay. Yet it was obvious that they, too, were close to panic.

Shots then rang out, irregularly, as the rear ranks fired haphazard into the crowd before them, while sounds of a general melee arose. Meanwhile, Captain Lawrence had frozen, in woeful awe at having learned of the loss of his entire command. It must have struck him hard, to know he had not been present.

"They can't be killed, sir! We mustn't remain!" I then pleaded with both of the officers. A soldier suddenly broke from the column and made to flee, before he was seized by the lieutenant, who delivered a hard punch to the stomach with the hilt of his sword.

"Back into ranks, or I'll run you through!" The officer threatened, yet through the blow the man was undeterred.

All fear of such simple, *mortal* punishment had long fled his mind. He actually wrestled with the lieutenant to slip from his grasp, and was soon followed by others who broke from the column in a great clump.

"Keep ranks! Hold fast!" The sergeant tried to force men back with his pike. Captain Lawrence lost control of the major's horse, which began to buck and run, nearly toppling him over in the process. Another, louder shot then rang out, as a zealous corporal shot a fleeing man in the back. He fell at my feet, his spine severed, gasping for air.

Nothing would do for it. The line was collapsing.

Within a blink, at least half of the column took to flight down the narrow street. Among those who stood, the frontmost men were keeping biting devils at bay with their bayonets. They were failing under the push of dead meat, whilst every moment stragglers broke through to bite and tear away at them.

Notwithstanding countless shots and bayonet thrusts, musket butts beating into them and an ensign's sword cutting away, our foe's indefatigability was quickly realised. With the major in unwitting flight atop his wiser mount, it fell to Captain Lawrence to take the command of whatever pathetic little band remained.

"Retreat! Break ranks!" Roared he atop the din. The soldiers capable of following such orders did so with all too much enthusiasm, save for a few who tried vainly to rescue some crony or other from the devils' grasps.

Among those at the very front, *unable* to retreat, the corpses soon fell atop them; their screaming was muffled beneath so many layers of necrosis. I found myself rushing at speed down the road alongside the captain, who urged the men to keep together all the while, and load as they ran. Few heeded him, but made for whatever path they could. Up ahead we saw the major, having finally given power over to his horse, galloping down the road with all speed past the scattered remains of his company.

Thus fell the garrison of Stowlham: in fear, confusion,

cowardice, and sick betrayal.

It was a terrible blessing that the first men overtaken were slow to die, having been so clumsily swarmed, for their corporeal stubbornness thus distracted the devils and permitted the remainder of us to gain some distance. Our advantage was not to last long, however.

As the wounded, scattered column fled down a wider lane, another terrible scream emanated from our head. While several devils pursued hotly from the rear, it seemed others were drawn to the general commotion, and soon came on from all around! I saw an old man, his jaw ripped clean off, come charging out from an alleyway to tackle the man before me. When Captain Lawrence made to aid him, I had cause to break my discipline in a most terrible fashion as I grabbed him by the arm and pulled him back.

"There's nothing for it, sir!" I implored over his aghast protestation. Just behind the jawless creature, two others then descended upon their victim, whose screaming was soon silenced.

All about us were similar scenes playing out, as the devils came on endlessly. They stumbled not only from the town's centre, then, but had evidently managed to infect every corner of the town. Nowhere was safe as the captain and I were preserved by little more than the sick whimsy of fortune; man after man all about us succumbed in one fashion or another to the biting masses.

The head of our 'column' had slowed, then, with many men doubling back as a particularly large group of devils appeared to the front. Panic filled every soldier's eyes, and the few who remained armed fired wildly in every direction.

We were truly surrounded, and hopelessly lost in the winding streets, lit only by the moon and distant fire. Soon even the major himself, attempting to turn his mount clear of danger, was set upon.

His attacker had stumbled from around some bend and seized upon his leg, desperately gnawing away at the thick leather of his boot. It could not bite through the material, but neither could it be extricated by the thrashings of man or horse. It was soon joined by another devil, and a third.

Before long, the poor horse was bogged down by biting devils, and overwhelmed. With every kick, which might have killed any mortal man, the steed merely provided greater openings for more assailants to shove themselves. They bit at its flank and underside, clawed at its face and pulled erratically at the major. All his cutting was futile against the mob, which had grown to a staggering four deep in parts. It was too much for the unfortunate animal, as ever-so-slowly it was dragged to the ground, beneath the chittering mass. The major was soon silenced; yet his horse was a stubborn beast, evidently feeling every bite and refusing to give up its ghost to the last. Its shrieking echoed loudly through the streets, and served to pull more devils into the frenzy, as they bathed in the heavy entrails of beast and man alike.

For those few men who were capable, and willing, to try and aid their commander, their stabbing and shooting into the crowd proved little worth. They were soon taken just as their officer had been.

Yet while I was frozen in fear of all these terrible events, it was Captain Lawrence who leapt at once into activity. The greater portion of our foe being distracted, he took the opportunity and made for the nearest home, attempting to force his way inside.

"Open this door!" Shouted he, pounding on it with his sword-hilt. Yet there was no reply. Turning away, then, he rushed along the terrace to the next home.

I made to follow his example at once, and coming to the nearest door likewise attempted to force it. Finding it firm and locked, I began bashing upon it with my fists, calling for any inhabitants. From within, though I could not see her through the blockaded window, I heard a small child wail in horror. No doubt they were clutching away at their mother's skirts, imagining me to be one of the dead.

"I'm alive! Please! Help us, please!" I pleaded with the door, yet its cracked paint yielded nothing beyond the sounds of terror within. Nor should I have suspected otherwise; for what parent would risk their child being ripped asunder for the sin of charity to a soldier? Still, in the chaos of that moment, I did not care a lick for their *potential* dangers, as I faced a very *real* one!

Fear, in that way, had driven all sense of soldierly chivalry from my mind, and numbed me to the horror of my actions. Blessedly, I had not long to terrorise those poor inhabitants before a joyous cry issued from across the road.

"Here!" Called a man, standing in the decaying frame of a door he had forced. "Come on, lads! Here!"

Without a thought I set off for the sanctuary, skirting past numerous gruesome scenes as I went. To one side, two men were overtaken and fell over each other when a devil boldly collided with them. To the other, the major's horse, half gutted and well spread across the street, had finally succumbed. The great heap of corpses atop it struggled, in their tangled limbs, to detach from the mob and haul themselves upright.

By the time I reached the doorway, many men were already clambering for a spot inside, jamming themselves unceremoniously through the narrow gap and receiving terrible deep splinters to their hands and faces in the process. Captain Lawrence was soon there to shove some of them inside, and with blood pouring down his arm from some unseen injury, waved the remainder of us in.

I was among the last to enter the little home, and the captain slammed hard the door behind us as a number of devils caught wise of our movement. Without hesitation they threw their weight against the door, already loose on its hinges and propped up only by the effort of wounded Lawrence, who called out for a blockade.

The nearest men soon produced numerous sizeable pieces of furniture which, with some difficulty, they wedged before the door. Soon every object of weight in the little sitting room we had found ourselves within was heaped against the entrance. Blessedly, it seemed the creatures lacked the wit even to ram our gates, but merely pushed continuously upon it with all their weight. Thus, with great fortune, their efforts proved ineffectual at overcoming our defence. Nor, however, did they surrender the effort, but piled deep around the home in the memory of our escape.

We had been laid to siege.

The Streets of Stowlham.

Part the

FIFTH

wherein

the devils are obſerved.

As I retreated into the home, I was finally able to take some stock of my surroundings.

The place was small, consisting of little more than an entryway leading to a sitting room, behind which another door presumably led into an equally diminutive kitchen. A rickety old staircase led up into a shadowy first storey. It was even darker than the outside, with scarcely any light glinting through our blockaded door and the window alongside it. As my eyes adjusted to the conditions, they alighted to a most pitiful sight. Torn up and bloodied redcoats lay collapsed all about the floor and strewn over the stairs. We were all heaving for breath, and in a terrible shock.

There were perhaps a dozen and a half of us then, none from my former company save Captain Lawrence himself. Nary a man spoke, though one wept quietly in a corner and was fearful of any who might come too close.

From beyond our little fortress came the sounds of so many scratching fingernails against jagged wood, as the devils attempted to claw their way through, uncaring of the splinters it brought them. Most chilling of all was the *click-click-clicking* of so many biting jaws. It was a brutal reminder of our comrades' fate, and possibly our own besides.

~ 67 ~

There was no doubt that many of those pressing bodies wore red coats, the same as us within.

"Right then." Captain Lawrence soon took charge of the situation, speaking softly lest he arouse greater attention from the devils outside. "Don't just laze about now, everyone, there's work to be done. Has anyone checked for other entrances? Inhabitants?"

It was only after a swift kick that the first man 'volunteered' his services, and this had the desired effect of spurring some others into activity. The men set about their business as quietly as possible, scouring through the home and contributing to our growing barricade. Another door to a back alley being found in the kitchen, it was likewise shuttered up with several chairs and an old table. Before any could venture to the floor above, however, our concern regarding other inhabitants was answered.

A loud creaking came from the wood above us, as it became clear someone- or *something-* was slowly moving there.

At once this provoked some distress among us all, yet cooler heads prevailed before someone could fire his musket into the ceiling. From around the corner, atop the stairs, the captain spied the glimmer of a candle. We soon found ourselves looking upon the property's owner: an old man, in equally old-fashioned clothes, looked down the stairway upon us with tired eyes that flickered dully.

All was again quiet, save for the pushing devils beyond the door.

"My good sir." Captain Lawrence moved to address the man. His voice was unnaturally quiet, and lacked all his usual gravitas. The extent of his injury became clear to me, then. His once beautifully laced waistcoat was stained all down the side with blood, and while he hid the pain well, his left arm clung tight and unmoving to his side. "I apologise for our intrusion, but your home has saved our lives. I assure you, I shall make good on the damage. We must remain here some time to regain our strength."

The old man kept silent, observing the captain without

acknowledgement for some time, before steadily descending the stairs. With an annoyed grunt he kicked aside one of our number who had collapsed in exhaustion upon the lower steps, and brushed past our officer as he made for the kitchen. All our eyes followed him, yet none dared shift their place.

The old man then paused at the kitchen door and, without looking over his shoulder, finally addressed Lawrence.

"Come on, then." He muttered gruffly.

With a look about the men, the gentleman confusedly followed after. In the ensuing meeting, our host proved well hospitable, if not outwardly polite. While none could offer anything like medical expertise, Captain Lawrence was at least given some ratty old cloth to clean and patch up his wound. So too was any man with a bite or scrape of significance, of which there were many, able to do the same. It seemed, by the end, that we had thus looted every napkin and tablecloth to be had in the home. Likewise the man's larder was soon opened, offering up to us what precious little he had. Of particular blessing were a few bottles of wine, from which every barbarous one of us took a long, unceremonious pull. All the while we kept silent as church mice, while the old man uttered no more than a dozen words altogether.

He was, in that moment, our saviour.

We sat and drank in the sad, lonely dark. Our only light was a dim candle in the kitchen, over which Captain Lawrence and our host huddled, as the officer rather awkwardly explained the circumstances of our arrival. They sat at the table which had been shoved so unceremoniously against the back door. All through that meeting, although he resisted any outward display of such, the paleness of my officer's face betrayed the seriousness of his condition.

For us private soldiers, however, there remained nothing more than to sit idle. Those few who were capable of it, or who had imbibed too heavily in drink, soon fell asleep. A few others muttered to each other in darkened corners. The one poor soul continued to quietly weep. The remainder all sat distinctly unnerved by the continued scraping outside the front door. At least any sounds of bloodshed had by then migrated to more distant parts of the town - not to say they were terribly far.

For my part I was utterly restless. Closing my eyes, I saw flames reaching with their spindly tendrils across the town to ravage our little sanctuary. I saw black shadows dancing across them, and ripping at flesh upon the ground. Flesh that held Richards' or Bennett's eyes, looking to me in pleading terror. Every rattle of a window from some breeze or faint rumbling cough forced me awake in fear of an incursion.

Though my body, cut up and stained, had yet survived, it seemed that already my mind had become terribly afflicted. I was then, as I now remain, a *living husk*, cursed and made low with the weight of so many dead souls. The tears upon my cheeks had mixed with so much dirt and gore that when I rubbed at them, the smear made it seem that I wept a black, tarry blood. I recall thinking, with an unhappy smirk, how I must have cut a similar image to that of so many devils outside.

Abandoning my futile hope of rest, then, and being more curious - or perhaps more numb - than the others, I soon found myself creeping up the little stairway whence our host had first made his appearance.

The home above was precisely as one might have expected, with a little bedroom, once finely decorated, having since fallen to age. A lone portrait upon the wall captured a beauty who must have been the old man's wife, in a happier time. Here, at least, above the chaos below, there had been no need to block up the few windows, and beneath one of them I saw another soldier had sat down to dazedly stare outside.

As I stepped forward, a creak in the floorboard betrayed my presence. The man's face snapped up from the glass in a terrible, though blessedly silent, fright.

"Hell!" He hissed at me. "Poor form, that. Sneaking up on a man."

"Sorry." I replied, spreading my hands in truce and coming up to the window. "I couldn't sleep, is all."

"No, I fancy not." The man's attention had already returned to the outside. "You're one of Lawrence's men, then?"

"I am." Indeed, I suspected I was then Lawrence's *only* man. That thought set me to grimace as I wiped again at my face. The corruption felt as though it would never brush away.

Lieutenant Farwell had *certainly* been killed, the same as both sergeants, while any survivors had at best been scattered to be plucked off, one by one, in their rout. I could only pray the same fate had not befallen the women and children, and that they had remained in their billets unnoticed. Yet, what were the odds? Some foul end seemed assured to meet them before long, just as it seemed assured to meet us.

Already I saw the glimmer of flames outside, illuminating the street below and casting long, vile shadows over the ghastly site we had only just escaped. I knew it would not be long before they reached the home and cooked us alive, should we remain.

The other man took no note of my distress, however, as he remained transfixed by the view.

"Is he a good officer?" Asked he quietly. "Can he get us out?"

Of course, I hadn't the faintest idea how Captain Lawrence might effect an escape. I could only attest to his being a fair and intelligent man. As my gaze followed the man's own, then, the scent of burning wood and flesh on the air became little disturbing to me compared with what lay below.

Military equipment lay scattered beside chunks of torn flesh; little islands amidst a sea of blood which covered the road whence we were set upon. Splashing their way through the gore were what seemed to be dozens of devils - mostly former townsmen who had rushed out to combat the fires, and not a few of my fellow soldiers as well. Any persons who survived within shuttered and latched homes would surely be the most innocent: women and children, the old, the sick, and infirm. Poor Stowlham had been struck at its most vulnerable, and stood now utterly defenceless against tooth and flame.

For the first time, then, I could observe the corpses from

some security. I noted with horror the severity of the wounds each wore. Necks and chest cavities had been ripped asunder. Eyes were gouged and noses gnawed off. Behind many of them trailed limbs half severed, or entrails gutted from within, upon which others frequently slipped and became entangled. Their subsequent uncaring thrashing, then, served only to draw out yet further viscera, or otherwise snap it away in terrible, squishy motions.

Regardless of their size or injury, each of the creatures was clearly unsteady and uncertain of itself. It seemed their steps were without direction, a struggling shuffle and limp. Without some prey to pursue, every limb fixed itself upon a variable point, hardly cooperating to fall from one step into another. Their hands were as disquieted as their mouths, opening and closing rapidly from the ends of snapping, probing arms, as if in anticipation of grabbing firm upon the living. Likewise their heads swivelled and shot about rapidly with wide, unblinking eyes, as they sought any sign of life. To our fortune, at least, the mere concept of *gazing upwards* seemed alien to them, for whatever lay beyond their immediate front was evidently of little interest. They made no sound, nor communicated in any way, beyond the constant cracking of their jaws.

Listening to it would be enough to drive any man mad, over time.

"Milling about like drunks." Muttered my compatriot. "Looking for us, I suppose."

"Not much sense at all." I agreed, transfixed by their every move. Intensely I studied in horror how they went to and fro, some twirling about in circles, while others merely stood staring at walls. That seemed to be the case for at least three devils, which evidently comprehended our presence within the home yet could not determine how they might go about entering it. One continued pushing itself bodily into the door, to no avail, while I could see that its fingers had gone red and raw from clawing at the wood in feverish desperation.

It was wearing a regimental coat.

"Some seem to remember us, at least." Joked my

companion, without humour. "That, or I suppose the bastards downstairs keep making some noise to keep his attention. Oh, poor man..."

The soldier trailed off, keeping some emotion at bay. It was surely a deeply affecting sight for him, to see so many former comrades in such a state. I wondered, then, whether he was close with any of them? Whether his feelings were deeper than mere curiosity, to keep him so affixed to the windowsill?

I found myself thinking once more of Bennett, and of Richards.

Where were they then? Did they shuffle through the streets in like fashion? The thought seemed more sad than frightening, as I stood solemn before the window.

"Was he a friend?" Asked I of my fellow mourner, regarding the particularly zealous once-soldier at our gates.

"No." Replied he after a moment's silence. "Never even spoke with him, really. He was transferred to us from the Lights after a row with some officer or other. I don't know the details - some trouble with drink, I think it was. Had a pretty little wife, though. She didn't come with him after we left Salisbury. Not a one for marching."

His face contorted briefly as he bit away his melancholy.

Thus we remained in silence for some while, until slowly there appeared the faintest light of dawn above, in stark contrast to the black smoke rising in ever-greater intensity. As more of the street was thus illuminated, so too was its horror all the more terrible.

Of particular note, more visceral than all the rest, was the state of Major Bray's poor horse. It lay gutted and well strewn across the ground. It, too, had become corrupted in death. Somehow it seemed even less aware than its human counterparts, for it was unable even to rise, but still I saw its limbs twitching weakly. It did not quite chew the air, as the others would, but its lips and tongue worked in odd contortions as its head lolled about senselessly. At that, I could not help but feel an even deeper pity than I did for the major, who lay frantically writhing beneath the animal.

I sat with the other soldier for some time, joining him in his melancholy. I found myself unable to look away from the horse. From its tragedy, however, came to me a thought of the slimmest hope.

"Cavalry." Said I, simply. "There will surely be a relief force. The smoke will be spotted soon, and word will spread of our plight. They'll send help!"

If the soldier set any stock in my prediction, he did little to show for it beyond a noncommittal grunt. Nor could he be blamed for any lack of enthusiasm, as it was not long before my little dawn succumbed to darker tones.

Who was to say, I thought with a terrible pain in my breast, that Stowlham was alone in this plight? Just as our fate was obscured by the dark, so too might that of every other surrounding community. Who was to say that these terrible assaults of the dead had not been launched throughout all England by then, and that there would be *no* aid at all? Or even, should the rest of our battalion come marching in, that they would not befall the same fate as us in the garrison?

My mind went to Lieutenant Farwell's stand, so noble and yet totally futile. To those many men so easily overtaken by such a small number of the foe, and to how the bodies of mere *children* had endured so many shots and bayonet thrusts undeterred.

It was apparent to me that the whole town had fallen, which would mean *thousands* of mindless daemons prowling those burning streets. What hope was there, then, for even the best prepared relief forces?

All of those dark sentiments and more seemed to cascade unending through my mind, whilst we remained in the window. Had I remained there long, I suspect I'd have been driven totally mad. Yet with a jolt, I was soon pulled from the brink as another weary soldier appeared in the doorway behind us.

"Sergeant?" I turned at the sound of his voice, yet there were no men of such authority in the room, as I informed him.

"No matter. Captain wants to see you." Slurred the disinterested messenger. He seemed a little drunk. Perhaps he had stolen away more than his share of the libations, or was merely weak in constitution.

There was nothing for arguing the point, so with a nod to my companion, who had already resumed his watch, I followed the messenger down to the kitchen where Captain Lawrence still sat with the old man. I approached and made to remove my hat, only to recall it had long since been lost. I fumbled awkwardly for a moment, then, before coming to my proper attention.

My officer's face was still pale. He seemed the most fatigued of us all. His breathing was slow and laboured, yet his eyes pierced through me with grim determination.

"Sir?" I inquired, nearly interrupting him as he wasted no time on such formality.

"Sergeant. Forgive the lack of a proper sash," spoke he in a dry, hushed tone, "but exigencies of the service, and all. We are in a hard position and I require a man I can trust. So far as we know, you and I are the last of our old company."

Thus I had received my most unnaturally rapid field-promotion, and I doubt whether one has ever been *less* welcomed in all the annals of military history. Though, naturally, I tried my best to conceal the feeling.

"Th-thank you, sir." The words eventually stumbled from me. "I will try-"

"Play your cards right, and you'll retire off a commission by the end of the week, at this rate." The captain tried to joke, although his effort to speak was not an easy one and, like all the jokes made in those terrible days, it was quite humourless. I figured, at the time, that the officer could address me as colonel, for all he liked. It would make little difference to our station.

"Now take the seat there, and look at this." He gestured to the table before him, where I saw in the faint candlelight a sort of rudimentary map, clumsily scratched into the wood with a kitchen knife.

"Are we to...sally out, sir?" Asked I, awfully frightened of the answer.

Lawrence's gaze never broke from me.

"I need not explain the difficulty of our situation, sergeant. Our position is untenable and we have no choice but to act. Now, our host knows this locale better than we, and it seems the alley behind this home might provide our best opportunity."

The prospect of returning outside was a terrifying one. Already I felt I had cheated death twice, and I fancied the bill was sure to come due any moment. Given the choice of burning to death, or being chewed to bits, I was not entirely certain that death by fire was the worse of the two. If nothing else, I could perish at rest, rather than exhausted in any misguided escape attempt.

The plan Captain Lawrence then spelled out was simple enough in principle. We could anticipate no *timely* relief, he explained, nor would it be wise to presume security in any part of the country before we got word from London.

That was a point agreeable enough.

As such, he assured me, the only *reasonable* course would be to establish ourselves within some bastion or other, until we might learn more. Apparently the old civilian had assured him, though he spoke not a lick in my presence, that the alley would lead directly to a little square near the edge of town, far from the fire's start. There stood a church, vitally encased in a stone-walled yard, which we might readily fortify.

"With any luck," rasped he through a pained, dry cough, "any refugees will have already found their way there for sanctuary, same as us. Major Bray's company was billeted nearby, besides, and I fear that without an opportunity to save their wives, these men will refuse any action. Already I've had a few of them grumbling to move on, and discipline will surely break if we sit idle much longer. Once we secure ourselves, and as many civilians as we might, within the walls, we might further evaluate our situation. Should it prove viable, we'll escape this infernal place and rejoin with our Colours."

The captain then shuddered at an unfelt chill. His focus seemed to slip for a moment as he fought against himself. Every breath and every motion seemed a terrible effort.

"So?" Asked he. "What say you?"

"Sir..." My response came unsteadily; I was thoroughly unaccustomed to *speaking* with my captain, let alone to the idea of offering my thoughts on his scheme. "I suppose it's all fair enough, but...supposing we're wrong? The church could just as easily have been broken into. It could well be *filled* with the things by now. What if-"

"You will learn quickly, sergeant," interrupted the dying gentleman, "that in commanding men there is little room for the hypothetical. If the church is overrun, there will be no chance to form a defence within the town itself. Certainly not one that the fires won't soon reach. I fear there would be no choice but to abandon the town entirely. Which means," he pointed to another vague, long scratch upon the table, which ran parallel with the square and churchyard, "that we shall cross to the river here...and learn whether the devils can swim or not. I suspect many of the men won't dare leave their loved ones behind, and we'll not be able to prevent their abandoning us. Truly, it will mean every man for himself, but we'll keep order as best we can. *Save* whomever we can. Circumstances allowing, we might even move downstream to our own billets to pull our own out, and hopefully gain a few muskets along the way...I only pray that the women and children have kept themselves away from all this...But above all else, sergeant, we need to regain some *stability*, and prepare to meet with whatever relief could well *already* be on its way. We'll need to warn them of the situation, lest they be caught unaware and suffer our same fate. Do you understand?"

What could I do, besides nod in agreement? My mind raced endlessly through a cavernous void, in which every thought was drowned. The panic which then gripped me was a silent one. The little candlelight burned a deep pit into my vision.

The captain's path seemed sound enough, and was likely our best chance at survival. Yet, could he make it? He seemed already to be knocking upon death's door.

Was he asking me to take up his mantle, should he fall? I knew I had not the strength for such a task. Glancing again at the old man, still he kept silent at the table's end.

Perhaps he had encouraged the captain with a *false map* to see us gone? Though, he did not seem angry. In fact he had, despite his quiet, been overly charitable in our time of need. The man merely seemed exhausted. Tired of life itself. Would he even try to follow us out?

"Only sir," I found my courage to speak only as Lawrence arose, "what if the men refuse? They won't all have families they're looking to save..."

The captain looked down at me with a stern, determined look upon his pale and haggard face. He laid a hand on my shoulder and squeezed with what little strength he had left.

The words he spoke have never left me since.

"We are still *soldiers*, lad. We have our duty, and by God, we'll see it through. Even to our last. The kind of men we *want* to have by our side, will follow. Now come, we've a siege to break, and enough time has been wasted."

I would have been proud to follow Captain James Lawrence into battle against the French. I was sure then, as I remain still, that he would have brought us all to great glory, had he been given the chance.

Yet just then, he seemed already condemned.

He was a hollow, fading man who had the privilege to speak of duty. Was he *truly* in earnest? Or merely hoping to salvage some glory in a pained, ignominious death? I realised that, just as myself, the madness of that night was the first true bloodshed he had seen.

Would he lead us to glory, then, or damn us in vainglory? It is with regret that I recall these thoughts, yet I was petrified, as any sane man must be in such circumstances.

Before following my officer, I looked again to the old man in hopes of some answer. He would not meet my gaze.

Our Defence Breached.

wherein

a ſtranger is met.

𝕮𝖆𝖕𝖙𝖆𝖎𝖓 𝕷𝖆𝖜𝖗𝖊𝖓𝖈𝖊 𝖍𝖆𝖉 𝖇𝖊𝖊𝖓 correct in one thing.

As we re-entered the sitting room to explain the plan, a number of men rose at once. They were eager to abandon the dark, cramped, and by then quite foul-smelling shelter. It was clear they had families back in their billets, and would follow their new officer so far as was necessary to see them safe. They soon dusted themselves off and took up whatever means were at hand to assail the enemy. Some retained their muskets, while for others a severed table leg, the wood of a fire screen, or a heavy mirror, intended for use as some rudimentary shield, would have to serve. To be sure, any object which might be placed between oneself and the biting masses was preferable to one's own limbs.

A particularly stout fellow offered me one of the table legs. Grateful as I was, still the prospect of clubbing a devil with the thing was thoroughly disturbing to me. Against that which countless bayonets and musket butts had failed to stem, I now wielded nothing more than a mere hunk of wood!

As our party readied itself, we attempted to maintain a strict code of silence, lest we attract any greater attentions from the outside. Still a number of bodies remained steadily scraping and pushing against our blockaded front door, and the faint sound of their working jaws could be heard from within. Yet as the plan was explained in greater detail, and the men divided themselves up into little teams for a leap-frogging dash through the alley, it became clear that some were less than enthused than others. They would not meet the eyes of their comrades, but huddled into corners away from the rest of us wherever they could. Before long, these would-be mutineers had formed themselves up into a party of their own, so far from the door as they might slink.

The big fellow then made to force a club into one of their hands, but it was violently refused, and soon clattered loudly to the floor. The sound made us all jump, and seemed to encourage the waiting devils just outside.

"Damn you all!" The shirker exclaimed too loudly, his eyes wide. His tone met with immediate, desperate *shushes* and muttered swears, yet he would not be cowed in his madness. "You're all mad, is what you are! Thinking to go out there!"

"Bleedin' Christ, shut it!" The stout one whispered fiercely, and made again to force the club into his hands. "You want to bring 'em on our heads? Come on, I won't die in a hole on your account!"

Yet I could see it in the afeared man's eyes. He was panic-stricken, and would not move by *any* accord. Nor could I blame him, or his fellow shirkers; for what protection might bravery and a table leg offer in such horrid circumstances?

Captain Lawrence, however, was not a one to suffer disorder or *cowardice* under his command, even before a cannibal horde.

"Sergeant, see to that man." He spoke to me in a grim, yet utterly determined, tone.

I would have no time to season into my new role. As I pushed through the mass of tightly-packed strangers, I found my legs beginning to shake. My breathing accelerated. I was no more prepared to effect a break-out than the man I was meant to discipline! My own cowardice was merely suppressed by the will of my captain, whereas this poor fellow was without his usual leadership. My mind raged in emptiness, a vacuous pit of despond. I was carried, then, as if by fate to stand before those two soldiers.

They seemed ready to come to fisticuffs, and I was at a loss of what to say. All the men looked to me, yet none with confidence. Never had a promotion been so unhappy as mine!

"C-come on, then." I stumbled over my words. How could I demand respect of a man more honest in his fears than myself? He knew it, too. They all did. "We're...still soldiers, aren't we? We've our duty to attend. Now, take up your weapon, and le-"

"You miserable wretch." Spat the coward, accepting nothing of my up-jumped pretence. "You'd go and get yourself ripped apart, then? Eh?"

He made no effort to keep quiet, and was soon joined by another of his assembled gang, who angrily gestured towards the outside.

"I shan't follow any man but Major Bray, and you *saw* what happened to him! You all *saw* what those things did to Sergeant Rivers!" He was nearer to shouting than those before, and this led to new tumult as another soldier aimed to silence him bodily.

"You're a bloody coward, Smith! Always have been!" Exclaimed another in the loyalist party, only restrained from blows by a cooler-headed comrade. The larger man had no such restraints, however, and soon seized upon his adversary - as if shaking him would quell the rising chaos!

The room at once erupted into bedlam, as half the men were but a moment from outright brawling, and the others desperately pleaded for quiet. Beneath the din, his voice rasping with long-dead authority, Captain Lawrence stepped forward to raise his sword high. It seemed he was trying for a speech, to settle the men's fears and rouse them up like we stood in some grand story. The only effect of his grandiosity was that a different soldier, being shoved back in an attempted grapple, knocked him hard to the floor. I hastened then through the jostling mob to the captain's side. He had landed poorly; his hands, which had become frail, clutched at his broken, bleeding nose.

It was all the spark many men needed. At once, numerous shoving matches broke out between the factions, and half-drunk shouting was heard. Hell was then unleashed upon our former sanctuary.

There came a fresh, loud *thudding* upon the door as new bodies crashed into the press. Then followed the rattling of glass. Some devils, newly aware of our presence within, had thrown themselves against the blocked window! Yet even as they scraped and pried away at our walls, the men inside would not be cowed. Many, in fact, seemed not to even notice until the sound of *rattling* and *thudding* turned to *shattering* and *splintering*.

One of the devils at the window collided headlong into a lesser-covered panel, breaking clear through and toppling the loosely-laid chair before it. At last, the whole terror of our situation had become clear. One fellow screamed, while another rushed to push the invader out with a musket butt.

Yet it was too late.

The devil with a foothold, despite its skull being repeatedly smashed in, soon forced the remainder of its body through the gap, which in turn widened as it went. With a point of entry to exploit, other corpses frantically fought for the space, and our barricade shifted and fell back one piece at a time. Soon a second creature had come through, while another's hand broke into the room to grasp at whatever it might reach. The dead fingers secured a hold upon one poor man, who shrieked pitifully whilst his comrades tried to wrest him free.

Then, a shot rang out.

As the first devil had risen up and made to grab at his attacker, the man turned his musket about and fired directly into its skull. The shot scattered the bone and set every *living* man's ears to ringing as the room flooded with a dreadful, acrid smoke. Yet even this brutality failed utterly to slow the cannibal's pace. Brushing aside the smoking barrel, the now half-headed beast, with brains all exposed, fell into its victim as the pair tumbled back into the crowd. Teeth tore open the soldier's neck through the simple roller he wore in lieu of a stock.

There was no hope of pushing the foe back, and our rout was immediate. Some of the men raced upstairs to a presumed safety, while others stampeded and fell over Lawrence and myself to get into the kitchen. Outside, every creature within earshot was descending upon our position. Those few men who stood at the window were grabbed, scratched, and bitten by innumerable bodies swarming their way through every possible gap.

The furniture at the broken-in door likewise was giving way, and I found myself locking eyes with a red-coated devil behind. What seemed like dozens of corpses had piled hard against the entrance, and nothing would stop the onslaught of their fresh advance. All their gross attentions were fixed squarely upon us.

Another blood-chilling scream pierced my ears as I saw one man, the first to have been grabbed, abandoned by his fellows. While one hand then tore open his waistcoat, another squeezed at his neck, and a third tore into his face. With horror I saw, between the panicked, rushing bodies which trampled over me in their attempt to flee, how the poor wretch's eye began slowly to split apart under the scratch of an over-long nail.

"Sir!" I looked back to Captain Lawrence, pulling at his collar and attempting to bring him to his feet. He seemed delirious, meeting my gaze yet uncomprehending of it. "Sir, we must leave!"

"Sergeant," his reply came as a dreamy whisper, "the line mustn't break...Reform the company..." He trailed off, and I realised that the wound at his shoulder had opened up again.

What little blood remained in him flowed fresh to stain his arm anew. By then, the devils had fully breached the home through the door as well as the window. What few men remained were attempting to stymie them, and falling quickly. Those less courageous of souls then stood clamouring all about the back door, through the kitchen.

They fought atop one another to remove its blockade, and undo the simple latch. One even attempted to force his way through a window that was too small for him by half, and had evidently begun to weep and panic as he realised he had become fastened in place.

There was nothing for it. I could expect no aid from my fellow soldiers.

Mustering what little strength I yet possessed, I hoisted my officer upon my shoulders, and made to drag him towards the kitchen. No other paths stood open to me, as the bodies piled higher just feet away on the other side of the sitting room. The exceedingly few heroes in our party beat away at the encroaching wave of dead meat with their musket butts and pitiful 'clubs', yet each were overtaken in turn. Still, many among them were true die-hards. Fighting to the last, through all their pains, they granted some additional time to their more *cowardly* brethren. Thus, by the time I reached the back door with the captain, the panicked mob had finally succeeded in clearing the way.

To my front, soldiers jostled awkwardly for their place through the door, and fled from the home in every direction. Behind, a stumbling wave of newly-deceased soldiers came stumbling alongside townsmen and women in their soulless, silent hunger. With Captain Lawrence across my back, I passed by two braver men who, rather than attempting to force their way through the press, turned to face the foe.

The first fired his musket directly into the mass of oncoming bodies, again clouding the air as he did so and casting the whole of them in white shadow. The second hammered away with his 'club', quick and brutal, to dash the corpses away as they came near. Yet those men's noble stand offered less worth than their deaths. As the biting masses took some time in rendering them into so many rough cuts of meat and broken bone, piling all atop one another as they did, they actually served to *block up* those devils behind them!

In a sick blessing, before the two men's sacrifice could be completed, the doorway ahead of me was finally cleared of men. Their frightful screams echoed loudly through the alleyway to accompany the tortured ones within.

At once I joined in their flight, and at the last moment I caught a fleeting glimpse of the old man. He regarded the whole of us with his same quiet, resigned countenance from the kitchen's corner. As three creatures leapt atop him, he first seemed to accept his death without protestation. Yet when the first set of teeth sank into his flesh, even so stoic a figure could not but cry out in pain.

In the sheer terror of that moment, I still cannot fathom whence I summoned the strength to stay with my poor captain. His flesh, although weakened, if cast unto my pursuers would surely have granted me more time to make my escape, to say nothing of lessening my burden. As it stood, I could hardly anticipate *my own* survival, let alone his. Yet onwards I pressed with the dying gentleman atop me, threading my way through the doorway, and into the alley beyond.

Was it loyalty to the old, dead military discipline that spurred me on? Or perhaps some naive, stupid prayer that by defending my last officer, my life might somehow restore itself to the way it had been before? That to save *at least one* man might keep me from the terrible fate which befell so many friends and comrades? The captain's final order had been to reform the company; we were all that remained of it.

Thus, seemingly overtaken with some queer sense of philosophy, I refused to abandon my charge and resolved instead to do *all I could* to meet my soldierly duty. Lawrence had gone entirely limp by then, and his breath was slow and shallow upon my neck. It was a miracle he was still alive at all.

My back had first been warm from his flowing blood, yet was fast becoming cold. It was only, then, by the grim Providence of a twisted Divine that we were able to escape that alleyway; for there came to the devils two final, tragic distractions.

The first came in the form of the man held fast by the window. Over my shoulder, I saw him screaming, and pleading with God for release - whether from the window, or from the mortal coil, I know not - whilst he endured every bite and abuse the devils might offer him from the other side. From his mouth spluttered great globs of blood, which mixed down his chin with so many tears. As the first devils then burst into the alley, their interest was soon turned upon his upper half in equal measure.

My second unwilling saviour then came from above, where from the home's upper floor I heard the fresh breaking of glass. Turning from my flight for but a moment, I saw a man attempting to clamber out of a window.

It was the man I had spoken with earlier. I had never asked his name.

Despite his best efforts, he was unable to gain a reliable foothold. Thus, whether willingly or not, he took his sole remaining chance and flung himself from the window. He fell at a poor angle and landed hard amidst the broken glass below. Even as I again turned to flee, I heard the horrific *crack* of a bone. He was soon followed by his pursuer, which threw itself uncaring from the height to land atop him. Of the remaining devils in the alleyway, they soon joined with their dead kin in tearing at the grounded man.

Thus I turned away, abandoning the remnants of Major Bray's company to their bloody fates. I ducked around one corner, and then another, to ensure that the witless creatures might not so easily pursue me.

My rushing then slowed to a laboured shuffle along with my disoriented charge, and it struck me how *silent* the town had become. It seemed the entire place had given up its ghost, and we remnants of the garrison had been last of all the living. The only sound then, besides the chaos I had left behind, was the roaring of ever-intensifying flames which continued to spread across the rooftops. The sky was blackened above as smoke battled the rising sun in its war to keep Stowlham in shadow. It would scarce be long before the whole of the town was alight.

I stood truly alone, then, save for my dying officer.

"The church." I muttered to myself, for the captain would

surely not comprehend my words. "The churchyard will be safe. We'll shelter there, and make for the river. Like you said, sir. Like you said."

Though I frequently had to rest the captain against some barrel or wall whilst I scouted a sudden turn or long dash ahead, we managed to avoid any of the wandering corpses. Twice I needed to crouch behind some little cover, waiting for one to face away, to then sneak by speedily, praying it would not turn about again. I realised that regardless of their former stature, and whether once a man, woman, or child, the devils equally lacked wit. They could but gaze about them and stagger, this way or that, in hopes they might encounter some living prey.

On one count, I was saved by a dog, whether a forlorn pet or feral I knew not. The poor, whimpering thing had rounded a corner it thought to be safe, and in so doing came directly into the sight of a dead roper. The poor hound could only speed off down the road, the corpse in hopeless pursuit.

Eventually, I found a stubby steeple rising above one of the houses ahead. In that moment, the *spiritual* implication of such a sight was utterly lost on me, for the salvation I sought was purely temporal, and more fixed upon the walled-off yard than it was the altar within. Even so, the irony that my yearned security might be found within a *graveyard* was prominent in my mind.

At least the dead there were sealed away beneath so much stone and dirt, thought I!

Yet the comfort in knowing my goal was soon at hand would not last long. For as I peered around one final corner, I was at once denied any prayer of reaching the churchyard.

Captain Lawrence had once again been proven correct; yet to an awful end. The church had indeed represented a sanctuary for many, who fled to the security of its high stone walls and iron gate. That sanctuary, however, had been stolen from them by way of an unyielding lock.

There had evidently been a great struggle.

The front gate was coated with blood, and the stones

before them were slick with entrails and severed limbs, whilst the little market square before it was a hellscape of collapsed and charred stalls. It was filled with a veritable horde of chattering corpses, suffering all manner of injury.

To advance upon such a field with even a *battalion* would be suicidal.

The air all about me then thickened and began to close in as an impenetrable, invisible wall of claustrophobic confusion. I felt then, for the first time, the full extent of my weariness and injury. It was all I could do to keep from collapsing beneath my captain.

I realised too how ragged his breathing had become, and knew that even if we *were* capable of crossing the square, to move the man such a distance, and in such haste, would be folly. A new plan was needed, and foolishly I imagined that some rest and medicine might restore Lawrence to some faculty. I had refused to see how near he was to his end.

Instead, I thought to seek shelter within another home. Moving away from the square, I went down the path whence I had come. As I was alone and unarmed, however, I could not presume that even a way previously explored was without danger. My progress was slow-going as I moved from home to home, peering through windows and keyholes to find some shelter untouched by the chaos.

As I tried the myriad little doors in the alleyway, unsurprisingly, most were latched from within. While I *might* have forced them with some strength, I was then quite weak, and knew not what I might alert upon the other side. After some effort, at last I found a side entrance to a well kept, and *unlatched* home. As I pushed the door ever so gently, the creaking of wood sounded to my ears like a great whistle blast, which would serve only to bring the horde down upon me. Yet standing in the crack, and peering into the darkness beyond, all was quiet save the roar of distant flames.

The door itself *had* been blocked up, but imperfectly so with only small furniture. A firm shove easily dislodged the blockage enough for a little gap to appear. Sliding through, I then dragged the captain ignobly after me.

I found myself in another dark little kitchen, the windows being shuttered without, and covered with layers of wet newspaper within, so that practically no light could penetrate its formerly still air. While there stood a narrow table in the room, upon it was a full setting, evidently long untouched, and I dared not risk the noise of shuffling them. Besides, I had little enough strength to lift my officer again. Thus I dragged him over the dusty floor into the kitchen's centre. With no other comfort to offer, I removed my belting and, casting them aside, stripped off my coat to roll into a cushion for his head. I doubted whether he was aware of the world at all, but it did not feel right to have him lay so hard upon the floor. If nothing else, I was glad to be rid of the extra weight of my cartridge pouch and an empty frog. In a moment of folly, I even tore away my stock to liberate my breathing.

Whether in reality, or merely in my foolish hope, it seemed to me that the captain's breathing had settled with his respite. He had lost a great deal of blood, yet still the hero resisted the call of mortality.

With exceeding delicacy I pulled aside his coat, and determined at once where the devil had bitten hard upon him. His shirt was torn at the underarm, just where his thicker waistcoat, which might otherwise have protected him, opened up. How tragic it was, for the captain to have been a mere few inches from preservation! His final altercation must have been a roughshod grapple indeed, to have been bitten at so awkward an angle. Yet I had no time to dwell upon such sentiment or conjecture. Though I had little hope, still I felt that I must act to save my leader.

Thus, sparing but a moment to re-seal the door whence I had come, I made to clean his wound. First I pulled aside the little strips of tattered linen, matted thick in the mire of sweaty coagulate, before tearing a wide hole in the cloth. Through the mess I could see the distinctly circular cuts of teeth. Already the wound exhibited gruesome signs of some vile infection, with a kind of festering humour that filled the air and set me nearly to gagging. Taking a napkin from the nearby table's lonely setting, I tried to clean the wound, yet found myself pitifully ill equipped to the task. I began to panic as the realisation settled upon me, that even should he receive the immediate attention of a *surgeon*, still there may have been no hope for Captain Lawrence. His every slow breath, dragged hard through dying lungs, seemed then a sad plea.

Death would have been a mercy for the man I sought to save.

In my panicked, useless dabbing at the injury, I heard no approaching footsteps; yet the quiet *creak*ing of hinges was as rousing as a bugle, and set me nearly to leap from my skin. In the exceptional dark, I had not noticed the second door in the kitchen, the presence of which ought to have been obvious to me. At once I halted all motion save to raise my eyes, suddenly aware of every haggard breath I took. I expected to see a corpse stumbling its way into the room, eager to fall upon me, unarmed and helpless; yet the creature which returned my gaze from behind the narrow doorway exhibited every woeful sign of life.

The young woman's eyes were wide with terror. At first unsure of my place, I slowly made to stand. Before I might explain myself, however, the door slammed shut in a manner too loud for comfort.

"Wait!" I hissed as I rushed after her, throwing back the door before the woman could latch it shut. I found her stumbling backwards through a little entrance hall, clutching a long, rusted-over knife in her hands. It glinted menacingly in the low light, which bled inwards from a tiny papered-over window at the end of the hall, near the front door.

"Stay back!" She spat her words firmly. "Get away!" Blood stained the front of her dress, and her hands trembled around the crude weapon.

"Please, miss, I–"

"No! Get out!" She was more forceful then, and brandished the knife in a threat to which I believed she would make good. Yet returning to the streets would mean certain death for Captain Lawrence, already so near to his end. There remained no choice for me.

"I am unarmed." I explained through my cracked lips and burnt throat. I only then realised before how dry I had become, from my panic as much as the town's burning. "Please, my officer only needs rest, we'll not b-"

"Your officer," her tone placed no honour upon the title, "will die. Once he dies, he bites. Now you take him, and leave here!" I saw tears beading in her eyes, yet her voice was unwavering. She took a step towards me, ready to attack should I try and stand against her.

"I cannot do that. I dare not." My voice was but a desperately whispered plea. For all that I had suffered, I had become blind to the reality before me. My captain's death had *long* been inevitable, yet he was my sole relation to a world since destroyed. To lose him, I felt, would be to lose myself.

The woman had not the luxury of humouring my triviality, however, and my second refusal of her righteous demand saw her lunge at me ferociously. With a start, I stumbled backwards into the doorway, missing the blade by only a hair, and causing a loud clattering in the process.

"Damnable wench!" The cruelty burst from my lips, unbidden and loud, as I fled her next blow. I soon found myself cornered, and tried to steel myself for a fight. "I'll not condemn him, nor be turned out! You know a man is more dangerous dead than alive, now!"

Yet my threat, true as it may have been, did nothing to deter the woman, as, with an equal curse, she plunged again with the blade.

"Leave!" Was her only cry.

The rusted steel nearly caught me again, but instead ended in the wood of the door to delay her recall. Thus, on my retreat was I able to grapple her arm, and twist it hard. The poor woman grunted in pain, but to her credit, still would not release her hold upon the blade.

Instead, more frantically than before, she wrested it free and half-struck, half-fell into me. I was weak, then, and terribly frightened. I could scarcely thwart the motion, but fell back, being painfully - though blessedly, quite thinly -

sliced across my cheek.

I did not release my hold upon her knife-wielding arm, and we toppled violently into a small shelf, dashing a fine porcelain service to pieces as we went. At last the knife skittered away from her grasp, and we both made a desperate leap for it upon the floor. She again proving more dextrous than I, quickly took up the weapon and brought it fast upon me, cruelly slicing my reaching palm.

I could not keep from yelping loudly as I recoiled from the injury, sliding pitifully away from the woman to my original place at the door. A fresh stream of blood coursed down my cradled hand to join that which had long dried upon the floor, whilst the same from my cheek-wound wetted my lips and warmed my face. Shamefully I huddled in the corner, laid entirely before the woman's mercy. I knew then how sorely I had failed the captain.

"To Hell with you and your bleeding officer, redcoat." Whispered the woman through harsh, haggard breaths, "Now you must leave, you mus-"

Her final entreaty was cut short by a most dreadful sound. A low *thud* came suddenly like a gunshot, and was promptly followed by a second, and a third.

We both wheeled to face the front door, at the end of the hall, and saw it shaking on its hinges under the pressure of corpses throwing themselves furiously into it. That the door was better barricaded than the one whence I had entered was but little comfort, for it was apparent that our commotion had brought a great mob upon us. Our eyes met again in wide horror at the mutual revelation. We ought to have then become allies in common cause, but I found myself utterly cowed. The pain in my hand was severe, and it was all I could do to try and stumble to my feet. Before either of us could speak, there came yet another sound, even more chilling for its immediacy.

From the nearby sitting room came a shattering of glass, followed by subsequent violent thrashings of limbs upon a wooden floor. It was obvious; a devil had thrown itself *into* the home.

The walls had been breached, and so it seemed our fate had been spun. I could only quiver in panic, a cold sweat pouring down my flesh as I tried to imagine an escape. Yet to her *glory*, and without hesitation, the woman I had condemned did not run, but took up her blade and rushed *towards* the noise.

Whilst I remained frozen, there began the sounds of a terrible struggle; of scuttling feet, grunting blows, and crashing bodies. I looked back with tearful eyes into the kitchen, where Lawrence lay still upon the floor. His arms hung limp at his sides and his head lolled in unconsciousness.

God did not answer my prayer, then, but the words of my captain echoed from the depths of my mind.

We are still soldiers.

A scream came from around the corner, laden with horror and pain, and the incessant pounding at the door matched that of my heart.

We have our duty.

I ran to the woman's aid.

The Woman's Noble Stand.

Part the
SEVENTH

wherein a tragedy
befalls the author.

As I entered the front room, I met with a horror all too familiar.

A creature had smashed through the once beautiful large window, and easily swept aside its paltry barricade. Then, dragging itself through the jagged shards of glass, it latched onto the woman's leg and was biting hard upon it. Her knife was buried deep between the thing's neck and shoulder-blade, yet its bloodlust was undeterred. As her flesh gave way under the assault she screamed, and in dwindling strength she stabbed and clubbed away at the devil with a fire-poker she had procured nearby.

Blow after blow rained upon the pulpy skull of the once-craftsman, yet as flecks of brain and bone fell about us, it *only bit all the harder.*

With a terrible cry I threw myself into the fray. Grabbing hold of the corpse's shoulders, I endeavoured to pull it off the woman, yet as I struggled against its flailing arms I could not loosen the powerful squeeze of its jaws. Teeth ground and pressed violently into the woman's flesh and bone, seemingly intent on splitting her leg, as cold fingers grasped at my arms, squeezing and tugging with terrible might.

The woman nonetheless persisted in her assault, thrusting down hard with the poker into the deepest recesses of the creature's brains. At length, I gained some little advantage in the grapple, and with my free hand took hold of the blade lodged in its neck. Violently I wrenched it free, the rusty steel grating against bone on its way out.

With a cry to rival the woman's, I plunged the blade soundly through the nape of the devil's neck, and twisted it as hard as I could. Yet, through a river of spurting blood, my efforts still did nothing to loosen the bite.

There seemed, then, to be no hope of extricating the thing from its prey. Yet I was soon struck by a notion which, in any other circumstance, must surely have branded me a madman.

"Wait!" I shouted. When the woman next retracted her bloody spear, and while still I laboured to keep hold upon its flailing torso, I dropped my knife and took a hold *inside* the devil's smashed-open skull. Broken shards of bone cut my fingers as they explored the chunky stew of its brains. Contrary to all reason, and in spite of its injury, still I could still feel the devil's muscles flexing and contracting as it made to bite clean through the woman's leg.

Ultimately I gained a firm grip upon some crevice or other, perhaps the opening of the skull to the nose or mouth, and I pulled back with all my strength. With this little leverage I found myself able to provide a little relief from the bite. The woman took quick advantage, and shoving her poker betwixt the jaw and her leg, pried herself slowly free. With a visceral rip of her flesh, the woman stumbled backwards to the wall, the meat of her mangled leg trailing before her.

At the same moment, having thus gained the advantage, I found myself mere inches from the devil's face. My eyes locked with its emotionless stare, unblinking and thoroughly glazed over, yet fixed upon me all the same. It had the countenance of a man long deceased, and it pierced my very soul. Beneath its eyes, however, rampaged a far more pressing concern - the devil's jaw. Now freed of its victim, it cracked away in enthused biting, the awful sound muffled only by matted strips of cloth and squishy flesh in its snare.

I have since had ample time to comprehend that terrible visage, as it frequently plagues my nightmares.

Yanking back the devil's head, I risked releasing my hold on its arms, which again flared out in their effort to seize my body, and took up the knife I had earlier dropped. I thrust it hard upon the attacker's lip, stabbing clean through the flesh and into the gums behind. Twisting the blade, I felt the devil's teeth pop away one by one in a bloody mess, and in the queer horror which only war might provide, derived some *sick satisfaction* from it. I withdrew the blade, and, weeping more than shouting, repeated the action.

Again and again I stabbed at the devil's mouth, cheek, and chin in a fury without aim. Having thus eradicated its lower half, I turned my attention to its eyes: they did not flinch as the knifepoint burst their retinas.

I was not alone in my struggle. Having liberated herself and taken a brief time to recover, the woman rejoined me with matching zeal and madness. With her good leg she pinned one of the wild limbs down, and commenced at once to hack it to pieces with the fire-poker.

Having done all the harm I could with the blade, I dropped it and took hold of the devil's lower jaw. Though it had lost most of its teeth, still with weakened and destroyed tendons it made to bite me. I pushed then against the lower jaw, whilst I pulled back with my hold upon the skull. It was a terrible, jagged *snapping* that separated the two in a mess of stringy muscle.

I could not help but scream at the terrible cracking noise it made when their connection finally gave way.

In spite of this abuse the devil remained committed in its assault - yet it was substantially weakened, and had become quite senseless, so that I was able to relinquish my hold. Feeling myself coated in its brains, as if I had swum in them, I slid away gasping for breath. I found myself at the far side of the room beside the woman.

We beheld the foul wretch in silence. It had lost all sense of itself, thrashing about madly on the floor as it struggled to move on broken limbs, and to seek us out with no eyes. Yet still it moved, and lost nothing of its erratic nature.

I realised, then, that *nothing* might kill them.

Though I found myself unable to speak, my thoughts turned to the woman and her injury. I saw her wounded leg was buried beneath a flurry of torn skirts matted with blood. It was only by the ferocity of her will that she remained half-standing against the wall. As I struggled to my feet, and to keep some distance from the blinded and broken devil whirling before us, I thought to secure some rudimentary bandage. The torn curtains from the shattered window opposite seemed promising, then, and I gingerly made to work around the wall for them.

I was interrupted in this motion by a stifled yelp behind me. Pivoting about, I saw the woman's eyes were wide once more with that queer tincture of hate, fear, and sorrow. Beyond the first abomination, still convulsing in the sea of its own gore, stood that vision which I had feared above all others.

Captain James Lawrence stood in the doorway.

The final bastion of decorum and dignity within that accursed town shook as he stood, pale and unnaturally wide-eyed. His jaw chittered like a starving beast.

I had no time to comprehend the spectacle's tragedy, ere my former officer lunged forward on unsteady limbs to attack the woman, who stood nearer to him. Again she brandished her iron spear and thrashed it hard against Lawrence's head, where once a fine cocked hat proudly rested. His flesh and skull caved in at once, further painting the room with red, yet no blow would deter him. The woman could only just keep the corpse at bay, beating his arms aside with the firepoker as she backed away.

Despite the chaos of the moment, I mustered courage enough to rush towards them both, evading the flailing body upon the floor as I went. I was thus able to seize hold of Lawrence's arm as it was only a hair's breadth away from the woman's flesh.

"Run!" I entreated the woman as I grappled with my former captain. His attentions pulled aside, his bloodstained hands at once tore frenziedly at my shirt to reach the flesh beneath. His jaws cut hard and fast, so near to my face as to frequently scrape into me, though blessedly he was unable to bite with a proper hold. From between his lips I could feel no breath at all.

I could but hope, as I heard the woman hurriedly limp away, that she might find some safety and be spared the fate which I had brought through her door. A fate I then seemed certain to suffer.

As I wrestled with Lawrence, desperately struggling to keep his fanatical teeth at bay, a relief suddenly came in the most providentially ironic fashion. For the other devil, though thoroughly mutilated, nonetheless discovered our place and insisted upon joining the slaughter. Yet with its broken limbs, unable to bite nor take hold upon my flesh, it could do little but entangle itself upon our legs, setting the captain and I both to tumble overtop it! In the fall, despite having little wind in me, I managed by some extraordinary fortune to place some part of the writhing cripple between myself and the greater assailant, wherein its flesh became a gruesome shield against Lawrence's teeth.

I took the opportunity to at once beat a hasty retreat, throwing myself from the clammy mess of sticky limbs. The captain's eyes were ever fixed upon me, though, blessedly, neither creature possessed the coordination to untangle and upright themselves quickly. The once-genteel corpse could but attempt to futilously grasp at me, whilst its blinded compatriot continued to flail overtop him in search of some life to slaughter. It seemed neither creature was aware of the other's presence.

Still, my newfound security would be short lived.

As I tottered back to my feet, a clamour drew my attention again to the window whence the first creature had come. Yet *another* devil had thrown itself onto the edge of the windowsill, and was forcing its body through the broken frame. In the street beyond, a band of them was steadily rushing forth from every direction. No doubt the earlier hullabaloo had drawn a great deal of attention from the surrounding area. The devils were swarming the home, and it was only by another miracle that they had not come up a moment sooner.

With no other path open to me, I darted out of the front room and back into the entry hall. The devils were then hot upon my heels, for as I turned to slam the door shut behind me, I smashed the newcomer between the door and its frame. The creature's arms grabbed out at me from between the wood as it tried to push its way through. With a heavy grunt I heaved all my weight against its advance, yet I could not overpower the devil, nor force its arms from within the frame.

The one devil was then soon joined by Captain Lawrence who, alongside doubling the weight upon the door, likewise snaked his arms through in the attempt to grab at my face and pull at my hair.

The moment compelled me to again meet the corpses' unbroken gazes, which stared emptily through the gap. Even from Captain Lawrence there came nothing of recognition whatsoever; nor did his countenance betray any rage, which might otherwise have suited the violence of his actions.

There was no comfort in my dawning understanding that the man I had called my leader was truly gone, as the foul daemon which overtook his corpse permitted little time for sentiment.

As I struggled at the door, slowly slipping back as a third and then a fourth devil joined the press, I knew my position was untenable. The snapping of so many teeth and the scraping of flesh against woodgrain so near to me were maddening. I wondered for a brief moment whether I might be, by then, the last of the garrison still alive. Perhaps I was even the last Christian soul in all of Stowlham, save the poor woman.

She was not in the hallway, I realised, nor the kitchen beyond it. A faint trail of blood revealed that she had limped around a corner just alongside the kitchen door, whence there stood a narrow staircase to, presumably, more rooms above.

These would offer my sole hope of survival, for there still remained my blockade upon the rearmost entrance whence I had arrived, and I would nary be able to clear it before being set upon by my pursuers. If nothing else, I thought, surely I could not abandon the woman with her grievous injury? Not after all I had brought upon her.

Thus, in attempting to justify my selfishness, and with my strength failing, I committed yet another condemning sin.

Surrendering my hold upon the door, I leapt beyond its bounds and ran down the hall. The door immediately gave way, and from behind me spilled the mass of bodies, one atop the other.

As I came to the hall's end, I saw them all tangled up amongst each other and again struggling to regain their footing. Still their eyes never broke from me, and it would scarce be long before the first of them managed to make some headway above its necrotic brethren.

I rounded the corner in panic, then, and rushed up the stairs and out of their sight as quickly as my legs could take me. Soon I reached the limping, bloody heel of the woman just as she was passing through a door.

Following after her, I turned to slam the way shut behind me as I heard the first devil begin to stumble noisily up the stairs. Without a moment to spare I spun about and braced myself against the door, waiting for another push, yet was surprised when nothing came.

A smothering silence fell upon the room. I struggled to keep my shuddering breath in check; it seemed to resound like a whistle blast in the dead quiet.

From beyond the little strip of wood, I heard the shuffling of the devil's feet and the awful chattering of its jaw, yet the latter then seemed to gradually slow from its anticipatory speed to something more idle. It had crested the stairway, yet it did not continue its assault. Within a moment it was followed by the awkward clambering of another - likely Captain Lawrence - yet still, there came no push upon the door.

I then realised that, while the devils had seen me rush up the stairs, they could not comprehend where I had gone afterwards!

It was as if some rudimentary memory yet remained within them, but they had not the sense with which to *understand* it.

For some time I stood there, aware of nothing beyond their terrible noises, as they scratched and dragged their bodies up and down the dark little corridor beyond in search of us, or any living soul. It was evident they would not depart of their own volition.

With trembling limbs and a stifled sigh, too loud for my taste, yet unheeded by the creatures, I relinquished my hold upon the door and moved somewhat away from it.

Nothing.

It was all I could do not to weep in that moment, knowing the slightest hint of our presence might alert the creatures and renew their assault. A third devil, I could hear, had started to crawl up the stairs, yet not a one, as they clumped and jostled about each other, seemed at all aware of our presence mere inches away.

For a moment I considered taking up some of the small furniture about the room and using it to reinforce the door, but quickly dismissed the prospect out of fear of the movement's necessary noise. I was so lacking in strength, I doubted whether I could lift anything beyond a small chair.

Finally having some room to breathe again, however, I found the fog of horror was gradually lifting from my vision and I was at last able to study my surroundings.

Though it was but an early morning hour, the tiny room was alight with an orange and red glow. I realised, regretfully, that it was not the cheery hues of a morning sun, but outside the little window opposite, Stowlham's fires had grown to a great and rapidly encroaching conflagration. Ash peppered the glass like snowfall.

In that dim light, I discovered the woman and I were not alone. There was a small bed pushed against the wall, and tucked beneath a pile of old blankets, was a man.

It was clear he was severely ill, and had been for some time. His flesh was pale and his head lolled to the side in incomprehension. I shivered at the similarity between himself and my captain. Upon the man's cheeks were the thick whiskers of some days' growth.

Perhaps, I thought with some relief, his illness was a natural sort. He certainly bore no marks of having been set upon by a corpse, although I could see little beyond his face. In any case, whatever plagued him, he had not yet succumbed to it.

The woman had laid herself down beside his yet living corpse. Her delicate hand, that of a lover, laid across the man's chest to slowly rise and fall with his shallow breath; her eyes regarded him as only a dear companion could. They flooded with tears in silent weeping at the inevitable fate of he who must have been her husband.

I froze then, not only in fear and sorrow, but in *guilt*. The woman's desperation to see me gone was not of fear for herself, but for her beloved charge. I came to her home, not a humble refugee, but a bearer of ruin. I wondered no longer at her extraordinary measures to see me gone, nor at her courage in racing to throw the first devil from her home.

I desperately wished then to plead my regret, yet I knew speaking would only rouse the attention of those devils beyond the door. The clacking of their teeth had since slowed to a steady beat, as if marking time on parade. Their sound mingled with the shuddered breathing of the woman and the distant roaring of fire to create a quiet discordance of misery.

I took a ginger step into the room, painfully failing to muffle the creaky floorboard beneath as I went.

"Please." The woman's whisper was barely audible. Her body had stained all it touched with terrible gore, both her own and that of the devils. "Leave us."

"I am sorry." Even to whisper was a great difficulty, as my lips were frozen in stifled sorrow. "I...don't know-"

"Damn you to *Hell!*" The woman exclaimed in fire, rising quickly from her husband's side with hatred bleeding from her eyes.

Numerous harsh weights slammed into the door immediately, and I nearly leapt from my skin. The chattering of teeth came louder than before, built up to a great anticipatory crescendo. Again, all of my world seemed to shrink inward and darken.

"If I am to perish, let it be at his side." She continued in a measured tone, laying back down in her defeat. "If you will not leave us to the fate you've brought, at least be silent. Die with *dignity*."

I could find no words to reply.

The little door began to creak and moan beneath the weight, as there came again the awful scraping of teeth and fingernails cutting themselves against the wood. The corpses were desperate to rip at our waiting flesh. I feared they would soon meet that desire.

"I am sorry." The pitiful words were all I could muster, and they went unheard. All *dignity* had abandoned me.

The woman whispered little comforts in her husband's unconscious ear as I trembled at the prospect of my fate. In all my brief time as a soldier, I had thought I might meet death upon the field of battle with something like nobility, yet as it pounded upon the door, I could think only of the terrible pain it must herald. For a time, my cowardly fear overwhelmed even my guilt.

Had I then retained my arms, I fear I would have blown out my own brains to escape it all. Another creaking came at the door, louder than before, as its latch slowly bent inwards.

Still numb to the world, I somehow forced myself into activity, and began dragging along a small chest-of-drawers nearby to create some barricade at the door. Yet as I did so, it was clear that such a blockage would not last long, and that once a devil gained even the slightest handhold about the door, they would overwhelm the defence just as they had before.

There would be no keeping them out; merely offering up slight impediments.

Establishing the futile barricade, however, my attention

was poetically captured by the outside fire's fanciful play upon the furniture's japanning, which seemed to echo the harrowing descriptions of Hellfire I had so often heard, yet never truly *understood* until that fateful night. Peculiarly, it was that very vision of Hell which reinforced some little hope within me.

Turning about, I saw that the room's window was, while tiny, perhaps *just* sufficient to slip a man through its length. *My escape!*

"Here!" I rushed to throw open the ash-stained glass. All down the street continued the signs of terror, as little packs of devils wandered up and down in search of prey, whilst at the home's door just below, yet more bodies still scraped and heaved. Above, however, I could see the roof was not far at all, and with a proper foothold against the thick sill, one might pull themselves up and over the ledge to some safety!

"Come with me!" I turned to plead with the woman, ever aware of the weakening doorway and the wretched biting sounds behind it. "Please, they'll be upon us in no time at all, now!"

In a greater narrative, there may come here a great speech on the woman's behalf. A treatise on the great power of her love and fidelity; an appeal to heaven and an insistence that she would never abandon her husband to the cruelties of fate. A man of superior character, then, might have joined her in this defence, and chivalrously borne the lot to safety.

Yet I am constrained by truth; burdened by it. The poor woman did not speak, nor move, and I knew no entreaty would be sufficient.

For a brief moment, I contemplated *forcing* her to follow me. She being so injured, and more weary even than myself, I could surely carry her away. I little doubted that her husband - were he a good man in life - would have insisted upon my doing all I might to save her. Yet while I might force her to the window, I could not force her to climb, and thus might only succeed in throwing her out entirely! Indeed, there could be no salvation for the poor woman, barring that which she herself sought. In any case, she had long accepted the fate I had so cruelly thrust upon her.

I had *condemned* her, in fact, the moment I came into her home.

More groaning, and a loud crack, sounded from the door. I turned to see its old latch had bent largely out of place, and was soon to give. Wriggling fingers began to appear all around the growing gap at the doorframe.

To pacify one devil had demanded a desperate struggle from both the woman and myself, with advantageous positioning and ample armaments with which to strike. But this time, I stood effectively alone, cramped within a narrow place, and unarmed against numerous foes. My only option was to stand and perish by the woman's side, or to save my own skin.

I recalled the sight of Ensign Tell. The sinew of his neck being pulled out in a stringy mess of bursting gore.

I recalled the shot I had taken to liberate him from the pain of slow-surrendering mortality.

Then I looked to the woman for the last time. There was no time to suffocate her, even if she wished it. She was utterly resigned to her fate. Did she know what it would entail?

Blinking back tears of pain and sorrow, I made to lift my way out of the window. It was then that the barrier finally broke, and through the gap, the little Fleshtide was released.

At once the devils rushed upon their nearest victims, laid so serenely upon the bed. The woman's screaming only began when the first dead teeth bore into her. The man made no such protestations as likewise he was overtaken, and his offal spilled forth.

I felt there was nothing I could do, and that it would not be long before the corpses came for me too. Thus, going headfirst out of the window, I forced my torso through its narrow opening with all my might. For every moment my legs flailed within, seeking some foothold, I feared the icy grip of stiff, dead fingers taking hold of them. I lost all vision of the interior, facing only exterior brick as I hauled myself through the gap, yet the terrible sounds within informed me of all that was transpiring.

Before long, the woman's screaming gave way to a kind of pleading, wet gurgle as she drowned in her own blood. Paired with the ripping of cloth and flesh and bone, it birthed an awful cacophony, the echoes of which have long lingered in the depths of my mind. Yet I knew that to pray for the poor woman's end to come swiftly would have been a damnable lie. It was my vile understanding that, so long as she refused to give up her ghost, she would continue to hold the creatures' attentions. To this day, it is with dour self-loathing that I recall how the woman's agonizingly slow end spared my life.

I soon managed to grasp some protruding brick, and gained the space of a foothold beneath me. With a final great heave, I thus attained a sitting position with my torso fully free of the gap. Perspiration and tears mixed with dried blood to run down my face and sting at my eyes, while I could scarce breathe through the smoke-choked air. Then at last, as I tried to gain a final foothold against the sill, from which I might push up to the roof, my vicious fear had become realised.

Despite all her resistance, the poor woman's pains had at last come to their end. Within a blink, then, I felt the first sharp pull upon my leg. Again I yelped at the sensation of so many stiffened fingers taking hold of me, yet I was also blessed as the creature's teeth were halted by my gaiters! Still, the sensation was a terrible one, as I was instantly cognisant of every little tooth which tried to bear down through the stout, blacked linen.

I kicked hard at the devil, feeling my heel connect with its face, though such action bought me little time as it - or a different corpse altogether - rebounded to again latch on. Then crashed into my legs yet another body, against which I was not so fortunate.

As I stretched and strained to pull myself beyond the window's confines, that second devil bit hard upon my leg, *above* my gaiters. I felt myself pierced by a half-dozen little bone needles, while the devil thrashed to-and-fro in ripping my flesh away. The warmth of my blood then burst free to coarse down my legs in little, throbbing rivers.

My vision quickly began to blur, and for a time I discerned nothing beyond my own scream. Kicking so hard as I might, I attempted to dislodge the devil while knowing that at any moment it would surely be joined by its daemonic colleagues to drag me back through the window and to my doom.

Was Captain Lawrence among my attackers? Or did he still revel upon a victim within, not yet fully dead? It was impossible to know, nor did I much care. For a moment I considered casting myself down entirely, imagining a fall to provide some end to my suffering. Yet beneath me, beside the height proving sorely insufficient to the cruel task, I saw there a veritable horde of grasping once-persons had coalesced in a great fervour to feast upon me. Dozens of soldiers and townsmen, women and little children, all biting and staring with their cold, unblinking eyes.

There was nothing for it, then, but to continue climbing.

My assailant within made another terrible twist, and I felt its teeth scrape violently against the surface of my flesh, carrying away another small part of it. Yet as it did so, there came a quick gap in its hold, the opportunity of which I could note even through the rush of my pain. Thus, with another heavy kick, evidently well-placed for the time it allowed me, I found a new foothold beneath me upon the sill. Pushing so hard as I might, and pulling from above, I rose further out of the window, and up along the side of the brick wall.

In but a moment I knew they would be upon me again - yet ironically, it seemed the jostling of so many bodies within that tiny room was to my aid, as all the creatures fought for space, clambering atop each other with no mind for strategy.

My pain was still terrible, and I felt faint from my blood loss, which I thought must have poured forth most heartily. Indeed I nearly slipped from my post from the gore there present, and were it not for my firm hold upon the roof's edge, I would surely have fallen into the waiting maws of the horde below. Caught thus dangling over the window, there was nothing I could do beyond kick and pull with all my might. As the devils reached for me once more, I was only just able to prevent their gaining any fresh hold upon me, whilst they attempted to bite through my gaiters and take hold of my flailing legs.

At length, I found myself able to peer over the lip of the roof, and with one final effort, hauled my torso over it. With a final strong kick at the devils, who then jostled within the little window for a place to reach me, at last I rolled up, over, and onto the roof.

My every limb screamed in pain, whilst my lifeblood flowed from the tiles to steadily drip unto the crowding horde below.

Yet from that terrible, sinfully miraculous action, I was alive.

Beneath me, my assailants continued to reach, unrelenting in their hunt, but could do nothing else. I was beyond their ravages, but they cared no more than the devils on the street, who likewise clambered along the side of the building as if they might suddenly be capable of scaling it. Thankfully, none had the wits to climb. As I saw them from the corner of my gaze, over the edge, they all took on an almost sorry appearance, so desperate they were in their singular, mindless desire.

I laid at the edge of that roof for some time, my consciousness withering. I looked away from the devils to a morning sky painted black with smoke. Falling ash peppered me and burnt little holes in my red-stained waistcoat and breeches. I heard only the approaching roar of the fires, near to hand, and the chattering mob below. I felt nothing, save the pulsing throbs of each wound on my legs, arms, and face, and the hot roof which seemed to sizzle beneath my queued, matted-through hair. In my mind's eye, there came the empty gaze of Captain Lawrence, staring through me in silent, condemning scorn. His mouth opened only to scream the woman's screams, and those of Ensign Tell, and of Richards, all mingling in an awful unity of suffering.

I had found some safety, yet could not believe myself deserving of it. Still to this day I cannot. So many good and noble persons having lost their lives in nobler pursuits, who was I to escape their fate? To be deserving of life at all? It had been through stupidity that I condemned an innocent, and through cowardice that I yet lived.

Beneath the burning sky I lay alone and damned, surrounded by the choleric dead.

I wept like a child.

~ 113 ~

A Soldier's Account

My Sanctuary Within Stowlham.

Part the
EIGHTH

wherein the cavalry arrive.

𝕴 𝖐𝖓𝖔𝖜 𝖓𝖔𝖙 𝖜𝖍𝖊𝖓 I lost consciousness, nor how much time elapsed before I was again roused with a horrible, wracking cough. It seemed as though all moisture had been driven out of me by the inferno which raged, by then, quite close at hand.

By some fortune, though my clothing had become thoroughly singed with fallen ash, I was not wholly immolated whilst absent from the world. The pain in my leg had diminished to a low throbbing upon those distinct points where teeth had pierced my flesh. Every inch of me was utterly exhausted, so that even sitting up proved a herculean task of both body and spirit.

With fingers trembling violently, I tore at the little punctures in my stockings to bear my injury witness, and felt blessed to realise that each mark, though horribly painful, was not overly deep. It was a disquieting comfort that the majority of the blood which coated my once fine clothing was not my own. I dared not fathom whatever vile distempers might have infested my body.

My sojourn, meanwhile, had done little to improve my circumstances.

That the fire continued to wreak havoc upon the little market town was obvious, for nothing could be smelled but burning wood and fabric, and something still more sinister. Turning slowly about, I spied the fires dancing erratically but a few dozen yards upon the very terrace I lay atop. The pain of the woman's blade across my cheek, and the little nibbling bites Lawrence had won against me, were at once overpowered by the red-raw heat. The fire was spreading rapidly, and not far beyond it lay the smouldering piles of former homes, shops, and public houses. Nigh a third of Stowlham must have been ablaze or burnt, by then.

Beneath me, however, remained a more terrible vision.

Uncaring of the heat and burning ash, and voraciously feasting upon every slow drip of my lifeblood from the eaves, many *dozens* of devils relentlessly grasped upwards whilst pushing against the home. Their eyes were firmly fixed on what little of my flesh was visible to them, and the sound of their chattering teeth rose to a din resembling an enraged beehive. They clambered atop one another, and over burning debris, with no regard for such mortal concerns as the searing of their flesh. Further down the road, I noted how some of them had been thoroughly scoured, and dragged their crackling entrails along on blackened limbs which crumbled as they went.

Yet for all these visions of pandemonium, none were so affecting to me as the sight of those arms just barely scraping the little eave's edge. Two of them wore a once-fine coat of scarlet with gold lace. Another pair, clearly losing in their struggle to gain a place at the windowsill, were shorter and more delicate, donning the remnants of a tattered dress.

I looked away from those reaching corpses with the deepest shame. I had no more tears to offer.

Slowly, then, I slid my way up the narrow roof, somewhat rolling myself over its other side in my desire to escape those cruelly empty gazes. Yet my relief would be a passing one, for I could little hide from the spreading fire. It was a most horrible predicament, as whilst I had no desire to continue living, still the fear of pain drove my body unbidden. It was as though I were nothing more than an *insect*.

My choices seemed only to remain and burn slowly alive, or to flee and again risk being shredded by so many teeth. Indeed, it is ironic that my fear of the latter had all but guaranteed the former in Hell.

Yet my decision would be forced. As the flames crept ever nearer, the heat upon my back soon became intolerable. It was as if a hot iron was being pressed upon me. Ash, too, continued to fall in great torrents all about me, to burn through my smallclothes and singe at my exposed neck like so many little needles.

Thus, I made to preserve my meaningless mortality by shuffling along the terraced rooftop. It was slow going, particularly as I attempted to remain low and quiet while retaining my delicate balance. Still, every step away from the flames offered some respite, and I found myself breathing more easily through the air tainted merely by the rot of flesh, rather than choking black smoke.

At length, I reached the end of the terrace which opened out to the square, and beyond it, the impenetrable churchyard. Still it sat unmolested by the flames, and still it was filled with a swirling horde of devils.

It took great effort not to scream out, which would serve only to pull the corpses all to me in a great throng. Yet there seemed no recourse, and my sorrow had welled into a mighty *hatred*. Not merely for the devils themselves, but for the foul town which they inhabited, for the church that refused me sanctuary, for the Army that led my comrades and me to so terrible a place and made a mockery of our dreams for glory. Above all else, I harboured a deep hatred for myself in every respect, and for the despicable choices I had made.

Why hadn't I *listened to John?* I could hear, through the crackling flames, the yet harsher crack of the lash upon his back. His stoically muffled groans of pain turning slowly to weeping; his snotty breathing through terrible whimpers. Why hadn't *any* of us listened?

Where was he then, I wondered? Had he been amongst our

number in the firing line under Lieutenant Farwell? Or perhaps he had secreted himself to some quiet corner to hide from fate, just as I had run from it?

As I tarried in disillusion, my mind transfixed by all that might have been, my indecisiveness was soon forcefully ended. There echoed, from the streets beyond the market, an awful sound the likes of which I had never before, and have never since, been so thankful to hear.

The rough and panicked bellow of a horse was accompanied by the sharp crack of a musket shot. Then came the cries of a man, and a yet greater rattle of musketry, and pounding hooves, all underscoring a panicked, pealing bugle.

Battle! The sounds began to echo through the distant streets, and I saw little clouds of musket-smoke begin to waft above the faraway rooftops to catch in the fire-bound wind.

So terrible were these sights and sounds in their own nature, yet they brought to me the queerest sense of *joy*, for with them came the singular understanding that I was not alone. That men did yet wrest against the terror which had consumed poor Stowlham, and that, perhaps, there might even be some escape from it! Not all was *fire* and *teeth*!

In more practical terms, whatever its meaning, the mighty fracas had garnered more than just *my* attention.

From the very first shot, the great mob then occupying the market violently twisted their attentions to the noise. First in a trickle, and then as a great charging mass, they surged onwards in a wave of flailing limbs, tearing past and overtop the ruined stalls and trampling each other underfoot in their silent desperation to meet the source of the noise. Likewise, those in the street and alleyway below had caught wind of the affair, and I found myself again ducking away as a second tide of churning flesh, that which had so hungrily clawed up at my unconscious personage, flowed from the main street and through the square.

Only a brief spell elapsed ere the ground before me was all but drained of bodies, save those slowed by broken, charred, and half-severed limbs.

The clamour of battle on the outskirts of town had only swelled in its intensity then, and with a sinking feeling I realised the terrible fate which must surely await the poor souls who had thus thrown themselves into the grinder. Yet I also realised, once more in a sickening relief, that their imminent doom presented the opportunity for my own preservation.

The way was not entirely secure, but I could nonetheless discern a potential path through the debris-laden square which stood away from the eyes of any straggling corpses. Thence, by some miracle, to a small cluster of crates sitting against the churchyard walls! With courage and speed, though I knew not how long the square would remain unoccupied, the safety of the churchyard was within my reach. From there, I might enact some part of Captain Lawrence's plan and beat my retreat to the quayside, down the river, and to my liberty!

The prospect of relief from my pains thus superseded all weariness and woe. My fatalism had been eclipsed, if momentarily, by opportunity. I set at once to clambering down a nearby drainage pipe to rejoin the grime and blood-soaked earth below. As I did so, the shrill screeching and guttural neighs seemed to reach a crescendo, as if a half-dozen horses had been suddenly set upon all at once. Their cries were matched by the hearty swears and shouts of men, rather close now, and the snap of musketry and pistol shots issued irregularly. The cavalry I had earlier set my little hope upon had broken the moment it arrived.

Having reached the ground, and with little time to spare, I examined the path before me and took stock of every little twist and blind corner I could see. By ducking around a nearby collapsed stall, and slinking down the lane alongside it, I saw I might have a clear rush to the churchyard wall with only a solitary, largely immobilized, devil to impede my path. It had long since lost its compatriots, stiltedly shuffling on half-roasted legs which still smouldered. Still, despite its weakness, the prospect of fending off another devil while in the open was deeply troubling. I realised then that my hands were trembling wildly, and my vision was becoming clouded by a fear which, mere moments prior, had felt so distant. Never in my life had I missed the company of old *Brown Beſs* so dearly!

There was nothing for it but to press on. To reclaim my former post would be to burn in idleness, while retreat would only bring me deeper into the town. I took up so large a stone as I could find, blinked away the sting of ash and perspiration from my eyes, and made my break.

The first narrow stretch was an easy dash, even as my injured legs were pained by every step. Diving into a little nest of collapsed wood and tragically dashed pastries, I took a moment to steel myself for the greater rush ahead. Thinking a spear superior to my present pebble, I wrenched free a length of broken wood, yet still my makeshift weapons offered little comfort. The crippled devil continued to drag itself along my intended path, while not far along the market's edge, another band of horrors was wandering into the square, their heads snapping erratically in every direction like so many birds as they confusedly sought out the distant noises. Steadily, the cacophony had been shrinking as what isolated pockets remained of the relief force met their final glory.

With a silent prayer I broke from my cover again to hurry down the path. The devil before me seemed entirely unaware of my approach, so distracted it was by the sounds of dying horses. It was only as I came near to passing behind it that the thing finally noticed me, and for a brief moment I locked eyes with the once-man. Its face was red and peeling from the severity of its burns. One of its eyes seemed half melted away in a raw socket. The devil tarried not in its assault.

Putting forward all my strength, I hurled my stone at the fiend, striking it hard on the jaw and certainly displacing some of its teeth. Yet there was no time to examine the results of my blow. With gangling limbs and broken teeth, which fell loosely in chips from its frenzied mouth, it made to lunge upon me.

Not daring to slow my speed for fear of what could, by then, have taken pursuit to my rear, I couched my mighty lance and with an unwise cry thrust it squarely at the devil's chest. I felt a distinct crackling as the wood pierced through weak, burnt flesh, and the creature tumbled to the ground. Its legs sloughed terrible black marks on the cobblestones as it went.

Following through with my attack as it fell, and still holding the length of wood with the creature laying before me, I was fiercely tempted to retract the weapon for yet another strike. My blood was up, and in that moment it was perversely invigorating to stare down into the uncomprehending eyes of my victim. I could have spat on its pitiful attempts to grab at me from the end of my spear. For the first time, I realised, I had taken the *offensive* against one of the abominations!

Yet there was no time for the succour of slaughter. Already I had been delayed by the creature more than was wise, and tamping down my rage, turned to continue my flight. As I went, I spared a glance to my rear and saw that already a few devils had noted my presence. Their advance was more rapid, slowed only by their colliding with each other and the occasional stray which still rushed on for the distant cavalry fight. Thus I rushed as quickly as I might, and reached the gated wall of the churchyard with little time to spare.

The great lock set within the gate's iron bars seemed to mock me, as I imagined it had done to many other would-be refugees, but I was comforted to see that the churchyard's interior was undisturbed by the chaos. While small patches of grass beneath the mossy gravestones were somewhat singed from falling ash, the grounds remained wholly unoccupied, whether by the living or the dead.

To my great displeasure, however, the stone wall blocking me from that peace seemed, from its base, far taller than it had at a distance! It towered at least an arm's length above my head, and I briefly, angrily, wondered how so tiny a churchyard, in so unimpressive a town, could come to be so impregnable!

Already the devils at my tail were drawing nigh, and others still had joined their pursuit. Even the creature I had speared was hastily recomposing itself, half-crawling, half-running towards me with the length of wood still awkwardly jutting from its torso. I had perhaps a half-minute, at best, before they would all be upon me.

Cursing whatever medieval architect had been so discourteous in designing that infernal wall, I made for the crates I had seen previously, and immediately began to clamber up them to gain some vantage. It felt like they might have shattered beneath my weight at any moment, which must surely have spelled my doom, yet I could spare no time on trepidation either. Perching atop their height, my fingers could just scarcely reach the top of the craggy stone. Thus with all my little remaining strength, I commenced my awkward scramble for the top.

In a more peaceable scenario, the effort would have proven simple. Yet it was only after a mighty struggle that I found myself barely peering over the edge, with my bloodied legs scraping along the side looking for some hold. It seemed I was taunting the fast-oncoming devils as one might a dog with a scrap of meat. The inches between my toes and the crates below seemed a great chasm, in that moment. Yet against all odds, through my panicked breaths I felt my foot catch upon some little crevice, and with only a blink to spare, I rolled myself atop the wall. My pursuers then crashed into the crates below.

The abrupt violence of their impact made me yelp most ingloriously as I nearly fell into the yard behind. I had suspected, however, the devils had no opportunity to reach me, lacking the wit for climbing. Instead they could only clamber overtop and through the crates, totally oblivious to their presence. Many fell headfirst in the process, and were roughly trampled into the rapidly crumbling wood by their comrades. It was with a disturbed shiver that I saw little spindly strips of wood piercing the flesh of so many men and women as they stared up at me with dead, unblinking eyes. Yet while they pressed themselves hard against the stone and reached up so high as they might, snapping their hands at me like babes in the throes of a silent tantrum, even the tallest among them could not manage to brush at me with their stiff fingers.

Having again gained some security, and now without the heat of the flames lapping at my back, I felt I could begin to breathe. The blur obscuring my vision began to abate, and I found myself resuming my prior study of the creatures. Had some greater feelings of philosophy then played upon my exhausted mind, I might have considered it a wonderful opportunity to moralise. Yet as it was, I could scarcely envision the devils as their former selves, so mutilated and alien and terrible were the mass of them. Instead I was only sickened by the sight of them, and their unique stench of rot. Had I a thimble of moisture left within me, I might have wretched atop them all.

Before I could drop down the other side of the wall, however, my attention was again pulled by something most unexpected. For as the sounds of battle had all but faded to an occasional, distant scream, suddenly a pistol shot rang out close at hand!

Looking to whence it came, I saw a horseman bounding into the square! He was soon attended by two others, and then five, before what seemed a band of some thirty light dragoons came charging full tilt through the desecrated market!

Their blue coats were stained black with blood, and they struggled to keep rein over their panicked horses as they fled before a great band of dozens, perhaps even *hundreds* of devils! They poured into the square as a great cavalcade of chaotic horror from all directions, as corpses from all around were alerted to the noise. I had not yet encountered such a mass of them, and the sight of them was all the more sickening for it. My breathing quickened and my head felt increasingly light. Among the dead, several fresh corpses wore the same blue coats and furry black helmets as those they pursued.

Their terror evident, these last samples of military potency called out to one another as they fired carbines and pistols blindly into the unwavering mass behind them, and hacked their sabres wildly at any devil which drew too near. For every foe thus *inconvenienced,* five others shortly overtook them.

"On, lads! On!" I saw an older fellow spurring the troop

onwards, his mount bravely knocking aside assailants as they went. His head pivoted wildly as he ascertained his surroundings, seeking any kind of sanctuary for his men. He found only waves of the dead.

As the soldiery made their way along the square, I saw that one of the rearmost horses was slowed by some unseen injury. Atop its back sat two badly beaten-up troopers. The man in front could barely keep his hold, while the other slashed with his one good arm into devil after devil. Their noble efforts, however, were futile, as some bodies managed to cut off the mount's path and it began to spin about in panic. The lot of them were set upon at once by the Fleshtide, which pulled the poor creature down under their sheer weight. The two troopers, try as they might, could resist but little. Their own shrieks soon joined that of their horse as the three bodies vanished beneath the pulsing swarm.

Deep in the fray, their comrades could not offer but even a moment's regard for the loss. They pressed on with their retreat, firing wildly in every direction as they went.

Captain Lawrence's words echoed again through my mind. The terrible fate of these troopers had saved my own skin, and I felt the burdensome weight of their souls upon me. Though I desired only to slink behind the wall, and succumb to the weakness in my limbs in rest, I forced myself to stand.

"Ho, there!" I shouted and waved my arms about. "Here! Here!"

At once the leader of the band spotted me, and with a bold kick to an attacker's skull, made again to redirect his mount. The whole mass of cavalry soon shifted and rushed for my wall, cutting their way through narrow lanes of broken market stalls as the fires of all Stowlham cast long their racing shadows. It was a heroic sight indeed as the old dragoon spurred his men onwards, waving his blade about whenever it was not cutting deep into the flesh of a foe.

"To the wall! Ride for the wall!" Bellowed he amidst popping firelocks and shrieking horses. Along the little column's flank, as they turned, another steed was overwhelmed by a mob and dragged to the floor. The trooper swore all the way down as he punched at the swarm with his hilt.

As quickly as they had burst upon the scene, the first dragoons drew near to the wall. Some of the devils beneath me had noted their approach, and were trampled underhoof as they made to intercept. A little mob remained between the first riders and the wall, however, just as the greater horde pursued them from the flanks and rear. Even the bravest of the steeds could but dance about in fear, refusing to come nearer as they realised that their riders' course of escape would see them left behind. They kicked and thrashed violently as one by one the devils came closer, with their masters forcing them as near to the walls as possible. Still, no amount of beating could coerce the poor beasts to meet deaths so painful and slow. Many of the troopers were but an arm's length away from the wall, yet they could draw no closer. Already, another two horses were drowning in the sea of teeth.

"Jump!" Called I to the lot of them. "Come on!"

The leader of their band had begun to position himself accordingly, but three devils latched heavily on to the flesh of his mount, and it thrashed uselessly against them in pain and distress. Standing precariously in his saddle, the fellow unhooked his distant leg and made to leap over the devils' heads in an extraordinary display of dexterity. Despite it all, he managed to clear the distance and grasp hold of my outstretched arm, soon getting a leg over the wall as I heaved him up. His other foot still dangled over the side, and was set upon by many biting corpses, yet the thick leather of his tall riding boots blessedly prevented their gaining any advantage. Though he was thoroughly shaken, the man was at length able to wrest himself away from them.

Before us, however, many of the other cavalrymen were faring more poorly. Some, fearing themselves incapable of making the jump, actually dismounted! To see their horses panic, as they became nothing more than fleshy shields for the men to whom they entrusted their lives, was a most affecting sight; nor was it easy for the troopers to so abuse their loyal, old friends, and despite that unwilled sacrifice, few made it far before being overtaken. The cobbles before us were quickly strewn with so many innards of man and horse alike.

Yet the living were slow to die, and in their throes, they offered some little distraction for their comrades still rushing on from the rear of the once-long column. Once a gap appeared, some men were able to push their steeds through, and I made to help the first dragoon lift another to our place atop the wall. He was a young man, and mad with fright. The chain of his fur-crested helmet had snapped free where a horrible gash sent a torrent of blood down his cheek. His mouth worked, yet he could not speak. Still, when my companion gave him a clap on the shoulder, he joined us in reaching out for a third trooper who had braved his way through the mob.

The third then became a fourth, and more, as every man to reach some security turned to aid his comrades. Before long, eight of the cavalrymen had made it atop to safety. They were the only survivors of their troop; the remainder lay buried beneath the thrashing Fleshtide, all piled atop one another in the frenzy, and in places some four or five corpses deep. The poor wretches beneath them all made known every injury they suffered before the slow mercy of their deaths.

I sat high upon the wall with the survivors, all breathing heavily and gazing out at the orgy of violence before us. Already there had appeared amongst them a number of blue-coated corpses. Not a man of us spoke, though one was soon sick, spraying the scene with further disgust. Likewise, the boy was utterly panicked.

"Peter!" Exclaimed he, being held back by two of his fellows lest he lean too precariously over the mob. That which had presumably been the boy's crony stood silent amidst the enemy, reaching wide-eyed for us with his mouth chattering. Its cheek had been torn to reveal rows of bloody teeth. "Oh God, Peter!" It was all the boy could choke out between his sobs.

Perhaps even more troubling to us, however, was the sight and sound of the horses. For unlike the men, they died slowly, and seemed to feel every bite and tear whilst their entrails were extracted and their organs were burst. I realised, then, just how *prodigious* was the volume of blood contained within a horse. It coated every surface within range of its spray.

Nor were the horses' slow deaths their end, but as with Major Bray's mount, while they did not *rise* to join the devils their horseflesh nevertheless twitched erratically in a continual, slow seizure. They frequently tripped up their former attackers. Not even the beasts would be spared the cruel fates of their masters, then. Their stirrings were merely of a weaker nature.

"We cannot stay here." I was the first to break the silence. "Nothing will pull them away, so long as they can see us."

Only a few of my new colleagues paid my words any mind, however, and they with confusion and horror moreso than understanding. They were utterly transfixed by the horrific spectacle before us; nor could I blame them.

"We stay here, and we wind up like him." I urged more strongly, gesturing to the man below us so sorrowfully dubbed Peter. It was a rude sentiment, I knew, yet there was no time for being well-mannered.

The elder among them finally broke the cavalrymen free of their stupor when, after a quick examination over his shoulder, he slid down the wall into the deserted churchyard behind.

"What are they?" He breathed quietly as I slid after him, grunting as I landed hard on my injured legs. I could feel already that some cuts had begun to bleed anew.

"I don't know." My words were stunted, and I sighed heavily, feeling again the weight of all that had transpired. One by one, the other dragoons descended the wall, looking about the churchyard with terrified glances. Those few who kept hold of their firelocks proceeded at once to reload them, as if they would prove any use.

"You're with the garrison." Another trooper realised when he saw what tatters remained of my military smallclothes. "Have...have you held up here? Where are the others? What has happened?"

He seemed to know the answer before I could give it. I shook my head. It was a struggle to speak clearly through my raw throat and returning melancholy.

"So far as I know, the others are..." *Dead.* I found myself unable to say the word, as if trying to escape the very thought. Indeed, I questioned whether it was truly apt, given their wretched condition. "I'm all that's left."

Even this reductive phrasing was crushing to speak aloud; nor did it provide any solace to the cavalrymen, who turned to me as one in fear.

"Damn it all. God damn it all to Hell!" The older one struggled to restrain his feeling as he took a few steps to nowhere particular. "...I fear we might say the same. We were sent before the advance force to reconnoitre. We came into town when we *thought* we saw injured civilians, but no French. Like *Hell* they were injured; they went and attacked us the minute we rode near! Then...they just started pouring in, and it all..."

He suddenly caught himself, sensing his emotions were of little utility to himself or the others. He bit his lip, and offered me a trembling hand.

"I forget myself. We are in your debt, sir. Sergeant Alan Wilkes, light dragoons."

I responded in turn, and took the liberty of assigning myself that noble title of s*ergeant,* before explaining the situation in brief. I told what little I knew about the risen dead, of Lieutenant Farwell's valiant attempt to face them, and how they seemed impervious to all our means of war. I spoke nothing of Captain Lawrence, nor of the woman whose name I would never learn.

The dragoons were horrified by it all.

"I only made it here just as you arrived." I concluded. "I thought to find some security in the church, and to escape down the river."

Wilkes made to speak again, but, seemingly as one, we realised there were more ideal places where we might discuss. From opposite the wall, we could yet hear the masses of the dead scraping away at the stone. Their clattering teeth resembled a hailstorm, whilst we stood amidst an ever-greater ashfall, which stung at our hands and faces like little needles. It was all beginning to take a toll on the men - not that I was totally numb to it, either.

"To the church, then. We'll get away from their stench and collect ourselves, then rejoin the others and stop their marching into all this. Right lads, Indian file, on me."

With a single step Wilkes resumed his role of the dutiful sergeant, sloping his sword over his shoulder and prepared to lash out at any to dare oppose him, be they devil or man. The others followed behind him in a line, one by one, eyeing every stone and tree in the little churchyard with suspicion as they went.

Despite my doubt to the value of firelocks, I was thankful to realise that still we counted three pistols and an Eliott carbine between our number. The remainder of our little band carried their sabres in like fashion to Wilkes. The youngest trooper, however, was without arms entirely. In any other world, he might have been censured for having dropped them in the fray. He trembled still, and upon his injured face blood mingled with his tears.

The trail we followed was small and gravelled. With every crunching step, I feared some unseen devil might be roused from behind some tree or stone. Perhaps, I even envisioned with horror, stretching up from beneath the very earth itself. Yet blessedly there came no such alarm as we approached our sanctuary, save the rattling of the firmly locked gate behind us. I made the mistake of glancing behind me, to see the horde of corpses pressed against it, reaching frantically between the bars. Many of their arms dripped fresh blood.

Before us, the little stone church and its squat steeple might have seemed serene, were it not for the black stain of a charnel sky above it. Before coming to the doorway, I made my way to the front of our 'column', feeling there was more to discuss with the head of our little band.

"You're unarmed?" Wilkes noted my empty hands as I came up alongside him.

"I lost Bess in the attack..." I recalled the final look in

poor Collins' eyes, and how he had screamed at the biting whilst I fled with the others. "They don't die, anyways. Not after you've smashed their skulls to pieces, even. Best you can do is fend them off and run."

All was silent in the little yard save the crunching of our shoes to meet the unusual ambience of crackling flames and chattering teeth.

"I've noticed." It seemed the only reply Wilkes could manage.

He and his men had experienced much the same as myself; they were among the very last of their brethren, and had witnessed their friends and officers torn asunder. I was scarcely fit to lecture them on the severity of their position.

"You said you were sent to reconnoitre." Said I. "That there was an advanced force of some kind."

"We could see the smoke for miles." Affirmed Wilkes, without meeting my eyes. "Reports flooded in from every which way, alongside orders that kept contradicting each other. It was thought the French had somehow landed and snuck their way up the river. Eventually our regiment found its way in with General Hawkins. He was organising the first defence, with a few battalions. We set out with his lot to figure out what was really happening. They're camped just ten or so miles from here. Most of them still think the Frogs are landed...or at least, they're acting like it. Last I heard, a larger force was being gathered around Cambridge to follow up behind us."

The thought of more men marching unwittingly into the terrible maw of Stowlham was bone-chilling. What hope might even ten thousand men have against an unkillable foe, after all? The dead could not die, and for every living soul lost, the enemy's strength only rose. Any hopeful vision I might have had of the Horse Guards racing through the streets and routing the daemonic horde had long since been dashed.

At last we came to the church at the end of the yard and, the unspoken decision having been made to enter, the bluecoats made their way all about the door before us. We would not use the great double doors at the church's front, but a little side passage which we suspected would be easier to sneak through.

Wilkes pressed himself against the wall nearest the door, whilst the others formed a concentric position to its front. Every barrel was pointed to the wood, quivering and ready to shoot at whatever might have awaited us on the other side. Being unarmed, I stood behind the lot, alongside the younger trooper. His bleeding had since slowed, and he held his breath.

Should devils lurk beyond the door, I recall wondering, what would I do? What *could* be done, save turning to flee once more? Would the others join me, or would I be abandoning them, also, to cruel fate? I found I was holding my breath, as well.

With a quick nod, Sergeant Wilkes unlatched the door and ever-so-gently creaked it open with the tip of his sword. He spied the dark interior to discern what he might, before throwing it fully open.

There came only silence, and Wilkes, or rather his sabre, led us into the sanctuary. I was the last to enter, half pulling the frightened younger man along, and sighed with a relief so deep I might have wept when one of the men barred the door behind me. Inside, we met with the same quaint vision that any parishioner might expect all across England.

In the absence of candles, the only light came from those narrow shafts which made their way through panes of stained glass. They cast long shadows across the pews, gently illuminating the dragoons as they skulked about to inspect every nook, cranny, and crevice of the building. The fur on their helmets ruffled in the dark like so many prowling wolves, while their arms shimmered and glinted in the blues and reds of the Biblical scenes overhead.

No devils appeared, and we gradually came to feel ourselves secure, if also alone, in the forgone House of God. We all began to breathe more easily, then. Yet our illusion of sanctuary was quickly shattered, when a sudden cry of terror echoed all through the nave. It was followed at once by a deafening pistol shot, and a sharp yelp of pain. Every man whirled about in panic, and soon clustered together in anticipatory horror. I nearly collapsed, while Sergeant Wilkes rushed onwards to the altar.

The Quayside of Stowlham.

Part the

NINTH

wherein the author

makes his efcape.

The church burft at once with activity, and little of it valiant. As Wilkes went forward with his most zealous companions, the remainder of us recoiled and sought our escape. Nor ought the men be blamed for such, as even the most diehard veterans must recoil in terror at prospects so bleak as we felt ourselves to face. The air alighted with panicked curses and desperate prayers; yet, ere we could unlatch the door, we heard not the rabid snapping of a corpse's jaw, but instead the pained hissing of a *living man!*

"You whoreson! You've shot me!"

There *certainly* was no devil, then.

"I- I'm sorry, I didn't know, yo-" One of the dragoons was stammering in confusion as the first voice continued its torrent of abuse. It was a voice I recognised at once. *But how could it be?*

The heavy smoke of the pistol shot rose lazily up the nave and made the place reek of sulphur. Despite their panic, the others likewise realised they did not face their end. Leaving them to their mutual embarrassment, I went behind the altar to discover the source of the argument which now flooded the church. It was a sound far more pleasant than that of tearing flesh, to be sure!

"Quit your whingeing! Now tell us who you are, before we put another one in you!" Sergeant Wilkes stood amidst his little party, one of whom shakily bore a still-smoking pistol, and made his demand of a figure pitifully crumpled in the corner.

The wretch clutched at his shoulder where the ball had given him a nasty scrape, staining a once beautiful sky-blue coat to crimson. It was a *civilian* coat, yet the fellow was anything but.

"Damn your eyes, breaking in here an-"

My old crony John was cut into stunned silence upon my sudden appearance. His expression morphed from one of anger and pain, to outright fear.

It was obvious: he had *deserted.*

The nave fell silent as the others slowly gathered around us. Nor did it take long for Wilkes to notice John's change in attitude.

"You know him?" The cavalry sergeant asked me.

At once my mind set to racing, though contrary to my usual thoughtless void of panic, a dozen questions bubbled along the surface of my cognisance.

What was he doing t*here*, of all places? Whose clothing did he wear? When had he deserted? *Why had he abandoned us?* The last of these queries, at least, had an obvious answer.

Yet through all my consternation, I was aware of one truth. That to reveal John's identity would see him hanged; assuming Wilkes did not shoot him on the spot.

"I do..."

John's eyes pleaded with me most desperately. He seemed a man on the verge of utterly breaking down. I couldn't stomach it.

"...Altmann. John Altmann, a friend to my brother back home. What are you doing here?"

The false name, conjured by a fearful glance about me, was

laughable in hindsight. Nor was my claim of familiarity, which had come from God-knew-where, particularly compelling. In truth, my only brother had died in infancy. Thankfully, more pressing concerns served to effectively cover my lie.

John's eyes lightened as if the Almighty had delivered him from fate. He sighed, though he tried not to betray his relief, and again realised the pain of his wound.

"Same as you, I imagine." He groaned. "I came seeking shelter. The place was abandoned by the time I arrived. The priest must have run out with all the other damned fools at the cry of fire."

Wilkes hardly seemed patient for the supposed civilian, cowering in safety whilst his men had fought and died outside.

"Well," said he through gritted teeth, "you're lucky that ball didn't go through your brains, skulking about like that in dark corners."

I must admit that my own feelings towards John were not wholly merciful either, in that moment. Pitifully he sat clutching at a tiny scrape where the ball had but grazed him, while I stood coated head to toe in *gore*. My gaiters and stockings were shredded. I bore a foul cut along my hand, and another on my face. I had long lost my hat, my coat, my arms, and my *dignity*, whilst so many others had lost their very lives...and there snivelled John, hiding from it all.

Even his *fingernails* were clean, save those lightly tinted of his own, fresh blood.

"I'm sorry." He mumbled. "When I heard you come through the door, I thought you might have been..." He wavered. That we may have been his former comrades? Men who might recognise him for what he was? "You know, one of those *things*."

"Well, consider yourself lucky." Repeated Wilkes. "Now get up and deal with your little scrape like a man." He turned to the rest of us to continue. "And all of you, quit your gawking. Finish searching the place. See if you can't find some water, and rest a spell. Matthews, find something to bandage Altmann here up. He's your mess, so you can deal with him."

The men saluted and muttered their acquiescence to the sergeant's orders before scuttling away. Their heavy cavalry boots thudded awkwardly over the ancient stone flooring, where the names of so many honourable departed were inscribed.

"You'll come with us, John." I tried to sound authoritative as he stumbled to his feet. "The garrison is fallen, and Stowlham is lost. These men came in to reconnoitre for a force that's marching on the town, and we're off to warn them. We'll hop the wall at the rear end of the churchyard and cross the river there. We should be safe, then."

Perhaps the reader shall question my offering aid to a proven deserter. No doubt those men of military bearing would decry my *duplicitous mercy*, just as they would the cowardice which secured my survival. Yet in such unprecedented circumstances, it did not strike me that revealing the truth of John's circumstances would benefit anyone.

Indeed, in the face of the choleric dead, few such *ancien* principles could stand; nor would that be the last surrendered by the end of those foul days.

I shan't pretend, however, that my intentions were purely in consideration for the service. Angered though I was at the betrayal of my brother soldier, I found myself equally comforted by the revelation I was not my old company's sole survivor. So long as John lived, I was not alone in my terror, or even my cowardice.

After he was crudely bandaged by means of a torn sheet, discovered by the trooper Matthews, I bade John follow me to the rear of the church. We passed by the others, by then all resting so well as they could in the pews. Glints of midday sun pierced the smoke outside, and the stained glass, to paint them in moody tones of blue and red. None could sleep, but sat silently amongst themselves, unable to voice their myriad feelings.

Even within that peaceable sanctuary, the air smelt of burnt wood and flesh from the outside conflagration. We would not be able to linger in the church for long, even defended as we were by its thick stone walls.

The baptismal font into which I thrust my hands and face was at once corrupted by the vile cruor which painted my flesh. John stood apart from me, his face etched with wariness and fear. He knew his life was forfeit, should I but say the word.

"Where did you get the clothes?" I whispered between my rushed ablutions. The fouled water dripped from my face into the blackened pool of water.

"Is *that* your concern?" The deserter seemed incredulous through his terror. I noticed he gripped his elbows and rubbed at his arms, as if to embrace himself. "You can't blame me. Not after all this, not after I was *right* all along, you-!"

The last bit was spoken too loudly for comfort, and John cut himself off as he glanced to see if the troopers had noticed. Of course, they were too deep in their own thoughts to mind anything beyond themselves.

"I do not blame you." I spoke slowly, and to my surprise, found I was being truthful. On some level, of course, I *wished* I could pin all my woes on poor John, who had so thoroughly escaped my own hardships. Yet I found myself unfeeling of anything but kinship with him. There was nothing he might have done to prevent my struggles, and had he been right alongside me, he would likely have long-since joined the cannibal corpses' ranks.

Indeed, every commander I had served, every companion alongside whom I had stood, and every charge I had taken, all of them had been torn asunder whilst I made my damnable escapes. Should John have even *killed* a man and *stolen* his clothes, could I rightly deem him a worse man than myself? For the consequences of my living stood far more severe than his own.

God, forgive the poor man. For all I knew of him, he certainly deserved better than I!

We stood quiet for some time, the only sound the steady dripping of foul water from my face into the basin.

"All of them?" John eventually broke the silence. His voice held the faintest tremor to betray the depth of his feeling for the men he had abandoned.

"To a man." The words were alien to my lips, stiffened as they were with melancholy, so that I could only whisper with difficulty. "Farwell tried to organise a defence, but it did not last. Captain Lawrence was with the major when it happened, and they suffered the same. We were all scattered. The only men I've seen wearing red since have all…"

I could not find the courage to continue. Visions of old friends with wide, dead eyes threatened to bowl me over on the spot, so overwhelmingly they assaulted my mind.

"Bennett?" John whispered, already knowing the answer. We had mocked poor John for his earnestness, to be sure, but all of us in the old squad had been good cronies. Together we had long toiled in labour and idleness, and formed a brotherhood amongst ourselves.

I could but nod. I dared not recount the horror of how I had found our friend. How his head had tilted towards the bells in the moonlight's glimmer, how he had grasped at the air like a broken child, how my bayonet had felt when it pierced and *scratched* between his ribs.

I was glad for the water, and the stains upon my face, for they obscured my tears.

"Come on, then." I spoke at length, attempting to shake off my useless feeling. "We ought rest before the march ahead. We won't long tarry here. Let us join the others."

"No." I was surprised by John's sternness. "You know I can't come with you, much less rejoin the regiment."

"Of course you must. I won't betray you, John, nor demand you abandon your course, but to remain here is madness! It's a certain death, and hardly a good one. Accompany us to the river, at least. Then you might go wherever you wish, but we stand a better chance working together."

That final sentiment was a cruel irony, given the fate of those who had stood with their fellows, stood with *me,* prior. They of the greatest dignity and courage, for all their virtue, had suffered only the worst of ends. My mind, unbidden, recalled the pain young Ensign Tell had surely endured, ere my shot pierced his skull.

John considered me for some time. He was just as afeared as myself, and perhaps all the more so. How had he managed to escape the billets? When did he take shelter within the church? These curiosities later plagued my thoughts, though I would never satisfy them. Only now do I understand how insignificant they were.

I might only hope that my friend had found the gates to the churchyard locked, just as I had, upon his first arrival. The alternative remains unthinkable, as I recall the great mass of slaughtered refugees upon the gates.

"Alright." Whispered he. "To the river, at least."

We then returned to the others, where I won some little respite, accepting a long pull from a bottle of wine which one of the troopers had liberated. The irony of imbibing Christ's blood was not lost upon us, though we found little humour in it. My limbs had been drained of all their strength, whilst the dark of the church and the comfort of living comrades all about soon joined forces with the wine to collapse me into slumber on a hard pew.

Of course I had hardly time to close my eyes, let alone to suffer the inevitable nightmare, before a firm grasp upon my shoulder started me awake. That terror in waking, as I feared the cold, clammy fingers of former comrades, far surpassed any I might have experienced in dreaming.

To my relief, the eyes I met were not glazed over in death, but burned intensely with life.

"It's time." It was all Wilkes said before moving on to rouse the others.

Rubbing delicately at my cut face with a pitiable groan, I grasped at the pew and hauled myself to my feet. I could feel every miniscule scrape, cut, and bite marring my flesh as they throbbed, untreated and scabbing over.

Taking fresh stock of my surroundings, it became apparent that, indeed, little time had passed. Those men who earlier were praying at the altar kneeled there still, making their final appeals to the Almighty. The wine even remained unfinished, and I was deeply grateful to the man who, acknowledging my condition as the worst among us, offered me the last of it.

Our limited preparations being made, we congregated before the door whence we had entered, and I realised how strongly the foul humours of the outside world had infiltrated our sanctuary. The dancing amber glow of flames shone all the more vividly through the glass saints above our heads. It was wise of Wilkes to evacuate us before all the churchyard turned to tinder.

At the sergeant's behest, I presented the plan once more to ensure every man was on a level. We took stock of our every arm and munition, while John and myself were given the largest Paschal sticks we could carry to serve as great maces. We cut rather ridiculous figures, yet I admit the *feeling* of armament, at least, provided some comfort.

Thus, being so well prepared as we might hope, we cleared the door for exit. Sergeant Wilkes was first to leave, and moved slowly to reexamine our surroundings in the odd chance that any devils had broken through. Little had changed since our arrival, save the addition of several patches of burnt grass, one of which was spreading a little flame quite readily. The smoke and rain of ash nearly sufficed to blot out the few corpses yet pressing themselves against the distant gate. They were at once emboldened by our reappearance, biting and strained with great fervour as the iron began to rattle. Surely others would be called to that dinner bell, though thankfully our path would carry us clear away from them.

Of the number in the square beyond, I could perceive how some stood within the burning ruins of a home, their skin all charring black whilst their heads desperately darted to-and-fro to locate the stimuli before them. A good few devils had outright caught fire, yet they took no heed even as the scent of their seared flesh soured the air.

Notwithstanding our would-be assailants' impotency, I was glad to move around the opposite side of the church, away from their obsessive, uncanny gazes.

Our advance across the boneyard there was slow and silent. The ancient stones and tired oaks, all enveloped in shadow by the blackened daylight sky and caked with a thick layer of ash, seemed to mock our vain protestation of mortality. Still, the sky beyond the rearmost wall, as it faced away from the town, was perfectly clear. It was as if the river would carry us to Eden, so peaceable the scene felt in relation to the Hell at our backs. Approaching the wall, however, we were soon divested of such foolish sentimentality.

"Wait!" The trooper at Wilkes' side, carrying the carbine, suddenly halted and whispered harshly. "I hear them."

Sure enough, as we crept forth to listen, we heard through the stones the faint, wet *click...click-click...click* of a corpse's maw. It did not seem agitated, for the sound was slow and irregular. We heard stunted, dead legs shuffle slowly along the wall as the devil sought some prey. It was chilling to be so near one of the vile creatures again, and to smell its unique, rotting putrescence so potently atop the foul humours of Stowlham aflame. Still, there was a blessing in its being alone.

"It hasn't noticed us." I whispered, hoping my words would not alter the scenario. "Wait, and it should pass us by."

My companions nodded their assent, though some were clearly more confident than others. The prospect of abandoning our relative security was enough to set the younger trooper to trembling. A compatriot placed a reassuring hand on his shoulder, though it was of little aid. Meanwhile, John shot me a glare of anger and fear, as if he were questioning the plan all over again. Still, all stood fast, waiting for what seemed an eternity in silence as, step by shuffling step, the *click-click...click*...gradually faded into the distance.

"Alright," Wilkes, at last satisfied, whispered to the man

beside him, "now's your time."

The brave trooper, evidently the most dextrous of the lot and a real diehard to boot, had earlier volunteered as our *Forlorn Hope*. He tucked his pistol into a belt, removed his heavy cavalry boots, and stepped bravely up to the wall where a crony knelt offering a foothold. The climber was delayed more by our need for silence than the vertical stone, as he pulled himself up to peer over the wall, legs dangling over the side. Every man held his breath, as I tried to ascertain any reaction he gave to his sight.

He was not long in surveying the ground, ere a quick nod signalled the others to assist him in clambering down. The scrape of a belt against stone set our hairs to stand, but after another moment's silence, we were satisfied that no devil had caught wind of us.

"We have a window. A narrow one." The man said as we gathered around. "A half dozen of them stand to either end, but the way before us is empty. If we keep quiet, I think we can make it without rousing any. No sailing today, though. Every boat save one has gone, and it's got a couple of the bastards on it. They shouldn't prove an issue, just steer clear of them."

"Well done." Wilkes replied with a slap to the scout's shoulder. "Come on and help me up top, then. As we discussed: gather atop, down as one, rush the water."

"And no shooting!" I contributed in a harsh whisper, whilst the others began removing their boots. Riding boots were of little use in climbing, after all, and even less in swimming across the river. Thus we made to ascend the wall, the first men being propped up from the base, before in turn reaching down to pull the rest of us. At the top, we all kept so low as we could to avoid any twitchy, wandering eyes.

At once, I saw that our scout's summation was astute. The quay directly before us was blessedly empty, while to either side there aimlessly roamed a smattering of corpses, oblivious to us. They had suffered the same horrific injuries as all their ilk, and stumbled about on half-severed limbs, all bled dry. One of them was missing near its entire lower half, and was half crawling, half rolling, out of a little storehouse. The heavy doors swung lightly in the faint waterside breeze.

Save one, all of the once-plentiful fishing vessels, narrowboats, and barges had slipped their moorings, by their owners or otherwise, in the chaos of the night. There would have been refugees all over Norfolk by then, I realised, and I wondered whether their assuredly panicked stories were being heeded by the outside world, or if Wilkes' vanguard still marched blind. Of the sole vessel remaining, then, its two sole occupants patrolled the deck like drunken officers.

One of them was obviously not a sailor, and had thoroughly painted the vessel's side with innards when it fell over the gunwale, onto the deck. The other, once a fisherman, peppered the deck with a fainter spray from a wounded arm and neck. The sailor must have been late in his attempted flight, when the more lubberly devil crashed aboard the moored boat to slaughter him. By the time I saw them, their former dispute had been long forgotten, as the two risen corpses were totally incognisant of each other. They merely splashed about the great pools of each other's blood in continuous patrol, up and down the gently rolling deck.

Momentarily transfixed by their state as I was, there stood no time for such morbid dalliances. The next phase of our manoeuvre would see us slide down the side of the wall, onto the stone beneath. Being again near so many of the foe, the full terror of re-entering the arena dawned upon me more fully. It seemed nothing would be so viciously poetic than to be set upon, torn apart, and baptised into the chittering masses, when my freedom stood so near. Nor, evidently, was I alone in such rumination, as some of the others seemed hesitant in dropping from the wall.

Beside me the younger trooper had likewise become transfixed by some of the devils, slowly shaking his head as if in denial of them. The crony next to him tried to offer a silent encouragement, but it would not do. Thus, when the waved signal came for us all to drop, he took a bodily hold of the boy to slide down with him. The two landed hard, nearly toppling over entirely, as did I upon my hard-used limbs. Still, we kept mostly silent. Myself by a hard bite upon my tongue, and the boy by his crony's firm-laid palm across his mouth.

The many *thumps* of our arrival, and the muffled whimpering of the boy, set us all to fright as we looked to the bodies surrounding. Still it seemed none had been roused to our presence, and slowly the boy was released from his hold. His breathing was hard, but he kept quiet, and upon another signal from Wilkes we began our crouching dash for the water. Beneath our feet, every pebble disturbed set my skin to crawl. Never had I encountered a waterway so silent, whence every slow scrape of a corpse's broken legs or dragging entrails flooded my ears like cannon fire. For all our speed, and the nearness of our foes, the narrow little quay felt akin to a mile.

Near halfway across, there issued from our right a thunderous great *thump* of bodies colliding with wood, as the devils in the boat caught sight of us. For the boy, the start was too much, and despite the devils' impotence as they stretched over the boat's insurmountable waist-high barrier, still he could not help but release the faintest yelp. His handler was on him at once with a hand pressed tight over his mouth, yet it was too late. Quiet though it was, the human noise was all our foes required. They wasted not a moment in comprehending us, but all at once twisted unnaturally to commence their pursuit.

"Run!" The cry came, as all our care for silence had gone. We all rose up and tore for the water. Pistols and the carbine were fired erratically, and most missed their targets entirely. Of those to land, of course, no effect beyond the further bloodying of the foe was to be had.

As we went, my own steps were painfully slow. My legs' every abuse bore terribly upon me and combined with my sudden panic. I struggled to catch my breath. Should I have halted but a moment, I felt it would surely be my end, and I could not help but take a quick glance over my shoulder to examine the condition of my pursuers. They were not so near as I had imagined in my terror, but still, those few arm-lengths would quickly be covered in their unnatural shambling.

It was then, in my foolishness, that my legs caught upon something. Likely themselves, in fact, and I fell hard unto the stone beneath me. Ignoring the further scrapes which had slid all down my hands and knees, I made to crawl forward and restore my footing as I went. Yet I found my legs poor in cooperating, as though I were already amidst the water, or in the throes of a nightmare. I found myself hardly able to wheeze out a desperate call, as my clambering resembled that of the corpses themselves.

Still, my plight was not unnoticed. While the cavalrymen, already well ahead, carried on in their flight to the water, it was my old comrade to risk a glance of his own. It was then that my earlier ponderings were answered definitively: John showed himself to be the better man.

Without even a moment to curse my name, he slid to a halt upon his heels, and came to the right-about. The nearest devil was close to my legs as he reached me. Still clutching his tall candlestick, he went just beyond me to strike hard at the erratic enemy and set it stumbling back.

"Get up!" His scream, though heroic enough, was filled with terror as he shoved a second corpse back from reach. With the brief seconds thus afforded to me, I was able to come to my feet. Scrambling only a short place away, I questioned with horror whether I would abandon the last of my brethren to his fate for another ill-deserved retreat. Yet I was spared from acknowledging the shameful truth, when suddenly there came a strong presence behind me.

"Come on!" John took me by the shoulders and aided in bearing my weight as we rushed for the water. He had lost his weapon, and a thin scratch sat just beneath his eye, but he had evidently succeeded in throwing off those assailants nearest us. Still, the others were not far behind, and it was only by virtue of the deserter's courage that I survived that final flight.

Courage had never been a word with which I associated my old friend. Excitability, to be sure, but never *courage*. I found myself respecting John in a new light. What I had once taken for stupidly mutinous skulduggery on the march to Stowlham,

I then learned was a genuine care for his fellows and our safety. Cares which we, his friends, had so wantonly decried.

Abused though he was, John safely bore me to the water's edge, where Wilkes stood waiting after the remainder of his men had dived to commence swimming across the river.

"Hurry! Come on!" The sergeant had evidently procured a pistol from one of his men, for with his sabre in the off hand, he lowered it to fire just beyond John and me. The crack of his shot landed true, for while I could not see its effect, I heard the telltale *squelch* of a bullet hitting flesh not far behind. Coming at last to his side, and ensuring we were well outside the reach of those devils still upon the boat, we leapt as one off the quayside.

The lazily flowing water was blessedly cool, and the fresh sting of it rejuvenated my ashen, blood-soaked flesh at once. Still it was only with difficulty that I first waded, and with the others' assistance swam, across the current. We had only just cleared a sufficient space before the first loud *splash* came behind us.

The first of the corpses had toppled headlong into the water, unaware even of the drop as it went. Its limbs thrashed and flailed all about as it bobbed up and down, unable to right itself in the water. Its rot mingled downstream with my own lifeblood, and that of the others. Nor was the devil long alone in its watery suspension, as the second at its tail soon fell right atop it. All down the quayside, as the devils were attracted by the noise, they ran, hobbled, and crawled their way into the water. Before long it seemed all the river was stained in black and red, as its surface became a churning rapid of desperate limbs.

For all their enthusiasm, however, the hope to which our fates were pinned had proven correct. Despite the relative easiness of the waters, its shallow depths proved wholly ill-suited to the dead. They could but weakly thrash and rotate themselves in the gentle current, entirely unable to propel themselves forward. Many simply sank straight to the bottom. The image might have been amusing, were it not so grotesque. That they could not drown was unsurprising; yet in my relief of having escaped, I spared not a thought upon where the corpses might wash up.

Escape! Safety! The meaning of such words had only just begun to dawn upon me as, more independently by then, I swam to the opposite bank where all the shoeless horsemen lay panting amidst the reedy, tall grass. Upon that bank there was no quayside, nor civilisation, but only a gentle rise into some flat, dying marshland. Yet as I clambered up to land, spluttering and choking up water, I found the blessed relief of security becoming fast drained from me.

Turning on my back to gaze upon the burning town, I began to drown anew amidst a sea of what I might only describe as *emptiness*. It seemed as though, whilst my *corporeal* being had escaped, my *soul* had been devoured.

I was near to weeping. Insofar as I could *feel* anything, there stood only disgust and shame, in a deeper melancholia than I had felt upon the sight of any friend's demise. I soon became transfixed by the distant fires, and I know not how long I stared into them. Even there, it seemed I could feel their heat upon my face, while the crackling echoed over the water to resemble so many teeth.

My stupor was driven from me as a hand grasped my shoulder. With a start, I looked up to see John kneeling beside me. His face was speckled with moving stains, as I struggled to blink away the fire's imprint, slowly revealing the similar sorrow ingrained within him. I knew, then, that I had *not* truly escaped, but suffered a different sort of death. The kind which only the living might know. In that strange and horrifying manner, I found my foul kinship with the protesting corpses, drifting steadily out to the ocean and God-knew where.

Neither John nor I uttered a word, but he helped me up, and together we ascended the riverbank to join the others, all wringing themselves out and likewise coming to terms with events. I realised that their walk would be a hard one, even with the marsh having become so dried out, given they had all abandoned their boots in the churchyard.

"Right then." Wilkes said at last. "I...suppose that's that.

We'd best be off. It'll be well dark by the time we reach the lines."

We spoke scarcely a dozen words the whole way, although it was hard marching and frequent stops were necessary. My wounded flesh was numb by the end, and I was hardly conscious of the many insects swarming and biting at me. I comprehended little of physicality save the next step before me, and the great smoke column looming heavy above us. Even there, it deposited the occasional fleck of ash upon us.

Stowlham's carcass, I knew, was not yet through with me.

Stumbling Across the Sentry.

Part the
TENTH
wherein the army is met.

It was indeed well dark by the time we stumbled across the sentry, frightening him near to death as we did so. Notwithstanding his musket barrel glinting in the moonlight as it was promptly squared on us, the sound of his voice as he called out his challenge was a deep relief.

Despite soon recognising Wilkes and the other troopers, the sentry had good cause to be suspicious of us. He and his brethren were little aware of the past day's events. For all he knew, and for all the falsities that had spread, we could well have been devils ourselves! Perhaps we had stolen the voices of his former comrades, or worse, been made into agents for the French! Many still suspected them of the whole thing, of course, as a few do even to this day. The only information the poor sentry had, as he stood alone in the dark, was that a routine patrol of cavalry had been dispatched and never returned. Then, in the dead of night, we came along in all our dreadful state!

At last satisfied of our identities, if little else, the sentry called more loudly to signal the others of his watch. Still, as he allowed us nearer onto the road where he stood, his musket never dropped.

Most of his attention, it seemed, was fixed upon myself. I

could scarcely fault him for his fear, or disgust. Given the rumours then racing throughout the country, I must have seemed like some terrible swamp-creature to him. I had no coat, nor hat, and my smallclothes had long since been torn to shreds and, even after the river, were every part stained with blood, mud, brains, and ash.

His anxieties aside, I cared little for the threat of his muzzle. Instead I was simply glad to halt, and at once sat myself against one of the few crooked trees near to hand. John and many of the others came to my side, all likewise exhausted in body and soul.

The sentry was soon joined by a corporal who made to briefly interrogate us, inquiring after the remainder of Wilkes' comrades - to say nothing of his boots! Before Wilkes might even *begin* to explain, so too had a sergeant hurriedly joined our cadre, announcing himself by way of a tired swear as his pike caught up on a dry branch overhead. With one arm he impatiently pulled the pike free, dried out leaves falling all about him, while in the other he carried a low lantern, which bathed the whole scene in an imposing glow.

Shortly thereafter we were made to follow both non-commissioned officers down the road, whence our escort was joined by no less than three officers! They likewise carried little lanterns, yet they held no function upon the watch. They had merely heard of some commotion and were *desperate* for information. At once they began to pepper us with questions.

"What the devil happened to you? Have you come from the garrison?" One gentleman was particularly brash in his interrogations. I could hardly hear him, despite his closeness. Thankfully, one of Wilkes' men was able to offer some stumbling, though unsatisfactory, answers in my stead.

I found myself little comprehending, and leaned against John ever more heavily with each plodding step as he assisted me onwards. We were by then evidently near to the vanguard, for soon a different sort of mob overwhelmed us. It seemed every officer with an excuse to be without his tent had come to join in the questioning, having heard tell of some reconnaissance men returned at last. In their excitement, all the usual decorum was totally abandoned.

My vision was blurred with copious gold and silver lace swirling about, and all a-glitter in the cavalcade of flickering lamps. Yet I saw nothing save the flames of Stowlham in that mesmerising glow. My ears were quite deafened in the commotion, yet I heard nothing beyond the screams of my fellows, while John pleaded for them to give space. I could little feel my limbs by then, even as a canteen of water was shoved into my hands, and I tried to drink from it through quickening breaths.

One question, still, broke through the chaos to my cognisance.

"Is it true?" The blue eyes of a boy ensign, no older than fifteen, flickered brilliantly between his finely dressed stock and well pressed hat. His lips seemed to tremble. "Have the dead arisen?"

Even had I possessed the wherewithal to speak, I am unsure what I might have offered in reply. My dreadful visage, and the cold blank of my stare, seemed distressing enough to the poor little gentleman.

Before long, the first signs of encampment began to materialise. The few trees along the road being supplanted by crude stumps, their bodies having been felled to fuel cooking fires, while we left the narrow country lane for a dry field, its grass thoroughly compacted by so many hundreds of trampling shoes, boots, hooves, and wheels. The emptiness of the countryside was replaced with a forest of white canvas, dimly glowing by the full moon above. From within the seemingly endless rows of tents poked the eyes and ears of curious souls, all desperate to gain some inkling of their fast-approaching fate.

Even through my haze, I could not help but be overawed by the scale of humanity which surrounded us. Not since my last regimental field day had I seen so many tents, as it seemed at least two whole battalions had been summoned to impose upon that unnamed field in the middle of nowhere.

While the quite-sudden appearance of this brigade is likely a tiresome fact amongst the majority of my readers, being well acquainted with the course of the so-called *Corpse War*, it may nevertheless prove beneficial for certain less informed others for me to step away from my usual narrative and offer some explanation for it.

As I had earlier suspected, the great conflagration of Stowlham had been spotted in the early morning by her neighbouring communities long before any knowledge of her *true* fate had spread. In particular, it was a farmer out for his cows who first noticed the smoke. Realising how widespread the flames must have been, he left the poor bovines without their usual relief to instead race to his village and raise the alarm. Soon enough, the local magistrate being convinced of the severity of Stowlham's predicament, there was assembled a little band of the village's most able men. They set out for the market town with buckets, spades, and not a few firelocks, some men having become fearful of once-foolish rumours, in hand. A rider was also sent ahead to ascertain the situation. By this time, I suspect I was contemplating the possibility of a relief, whilst in the upper storey of the old man's home.

Those good farmers and tradesmen were spared the fate of my comrades when, as they came to the river, which runs along the road into Stowlham a few miles distant from it, they encountered a bargeman. Though half-crazed, the man was otherwise unharmed, unlike the poor draft horse which he had beat nearly to death in dragging his boat up the current. The man was first detained by the villagers on suspicion of having flouted his civic duty. Some heated debate arose upon his spluttering explanation of the horrors which had erupted in Stowlham. In its course, many of those villagers with lesser stomachs soon abandoned their cause and returned to their families, while the bargeman was left to continue his flight.

Among the most zealous men, who forged on either in denial of such stories, or braver yet in spite of them, there soon came another distraction more difficult to ignore. The second refugee was a young woman cradling a babe in her arms and severely cut up. The party again halted, both to render her aid and inquire after her injury. She told, in utterances barely comprehensible, of her husband viciously attacking her after suffering a terrible wound. Even had her frightful account not convinced the remaining men, the sudden reappearance of their mounted scout quashed any lingering doubts.

He had come on at a breakneck speed, and could only keep control of his horse with some difficulty. He corroborated the refugees' tales of swarming devils at once and without prompting, for they had attempted to seize upon him as he entered the town. Evidently, he had only barely escaped their clutches.

With this final confirmation, the remaining men deemed any effort they might exert to be folly, and understandably went to the right-about to flee more hastily than they had advanced. Upon reentering their village, they raised a more general alarm, with riders going out to warn all their neighbours against ghouls in the night.

Similar events were occurring all throughout the surrounding countryside, as bands of men went out and were inevitably turned away, either by the warnings of refugees, or upon sighting the devils themselves on nearing the burning town. Each locale, then, disseminated their reports in every direction, save towards Stowlham. Within a few hours of daylight's first flirtation, dispatches containing every variety of truth, half-truth, and falsity were pouring so far as Cambridge, Peterborough, and Norwich. The effect of these being that, whilst everyone was soon aware that *something* had happened, and an enemy was upon British soil, few could agree on *who* or *what* said enemy was.

Thus, while rumour and confusion spread like wildfire, real action was sluggish. Many ministers, doubtful of the rambling, inconsistent reports they received, refused to call out their militias until concrete *evidence* might be had, instead dispatching their own messengers to further muddy the narrative. Meanwhile, others seemed to race out with the news at once, calling their militia and every able-bodied man besides to arms. No doubt many were quite glad for the opportunities of advancement which a possible French invasion necessitated.

Indeed, those men with greatest responsibility generally assumed the *reasonable* threat to be the truth; that a French force, of unknown size, had somehow secreted itself past the navy and come to land in Norfolk. Thence, they had snuck up the river, and attacked Stowlham in the night, soon overwhelming we few of the garrison, and firing the town before marching on to some other rapacious business. The real concern, in their minds, was not in liberating Stowlham, but discovering the *Frogs'* whereabouts. No doubt, many fancied, that *planted anecdotes* of walking corpses served well to disguise their route of march!

To such an end, those preparations which *were* undertaken, were in countering Continental phantoms rather than the devils of reality. Villages were forcefully evacuated by the militia and other garrisoned troops; some residents nearly rioting in the process. Trees were felled and thrown across roads, ditches were dug along the same, and one 'enthusiastic' militia officer even went so far as to destroy every bridge on the road down to London he could find. In more believable times, such activities might have garnered praise as 'alacritous sacrifice' in defence of King and Country, yet in truth, they served only to delay our Army's reply.

By the time word reached London, the whole of the Southeast was mired in a state of terrible confusion and anxiety. The Admiralty, ashamed of their presumed failure to thwart an invisible French fleet, at once commenced assembling all possible shipping to meet them. In the process, of course, they only caught out a single unfortunate Dutch dogger.

Horse Guards, meanwhile, set itself to gathering whatever regiments were nearest at hand and throwing them to some vague point of assembly near Cambridge. There, they would fall under the hastily appointed command of General the Lord Edward Tomlinson, to march out to throw the enemy back into the sea.

The result of it all was that a series of little bands, ranging from individual companies of embodied militia to entire regiments of regulars, found themselves racing down the ravaged roads to join up with others wherever they might be found. Those little bodies most quick to reach Tomlinson, were then immediately dispatched as a vanguard to the 'Frenchmen's' last known location. Thus, by that late afternoon, as I had found myself staring down into the mobbed market square, were Sergeant Wilkes and his troop sent out to reconnoitre for said vanguard, never to return.

Until, of course, we unhappy, bloody, and brutalised few came stumbling in on them. It was little wonder, then, that we were so eagerly mobbed by every officer in the camp, all desperate for some morsel of information.

"Enough! Enough of this!" An authoritative, high voice came from the head of our jostling entourage. Steadily, it fell silent. The newcomer, in the finery of an aide de camp, forced his way through the throng. "Retire at once, gentlemen! Lest you bring further shame to your corps!"

Thus admonished, the overeager captains and subalterns began to disperse, many doffing their caps or saluting as they did so, whilst others sullenly tried to hide their faces in shame. Before long we stood alone, at the centre of the camp beneath a set of Colours. I found myself better able to breathe, and my presence of mind was steadily restored.

My earlier estimation had proven correct. I had never seen such a collection of tents in all my life! They lined the once-green field in their hundreds, sufficient to house a small town, and I realised there must have been near a thousand soldiers present! Yet there was nary a sound, save the soft patter of retreating officers' shoes, and the gentle flapping of so much canvas, cotton, wool, and hemp in the lazy evening breeze. It was accompanied by the occasional clang of kit, or the creaking of a wagon, overtop steady insect song, to transform the earlier pandemonium into a kind of peaceful melody.

The aide was a dashing young officer, whose long hair poked unceremoniously from behind his hat, in a betrayal of the haste he had made in coming to meet us. He pressed close to Wilkes with a wild, wide-eyed concern.

"Good God, man." He whispered harshly. "What has happened?"

The sergeant replied with a weary, yet fully earnest, salute.

"We were...set upon, sir."

"Set upon?" The aide's voice rose in concern before he could check it. "By...whom?"

Did his voice waver, then? Did he worry that the question he posed, of '*whom*', was less appropriate than of '*what*'? Wilkes was clearly hesitant to reply, and rightfully so. For what sort of truth could be believed by any save the mad, or those who had bore it witness?

"With respect, sir, I believe I need to report to General Hawkins straight away." Wilkes swallowed, hard. "Directly, sir."

"Very well." The aide saw little fit to argue. "Come along, and then we'll see after your men. It seems you've all been terribly used up."

Given our state, it was quite the understatement. Not one cavalryman retained his full uniform or stood without injury. We were each of us caked in filth, and I could only stand with difficulty, still leaning heavily on John for support.

Before he carried on, the aide could not help but ask after one final curiosity.

"Sergeant, you and your men, are you...all that remains?"

There was a pause. As if to voice their sole survivorship would finally make it *real*. How many troopers had been sent out, for but a little over half-a-dozen to return? When Wilkes replied, there lay a deep regret beneath his thin layer of placid professionalism.

"I believe so, sir."

~ 161 ~

Brigadier General Hawkins & His Staff.

Part the
ELEVENTH
wherein the truth becomes known.

As we were led a little way to the camp's headquarters, Wilkes made sure to keep a slight distance from the aide de damp, as to secret some words to the rest of us.

"The spread of panic won't do us any good," he explained cautiously, "and we still don't understand what any of this means. So all of you keep your mouths shut. *Anyone* asks you a question besides the general himself, you're *not* at liberty, you *don't* know anything. You just tell them to ask me. That goes for any bleeding *officer* the same as your *washerwoman*, understood?"

The troopers all nodded in assent. Given their state, it seemed few desired to recount their terrible experiences, and Wilkes was correct that to loosen their lips could spell disaster for an army already at the end of its wits. Not that the wretched state of our arrival was much consolation to them, either.

"Sergeant Wilkes." John cautiously inquired. "What about...me?"

I realised for the first time, then, how petrified my former comrade-in-arms must have been. Surrounded as we were by military men, it would take but *one* recognition to brand him a deserter. The only question then would be whether he was shot, hanged, or whipped within an inch of his life and forced back into ranks. The latter was perhaps a fate worse than death. The poor man was ruined for a soldier the moment his back was first torn by the lash, if not earlier.

While John had escaped the terror of Stowlham, he had hardly saved his skin. If anything, he now faced a cleverer, even *crueller*, foe.

Had I not required his aid, he could certainly have escaped from us in the night, well before we stumbled across the sentry. Yet now, terribly weary and without friends or direction, he had little hope of escape until dawn. I doubted whether any sane man would desire to be alone in the countryside at night, either, after all we had endured.

He faced all variety of terrible ends, and it was entirely my fault.

Wilkes considered him for some time, still presuming him an innocent refugee caught up in the chaos.

"I suspect your testimony may be of some use." Said he. "Afterwards, well, the general has been loath to release any able-bodied man, and I don't suspect he'll be able to petition your magistrate any time soon for *legal* permission to draft you in. I'm sorry, but, you'll probably be stuck with us for a while. You might consider volunteering with one of the militias for the duration, if you want to avoid any ditch-digging. We're all headed to the same place, anyway. Do you have any shooting experience?"

"A little…" John's reply was quiet as the aide halted just outside a long marquee, presumably the brigade headquarters. "I'm not a very good shot."

Before ducking inside, the aide bade us wait with the marquee's sentry, who did his utmost not to stare at us. We were left in silence for only a breath ere the aide returned, quickly gesturing us within.

The tent's air was far warmer than without, and smelled of oil and wax from the half-dozen lamps and candles scattered about. They lent the scene a steady glow, casting deep shadows along the canvas walls. At the centre stood a fine large table, its surface buried beneath a pile of maps, reports, writing tools, navigation implements, and not a few grand tomes.

Did the officers find much time for reading, I sourly wondered? Perhaps they were attempting to find answers in *natural philosophy* to account for the refugees' tales.

Behind the table was a veritable wall of scarlet coats and gold epaulettes. Staff and senior field officers stood expectant with hands on swords and hats underarm. Adjutants and surgeons, likewise in all their finery, hovered anxiously over this report or that. In the corner was one of the chaplains, wringing his hands for want of something to hold.

Standing like Christ at the centre of his disciplines, then, was a man of dark countenance; unblinking as he beheld our foul beings, as if resolved to display no emotion whatsoever.

"Thank you, Captain Russell." He spoke lowly to the aide. "If you would please, dismiss the guard and keep watch yourself. Any man so much as steps within earshot, and I'll have him flogged. Any officer, cashiered. Go now."

Such was my introduction to Brigadier General Albert Hawkins, whose stony gaze never left us. Nor did those of any other within the tent. Half the senior officers of the brigade must have been crammed behind that table, and I had never felt more cognisant of the grime coating the brutalised remains of my uniform, or the beard which had begun to tinge my cheeks.

None of the troopers seemed particularly comfortable under the scrutiny, either, and I noticed an officer of their regiment in the collection. His mouth was agape in shock, which he little bothered to hide as his eyes darted from face to face. Perhaps he was the man who ordered their troop on to Stowlham? It seemed as though this was the first time he had ordered men to their deaths, and he found the revelation of their fate smothering.

"Sergeant Wilkes," General Hawkins continued as the two men took post outside, "your report."

"Sir!" The old bow-legged cavalryman stepped forward, still in his stockings. His confidence soon evaporated, however, as he was faced with recounting all that had transpired. He stumbled over his words like a nervous recruit.

"I...I regret to report, that..."

"Out with it!" The sharp crack of Hawkins' palm on the table made every man flinch. With a swallow and a breath, Wilkes regained something of himself, and his words poured forth.

"To report that Captain Stuart is dead, sir. As is Lieutenant Campbell, and Cornet Evans. To my knowledge, I am the only remaining non-commissioned officer of my troop, and these with me...the only men. Sir."

All was stiff and still between the claustrophobic canvas, our shadows quivering in the little light.

The cavalry officer seemed faint. The chaplain signed the cross. Brigadier General Hawkins uttered one word.

"*How?*"

His meaning was clear. Had the cavalry succumbed to French bullets, or *something* else? With another heavy pause, Wilkes continued.

"On approaching Stowlham, it was evident the town was done for. We suspected it was purposefully fired, but saw no French. No motion of any kind, really. Nor was there any shipping upon the river, or indication of a landing. Captain Stuart ordered us to advance. Still we saw nothing on our approach, until..."

Every man hanged upon the sergeant's words. One might have heard a pin drop.

"Coming just to the outskirts, we thought the town abandoned, sir, until Cornet Evans swore he heard a woman scream. So we made to continue our reconnoitre, and search for any refugees. The lads weren't happy about it, but the prevailing thought remained that the enemy had sacked the place in the night. Survivors might carry information, the captain figured. So we rode within, and began to call out.

That was...that was when we saw the first of them, sir."

As Wilkes neared to the pivotal point of his recollection, his speech became laborious. I could not see his face, but saw that it was only with difficulty that the old sergeant kept his palms open at his side, as was proper.

"*Them?*" The general hissed. He had not the luxury of patience for past traumas when the future's survival weighed on his shoulders. "*Who*, by God, *who?* Quit your dithering, man!"

The cavalryman could find no sensitive means to speak the words, nor way to evade their outlandishness. Though in any reasonable world they would see him branded a madman, he spoke the truth.

"The dead, sir."

The dam of silence collapsed at once. The marquee flooded with gasps, exclamations, and accusations. Some of the officers had obviously believed the rumours of revenant dead from their onset, and had been waging a war unwinnable to that point. Now they gesticulated wildly at their maps and figures, insisting upon some prior rejected course of action. Many others still refused to believe it as anything beyond folly, and threatened Wilkes with reduction to the ranks. Each man spoke over every other with a fear transcending all the usual decorum of their class; save, of course, the brigadier general himself.

His eyes had widened, to be sure, and he struggled to hide the fear behind them. His hands pressed all the harder upon the table, to keep them from shaking. I had long since clenched my own, for the same purpose. None cared, by then, for maintaining the *proper* position of a soldier.

The chaos continued for some time. The officers argued amongst themselves whether they should wait for the main force, or continue forging onwards. Many made immediate, and utterly foolish, claims as to the nature of the foe. One gentleman even insisted they might advance into Stowlham outright, and 'put an end to this nonsense once and for all' overnight!

Still, I could only stand and wait. I felt tears upon my cheek, as I tamped down the urge to insult all their crass ignorance. For all the fear it induced, yet greater was my anger upon them. Closing my eyes, still I could see the stains of Stowlham's fire.

Eventually, as he regained his own bearing, General Hawkins raised his hand to try and silence the babblers.

"Gentlemen!" His tone was loud to transcend the din. His face had gone somewhat red in the flickering lamplight, a sign of anger he could not disguise. "Gentlemen, peace! That's enough!"

The space quieted, and the air felt all the more stifled for it. I could hear the younger trooper breathing heavily behind me, as he struggled to maintain his composure the same as I.

"Sergeant Wilkes." Continued Hawkins. "Do you mean to tell me your troop was unhorsed in a bone-yard? Ambushed by waiting skirmishers?"

His tone was that of a man hiding behind the veil of disbelief, and praying it was in *incompetence*, rather than devilry, that his answers would be found.

"No, sir." Wilkes worked to unclench his jaw and speak with respect. "We came across a little clump of them scattered in the road. Probably ten or so bodies, sir, all badly cut up. Some were even missing limbs. All the same, on our approach they ran towards us feverishly. Two of the lads dismounted at once. We..." Another hard swallow, and a blink through his sweat. At last, the sergeant's fists were balled tight. "We assumed the civilians to be injured, and in need of aid. They never spoke a word. We only realised their...unnaturalness, too late. The bodies swarmed over the first men they reached and began tearing at them. We tried to cut at them, and shoot them, but they just wouldn't stop. Before anyone knew what was happening, more had appeared, and we were near surrounded. They set upon us, upon the *horses*, even...and they just stowldn't die, sir. We could only flee, and found ourselves pursued by a mob of them. The formation split apart. They came from every direction, an-"

Wilkes' increasingly harried tone was abruptly cut, and he turned away from the officers towards me. His eyes, normally so stern, were bloodshot and weary.

"We few only escaped by virtue of this man. When we came to a walled-off yard, he helped carry us over the top and beyond the grasp of them. They were strong, but stupid and unsteady. They couldn't climb after us. Thence, we effected our escape from the town, and came straight here to report, sir."

Silence reigned again. I felt every eye cast to me, and my particularly dilapidated state. Many of those eyes had grown more fearful than before. Those with disbelief held it in resistance to our terrible new reality, moreso than any honest conviction.

"And who are you?" Inquired the general of me with a sharp-raised eyebrow.

Taking my own deep breath, I threw aside my disgust as best I was able, and stepped alongside Wilkes to begin my own awkward report. Identifying myself as a man of the garrison, I struggled to explain in brief all I had witnessed; discovering Bennett's corpse, the fires spreading, Lieutenant Farwell's stand, and my escape with Captain Lawrence before he appointed me his second.

My story was one of choking sorrow, and it was only with difficulty that I could recall all that had transpired in its proper sequence. With every word I spoke, I seemed transported in some way back to the very moment, as all my awareness of the men about me faded into visions of my former comrades being set upon in the night. I could hear their screaming as I described them, and felt the heat of fire upon my face. It only grew in intensity as I continued my tale.

"By all rights they *ought* to be dead, sir."

Bennett came stumbling towards me, his face shredded and hardly recognisable.

"Yet when a man should fall, well, some devilry seems to...resurrect him, and without any sense of himself."

Captain Lawrence stood in the doorway, cold and biting.

"It seems they attack anything living they might find. They're like...starved dogs to pieces of meat."

Intestines and bones were ripped from horses and men alike, mere feet before me as I sat atop the churchyard wall and could do nothing but watch.

"Nor might any injury, not to the heart or head, stop them."

My bayonet scraped between bones. A knife plunged hard into eyes which burst.

"We escaped only through fortune, sir. The devils, for all their strength, are without minds, and were unable to pursue us past the river."

With my conclusion, and a quick account for having found John, whom I identified merely as a refugee, I was again restored to the present. Every officer looked upon me in horror and deep contemplation. I wondered, then, whether any of them had known Captain Lawrence, or Major Bray. None of my own regiment were present then, but the officerial world was a small one. I was assuredly not alone in my loss.

"Without minds..." Another voice rose then from the side, as an infantry officer made himself known. He was somewhat enfeebled by advanced age, though was still sound of bearing, and seemed to be one of the few not entirely put aback by the terror of it all. "So they are without organisation? Without leadership?"

"None as we could ascertain, sir." Wilkes replied, somewhat restored.

"Well, that is good news, at least. It seems you men have ridden into the very maw of Hell, and come out for it with knowledge that may just save all our hides. We owe you a debt."

A general murmur of agreement followed amongst the gentlemen, save Hawkins, who seemed displeased by his subordinate's presumption of liberty.

Notwithstanding such useless gratitude, and our obvious

need of rest as we stood near-collapsing before them, the officers continued in their preoccupation with more pressing concerns. There ensued a barrage of questions as they were desperate for more information concerning the impending struggle. Though unsteady and nerve-wracked, Wilkes and I did our utmost to answer their inquiries. Of course, to the majority, we could offer but little.

When we described the beasts as senseless, what precisely did we mean?

Can they hear? See? Smell?

Had they any memory?

How many were there?

Did they have a herding instinct? Or were their groupings purely coincidental?

Might they be killed by this, that, or some other means?

And of course, *what of these reports, from some source we had never heard of, detailing events entirely unknown? Might they contain some truth, and if so, what would the implications be?*

We stood before our interrogators for what seemed an eternity, though given the circumstances, the officers surely felt they had no time at all to ready their brigade for the impossible task before them. Despite the protestations of my every limb, and the weariness of my mind, there was at least some comfort in the seriousness with which the officers regarded the situation. Doubts as to the foe's true nature, regardless of any flawed interpretations of niggling details, seemed piece by piece to vanish in light of our consistency and earnestness.

Near the end of our interrogation, some little attention was even paid to John, who throughout the occasion had steadily shrunk himself to the rear of our tightly-packed party. It was the older officer who first asked after his story, and how he had come to find himself in the church amidst the chaos.

"I was...praying, sir." Replied John plainly. He had little interest in speaking, and sought to hide his face as much as possible from the gentlemen. I even attempted to shuffle myself in aiding his effort, between the officers' arguments. It was my pitiful attempt at aid for the man who had saved my skin.

"Well I should imagine so, at such a time!" The grey-haired gentleman actually smiled, dry lips stretched taut across his weathered face. "But you did not run out at the cry of fire, like the others?"

"No, sir. I made to do so, of course, but on reaching the churchyard gates, I saw one of...them, you see. It was running down the road, stumbling over itself in excitement about something. Only now I suppose it was in pursuit of someone. I had heard the rumours and, well, I thought myself at the end of the world. So, I ran back, and I prayed, until the others found me. At the time it seemed my best use, sir.

It struck me that his prayers may have been for *forgiveness*, as much as they were for mercy to the world.

Again, questions swam to the forefront of my mind: How had the gates come to be locked from within, when no churchmen stood within the walls? Had John done so, after witnessing his nightmares become reality? If so, his cowardice had nearly cost me my life, and ensured far worse for many others. Yet I found myself unable to fault him, for within my own preservational deeds, one might find sins equally severe, while John had shown great courage in my own rescue when the risk to his flesh was at its greatest.

No, he could not have locked the gate himself. I knew, and still know, there stood another answer, though it be known only to God.

Nor could I blame John for not racing out to seek his old compatriots in the chaos. Even as I could *see* him, hiding away as so many stood outside against the Fleshtide, as I could *hear* the rattling gates whilst pleading faithful were chewed to pieces, I could not imagine I would have acted differently.

I loathed myself all the more for that realisation.

"Then you might consider it a favour from God that my men found you." General Hawkins returned to the conversation. "Now, you shall repay that favour. You may consider yourself pressed into the service of His Majesty's army. I'll not give you a firelock, but I will give you a spade. You'll be with the other civilians under the pioniers, until I grant you leave."

John's already anticipating the words provided him little relief, and he was thrown at once to a near panic. His mouth worked wordlessly. Without the approval of the civic authority, his impressment was undeniably illegal, yet it seemed our commander had little interest in the *formalities* of British Liberty, at the time.

"General, sir, you don't mean to-" John began his feeble entreaty, but was at once cut off.

"I am in need of every able-bodied man I can find, I'm sure you understand." Hawkins overtook the poor lad. "If you've a complaint, you might bring it before the local magistrate. In the meanwhile, you'll be clearing the roads. You are also to remain *silent* as to all you have witnessed, until such a time as I see fit to explain the situation to the men. All of you are. Am I understood?"

There was little room for misunderstanding, and at Hawkins' behest, Captain Russell was again summoned to lead John away. I did not have a chance to speak, but met his eyes with the deepest fear as he was pulled away. Yet while mine bore also regret, his carried the scornful seeds of a friend betrayed. He would be right, I knew at once, to blame me for his predicament. I feared that in his inevitable escape attempt, he would conduct himself poorly and be captured. My duty as a soldier was to the army and my regiment, yet I felt my duty as a *man* to be quite different then, and I foolishly resolved to be as great an aid to my old crony as possible.

Wilkes and the other troopers were thanked again for their service and sent out to return to the remains of their regiment. They would no doubt be reassigned to some other troop, and watched over with exceeding delicacy, lest they disseminate their stories and cause the panic which would surely follow.

As for myself, there were no such convenient paths available. I was informed that the remainder of my regiment was assembled with the main army, and would meet Hawkins' Brigade in the coming days. Until such a time as I could rejoin them, upon which a favourable reference would be given for my *formal* appointment to the rank of Sergeant, I was tossed to the authority and care of Captain Penn - the older officer I had earlier noted.

As I was led from the marquee, some heated discussion regarding the next course of action recommenced within. Another officer had been booted outside to play sentry. The last words I heard were from General Hawkins, as he damned the dead and proclaimed the advance would continue at double the pace.

Outside the marquee, all remained quiet, even peaceable.

"He's a firebrand, to be sure." Whispered Captain Penn to me with the same papery smile. "But, a decent enough officer, when you need men to move fast. He doesn't much like me, though!"

The gentleman's friendly chuckle betrayed him as that rare sort of officer who might view his men more as compatriots, than as petulant children. Indeed, Captain Penn was an uncommon man in numerous ways; his holding a junior rank at so advanced an age included. I later learned, from the man himself no less, that he had languished too long as a lieutenant with neither funds nor favour to acquire his promotion, which had only come with a free commission on the death of his predecessor during the American War.

I realised also that it was his very aloofness, and the resultant friction with his sterner commander, which led to his being saddled with me. Yet he seemed to bear me no ill will, and in fact, later became so great a champion for my cause as any I ever had.

"I am glad to hear it, sir." I replied wearily and warily. "That he is a good officer, I mean."

Captain Penn clapped me lightly on the back and led me through the ocean of canvas. He offered little remarks as we went about the camp and where I might find its various amenities. It was odd to again be amongst friends, and my heart knew not whether to take solace in the security they offered, or to anticipate a horde of devils that might be awaiting behind every shadowy corner.

Every quiet creak of leather set my skin to crawl, and the distant snapping of a lock set my face to twitch uneasily. What fool would be checking their spark so late in the night?

The captain observed all my poorly-obscured cowardice with the wise eyes of a man who had seen it before.

"You've had a hard time of it, then." He mused as we reached the section where his company was encamped. I could sense the many ears pressed against tent-walls all about us, and even spotted a few eyes poking through their flaps. The poor men were hungry for information long withheld, and were evidently little afeared of their officer.

"Yes, sir." It was all I could manage in reply.

"There's no shame in it, lad. Here," he came to a tent, "we'll throw you in with Sergeant Morse for now. He's out on watch anyways, and I'll make sure he's made aware of you. Don't mind him, or any duties tomorrow. Just come right and see me before the march, and we'll fix you up. I'll have some clean clothes and water sent for your ablutions, and something stronger to drink besides. You've earned some rest, but I'm afraid you won't get much."

He paused then, his kind eyes flickering deeply in some little, distant lanternlight.

"I cannot begin to fathom the things you've seen." The thoughtfulness of his words, and the sorrow of their sentiment, nearly set me to weeping.

"Thank you, sir." I murmured, feeling more than ever the great weight upon my shoulders, though they carried only a worn-through shirt and ruined waistcoat. "Though, I fear you will understand it quite well, before the end."

Captain Penn considered me for some time in silence.

"Yes." Replied he in equal tone. "I suppose I shall."

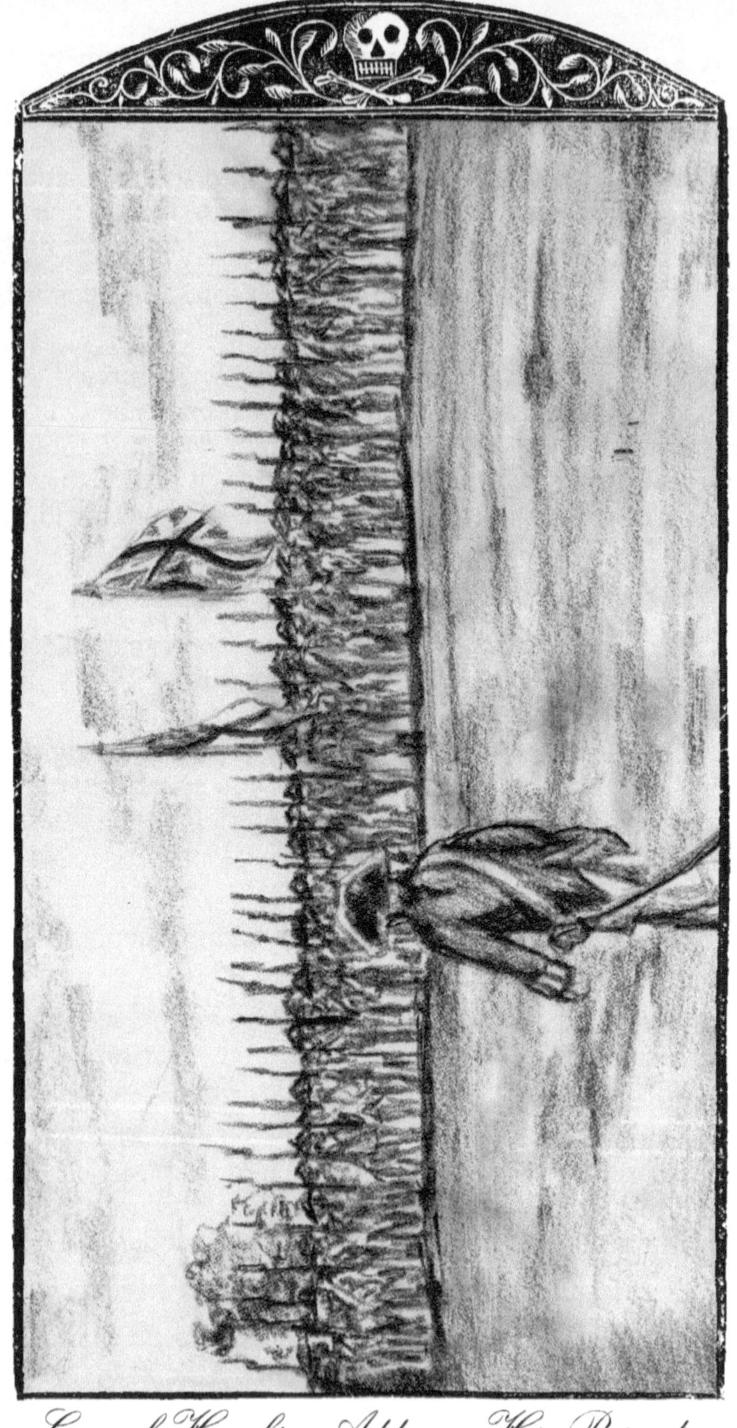

General Hawkins Addresses His Brigade.

TWELFTH

wherein Hawkins' Brigade advances for Stowlham.

𝕯𝖊𝖘𝖕𝖎𝖙𝖊 𝖙𝖍𝖊 𝖒𝖞𝖗𝖎𝖆𝖉 𝖙𝖊𝖗𝖗𝖔𝖗𝖘 which infected my slumber, the extraordinary weariness of my body would not allow me to wake. Though I spent many an hour *feeling* myself to be so, it was by my being utterly frozen that I knew myself to dream. Still, my assurances were of little comfort as I saw the impossibly long, stiffened fingers of my comrades reaching, slowly, into the tent. Inch by inch they slid over the ground, dancing first over my feet, then my legs, and coming to settle upon my neck. They were cold as they wormed about my flesh, and cracked with their every flex. I attempted to scream, but found them shooting down my throat the moment I opened my mouth. As they reached my heart to squeeze it hard, *then* was I at last permitted to wake.

I felt my body thrusting to sit up, while in a blink the cold night air was replaced with a harsh morning light, diffused by the canvas all about me. There were no fingers at my throat save my own. I struggled to catch my breath, as though I had been drowning, while my heart pained for how quickly it raced. For but a moment, I was confused as to my location, but glancing all about I came to accept my security. The fingers had faded at once with my waking, and outside I heard all the usual, comforting sounds of an encampment in the early morning. Men were fetching water and wood, cooking their breakfasts, and rubbing away at their belts and brass.

For the first time in my service, I had missed the call of *reveille*, and possibly even the morning inspection. Yet with the sudden panic of my waking, I was uncertain if I had truly rested at all.

Looking about the tent, there were no signs of Sergeant Morse. If he had reappeared in the night, I had been incognisant of him. At my feet, however, I saw Captain Penn made good on his word, for there sat a large bucket of water, a razor, and some fresh smallclothes alongside a little beef, a filled canteen, and even a bottle of wine finer than any I could afford.

I wasted not a moment in devouring the rations, little appreciating their finer cut than the usual fare of a private soldier. Though I might have drunk the whole bottle on my own, I was spared such indiscretion by its being already half gone - my first introduction to the elusive Sergeant Morse, I presumed.

Likewise, I do not believe I ever savoured a wash and shave more in all my life. Slowly, and painfully, for all my scabbing, I peeled away the charred and torn strips of cloth that remained of my smallclothes, and purified my body of the grime which had so long corrupted it. I could but shudder in recollection as I cleared the stains away from the many shallow tooth-marks dotting my flesh. The wounds were not so deep or severe as they first felt, I saw with great relief, yet still their distinctive pattern was a woeful reminder of their cruelly unusual origins. Many of them I could not even recall, for in the chaos of their acquisition I had not felt a thing. It would be prudent, I knew, to visit the surgeon after reporting to Captain Penn.

My new smallclothes were in some parts too large, and others too small, and made for a rather awkward appearance. Yet their being clean was sufficient to somewhat rejuvenate both my body and soul. Penn had even arranged for fresh shoes and gaiters to be laid out for me, that I need not clean and reblacken my own.

When finally I crawled outside the tent, even my abused limbs forgot, for a time, all their awful pains. Blinking at a harsh sun, still low in the morning sky, I nearly felt myself to be a new man; though such undeserved comforts would be short lived.

"Well, it's about time." A soldier soon appeared at my side to give me a start, thrusting a cup of something upon me before I could fully comprehend his presence. "I'd thought you'd died in the night!"

The private soldier cut a fine appearance, and my eyes were dazzled by brass that shone too bright. His cocked hat was reversed and folded over, for protection from the rising sun.

"What?" I must have seemed ridiculous as I glanced from the fellow, to the cup, and back again.

"It's only some tea, sergeant. Well cold, by now." The man seemed annoyed and amused with me in equal measure, though a great *curiosity* lay overtop them both.

"Oh, yes." I stumbled over my thoughts, nor did the half-bottle aid me in comprehension. "Thank you, ah-"

"Harris, sergeant." The soldier identified himself. "I'm Captain Penn's batman. He sent me to fetch you once you woke, and bring you his way."

I said nothing, but gratefully drank down the tea before following the soldier-servant, who was already proceeding through the tent rows. All about us the ceremonies of camp life continued, and many men had commenced the delicate process of dismantling their tentage. As we passed, to a man they would pause in their work, and make no effort to hide their staring.

Even *without* my presence, I realised on the brief walk that a queer *foulness* lingered about the air. Every man seemed unsure of himself. Here one would idly drop a hammer upon his feet in moving between the tent-stakes, there another stared into the distance whilst he rubbed vacantly at a belt plate long since eradicated of rust. The air bore a weight I had only felt once before, when marching out of a quiet little village in Wiltshire.

"We'll be marching soon." The batman explained. "Word is, General Hawkins wants to address the brigade beforehand."

Harris was spry on his feet, spinning about to walk backwards as he beheld me. It seemed curiosity dwarfed his annoyance at the lateness of my hour.

"So, it's not the French. That much is obvious." He stated plainly.

"No." I replied, though I oughtn't have said anything at all. I was overwhelmed, not only by all I had experienced, but by the organised chaos of the camp being packed away on too-few waiting wagons. I had never been in so large an encampment, nor felt so oddly out of place. A whole *brigade!* Yet I had little time to dwell upon such half-senseless amazement, as my guide continued his babbling.

"The stories are true, then? You were with the garrison, right? What did you see?"

I could find no words to adequately dismiss his concern. His questions were overly direct, and my discomfort only encouraged his pushing. Had I been accustomed to the concept of *sergeanting,* I might have threatened him with extra duty, but instead found myself stammering half-truths of little comfort to either of us.

I was spared such awkwardness, then, by a magnificent and altogether woe-inducing sight. From across the way, there rode a brilliant column of blue coats atop tall, trotting horses. They weaved through the camp towards the road along which the force had sat, as their canteens, helmets, swords, and firelocks all clinked and clanked, and glittered in the morning air. Another troop of dragoons was headed out, then, and alongside them I saw several others in civilian garb. Evidently, the local guides' crazed ramblings of wandering dead were being heeded at last.

Was Sergeant Wilkes in their number? His other troopers, mayhaps? What courage and horror must have spurred those men to ride out in further reconnaissance, when their compatriots had suffered so cruelly! What they intended to uncover, I knew not. I could but hope they went with better instruction than their predecessors, and respect for the lessons so bloodily learnt.

The batman then had no time to interrogate me further before we came across Captain Penn. The old officer was negotiating with one of the camp laundresses, who stood with sleeves rolled to her elbow and stout arms crossed in defiance. The others of her trade, just behind, were all working to prepare their equipage for the march. It was extraordinary to see the hardy women lifting great washing tubs, crates of soap, and heaps of linen as if they were weightless.

"You know that lot never pay on time!" She exclaimed. "I'm expected to keep up with a thousand men's linen, twice a week. The general won't let us stay put for more than a night, and the countryside's all run dry. Then, whenever I *do* find a scrap of lye, I'm expected to pay for it out of my own pocket! It just won't do, *sir!*"

Had one of the camp women ever spoken to Captain *Lawrence* so bluntly, she would surely have been drummed from the camp! Yet Penn merely smiled and nodded as she spoke, in complete disregard for the usual decorum. He was a kindly officer, indeed.

"I understand, Mrs Norton." Said he. "I assure you, I will speak with Corporal Hamley about his squad, and repay you their debt with interest. But you must understand that the men cannot be without their linen. It simply won't do to turn them away. Not for any reason."

With a sour grunt, the woman nodded and turned back to her business, shouting at a younger lass to pick up her pace. In the captain's defence, should *any* woman in an encampment be given deference, it *must* be the chief laundress. After all, without her like the Army would immediately collapse in a great, stinking, disease-ridden pile.

"Captain Penn, I've brought the sergeant, sir." The batman saluted lazily on our approach. I likewise saluted, more sharply, and somehow felt the fool for it.

"Thank you, Harris." Penn replied. "Now go and see

after my things, please, and make sure they're done up properly for the march."

Away the presumptuous soldier-servant went, leaving me to follow after the captain whilst he continued his rounds.

"I trust you're feeling better rested now, sergeant?" Said he.

"Yes, sir." Said I in return, still feeling somewhat dazed.

"And the clothes - they fit well enough? They certainly look better than your old attire."

"Yes, sir, and I assure you I shall make good on my debt the moment I am able."

Of course, there stood little prospect of such repayment in any good time. With the loss of my old company came the loss of our records, and assuredly the question of pay would be delayed even when I rejoined my regiment; notwithstanding that such monetary concerns were low on *any* officer's list of priorities, just then. Yet the gentleman seemed almost offended by the suggestion, and my worries would come to naught.

"No, no." Replied Penn gently. "Consider them a well-earned gift. You've been through enough trouble, I should think. Certainly beyond the service's usual exigencies. Likewise for the surgeon, I'll take care of his payment. Have you been to him?"

On learning I had not, Penn naturally insisted on bringing me there himself, and on reaching the appropriate section of camp he imposed upon his regiment's surgeon to step aside from his packing and glance over my wounds. The man was little happy about it, but saw the necessity and contained his grumbling; thus I was sat unceremoniously upon the ground and half undressed, whilst my various wounds were poked and prodded at. The surgeon cursed my carelessness in keeping them clean, and the need to rummage through his otherwise packed chests for the appropriate poultices, but otherwise went about his work dutifully and competently. His annoyance was likewise soon allayed by curiosity, and, little comforting to myself, by fear, regarding the nature of my wounds. The man was most accustomed to treating venereal diseases and fevers, and was certainly less acquainted with *human bites.*

Captain Penn continued to speak with me as the surgeon worked and muttered to himself.

"I'm sure you're aware by now that General Hawkins will address the brigade before we march." He explained. "He's loath to do it, but I suspect he'll bring the men up to speed on our little operation. No choice, really. He's all but told the cavalry everything, and oh, how *they* chatter!"

"Do you...know our route of march, sir?" I was cautious of any men nearby, lest they overhear. At least the surgeon had been present during the prior night's meeting, and no discretion about him was necessary. Captain Penn, however, was less wary in his speech and its volume. Perhaps he simply cared less for the secrecy of it all.

Of course, our path itself was obvious. The very *idea* of taking a single step nearer that accursed town horrified me, but I could hardly expect the comfort of a retreat. Nor had I any choice in the matter but to follow. Even if I returned at once to my own regiment, they were just behind us, on the same course.

"Straight on, to be sure." Penn's reply was predictably dreadful to me. "Hawkins will insist on investing the town even before the main force arrives. Looks better that way, of course, but I wouldn't say it's unwise. We don't know how far the devils may have spread, if what you say is true, and they wander without aim. Better to start the works as quickly as possible."

What those works might consist of, and what *use* they might be against a foe unbeholden to any material concerns, was beyond my comprehension. My mind was utterly enveloped by the mere *prospect* of advancing, let alone standing to *face* the devils! Still, the captain had raised a fair point; how far might the corpses have wandered? The prospect of our column stumbling across a great horde on the road set me to shiver in a cold sweat.

"You mean we are to lay siege, sir? To fight them?" I could see no path to victory against an unkillable foe, nor scarcely believe, given all that Wilkes and I had said, that any officer could feel differently. My fear came as no surprise to the captain, of course, who well understood my situation. Yet men of his position held not the privilege of *defeatism*.

"Well, as you yourself described," he spoke at length, for the first time mindful of his words, "they may be hard of dying, but they can be...broken down. They can be stopped, and so they must be. We can't just leave them to linger on British soil, after all."

Such was naturally the case. What alternative was there? To surrender all the nation to their slow advances? To merely sit and pray they would not eventually wander to whatever corner we hid within? They would certainly not depart under any flag of truce! Though every part of me rebelled against the idea, there remained nothing to it but to isolate the plague; to eradicate it, at the source, with fire and steel.

Still, such military necessity was of little consolation to me, as I was forced to help enact it! The wine and beef, earlier so restorative, then sat heavy in my stomach. Once, I had dreamed of heroics; just then, I wished only to be so far from them as possible. I thought it preferable to allow better men, of better means, to carry that duty out on my behalf.

I little welcomed such feelings, though I could not deny their presence.

I could think of nothing beyond Lieutenant Farwell's cries to *fire!* Of Ensign Tell being crushed beneath corpses, and weeping as he reached for our line. My shoulder ached with the memory of *Bess'* recoil; my heart, with the boy's merciful slaughter.

What could all the armies of the *world* do against a foe that *would not die?* While there we stood as but a single brigade! Our numbers felt far smaller to me, then, as I thought of marching against all of corrupted Stowlham, with its perhaps *thousands* of devils! I could but hope that General Hawkins, for all his 'firebrand' nature, would know better than to come within sight of the place.

I might have inquired further about the plan, but the opportunity was stolen when another, mounted, officer rode suddenly before us. He was perhaps Penn's major or lieutenant colonel, and two other gentlemen were likewise mounted near his side.

"Captain Penn!" He barked lively as my host leisurely saluted. "Is your company ready to move? By God, sir, I won't have Hawkins' wroth upon me because of your dawdling, again!"

"I believe they're ready, sir." Penn replied. His ease was not met by the superior.

"I'll not bandy with you about *belief*, Penn. Get yourself to them and be *sure* of it. We're already behind schedule." With that, the trio sped off to attend some other business, their poor steeds already well worked before the day had begun.

All about us, the brigade was in its final stages of preparation. The last wagons were loaded and men assembled into their sub-divisions for a final inspection before the march. As the camp steadily lifted to the road, its deep scars remained in the dry soil it had earlier occupied. Little plots where tents had stood remained largely untouched, but the roads and alleys between said tentage were thoroughly churned up. Throughout the camp, those few trees formerly present had been cut to stumps, whilst strands of hempen rope and spent flints, stray buttons and replaced nails, and countless squares of hastily-replaced topsoil where fire pits had been dug, all corrupted the scene. It would be some time before the memory of us would fade from that place, where we had lain but a night.

"Well," Captain Penn turned back to me, "I suppose that's a firm enough summons. I must attend to my men. When you've finished here, you can join the company on the road. I'll have my sergeants give you a primer on the job, as we march."

I thanked him again for his generous hospitality, and watched as he limped steadily away. He had been kind to me, yet the encounter well demonstrated the effective limits of *laxity*. We were then in desperate and unprecedented times, after all, where intensity, and even cruelty, was necessary. Nor had I witnessed the half of it, by then.

It was a principle well thrust upon the army, during our short campaign, that inordinate kindness was *not* a mercy, but a gap in the line through which yet greater privation might rush. Captain Penn was a good man, and on my escape from Stowlham, his was the care I personally required most; but a good *man* does not necessarily make a good *officer*.

Shortly thereafter I was cleared by the surgeon as, against all odds, being without any serious infections or other ill humour. I was instructed to stop by and see him on occasion, that he might ensure the wounds remained clean and replace the bandaging. There would be no easy excuse for a discharge, then!

Thus, I made my way to the brigade's point of assembly, they being formed in a line down the little country road, facing back towards the abandoned field. I felt rather awkward moving down the long ranks of men, feeling myself rather naked. I was a sergeant without a regiment, a coat, a sash, or even any arms. Every eye seemed to fall on me, from the highest officer to the meanest private soldier. All their whispering was palpable.

I saw clearly, in the light of day and with them all together, that this advance brigade consisted of two battalions of foot, with a little smattering of cavalry, as most of their number had gone out on reconnaissance, at their head.

Above the senior ensigns, the Colours drifted limply in the breeze, marking the space of each battalion. At least they seemed near their full complement. Still, it was nothing near sufficient for taking the town. Perhaps, in some ways, that was a blessing. Even the most *braggadocious* commander could only realise the same, and not advance too far, too quickly.

Between the cavalry and infantry stood the pioniers, as well as their rather sizeable clump of civilian 'volunteers'. They comprised perhaps fifty or sixty men of every age and disposition. They seemed even less enthusiastic than the soldiers, who likewise wore grim countenances. Tight packed as they were, I was unable to spot John in their number.

Finally, to the rear of the line stood the women of the regiments, and their children, alongside the myriad wagons and carts of our baggage. Several were still being clumsily hauled up from the field. Only one sutler saw fit to carry himself with us to ply his trade, and I saw an unnatural number of wagons being driven by soldiers, rather than the civilians generally hired on for such purposes.

It seemed, then, that few with any *real* choice in the matter were following the Army on that cursed campaign.

About two-thirds of the way down the line, I came before Captain Penn's company. On his invitation, I nudged myself behind one of their sergeants, attempting to avoid the men's glances as I did so.

Thus the whole brigade stood silently for only a brief spell, ere came the orders from each battalion commander to first *Handle, Firelocks!* and then to *Shoulder, Firelocks!* Some time later, from between the layers of cocked hats and arms, I saw the Brigadier General and his staff trotting along the line, surveying the men. They had steely looks about them, too purposefully held. They were anxious, the same as their men.

Going up and down the line twice in his half-hearted inspection, the general finally wheeled his horse before our centre, and dismounted in a poorly effectual attempt at relatability.

"Men!" He strode close, elevating his voice for all to hear. There was a kind of solidity in his volume, if not confidence. "No doubt, many of you feel you've been cursed!"

It was a curious opening. Indeed, there was a feeling of wretched *witchery* all about, even before the men knew the true severity before them!

"Cursed," he continued, "with lives of idleness! Of tedium, whilst so many of your fellows march through Flanders! Yet I am appointed now, to tell you all, that your days of idleness are over!"

Only a few days prior, such words would have swelled my heart with excitable pride. Yet I then felt it sink, deep and heavy, within the confines of my chest. The air felt thick with the unseasonable heat, and a shuffle of my foot stirred a small cloud of dust, most unbecoming of my rank. I found myself studying that cloud as he continued.

"You have all heard the rumours! That a foe, most vile, has *infiltrated* our country! The very soil of England itself is *defiled*, men! Defiled by an evil yet greater than even the French! Yes, lads, I say to you now, the stories are true! Some bedevilment has taken hold in the once fair town of Stowlham. The mortal remains of our heroic dead, have been forcefully resurrected and corrupted, to walk the earth as slaves to dark designs!"

Instantly the ranks filled with chatter of confusion, awe, and terror. Many men cared not how obvious their breach of discipline was, offering prayers and blasphemies to God and our officers in equal measure. In one place the line even flexed as men shuffled, to call after other fellows in the ranks, and seemed even to threaten running. Even the horses of the cavalry, and oxen of the baggage, seemed somehow dismayed. It took some time for the sergeants and corporals to silence the lot, shouting them down and shoving them back into ranks. I offered no assistance, but merely stared at my little dust-cloud. It lingered long in the still, hot air about my ankles.

"Enough! Enough!" Hawkins' expression was one of little-obscured rage. "By God, you are *soldiers*, not housewives! The foe stands before you! He has slaughtered your countrymen! Stowlham lies ravaged, with all this Kingdom to follow, save you do your duty! Would you surrender your wives? Eh? Your children? No! No, you Britons! You will *stand*! You will *fight*! And you shall cast this *French witchcraft* back into the waters whence it came!"

The heroics of this speech elicited a very few angry cheers from the ranks, but these were confined to the most zealous troops. The great majority stood deadly silent.

"Mark me well!" He continued with rage still boiling through his words as he made to remount his horse. "For in the coming days, the heroes amongst us shall win laurels the envy of all Europe! But of the cowards, of shirkers and *deserters,* there stands only the noose! Now we shall march unto Stowlham, and commence at once with putting her to siege. For our Country, our King, and our God!"

The brigadier general then made a great motion of drawing his sword, twirling it elaborately to gesture up the road to not-so distant Stowlham.

"Brigade! By companies! To the *right wheel-!*"

Upon the elongated tone, the pivot men within each company turned on their heels like automata. The officers and sergeants took their post to the new frontage, whilst I stood idly amongst the men, a queer sort of supernumerary's supernumerary.

"*March!*"

Hundreds of heads snapped to the left as one, as every company *looked out* and *leaned in* to twist itself, with stamping feet at the quickest time, into a column facing down the road. It was a remarkable display of precision, of which I felt not-at-all a part.

The general then trotted with his little staff up to the column's head, and with the order to *quick, march!* the whole of us set off down the road like a mighty clanking, pounding millipede, betailed by great clouds of dust which hovered over the pummelled dirt road. Thankfully, we soon reached one of the many turnpikes in that region, thence making a great, and far cleaner, speed. By the day's end, we would surely reach the place of our destiny.

Never before had I been so distressed to tread a more expedient route, nor endured so unhappy a march, short though it was. Our corps lacked utterly the zeal and alacrity otherwise so common amongst British soldiers. Whilst some fellows carried on in fatal determination, having taken the general's words to heart, most seemed surprised at their own legs for carrying them towards the waking nightmare. They looked to their comrades, as if wondering when someone might halt all the madness, only to be censured with an *eyes front!* by the corporals. Nor did any man suffer so great as I, being all the more aware of the little bites, scratches, and cuts peppering my skin with every step. Indeed, I found the answer to my earlier question, that my long sleep was little restful. From the corners of my eyes, I continually mistook my new companions for those I had lost to the devils, and had to physically shake myself free of the apparitions.

One of the regiment's grenadier companies being present, their fifer were soon brought up to the centre with some drummers to play music for our advance. The rousing tones of *Lilliburlero* did little to lighten our pace, however. My only consolation came from a light company being detached from our column to screen the advance in a long, open-order line over the surrounding countryside. This, combined with regular reports from the scouting cavalry, proved sufficient to quell my fear of stumbling across a horde of devils.

Still, I was at one point rather shamefully startled by the surprise appearance of a grazing sheep, which rustled about behind some brush. Nor was I alone in such, though thankfully none of the men were loaded, lest they try a shot at the poor animal!

As we went along, Penn introduced me formally to his senior sergeant, Morse, who awkwardly attempted to provide some basic instruction regarding his occupation. Still, I had little interest in the finer points of filing returns or *tossing the pike*, and Morse's dull, droning tone was of little help in that regard. Most of his words fell deaf upon me, nor did my instructor seem particularly keen to vie for my attention.

All along the route, which I recognised from my *first* advance to Stowlham but a few days prior, we passed a number of farmsteads and a small village, host to a most stately manor home, yet we saw not a soul beyond a lone abandoned goose. It was quickly snatched up by one of our number for dinner that evening. The fellow's escapade in acquiring said fowl was a lone source of half-hearted amusement on our journey, and short lived. Just as I had seen before, no children ran out of homes to greet us, nor were there any maids sat in their windows to ogle. There was but the clanking of kit, the snorting of pack animals, and the ironic trilling of an unenthused fifer amidst the sea of bobbing red.

We were alone with our fearful thoughts until our first brief halt. It came not owing to any weariness, for the route was short and Hawkins insisted on a speedy pace, but to our stumbling across another band of troops.

Two independent companies of the embodied militia, advancing to what they knew would be a point of confluence with the main force, came to a major crossroads at the same time as ourselves. Thus we were stood-to for a time, that our officers might converse, exchange orders, and the smaller body ultimately join with our own.

The militia were lesser equipped than we regulars, yet their attitude was conversely far more zealous. We *professionals* had been pulled from every corner of the Isles to that cursed place; the militiamen were conversely locals, and their fight was of far greater purpose. In addition to having long heard the tales of wandering dead from their countrymen, I was certain that every word Wilkes and I spoke to Hawkins had already been disseminated to every local gentleman of military bearing, and thence to the militia. Indeed, the citizen-soldiers were more keenly aware of their duty than the regulars. Nor were they the only of their sort to eagerly join our ranks over the coming days.

I took the halt as an opportunity to depart the ranks, with Captain Penn's leave, and move up the column to the pioniers and their 'mates'. They all sat sullen upon the road, in stark contrast to their large, bearskin-becap'd overseers. We had not encountered many obstacles on the road necessitating their attention, save a few logs hastily thrown over the roadway in the earliest hours of the 'attack', but their weariness was not owing to purely physical concerns.

Finally among them, it did not take me long to find John. He was still in his old clothes, having gone dull with the stains of blood and mud. Without money or patronage, he was clearly unable to secure cleaner clothing, as had been so generously given to me. Nor had he shaved, and the growing stubble lent him an air of madness or stupidity as it paired with his uneasy eyes. His countenance was not so sullen, as it was actively frightened. Though he sat amidst the others, he made a concerted effort to avoid their glances. On my approach, it was clear my old friend was little happy to see me. He looked up from my shadow and said nothing.

"I'm glad to see you safe." I was first to break the silence. John seemed unaccepting of the word, and chose his reply carefully.

"Do you require something of me, sergeant?" There was the faintest hint of bitterness in his tone. I stood clean and well appointed, while Hawkins' threats for shirkers surely rang like thunder through his mind. Had it not been for his rendering me aid, he might have escaped the night prior.

"I was hoping to speak with you. Privately." Said I, unable to grasp the suspicion I might have aroused. The foolishness of my actions were not lost on him, but he could little show it. After some prolonged staring, from eyes heavy in wariness and weariness, John allowed me to help him to his feet. We made for the side of the road, the pioniers making no trouble as I brought their man away, for they were evidently aware of my identity.

"I wanted to make sure they are treating you well, and to ask after your...intentions." I finally whispered, as we gained a safe distance.

"They've fed me, if that's what you're asking." His tone was strained by a continual pressure, from which there came even less relief than my own. "No one has been so interested in my account as yours."

"Well," I replied with but little optimism, "we must count that as a comfort, at least. None suspect your past, and you're not expected to fight. Perhaps you might continue hiding out, amidst the labourers?"

"A *comfort?*" He whispered in the harshest disbelief. "They're forcing us back to that *Hellhole* at bayonet point, and the regiment is coming up from the rear *bearing my noose!* If I stay here, I am dead. Hell, if *you* stay with them, you'll follow after me! My *God*, man, look around you! The general is a madman!"

It became apparent to me that, for what little rest I had, John received even less. Even his injury seemed to fester in a worse state, its bandage only being crudely replaced. It must have brought him an intense pain as still he was made to work.

"I am with you, John!" I implored him to return to sanity. "As much as I am able. But, you are in no state to flee. We can speak with Captain Penn, he has been kind to me, maybe he will-"

"Christ!" My old friend spat. "Don't you get it? You heard what the general said, and you want to bring me before an officer?"

"No, I-" I fell back from the position. "I only mean that you're in no position to flee. I know it sounds mad, but you're *safe* for now. Even when the regiment comes up, it's not like they'll be searching amidst the refugees!"

"*Nobody* here is *safe*." His tone sank low. "Every step we take, every inch closer to that *place,* is all the more condemning. They *can't be killed!* I'd rather take my chances out there, in *any* condition, than throw myself back into the maw; nor shall I debate the difference between *Christian sacrifice* and *witless suicide* with you, s*ergeant*. You never listened to me, anyways. Nobody ever did, and now look at where we are. I'm done placing my faith in soldiers. If you wish to stay the course, then fine. But be damned if you try to keep me from my own."

The thick venom of his words were all the more potent for their truth. How could any be blamed for the poor man's predicament more than myself, and all his supposed cronies wandering stiff and cold in Stowlham? A fire blazed deep within John's watery dark eyes, and try though I might, I had not the resolve nor the words to calm it. Had he gone mad from all he had witnessed? Had I?

We have our duty.

The words of Captain Lawrence ever reverberated through my mind, yet whilst I tried to ascribe some *meaning* to them, some course I might take to save my friend, I found only emptiness. I no more knew my duty than I knew myself; in that way, I felt myself already dead.

"I am sorry, John."

They were the last words I ever spoke to him.

Preparing the Defensive Works.

Part the

THIRTEENTH

wherein the Siege of Stowlham is prepared.

J ſpent the latter half of our march much as I had the first. Alongside Penn and Morse's introduction to their more lackadaisical forms of soldiering, however, I also found myself playing host to little bands of officers from every corps, regulars and militia alike. Their questions regarding the fate of Stowlham and the garrison, the devils themselves and how they might be fought, and my own survival were all incessant. The long-rotted cat having been let out of its bag, I had little excuse for secrecy, and was forced to recount my pitiful tale many times over.

Even the surgeons called on me, and insisted, *as we marched,* on rolling down my stockings so they might poke and prod at every little toothmark whilst interrogating me regarding the nature of injury they might expect the men to suffer, if set upon. That was the most toilsome conversation I endured, and it was likewise unpleasant for the private soldiers marching nearby. At least one of them became visibly sick, and passed out of the column for the purpose of expulsion. Not that the surgeons paid him any mind!

The most *challenging* discussion, however, came from one of the regimental chaplains - the man who had been present at Hawkins' great late-night war meeting. On finding me in the column, he beheld me in quiet, distant contemplation for some time, as if he wondered whether I were corrupted by the same putrescence as Stowlham itself. He kept the Book of Common Prayer tucked near to his person. At length he, too, approached and began to ask after certain *metaphysical* and *theological* concerns, for which I could little answer. He even fell into a poor habit of quoting Greek or Latin texts in his interrogation, rudely assuming I might comprehend his meaning. Ironically, I found his presence the least comforting of all. His were the only questions not concerned with the immediate reality, so harshly thrust upon us all, but with the greater implications thereof. I preferred not to dwell upon such matters, then as now.

The most consequential of my conversations, however, was also the briefest, coming from Captain Russell. He waltzed down the line as if going to Camden Town, instead of Hell, and paid the most minimal respect to his least-favoured captain before turning to me.

"Do you know of the Baron de Steuben, sergeant?" Were his curious first words.

"Sir?" I was taken aback by the question's oddity.

"The Baron de Steuben. A Prussian fellow who threw his lot in with the American rebels." He explained. "When Washington wintered at Valley Forge, his men were nothing more than a rabble. De Steuben rather whipped them into some shape and taught them how to soldier. Did a fair decent job of it, too."

The reason for Russell's little story became at once apparent to me. I knew not whether I should be relieved at having some occupation to distract from the terror, or be sickened by a role I was little fit to assume.

"He did it by introducing the Exercise to the best men of every battalion, who in turn taught their fellows. De Steuben had quite little time, and we've even less. The men all know their trade, but nevertheless face a...novel scenario, and the general appreciates this. You've faced the foe already. You know something of how they fight. When we halt, you are to report to General Hawkins immediately. You shall work alongside your fellow, Wilkes, with the staff to assemble a new Exercise. Beginning tomorrow morning, you shall provide instruction in it."

Thus I learned of my fate in the coming days, and found myself overwhelmed merely with the thought. I could but nod and salute, to which the aide promptly darted back up the line to his master. As he went, he seemed to recall something, and spun about on his heels to call down to me.

"Oh!" His voice was cheerier than before, easily transcending the trilling of fifes and percussion of heels. "We've made arrangements with your regiment to see your promotion through, and we're having a coat made up, as well. You'll be a proper sergeant, before long!"

At least I would be less gawkish, then, as I presumed to instruct the men in that mode of combat I had so often *fled*. Captain Penn's proud pats upon my back, and continued ramblings of which I was hardly aware, contrasted starkly with my emotions then. My stomach seemed to confirm my every doubt.

Thus the march continued for a final few hours, and as the sun began to approach its death over the horizon, we saw in the dwindling light a faint plumage of smoke rising up ahead. The fires, it seemed, had largely burnt themselves out, and the once mighty conflagration only leaked little tendrils. They weaved low together in the sky, an ominous forewarning of what slow deaths lay ahead for those who might stray too near. Stowlham was but a few miles away, then, though just out of view from what little undulations, curves, and copses stood in the otherwise flat Anglian fields.

There, at last, we were halted, but the men were given no respite. The march having been an easy one, they were set at once to work. Not merely in establishing a camp, but in digging out our fortifications. Of course, I took no part in these preparations, but after Captain Penn's assurance that I would again be given a place in Sergeant Morse's tent (though he was little pleased by the prospect) I was immediately sent up the rapidly dispersing column. As I passed the pioniers, I hoped to catch another glimpse of John, but his party had been among the first marched off, shovels and axes in hand, to begin digging ditches and felling trees. There were greater earthworks to be dug than mere latrine pits, after all. I could but hope the work would be easy on my old comrade.

At the column's head, I was made to wait patiently at General Hawkins' distant side while he and the staff saw to the myriad dull businesses of oeconomy. It was a curious thing, to stand idle whilst, all about me, men bustled in activity.

I was soon joined by Wilkes, who offered me a knowing nod. He had returned with the scouting cavalry, and I saw his officer briefing the general just outside our earshot. The old sergeant was clearly weary, but still steady. He seemed to have returned to his regular duties more gracefully than myself.

"What did you see?" I asked quietly, assuming the role of interrogator I had so recently scorned in others. The din of barking non-commissoned officers, packs being hauled off groaning wagons, and tent stakes hammering into dusty soil had already begun to rise.

"Not much." His voice was steady, and I was surprised at how much comfort I derived from that. "We dismounted just outside town, on my suggestion, and went the last few hundred yards on our bellies. Some went up in the trees for a better view, and to keep out of *their* sight. Through our glasses, we only saw a few of them straggling around, wandering this way and that. A little clump of the bastards was trying to get at a bird sitting atop some ruins."

His mouth tightened, as if he recalled some worse detail that he would not speak to. Perhaps some of those creatures wore the same blue coat as Wilkes, and stumbled comically about in tall cavalry boots?

"The town is near totally gone." He continued. "Few structures were spared the fire, and a few of the streets are blocked up with debris. Clearing them all out will prove a bloody hard time, however they decide to go about it."

"Have there been any in the countryside?" I asked hesitantly. "Does it seem any have wandered out?"

Blessedly, the cavalryman shook his head.

"Not far, it seems. There were a few of them a couple yards from the edge of town, but they moved with no purpose. They were equally likely to stumble backwards and turn themselves about, than to step further out. They're awfully slow, when they haven't got anything to go after."

He turned to look at me with deep, brooding circles around his eyes. I imagined my own visage looked much alike, and worse.

"For some reason or other, I think they've been collecting at the centre of town. Drawn further in, instead of out. We can count ourselves lucky there, at least."

I shivered at that. The thought of all the devils congregated was frightening, but Wilkes was right that it was a blessing they hadn't already scattered to the wind across the county.

"Perhaps some noise drew them in." I wondered aloud. "The collapse of a building, or...a shout. Then, after all jostling in a great clump, they can't find their way out. Perhaps they've trapped themselves?"

It was one of few comforting thoughts I would be permitted in those dark days. Nonetheless, I saw Wilkes shudder at some unspoken thought. His fists clenched as he resisted it.

"Damned unnatural, is what they are." His speech was stilted. "They're never still. They *twitch* and contort every which way, all the time. It isn't even like they've forgotten how to walk, it's...as though their *souls* are trying to escape. Thrashing their way out of the bodies. The mouths were all working, too, even without any prey before them. The whole town was quiet, but I swore I could hear the teeth chattering. Thousands of them."

I could well recall the eerily soft sound of a few dozen devils grasping for me when I laid atop the roof. The chattering was incessant, rabid even, as their stiffening fingers snapped out of reach. To hear all of them at once must have been maddening. I shivered just as Wilkes had, and bit my tongue hard enough to taste a faint trail of blood.

I was roused from my imagining by the sudden approach, yet again, of Captain Russell, who bade us follow him. Hawkins and his staff were evidently ready for the next stage of their preparations, and their great marquee had been erected at the growing encampment's heart.

Once inside, we were sat at a table with a select few of the general's most senior officers, including Captain Penn, while the sergeants major and other senior non-commissioned officers stood crammed, wall to wall, behind us. To accompany our thus inflated importance, we were given officerial luxuries of food and wine from the general's own mess, though neither Wilkins nor I could summon much in the way of appetite.

This great meeting on the military science was then commenced when General Hawkins, casting formality aside, instructed we *veterans* to again recount our time with the devils. In the most *thorough* of detail, he specified.

As usual, this proved no small feat, though I had grown at least somewhat accustomed to describing the events without suffering my usual panic. Many of the men about us, despite being hardened by long years of service, were visibly disaffected and even sickened by particular aspects of our tellings. One sergeant was compelled to step outside for fresher air as I recalled separating the jawbone from the devil which attacked the woman, whose name I had never learned. None could fault him for his squeamishness.

After our accounts concluded, the discussion turned to how we might best meet the foe in open field.

In open field! I could not believe the words as they were spoken right before me.

Hawkins wasted not a moment in detailing the folly of confronting the enemy within Stowlham itself, and explained that General Tomlinson was in full agreement with this summation. The enemy *must* be met upon an open field, he declared, that it might be exposed to the greatest extent of our fire. This was to say nothing of how disastrously the previous urban encounters had gone.

There remained, then, but a few primary considerations. For the cavalry, the question was how best to *lure* the foe from within their desecrated fortress. Wilkes and the other cavalrymen present were heavily interrogated as to the enemy's speed, the reaction of horses when near to them, and the like. The aim, it was rapidly determined, would be to corral and pull small bands of the devils, one by one, towards our infantry's established lines, where they could be destroyed in turn. The cavalry would achieve this corralling through riding in small groups, and near enough to the town to create great noises through firing their carbines, sounding bugles, and otherwise simply shouting. As packs of devils appeared to pursue each party, then, they would ride off to predetermined, separate rally points, and thence return to the main army upon their appointed times. A horse being able to easily outpace the clumsy devils at nothing more than a trot, with time to rest besides, it was agreed there would be little risk of them running too tired in the process. The hope was to lure not merely those devils within the streets and market squares, for whom the sight of horseflesh would be alone sufficient to drive them, but even those caught up within the homes and little alleyways, to ensure a most complete victory.

The niceties of all these points were discussed at great length, in which course I was only horrified. For every point made, I could only imagine a dozen ways it might go wrong. Nor was Wilkes much at ease, either, although he hid his feelings better. The very thought of attempting to *control* the corpses, by *any* means, struck me as arrogant at its best. Yet, even had I spoken out of turn, I was certain my words would go unheeded. The officers held not the same luxury of *pessimism,* as I had.

With time, the conversation turned to the infantry and the artillery. Though the latter arm was not represented at the meeting, a fair number of field guns were already with Tomlinson's main force, and heavier pieces were even being hauled from Woolwich. In all it seemed a most extraordinary number of guns had been wrested from the arsenal, even with so unclear an initial understanding as to their purpose. Upon those guns, all agreed, would sit the greatest importance.

They would be evenly distributed all down our lines, and fire upon the devils the moment the cavalry became free of them. Should their shots land true, it was even hoped they might cut every corpse to ribbons long before they came within musket shot.

Should either the cavalry or the guns fail, of course, it would invariably fall to us of the infantry. Thus General Hawkins insisted upon a new Exercise based on the principles I had introduced of the devils and their function. In this formulation, despite my being frequently consulted, none of my anxieties found answer. I became convinced that, should they be put to the test, they must surely fail.

Naturally, a long description of the exact points of this doctrine would prove, to the common reader, dull and ineffectual. To the military mind they would be utterly unnecessary. Already many great accounts, narratives, and treatises have been, and are being, written regarding the conduct of our forces at the great *Battle of Stowlham*. So, too, have flowed many a critique on how they might have been *marginally* improved in *this* way and *that*. As is generally the case, those minds least in need of swords or bayonets have seen fit to proclaim their *wits* the sharpest of tools, and to offer the '*true methods*' of '*dispatching the malevolent fallen*' regardless of the reality. For such debate, I have neither mind nor care; thus I shall relate only the conclusions we *soldiers*, who were *there* for the day, ultimately reached.

Should the worst of possibilities transpire, and the devils come to our line, it was determined the Foot would fight in the following manner:

The men would be formed in the Continental style, as formally prescribed by our regular Exercise, in three ranks. The enemy coming into effective range, they would immediately commence with firing to aid the artillery in *disrupting* the enemy. Should they reach the lines, then, the front rank would stand and charge their bayonets. To them would fall the duty merely of *holding fast*, keeping the presumably small number of remaining devils at bay.

To the centre rank, then, would fall the most grim task of

continuing the corpses' *deconstruction*. The men would *club* their muskets and employ the butts to either crush the dead skulls outright, or at least knock out their teeth. Afterwards, they might employ their bayonets in targeting the devils' eyes, and any vulnerable parts which might reveal themselves, with the aim of rendering them inert.

The rearmost men would then serve to reinforce whichever purpose seemed most pressing. In the absence of such opportunities, they would simply continue firing so quickly as they might into whatever opponent might favourably present itself.

Above all else, it was of the greatest importance that *not a single devil* pass through the front; for a single man falling victim, I stressed, might spell the rapid collapse of even the firmest ranks. Though I did not appreciate it at the time, *this* concern of mine, at least, wound up most heartily understood and respected by the gentlemen.

The result, then, of our great war-meeting was not so much a whole new Exercise, as it was a new form of *instruction* upon, mostly, established principles. Thankfully, the plan was found simple enough, and acceptable to all present. Naturally certain men of importance debated here and there about facings and the like, but the general novelty of our predicament prevented much in the way of intense argument.

The matter which followed brought far more comfort than the thought of battle on open field: the question of fortification. Though neither Wilkes nor myself could offer much advice on the subject, many more seasoned soldiers had seen combat at the likes of Yorktown and Gibraltar, and were well acquainted with the value of earthworks when facing overwhelming odds. Through longwinded accounts of such engagements, and a great many references to the likes of *Lochee* and *Pleydell*, a plan of firing lines, bastions, and ramparts was soon assembled, with orders going out for their commencement ere our meeting concluded. This ensured that any rest the men, particularly the pioniers and their *volunteers,* may have won, would be short-lived.

As before, any great detail of the plans drawn up should

prove unnecessary in a narrative such as my own. Nonetheless, understanding that some value may be derived from a general awareness of the field upon which the army ultimately stood, I shall aim to provide some little description.

The place where our column made its final halt had not been on the turnpike, but off a smaller side-road which ran parallel to the wide, lazy river by which Wilkes and I had made our initial escape. Our encampment was centred upon the road, and ran directly against the river upon our left.

Before us, then, the field upon which we settled was blessedly flat, sloping ever so gently up for the miles towards Stowlham with little by way of hills. Having kept animals before our arrival, the field's dead grasses were also rather short. Though not disadvantageous to our foes, neither would the landscape thwart our firings.

Were the landowner present for our arrival, he would certainly have been severely cross with the Army for our ravages. While he had apparently fled with the majority of his flock, in the haste of his retreat an occasional little cluster of sheep were left abandoned upon the field. These were quickly pulled in and put to immediate use by the forces. Fresh meat was a wonderful boost to morale. Likewise, what little fencing stood about the property was at once torn down and applied for our own purposes, as was every tree for a great distance in each direction, save towards Stowlham, where few fatigue parties dared to venture far. Every piece of tool and supply from the farmstead was confiscated for employment in our works.

From the field's descent into the river, and extending for a great distance to the right, a mighty trench would be dug some four or five feet deep, with an equal height being piled behind it, to craft a great embankment upon which the men would stand. The earthworks would then be reinforced with whatever wood was at hand, and the trench filled with abatis and sharpened stakes. A whole palisade might have been constructed, had only the resources been available. Instead, the sparseness of that countryside would permit but a faint layering of debris. To a *living* foe, employing axes and fascines, it would have been largely useless; yet against the thrashing mindlessness of our enemy, we hoped it would prove *insurmountable.*

Interspersed between the regiments of foot, then, would be gaps in the earthworks for the artillery to establish their own positions, behind thick walls of stacked gabions. There would also be narrow defiles, leading into the field beyond, for our cavalry and skirmishers to sally.

For the lattermost, there was also to be dug a forward line some two-hundred yards in advance of the main one. It would be similar in construction, yet reduced in scale, being only two feet deep and a further two tall. Likewise would the abatis there would be slim, for want of materials. This line was not intended not to withhold the enemy; rather it would be a firing step for the light infantry, who might lay on their arms and uselessly pepper the foe whilst the artillery played on them overhead. Some doubts were voiced as to the efficacy of such skirmishing, particularly as related with the necessary labour in constructing the forward line, and the risk it would prove to the light infantry, but their officers would hear little of it. They would not be deprived of their opportunity to dash like mad Indians across the field, ere we *hat-men* had our turn.

Mad bloodhounds, all! It was with a dark humour that I recalled Richards' admiration of the lights, and praised their particular zeal in flying after American rebels.

Finally, between the two lines, a more novel series of fortifications would be dug, as envisioned by some officers of the cavalry in a stroke of genius likely inspired by the usual, literal, pitfalls faced by their arm of service.

A series of elongated pits, some six feet deep, would be dug at regular intervals all down the line. The dark irony of the latter figure was not lost on anyone present. The initial proposal was for at least *eight*, but this point was argued against by Wilkes, being more courageous than I in speaking when not otherwise addressed. While a man, he argued, might easily extricate himself from such a grave, the devils, being wholly witless, would be capable only of grasping at its sides. They had no faculty for climbing, much less for jumping, seemingly rendering such a depth superfluous. The time spared in digging, then, could be employed instead upon other works.

Nor was any sophisticated pattern, or other obscuration, required for the pits. As I had explained in the course of my story, the devils would care little for the ground just before them, but pursue their prey mindlessly. They would simply fall into the pits wherever they lay. Thus it was hoped that, even should the enemy come beyond the light infantry, they would surely never reach the primary lines in any unmanageable quantity. Indeed, some of the officers seemed to take a sick delight in establishing so straightforward a killing field. *Satisfying,* one called it. The word made me shiver.

Finally, the great surplus of dirt thus acquired would be used to further shore up and widen the infantry's ramparts, that we might have a smooth platform on which to fire, and also towards constructing a series of taller bastions behind the line. There the heavier guns might be placed, and the skirmishers retire, if need be.

Though the severe extent of digging required for these pits was certainly the hardest labour we then faced, it was also the simplest when compared with preparing *abatis* and stabilising earthworks. For which reason, it was promptly assigned to the *civilian labour corps,* as the officers had taken to calling it.

Thus the plans were set, and it was late into the night ere I left the officers' marquee with explicit orders to rest before the next morning. Then, my duties would commence in earnest. As I went, already I saw the once bucolic scene of idyll, upon which we first halted, was morphing into one of harshly militant *industry.* The tents having been pitched and a small dinner had, at once the work had begun with digging. All down the camp's length, and for some distance to the right, I could see little clumps of dirt tossed high into the air as the men carved out the great trench. The work was thinly distributed, at first, but the majority of the army was but a few days away.

Upon their arrival, General Hawkins' Brigade would

represent the extreme left. The reinforcements would all *right face* at the road's end to fill in the position for as far as I could see. The property's few buildings, then, would invariably be torn down for supplies, fortified as strongpoints, or in the case of the farmhouse itself, ultimately serve as General Tomlinson's headquarters. Thus, not only would the poor farmer return to find his abandoned animals slaughtered and his fields churned into ruin, but his home pocked full of loopholes! I spared a moment to wonder after the Army's generosity in their reimbursement of him; though I could scarcely muster pity for a man's livelihood whilst he was safe in some faraway place, and *we* stood upon the precipice.

Above all else, in my mind, there was the matter of John.

With the main army would come our regiment. What could the man do? Still I hoped he might find some security in the sheer size of his *civilian corps*, and that he might remain unrecognised without necessitating any foolhardy escape attempts. I worried that my old crony had devolved into a man driven by fear, much like myself. Yet his was a different sort of danger. There could be no reprieve or comfort from it, for he was condemned, should his secret be outed. Indeed, my worrying after his safety at the hands of the *living* was my only distraction from my fear of the *dead*. Constantly I thought of him, yet could never imagine a solution to his quandary, save the both of us casting ourselves to the mercy of Captain Penn, which John would never permit.

Perhaps I could make him understand? Even General Hawkins could surely be persuaded into mercy, in such circumstances. John had not been under *his* command, after all, while so strange and terrible a foe, as had stumbled upon us in Stowlham, was certainly enough to ruin the heart of *any* man! Indeed, as the sole survivors of Stowlham's garrison, *neither* of us had escaped the town with his conscience free. It would be simple enough to think of some excuse regarding John's civilian clothes, and our little lie upon coming to the camp.

Through these theoreticals and possibilities my mind would race all through the night. Yet, I would never have the opportunity to plead the case. My anxiety for it all, and

John's rightful fear, were not long to last.

The Death of a Brother.

FOURTEENTH

wherein a friend and brother is loft.

In the following days my role extended well beyond the typical purview of *sergeanting*. While others of my rank were arranging work rotas, inspecting men, and filing returns, I was thrust into the role of the great *drill-master*.

In this, I was not whisked hither-and-tither between the various regiments to instruct the men directly; rather a sort of overlarge *fugle-division* was formed by the most senior, sober, and skilled men from each company, the militia included. They were not merely private men, but mainly sergeants and corporals, and even a few ensigns, all jumping to my whims as common soldiery whilst I led them through the *'New Exercise'*. I did not necessarily command their respect; but their fear of our unkillable foes was sufficient to demand their attention.

I was not alone in this task, as a series of junior officers and some sergeants major were joined to me in council, aiding me in all the little niceties. I was comforted to see my charges taking their new duties well to heart. None balked over what must have seemed rudimentary instruction from a fresh sergeant so obviously out of his usual depth. Every one of them seemed possessed with a fresh, albeit anxious, desire to see the thing done. After all, the same task of instructing their fellows would fall to them, once they returned to their usual stations.

The fate of the army, and all of Britain, seemed to rely on our work. In more cynical terms, the men's selection for additional drilling exempted them from the far harsher and more menial work of ditch digging, tree chopping, and abatis building. Theirs was a cushy position in those difficult days, and they did well to retain it with enthusiasm!

For the remainder of the army, every moment was one of fatigue. All down the line, clumps of unseasonably dry, loamy soil were thrown up in great waves by endless ranks of locally 'procured' shovels. Axes sounded every hour as they cut down and shaped any greenery at hand for the abatis, rendering the whole of the countryside to a most dismal condition. Likewise were men labouring beyond the front in little clumps to establish our forward line, and moreover digging pits within the two-hundred yard gap. Makeshift paths were shortly formed as the grass was trampled underfoot by marching and counter-marching workers, alongside the constant movement of wagons brimming with soil for the bastions. Besides all these went the women and children of the regiments, busying themselves with hauling water to men who might otherwise have perished beneath the heavy sun. Indeed, quite a few soldiers were only spared from total exhaustion when the women took their case to the officers, insisting they be allowed a spell of rest.

Alongside its military necessity, the severity of our labour was also beneficial in buffering our anxieties. Still, even the hardiest cannot toil forever, and every pause allowed the anticipation of action to pierce even our harshest weariness. Few men slept well, in those days.

The air of a camp before a battle is always a curious thing, and ours was no exception. Even in a more customary fight, wherein a man might hold high the prospects of glory and booty, there is always the chance a ball might find its way into his belly. Still, the annals of regimental histories and the wisdom of long-serving veterans could well allay the worries of any recruits.

"Never fear," the one might say to the other, "for I've seen a scrap or two, and come out fine for it! After all, should every shot find its mark, how might the world's kings ever keep their soldiers?"

In the instance of our present campaign, however, there were no veterans save Wilkes, his troopers, and myself; nor could any comfort be derived from our uneasy eyes and jumpy attitudes. Nor had we any glorious histories to warm our spirits, or even the prospect of loot to satisfy our baser desires. The sole element protecting us from the dark pit of despondency was our industry, and the prayer it might save our skins on the fateful day.

Far be it from me, however, to imply our efforts were lacking in that all-important task. In spite of our fears, the army had not *wholly* given itself over to melancholy, but poured all its energies into the task with vigour.

I prefer to imagine that my own efforts, and those of Wilkes for the cavalry, were of decent effect in readying the men for the coming trial. They took quickly to their new Exercise, with the exemplars soon dismissed to their usual parties whence they, in turn, became the instructors. Some enterprising men even fashioned a few hay bales and sticks into corpse-dummies! They were quite comical in appearance, and the men were enthused to shoot and bash away at them. It offered an outlet for their rage, and a sense that they were better prepared for the imminent horrors.

As my initial party gradually improved, then, I spent more time floating amongst the brigade and providing assistance wherever it might be needed. It was a comfort to see so many taking the preparations with the appropriate gravity.

While the fear never left us, then, it would at least settle. The officers, soldiery, and even the civilians of our camp seemed to take ownership of it. They moulded their discomfort into a more righteous fury, being impatient to see the matter through. Even my own spirit, crushed and ground though it was, could not help but be somewhat lifted alongside our ever-rising earthworks. A great, protective killing-field, more vast in scope and complexity than I might have ever imagined, was being rapidly formed before us. By the first day's end, the outline of our works was clear, and by the following evening, the initial sections were nearly complete.

On one occasion I stood atop the early heights of a bastion, and, observing the hive of activity all about, was humbled and overawed by so many hundreds of bodies simultaneously working in common cause. It even inspired some hope that victory might be had after all. I recall how, for a precious few hours, I fancied I might redeem myself to the memory of my comrades; that there might be hope not merely of victory, but of *salvation*.

This feeling was fuelled all the more by my improved condition, for I was not long consigned to my poorly fitted, hastily fetched smallclothes. Captain Russell had made good on his promise, and the officers of the brigade had generously collaborated to ensure I received a sergeant's scarlet coat in record time. It even bore the proper facings of my regiment, albeit with many a plain button that would need replacing, alongside a fine sash, a pike to sit upon my shoulder, and a cocked hat finer than any I had worn before. Likewise, Captain Penn had been kind enough to personally pay the tailor of his regiment to better fit my waistcoat and breeches. By the close of our second day investing Stowlham, I cut a rather fine and authoritative figure.

Yet, all the while, there loomed a spectre behind my comfort; vile and cold, with its stiffened fingers ever laced across my neck. Lord Tomlinson would arrive with his army on the third day, and with them would march my regiment. The odds of John being recognised amidst the labourers were slim, of course, but would he dare to risk it? It would take but one keen-eyed corporal, perhaps transferred out from our old company, or with a memory from a Regimental Field Day, and the deserter might at once become forfeit.

A most severe dread had taken hold of John, and I could scarcely blame him for it. I hadn't seen my old crony since the march, for he was digging ditches alongside the other unfortunates, as I stood always behind the rising ramparts with my trainees. Try though I might to escape my duties, the opportunity never long arose. Going often to the place of the *volun-tolds'* encampment, always I found John away on a rota; nor were any of his compatriots ready in offering me his location. Although, even if I could catch him, I feared he would reject my parley.

Had I wrested him from the fires of Stowlham, only to meet a noose or firing squad? To be made an example of every coward's fate?

I was the coward. Yet nonetheless I stood, in all new finery, with authority over men and prospects for advancement. Poor John was six feet beneath the ground, toiling in the heat with no hope for relief. He was not the only one to flee his Colours before the terrible Fleshtide. Indeed, his only sin was that he was smart enough to discern Stowlham's fate before the rest of us. He had tried to *warn* us, to convince us of the truth which none dared believe, and he had suffered all the more for it.

There was no consolation for his suffering, nor justice in its end. There came to him only pain; for poor John's fate was the most tragic of all, and the least deserved. It came late on our second night, as he must have laid upon the precipice whilst I did naught for his cause but wring my hands and furrow my brow.

I was the coward. Not John.

The thought rolled over me, again and again. I had slept but little, telling myself of the need to find a solution whilst all my faculties were frozen up. I could not recognise the unravelling of my wits; yet I would not forever sit in such cruel, circular idleness, as the fates again wove their thread down a musket's bore.

The crack of its shot at once roused me from my stupor.

Then came another, and a third.

They were hardly perceptible in the distance, yet pierced the night air like little needles. What followed were sounds more terrible still.

Screaming. Shouting. Swearing.

Evidently I was not alone in hearing it, for at once the air was flooded with commotion. As I came to my feet and flew outside the tent, so too, all down the line, were men scrambling from their billets and fumbling with their musketry. Fear and confusion plagued every soul as they cried out to one another, desperate to make sense of the cacophony.

"To your arms!" A panicked voice transcended the din, and was joined at once by a half dozen other corporals and sergeants all about me. "Stand to your arms! Form your ranks!"

Somewhere a drum was struck up, and its long roll moved quickly towards the camp's centre. Little lanterns flickered to life all through the camp to cast dim yellow glows and rushing shadows across every inch of tentage. Already Colours waved over that glow, as men rushed for their positions in every state of panicked undress, muskets in hand and belts hastily thrown over-shoulder.

I could scarcely comprehend what was happening ere another musket shot punched through the chaos to my side. I nearly fell aback at the shock of it, for it was close enough to nearly set my ears ringing! I saw a trembling soldier with the discharged piece in hand, smoke still pouring from its barrel.

Another man lay at his feet, stunned into silence by the blood spurting from his stomach. In a moment of madness, not yet feeling the extent of his injury, he tried to stand. Thus, as hundreds all carried on this way and that, bowling over camp furniture and foundering in the dark as they did so, some half-dozen fellows were put aback at his sight and would not cross his path. They levelled their pieces upon him, though none seemed brave enough to shoot. One man, in a cruel show of ignorant courage, stepped forward to strike him as he reached out in a desperate plea for the still-warm muzzle of his killer and friend. His prayers for mercy shrank in coherency as pain overtook panic. He collapsed to the ground with a shriek, and could not rise. Nor could any of the men comprehend his state, fearful as they were.

"Wait!" I managed to regain some composure, and stumbled towards the scene. "Hold yourselves! Hold, there!"

Blessedly, I gained their attention before any further

violence transpired, and, unthinking, threw myself before the muzzles.

"Damn you all!" My reprobation dripped with mad scorn. "He's alive!"

The men were wide-eyed with alarm. The scents of urine and sulphurous smoke stained the air. I knew that vile humour well.

The man on the ground was by then clutching his guts in agonising contortion.

"Oh God!" He cried to me with mad eyes. "I shall die! Oh, *God*, I shall *die!*"

His smallclothes had already gone red as he gripped at the wound, already obscured in a bubbling mess. I could offer no consolatory words, but failed to lift him as my hands trembled madly. My effort elicited a pitiful yelp of pain, and I was at once joined by two others, who slung their muskets and took him up by the shoulders and legs, despite his protestations.

The poor chap was as panicked as he was pained, while all about us the din neared its crescendo as the camp continued in hasty assembly. I heard another shot ring out, followed by a loud curse and what seemed like a scuffle. From further afield, yet another musket fired to accompany the loud whinnies of a horse and trampling hooves.

Yet through all the madness, I saw no devil.

"What did you see?" I demanded, likewise in panic, of the stunned man with the smoking gun. His mouth moved without sound. While the others succeeded in hoisting their charge, I took hold of the firer to shake him and again demand a report, yet nothing would restore him.

"I- I don't- I-!" The lad could only stammer.

I then realised that, had he *truly* seen a devil, it would have long since set upon us. Nor was it likely to have been alone, for whatever might attract one to the encampment must surely lure others. Yet there were no raving corpses, and those men who had jostled each other into ranks, just outside of the camp, found no targets upon which to fire. Instead, things were gradually quieting down.

"Get him to the surgeon! Quickly now!" I ordered the bearers with all the little authority I could muster, my voice cracking uneasily. Still, needing little encouragement, they set off, while the other men ran on to join their divisions. I could but hope the surgeons, equipped with better wits than the others, would also take their post in good time. Whether the casualty would even survive the short journey was doubtful, given the prodigious trail of blood laid behind him.

Just as quickly as it had risen to a panic, the camp was settling into stillness again. Those few men not yet in line were darting for the ranks and struggling to regain their breath. I watched as one young soldier, his musket and belting clumsily carried in a pile, caught his foot on a tent stake and tumbled to the ground. Profanity accompanied the clatter of his kit.

Yet there was no more firing, nor screams of fresh pain.

It became obvious what had happened. Some men had panicked, likely from nothing at all, and the whole brigade followed after them in hysteria. I stood dumb for a moment, my legs quivering from the sudden start, and rubbing my eyes hard to remove the dull white clouding which ever threatened to overtake them.

By the time the other non-commissioned officers had wrested back control over the lot, the first officers were already running onto the scene from their own encampment in equally myriad states of dress and alarm. Though it seemed an eternity, perhaps only a few minutes had passed. The juniors rushed at once to their assembling formations, while the staff clumped at the line's head to ascertain the situation. As I was yet a supernumerary, and regaining myself somewhat, I made to join those others within Captain Penn's sub-division.

Upon reaching the point of assembly, I found them all severely disordered, standing about in little clumps merely *resembling* ranks as the sergeants and corporals attempted to corral them into order. Not a few soldiers had found their way to us from other sub-divisions entirely, managing to lose themselves in the dark and simply attaching themselves to whatever band was nearest to hand. It was a poor showing, and I thought of how disappointed Richards would have been had he lived to see it. He had always stood steady, an exemplar of sober soldiering.

As the men thus shuffled into their unsteady ranks, I saw large groups of cavalrymen scouring every inch of the camp, and riding out into the surrounding country. The horses were no happier than their riders with the turn of events, and skittered unwillingly in the dark.

Though I could not hear him, I saw our Brigadier General ride up to the lines, failing to pacify his distressed mount as he gesticulated wildly to his staff. He was clearly incensed at the abysmal lack of discipline which had birthed such a disarrayed assembly. Still, I could tell that in spite of their necessary anger, the other officers were relieved to find the alarm was false. Few prospects were more terrifying than our being set upon, alone and in the dark, by ambushing devils.

Nonetheless, I found an even deeper fear as Hawkins turned and went along our lines. It was not in the barrage of scorn he issued to us; rather, my heart sank to hear the truth of what had occurred.

There were no *damned corpses*, we were told with no uncertainty. The first *bloody* shots had rung out when the sentries happened across some *damned shirkers* who would not answer the challenge. The sentries then *did their duty*, unlike the rest of us *horrid lot*, and made good example of them! *Cowardly whoresons* of the civilian corps, is all they were, who had attempted an escape in the night, deigning to *abandon* their countrymen to the *devil*, rather than endure some *honest labour* in service to *King and Country*! In light of this *justice*, the rest of us then *panicked* like *damned Frogs*! The *chief cowards*, the commander swore heartily, would be identified and punished for their *insensibility* with additional fatigue. Those who had harmed a comrade were to be *flogged*, if not *hanged* for all their murderous stupidity!

With this final threat, Hawkins spat before us, and slapping his horse about made to return to his headquarters with his staff. Stunned into silence, we lingered with orders to keep ranks for some time while the cavalry confirmed the area was secure. Several sergeants hunted along the lines to yank out sacrificial lambs by their ears. Yet I could spare no mind for them, or all our mutual shame, for I had but one terrible thought.

It must have been John. He must have proceeded with some foolhardy escape attempt, and brought others along with him. Images flashed through my mind of him being thrown into the black hole, of his flesh ripping beneath the lash, and his neck hanged at the gallows for all the army to see. Again I felt near to collapse for all my sorrow, so that a confused nearby soldier had to prop me up. I could not hear his concern for the ringing in my ears, and the pounding of my heart. I felt I might break apart entirely.

We were thus stood upon our lines, in the dark, for some two hours before at last being dismissed. Yet upon the order, I did not return to my tent, as the others did, but instead pushed rudely through the crowd without heed for whomever I brushed aside. In my mindless daze, I even found myself pushing past, or rather, falling through, Captain Penn, who at once took a surprisingly firm hold upon me to halt my intended folly.

I believe I had intended to stumble directly to General Hawkins himself, there to plea upon his humanity for my friend's life. Of course, there was nothing to my 'plan' but stupid fear. I would have been lucky to escape such an indiscretion being merely reduced to the ranks, so eager he seemed for a flogging. While I had been hailed an indispensable ally to the brigade, still I was a mere sergeant, and Hawkins' blood was up.

"Sergeant, wait." Penn's kindly voice echoed to my awareness through the crack of leather against John's back. "Captain Russell has just given me some unfortunate news. I'm afraid it's about the man you cam-"

"Where is he?" I interrupted the officer, knocking aside his hold and grasping his arms myself. I saw nothing through my haze but his soft eyes, yet they brought me no comfort. A deep worry was etched into his skin beneath the dancing shadows of passing lanternlight. He paused for a moment, and my heart sank all the deeper.

"I'm sorry." He spoke slowly, careful in his words. There was nothing of the contemptuous anger that a man of his stature well deserved at being thus abused by his inferior. "It seemed like he was something of a ringleader for them. When the sentry caught him out, there was a scuffle, and...well, he isn't in a good way. He's in hospital, his fellows are under guar-"

Cruel though it was, I cared not as to the fate of any co-conspirators, and at once pushed the captain aside to hasten on my new course. Even if the old gentleman had desired to stop me, he could not have done so; no authority, mortal or divine, could then have deterred my intention.

My race across the camp was but a blur. Men confusedly saluted my passing whilst they ducked back into their crowded tents. I nearly collided with some pioniers in my stumbling dash, and tripped over a poorly-placed stake amidst the light bobs, yet unceasingly on I went. I hardly even noticed the trail of blood I soon came to follow, which had come from the belly of the poor man I had previously aided.

Our field hospital had been established just outside the camp in a disused barn. It sat quiet and dark, with only a little candlelight bleeding out of a small window in its side. Pushing myself through its wide front doors, I saw how its interior had been utterly gutted and repurposed for military function. All along its side, and in its stalls, lay rows of tables and cots, and beds of straw upon the ground. A few other tables stood at the centre for surgery, and one, it was evident at once, was recently used. There was neither surgeon nor patient upon it, but only shallow little pools of fresh blood. One of the regimental women, acting as a nurse, was struggling to clean it with a rag already saturated. Her arms and stomach had gone red with splatter from the earlier surgery, and the water bucket at her side had gone black.

Whether that shadow of earlier sorrow came from the man I had aided earlier, or from some other injured man, or John himself, I did not know. I noticed no other patients in the dark corners of the barn, for at its furthest end I saw the cause of all my anxieties.

John lay on one of the low tables. A tight bandage was wrapped about his head, already soaked through; a ball had evidently pierced his skull. His clothing had been violently cut away, and across his chest was another bandage, though it was less well wound than the other. I gathered that his care had been abandoned upon the other soldier's arrival, and not revisited. Larger swaths of red on his chest, just visible beneath a thin blanket, showed that he had taken a second ball there.

As I went to him, I saw his exposed eye was closed, and his breathing faint. His face had not been cleaned of the dirt and dried, crackly blood which covered it. It seemed he had long since lost all consciousness. It was only by a miracle, or perhaps one final curse, that he lived still. I needed no physician to tell me he would not last the night.

"Oh, John." It was all I could whisper as I neared his side, and dropped my hat between clenched fists. "I am so sorry."

Worse even than his poorly tied bandages were the two thick belts tied above his blanket, as if he were a beast to be contained. His blanket, therefore, was no warming comfort in death, but a great bind against his rising again. The surgeon must have feared John's avenging himself, though he was clearly cut down by mortal hands.

Oh, what cruelty it was! To treat a dying man as a *danger*, more than a *Christian*! To see him secluded in a dark corner, abandoned, and tied like a madman! I could contain my feeling no more than Peter upon the cock's crow. I sank to my old friend's side, and wept.

There came no answer to my tears. As my comrade slowly passed, so, too, concluded the desolation of my soul, and any vile delusion I might have harboured of salvation. I had failed in Captain Lawrence's final order, to restore whatever remained of our old company. My body became then naught but a foul reminder of happier times, and of better men long since burnt alive in the fiery maw of wretched Stowlham. I am no more alive than the corpses which wandered that place.

Only now, upon these recollections, may I console myself with the knowledge that my old friend's fate was in the end, perhaps, kinder than my own. For soon after my arrival did poor John's breathing slow further, and further, before ultimately ceasing altogether as he passed from our corrupted world into perfection.

His suffering ended ere the sun rose. Never again would he be plagued by thoughts of devils, the cat, or a noose; his final countenance was a one of peace and gentleness, the like he had not worn since before that tragic night in a little Wiltshire pub.

Now, with the conclusion of his story, I must answer for one final concern: my insistence, which the reader has certainly long ascertained, upon using only John's *Christian* name, in contrast with all others in our old squad. In fact, this name, despite its commonality in our times, was owed to no man within my old company. Nor, with all of its returns and rolls having been lost to fire, might my old crony's true identity ever be deduced save *I* should reveal it. Of all my sins, I trust the gentle reader shall agree this obscuration ranks low among them, for its nature has been purely nominal, and made in defence of a good man who might otherwise be scorned by those ignorant of privation.

For all the world might know, the man I have thus falsely named could have fallen more courageously than any other, in perfect lockstep with his fellows. In thrusting forth his bayonet, *he* may have withheld the Fleshtide, whilst *I* fled in cowardice. *He* may have rushed to rescue comrades and innocents, as *I* abandoned him to his fate. *He* may have been steadfast and loyal and *indefatigable* in the face of Hell itself. Nor might *any* man speak ill of *any* soldier within the noble garrison of Stowlham, where stood such gallant heroes as ever have lived.

Save, of course, the *revenant coward* who offers this humble narrative.

Even the deserter, who thus lay ignobly before me, whoever he truly was, had harmed not a soul. His aim was to save our skins from the start, and had thought to preserve himself only when it was clear no others would follow. He, alone, cried out against the madness of our world; and despite all my cruelties towards him, still, he had stood by me whilst we fled Stowlham, and saw me, in my pitiful condition, to safety. I cannot believe any man, while they judge from the luxury of comparative comfort, unknowing of the cold grasp of *dead hands,* could have acted contrary to our deserter. Indeed, most would surely comport themselves in a far inferior fashion, against so novel a horror as that which we faced!

It is my earnest belief, then, that my friend committed *no other sin* than that of failing in his noble efforts, for which he paid the dearest price - and *damnation* to any who would assert otherwise.

With a trembling kiss, I offered the only meaningful prayer which John might receive in death. I, alone, knew his struggle. I wept my final apologies as several soldiers, acting as orderlies, came to take him away. They untied the belts which restrained him cautiously, as if still fearful of the body, despite its laying stiff.

My tears, being the last I would ever shed, mingled with the blood which stained him. A shallow grave had already been dug some distance from the camp, and in the hollow lamplight, in an unknown field, he was laid to rest.

We buried him with but a shroud, and no stone to honour his memory.

The Dragoon Pleads with his Former Comrade.

A few hours later, the morning sun was fully risen, and our camp teemed with excitement as our reinforcements arrived. They were heard before they were seen, as a full military band trilling a martial tune heralded their approach. Soon, one could glimpse flashing streaks of colour through a distant copse, one of precious few not yet ravaged by the army, and from around its corner issued the first of the column.

At once there arose a general cheer among the men, and on my return from John's fresh grave, I observed them all abandoning their breakfasts to rush forth and greet the newcomers. The non-commissioned officers could hardly deter them, but many rushed on to join the roadside celebrations instead, lifting their hats to *huzza* the entrants. From their fright and confusion the night prior, some hope had come at last, and that sudden lunge of joy was extraordinary to them all.

Still feeling numb, I tarried away from the throng, and instead clambered up one of our diminutive, unfinished bastions to observe the column upon which the fate of all Britain would rest. There, my senses were at once flooded with a vast and noisy river of madder red and royal blue, while betwixt all the tramping shoes, boots, and hooves, great wagons, gun-carriages, and caissons rumbled along. They cut and scuffed the dry dirt path, throwing up great clouds of dust to obscure the whole and offer it a dreamlike quality. It seemed the column emerged unceasingly from a great void behind the trees.

Shimmering muskets came on in great, bristling ranks. Waves of bearskins and plumed helmets from the flank companies interspersed a sea of cocked hats, all befeathered and flowered. Colours towered proud above their regiments, lazily drifting in the little wind. Batteries of the Royal Artillery rolled along with shining bronze barrels of every size, from small four pounders to giant *twenty-four* pounders, all winking in the morning's orange glow. Cavalry horses swished their tails and tossed their manes, swirling the dust clouds about them as they pranced in tune with the music at their head, all excited by the fresh commotion.

It was a militant panoply of colour and sound; a jingling johnny above whinnying horses and grunting bullocks, bassoons and serpents weaving between clattering canteens and squeaking wheels, pounding drums accentuating thousands of rough leather shoes cracking down on the hard-packed road. As they marched to view of our own cheering brigade, so too did the force hold high their hats, and offer great unified *huzzas!* At such heroic tones, even I could not help but derive some *inkling* of inspiration, as I thought that so mighty a force might serve our purpose, after all.

Still, there was nothing so affecting to me as the sight of my own regiment, which I first spotted by the Colours so often trooped past me before. It seemed the whole of the surviving battalion was present, with our flankers besides. I would soon rejoin them, though to which company I knew not, and would no doubt have to answer for the fate of many a lost crony and brother. Unlike the others of our army, they did not acknowledge the cheer and welcome of the advance brigade, but kept their eyes firmly fronted. I had always known my regiment to be a good-humoured and devil-may-care body, yet there was nothing of mirth in their lockstep. Each man of them seemed to bear a weight beyond his pack; a deep-running *hatred* for the enemy, and all it had wrought upon their regimental brothers.

I found myself sharing their feeling, and redoubling it, as rage came on to fill the great void that sorrow had left in my heart. It was a queer sort of comfort; a cruel warmth that alone carried me through the loss of all I had known.

The mighty procession did not end with my regiment, but continued on in ever-greater strength. At its centre rode old General Tomlinson himself, with all his staff. The great assemblage of generals and colonels, lords and gentlemen, sat austere in their saddles, with gloved hands on their hips and eyebrows raised, as they observed the curious disposition of Hawkins' excitable advance brigade. Hawkins himself had soon appeared as well, riding up to join the gaggle and offer his report with a curt salute.

It was more vast an assembly of humanity than I had ever before seen. So too trailed behind the soldiers an equally-sized slew of civilian waggoners, sutlers, and regimental wives and children, all toiling beneath heavy burdens or atop overladen carts. In short time, then, our camp would become a veritable *city*. What small areas of still-living ground we occupied would be thoroughly trampled, crushed, and beaten into submission beneath innumerable bodies and baggage.

As the column's great tail finally arrived, its front having reached our lines and the warm embraces of Hawkins' men, I suspected I had seen all there was. Likewise, I knew it would behoove me to force *some* food, even if but a morsel, down my throat, ere my labours were thus redoubled with the new arrivals. As I descended the bastion's slope, however, I was alerted to a new sight which left me utterly in awe; for no sooner had the first grand cavalcade concluded, than a *second* column materialised over the rise!

These men moved with no music, but were kept in rougher-shod pace by a single drummer alone. As with the regulars, there could be no doubting their military cut, but they marched in route fashion with arms in myriad positions, and in smaller groupings than the battalions preceding them. I realised at once that they must have been the embodied militia.

It was not their presence alone which so overawed me, however; for behind the militia then came up a brigade more peculiar than any I had ever beheld, boasting warriors of quite a different sort. They wore no uniforms, but were clad in the dress of farmers and labourers, weavers and cobblers, some even in the fine clothes of bankers and merchants! They did not march in precision, but sauntered bold and independent. Over their shoulders and under their arms they toted shotguns, fowling pieces, pistols, and even, I saw with a start, axes, knives, and crude pikes fashioned from the tools of their trades.

They were like so many medieval levies, ready to embark on Crusade! In some respect, they rather *were* Crusaders. I would later learn that these men came not merely from the surrounding countryside, but had flocked to the army from every village, town, and city for a hundred miles and more to join our siege.

There were country gentlemen and noble scions clad as if on a hunt; two eccentrics were not even armed with firelocks, but carried *bows and arrows* for their sport! Young apprentices had deserted their masters, not daring to miss so abnormal and perilous an adventure. Shepherds and fishermen, butchers and blacksmiths - all had cast aside their trades to take up the art of soldiering. Even some students from Cambridge, evidently roused by the martial airs which had so thoroughly inundated their town, formed a little corps all their own. They were presently trailed by an equal band, I later learned from Oxford, which had raced across the country in extraordinary haste as not to be outdone by the *upstart* university.

This mighty host of citizen soldiers was perhaps the proudest of them all, and as they came near the camp, they, too, raised up their hats and arms in jubilation, to be welcomed with all the more elation. While the soldiery was naturally comforted by our newfound multitude of arms, there seemed even greater confidence in the knowledge that we had not been forgotten at the lip of Hell. To this day, I fervently believe *this* segment of the procession, though lacking in all discipline and military bearing, nonetheless embodied a display of courage wholly unrivalled in the long history of these Isles.

Behind the lot of them, at last, came the roughest of the lot. Though these fellows were under military discipline, they were not soldiers, but rowdy jack tars of the Royal Navy. Like the civilian-warriors before them, they were clearly unaccustomed to marching, or even, it seemed for many, donning shoes at all! Yet on they came with good spirit and alacrity alike. They carried sea-service muskets and boarding pikes, pistols and cutlasses, and even hauled behind them some naval cannon! Theirs was a fierce image, with their tattooed flesh and roughshod sailors' slops. At their rear marched a company of His Majesty's redcoated marines, stepping to their drum in a more dignified manner.

On that day, it seemed all of Britain marched ready and eager to defend their country's cause, unheeding of and undaunted by any devilry! As I finally made my way back into camp, I found it miraculously transformed. Men previously lethargic in their every motion, moved with newfound zeal. The peculiar silence which had smothered us was suddenly vanquished by lively chatter on myriad topics, all permeated with undertones of *hope* and *glory*.

How many men had arrived in total?

All those new hands will make for easy digging, now!

Which was the ship those sailors belonged to?

Those dead bastards won't know what hit 'em!

Even General Hawkins himself seemed somewhat comforted by the lot of them, as orders never came for the mass punishments he had promised the night before; nor were any of his subordinates keen to press the issue. Rather, the affair was largely laid aside. Only two men were flogged, and then only lightly, given the severity of their offences. None were hanged.

My own regiment was then fixed within the centre-left of the line, just alongside Hawkins' First Brigade, which stood as the extreme left against the river. The remainder of the army, then, extended for some distance to the right. General Tomlinson established his headquarters within the old farmstead, as was to be expected, while our militia and the *proper* civilian corps, to whom Hawkins' own *volun-tolds* were soon transferred, were scattered as little attachments onto each of the battalions to expedite their labour.

Indeed, our prospects seemed to improve by the moment, as the isolated and thin-spread works deepened and expanded at breakneck pace. The occasional small plumes of dirt I had earlier noticed behind the embankment exploded into a continual stream, poured forth from an army of shovels. The bastions, once mere shallow mounds, rapidly rose to the skies, and the largest guns were laid up within them. The ground beyond our line appeared as though stricken by a terrible pox, as great ditches steadily materialised along its length.

Many of the civilians, little enthused by the *realities* of military service, but nonetheless keen on partaking in the coming fray, even volunteered for service with the regulars. The more keen staff officers, then, pulled heavily from their accounts to fund recruitment bounties and fill out their ranks. Daily there came yet further shipments of cannon, muskets, bayonets, and ammunition to accompany a steady stream of fresh troops.

Yet through all these chaotic preparations, I could little share in the excitement. It was a comfort that our flanks were secured, to be sure, and I was kept ever busy in moving from one band of fuglemen to another; but always beneath my labour was the wretched pang of loss, and the seething hatred for its source.

Though Captain Penn had graciously restored me to my Colours, I felt myself an outsider. I had borne witness to, and was the sole survivor of, the terrible fate which every man feared and anticipated. In addition to my usual duties, I was continually ferried to-and-fro from one officer or gentleman to the next, and repeatedly made to recount my tale of woe. Colonels and majors, artillerists and dragoons, country gentlemen who had brought their sons to *this great hunt,* even natural philosophers, anatomists, and physicians from every corner. A band of three doctors had somehow found their way from *Pariſ*! Indeed, I later learned that a great deal of my words had been mistranslated, in a most awkward fashion, for their *revolutionary* audiences. At least I was not alone throughout these interrogations, as Wilkes also was generally summoned to the same. Along the way, he had become something of a friend through our shared experience.

Even General Tomlinson, frequently conducting great war-meetings, would often demand our presence so we might advise on the nature of the foe. So too were the various scouting forces called upon, and, steadily, their reports corroborated our own. Before long, a rather thorough understanding of our foes' *capacity*, if not their *nature*, was thoroughly promulgated throughout the force. Although until the men could all gaze upon the devils themselves, and truly surmise their mettle, a sense of uncertainty would linger beneath all our burgeoning confidence.

Often I found others staring at me uneasily; certainly, my behaviour did little to inspire confidence. Having been restored to some queer approximation of my former life, surrounded by visions so alike those of happier times, my existence became a kind of phantasmagoric display. My every motion, and every word, seemed somehow disconnected from my own awareness.

From the corner of my eye, I might spy my old crony Bennett toting a water bucket or cooking up some beef, though on my approach, he would be gone. On another occasion, an old soldier, blacking his shoes, cut the precise image of Richards; until he glanced confusedly up to meet my stare, and I saw their faces were nothing alike. John would suddenly address me from behind, and I spun about to find only some unnamed private man.

Being still a kind of supernumerary sergeant with no *real* experience, I was thrust under the tutelage of a new officer, Captain Thomas Conway. He was the last of my officers, though we seldom interacted. Nor, as it were, did I pass much time with my brother sergeants in the new company, but remained ever an outsider to those whom I ought to have been closest with.

Nor would the camp's grandly surreal spell of courage and anticipation last long, lifting the very next day after

Tomlinson's arrival. It was the beginning of the twilight hour, ere the taptoo was sounded. It should not come as a surprise that I was nowhere near my own Colours, but stood before some ranks of sailors and marines of His Majesty's Ship *Torrent*. The sailors, in particular, were the most obstinate of my students. Even their officers spoke in cryptic nautical terms, with little respect for the purported authority of a mere *landsman*.

I was in the process of poorly re-explaining some minor point regarding one's footing whilst firing in ranks, when everyone's attention was at once snapped to the distant call of a bugle. Its deft tones soared over the usual cacophony of hacking axes, pushing shovels, and clacking muskets. There was but a half-moment of stunned silence across all the camp, before the first soldiers, more familiar with the signal than their own mothers' voices, leapt into action.

"Stand to!" The cry was taken up by every man of authority, and a mighty wall of madder red rushed to snatch up their stands of arms and claim their places. The distant bugler was soon joined by the duty drummers and not a few piercing whistles of light infantrymen, a sub-division of whom I saw dashing beyond our lines to their advance posts.

"Come on, *Torrents!* We'll show 'em what for!" The naval lieutenant, earlier deathly bored as I lorded over his men, rushed on in a most gallant fashion, his sword in one hand and a sea-service pistol in the other. With a great *huzza*, every seaman and marine followed after him, leaving me briefly dumbfounded and alone in the field. For my part, I knew not whether I should rejoin my regiment, some distance across the camp, or merely take up a nearby place along the battlements. Despite the numbness overtaking my mind and limbs, I settled upon the latter, and, shouldering my pike, made to follow the seamen.

It was yet light enough to see clearly, and as the men were in overall better spirits, I knew the odds of *another* false alarm were slim.

Could it be the corpses?

Had they encroached upon our encampment at last?

Perhaps they had set upon the cavalry, and followed them to us!

My mind raced from possibility to possibility with an ever-mounting intensity. Before me, most of the seamen stood to a long battery of naval guns which protruded out of the gabion defences, just as they might poke outside a ship's hull. Surrounding the placement of the gun batteries, on the elevated ramparts, stood the marines and sharpshooters, eager to support their naval artillery. I knew not the source of my will, but at once I crested the works, and, heedless of any annoyance I caused the foul-mouthed sailors, jostled my way to their front.

Perhaps it was not courage which bade me see the devils again, but my resignation to whatever course the Fates had spun for me. In any case, I moved as though under some great compulsion, and with palpitations fluttering in my chest I looked to the horizon.

By then, the field was a great mess of half-dug pits hastily abandoned by groups of labourers, civilian and military alike, with picks and shovels scattered all about. As waggoners frenziedly whipped their mounts down our makeshift roads, the working parties paid them little heed and so were nearly trampled in their rush for safety. Meanwhile, to the blaring of countless whistles and twirling swords, the light infantry ran past the workers to the fore. Theirs was a heroic cut indeed, and I finally understood why Richards had always spoken so highly of the *Bobs* he'd encountered during his service in America.

For all that great bustle of activity, however, I had little mind to pay. A portion of the light infantry had already been stationed upon their forwardmost line, which was shorter and more thoroughly completed than the main. To a man they stood, sat, and lay with muzzles poking through the brambled barricade before them, eyes fixed firmly down their sights.

What could they see? My imagination raced with myriad terrors, as I blinked away the salty sweat which stung at my eyes.

I could only just make out one of the light's officers waving to his men and shouting some indiscernible words of command. It must have been an order to save their fire, for not a man among them pulled his trigger.

Every second passed me in agony. The field before us was soon totally bereft of life, save upon the forward position. Yet from that long, thin line of red, obscured between so much thorny brush, there came neither movement nor firing.

What was happening? The thought held even the rowdy *jack tars* about me in the grip of an eerie silence. After what seemed an eternity, our spell was at last broken by the finely-pressed lieutenant, standing not far from me with a glass pressed tight to his eye.

"Cavalry!" He exclaimed excitedly, and sure enough, just beyond the opening in the forward lines I saw a dust cloud slowly rising. Though I could not see the cavalrymen themselves, it was obvious something was very awry, for them to be riding so hard for the lines.

"What's happening? What do you see?" I came alongside the lieutenant in a daring press of my authority. The novelty of the scenario, and all our excitement, prompted the officer to answer my demand all the same.

"It's one of the scouting platoons!" He replied. "I can't quite...they're out of ranks, to be sure, and pulling fast for us. It seems that...yes, one of the horses is without a rider! Another man is leading it...I can't make it out, but, it seems their officer is shouting something. God's blood, but they're in a *hurry!*"

Indeed, the horsemen slowly came to my naked vision, numbering perhaps no more than a dozen, and riding fast for the little gap. On coming up to it, they did not pause for a report, but were waved through by the officer and continued down the central lane, which by then was blessedly empty of cattle and cart.

"There!" The lieutenant gibbered excitedly on spotting some greater detail. "Yes, one of them is surely hurt. Oh, badly cut up. I can just about - there's blood all about his face! Christ, but something got at him!"

The mumbling of the sailors about us turned to excited

chattering, and had nearly to be whipped back into order by their boatswain. Though I was hardly cognizant of their being loaded, from below the ramparts the heavy naval guns rattled loudly as they were run out, ready to fire. *Torrent's* captain, an old sailor with a heavy limp, paced up and down the line of gun crews in grim silence, a cluster of officers and warrant officers at his tail.

The individual figures of the cavalry were becoming clear to me then, and soon reached within a hundred yards of our primary line. The men were all hunched over, nearly standing in their saddles as they spurred their mounts on to greater speed. The horses, likewise, needed little encouragement. The one to have lost its rider had a red stain across its back and was most panicked of all. Another beast struggled to keep up with its companions, being burdened by two troopers. One of them, the forward man, was slumped totally over. That he was badly injured was obvious, though in what manner, I could not then see.

"-urgeon!" The panicked shouting of their officer, at the group's head, gradually grew discernible as they neared. "Fetch the surgeon!"

I realised they did not flee in terror, then, but raced in a desperate, heroic desire to save their comrade! By then I could recognise some finer details of the horsemen. The injured man had taken on a pallor, and the fine blue of his coat was stained a deep, blackened crimson. These were signs with which I had become all too familiar; as was the vision soon following, for which it seemed all the camp had gathered to observe.

But fifty yards afield, every detail had become visible to any who desired bearing witness to the horror. Alongside all the soldiery, a number of bold followers and labourers had made their way to the lines, so they might peer between the gun batteries. Several others, with some officerial connection sufficient to grant them the liberty, even clambered up the ramparts for an optimal view. Many women stood among the civilians, and even some children too bold to be ushered away. Had I desired to look behind our ranks and along the line, I would assuredly have seen Lord Tomlinson with all his staff, hurriedly riding along the ranks to ensure their satisfactory placement.

Of all those keen eyes, mine must have been the first to realise what was happening.

The wounded man had gone to his maker, though the movements of the galloping horse disguised it well. The flight of his poor spirit permitted but a moment's peace for his remains, which soon began to stir anew in dark restoration. First came the twitching and bending of its legs into unnatural contortions. Its arms followed suit, and by the time the once-man's living comrade caught its wind, it was too late.

With the final pulse of daemonic genesis, the corpse threw back its head in frenzy, and noting the prey before it, clamped hard upon the horse's flesh. It bit with a heinous enthusiasm, trying to tear at the beast's thick hide to set steed and rider alike to immediate alarm. The horse released a hideous scream as its rider attempted to both retain control, and restrain the devil. Yet the horse, in its animal panic, bucked and kicked furiously to dislodge its unnatural attacker. With a guttural neighing, at last it succeeded, casting devil and rider alike to the earth, ere the other troopers saw what was happening.

All about me, the line erupted into chaos. Men swore most heartily and cried their shock to the Divine. Others kept deadly quiet, and one man fell sick. I could but look on in slow dread as my gruesome warnings came at once to fruition.

"My God." It was all the lieutenant at my side could whisper, unblinking through his glass. "Oh, my God."

The living cavalryman lay dazed for a moment after his hard fall. He struggled to free himself from his scabbard, which had caught between his legs, and to tear off the large helmet which had twisted askew atop his head. The corpse, meanwhile, suffered no such mortal discomforts.

On its own impact, it immediately spotted the poor cavalryman and began its cracking, disturbed crawl towards him. It stumbled to its feet as it went, ignoring a broken ankle to stamp on with bloody arms outstretched. Even from our distance, one could see its teeth working like mad.

The men about me fell quiet, in awe as much as fear.

The victim soon understood his fate, but would not accept it. He seemed to have injured his leg, for he could only clamber and slide back awkwardly, continually falling over himself as he went. He raised his arm as if to ward off his killer, forgetting the sword at his side. Though I could not hear his words, it seemed he was pleading with his former brother, hopeful of some merciful recognition.

It never came. The devil fell upon its victim in the bat of an eye, ripping and tearing in all their usual gory fashion. The poor man's shrieking echoed like a whistle blast through the valley of our defences. It was the sort of primitive sound that might violate any man's thoughts for years to come.

The other cavalrymen, realising what had transpired, did not delay in whipping their frightened mounts to the about-face. Their comrade was still embroiled in the grapple when they arrived, and a jostling crowd of horseflesh soon surrounded the pair to obscure them from my view. Through the billowing cloud of dust still came unabated sounds of panic, overlaid with so many pounding hooves and bellowing cries. "Take it down! Kill it! *Kill it!*"

The mounted arm had been well equipped, and repeatedly there came the glint of flashing sabres as they cut at the body below, before rising up again wet and ruddy. Pistol and carbine shots rang out, one after the other, and their white smoke mingled with the yellow dust. Yet even four or five well-placed shots did nothing to stem the attack. The dragoons' panic rose, and still came the pleas of their comrade. Looking to the officer beside me, I had half a mind to snatch his glass away for more direct observation. Beneath the long tube, his face was all of disgust and illness.

Though the full reality was obscured from those of us upon the ramparts, in a short time something had evidently altered the scenario. The already-panicked horses began to rear and kick all the more, refusing the commands of their masters to keep close at the grappling pair. With a wave and a shout from their officer, the cavalrymen abandoned their friend, and gave in to the flight of their steeds.

As they cleared the area, their reasoning was made evident. Even amidst the dense clouds of dust, one could see that the devil, resistant to every manner of mad injury which had broken its back and skull, had at last gained advantage over its former comrade. Dead teeth had sunk hard into some exposed flesh, and the ground surrounding the pair was muddied by blood and churning hooves alike. The still-living cavalryman's arms clutched about the devil's torso in a tragic, dying embrace. He had neither strength nor will to fend off his assailant. Though his screaming had ceased, I could imagine the awful gurgling which the blood escaping his lips must have made.

He seemed, then, abandoned to his cruel fate as so many had been before; yet one courageous soul, who had refused the order of flight, spurred his mount with a harsh beating towards the pair. That corporal of horse, whose name has since been cast into cruel ignominy by those uncomprehending of warfare's cruel nature, was I believe, among the most courageous souls in all our army for his next action. For his was a cruelty borne of kindness, and necessity. The very same I had dealt unto Ensign Tell.

Riding so near as he could, undoubtedly with a tear in his eye and a prayer upon his lips, the corporal raised up his heavy pistol and fired one final shot: not to the devil's skull, but his *comrade's*. The merciful ball rang true, and at once all torment was ceased. About me there rose nary a sound, but a shock seemed to paralyse every body.

There remained for him no time to moralise over the issue. The devil immediately rose as its kill was stolen away, and taking sight of the horseflesh before it, leapt anew for the animal. Blessedly, as his mount was already eager to flee, the cavalryman had only to release his reins to manage a hasty escape. Of course, as he galloped back towards our lines to rejoin the others of his platoon, the devil did not abandon its fruitless pursuit.

Thus, once more, was nigh our whole force to view a most

terrible and *necessary* sight; for though all had heard tell of the devils' horrid nature, there could exist no substitute for bearing them direct witness.

The corpse hobbled quickly for our lines on its broken limbs, thoroughly cut and shot up as they were. Its head was perhaps one-third severed, listing to the side, whilst only half of its skull remained to leak fluids all down its face. It strode in callous insult to every law, natural and divine. While the sailors and marines around me creatively swore in their disbelieving disgust, both physical and moral, I could think of nothing save the horrid clicking of those distant jaws. All my world, beyond that cut flesh and the cold eyes amongst it, faded to a blur. We stood then within the devil's sights, and it cared not for our numbers or fortification, but came on unceasingly in a grim portent of what was later to come.

Then came the time for our Royal Artillery, and specifically the centre battery, then to my left, which stood nearest the foe. I could not hear their commands of loading and elevation, but the effect of the gun's firing was inescapable. The sudden *boom* and distinct twang of the iron shot leaving its bronze barrel echoed through the empty field, as a ball of four pounds weight tore through the air at the head of a long, white cloud. At so close a range and tight an elevation, the perfectly aimed round met the devil's flesh at once.

The resultant sight was awful.

The ball was not impeded by the foul body, but carried off a full quarter of its torso in a vile spray of bone and gore, before ultimately crashing to the ground behind, skipping along the dirt a few times before rolling into one of the ditches.

The devil found itself thrown off by the shot, though while it stumbled, it did not cease its stumbling advance; not even as its head, torn further astray by the collision's great force, remained attached by only a thread.

Those seamen not retching then engaged in more violent swears, shaking their fists and offering crude gestures to the distant corpse. Their reply to abject horror, the sort that even the eldest veterans of storm, fever, and battle could never know, was a one of combative rage. The boatswain and his mates saw little function in quieting them.

The second cannon shot was lower aimed, and skipped repeatedly across the ground to meet the devil harshly above the knee, cleaving its leg in twain. The devil fell to the ground as many a boisterous *huzza!* erupted from army and navy alike. Many assumed the devil had finally been bested; but the reader shall know, as did I, that they were mistaken.

The grounded devil first reached out with bloodied hands to haul itself forward. Thence, with but *one* leg, it clambered up to an awkward, limping crawl. It rolled, fell, and strode forward with twitchy limbs which seemed impatient of their fellow stump. Though it could not restore its footing, still on it came.

No *huzza* rolled long, but another grim silence descended upon us; the seamen's sails were well shot through and their wind lost. Even the heartiest of profaners could but little comprehend that which came on before him. At last, all fathomed what it meant for the devils to be unkillable.

The gunners, at least, were evidently undeterred. They refused to be bested by any walking corpse, and I later learned how their captain, in a fury, had belayed the latter guns of his battery and ordered the first reloaded. Brushing aside one of his men, he, *himself,* strode forward with the next shot.

"Canister, by God!" Exclaimed the startled officer. "It will be canister!"

Thus, across a field already well obscured by lazily drifting smoke, was launched a third great cloud. It bore not a single, heavy ball, but *dozens* of smaller ones whizzed at its head. They reached and broke hard upon the devil, rushing it firstly with a wave of dirt and debris it churned from the ground, ere riddling its flesh all at once with so many sundering blows. They forced the already-unsteady creature to the ground, and through the devastation, I saw its head was at last fully rent from its body, and rendered a mushy pulp. What remained of its other limbs were flayed to the bone, which shattered within the stringy remnants of muscle. Before the first shot had concluded its course, a second roared and sang through the air to mimic the butchery a second time over.

When the smoke cleared and the dust settled, all that remained of the once-dragoon was a pile of churned-up meat and scattered, sinewy bits. From our vantage point afar, it seemed all its movement had ceased, for there remained no limb attached or intact. Yet for the sight of our hideous victory, none made a sound. Those without the stomach to abide it had long since emptied theirs of any sickness, and the stench of their bile filled the air as it dripped slowly down the rampart.

Not one officer, soldier, sailor, or civilian dared speak. Even the animals in camp, as if understanding that some grave event had transpired, were not heard.

All was silent as the grave.

The Cavalry Depart the Lines.

Part the
SIXTEENTH

wherein battle
is prepared.

For some time there was not a stirring; thousands of souls held their breath, not daring to cut the thick stillness which encased us. Steadily, several misplaced persons began to slink up and down the line to assume their proper places, and I knew I ought return to my own corps, though I found myself rooted to the spot. I could but stare at the distant heap of red streaked long across the ground, pooling atop the dry soil which refused it. As had become my poor custom, I was only wrenched from my stupor by a sudden grasp upon my shoulder.

I spun about with a quick gasp, only to see the naval lieutenant, the glass still clenched in his fist, and pale as a devil. He did not speak, but gestured behind us. Looking down the embankment, and blinking away the blurriness of my vision, I saw the aide de camp Captain Russell sitting anxiously upon his horse. He kept a second, riderless, mount in rein, and had evidently been trying to gain my attention for some time.

"Well come on, then!" He urged with another frustrated wave.

It was only with difficulty that I stumbled down the height of our unfinished defences, though the embankment's rear sloped far less dramatically than its front. My pike assisted in the manoeuvre, but when the aide bade me mount the empty saddle, I could but fumble the polearm - and my limbs besides - in a most awkward fashion. To that point, I had never ridden a horse, and the beast was little patient for the ridiculous hopping I made while attempting to swing my leg over it.

With an impatient swipe, Russell took my pike from me, and ordered two nearby seamen to come and hoist me to the top, in which their manhandling succeeded after some difficulty. Despite the comedy of it all, even the jolliest of jack tars had become numb to good humour.

My unsteady place thus gained, and without a moment for explanation, the aide prompted his beast to trot vigorously down the line. Unbidden, and with little mercy for my discomfort, my own mount followed at once. While the young gentleman ahead held his reins with ease, my pike at his side like a knightly lance, it was all I could do to hold on. I had never known horses to jostle so, and was hardly in an *athletic* state!

Blessedly it was a short journey to our destination, the farmhouse-turned-headquarters, where an assortment of all the mightiest officers had assembled. Lord Tomlinson was at their centre, and for the first time, I could observe our peerless leader more closely. The old veteran's cut was one of the grave, as his skin seemed too small for the body across which it stretched, and the occasional thin strand of white hair poked from beneath his hat to stick firm against a thin, sweaty scalp. He seemed diminutive in his uniform, as it had perhaps not been worn for some time, yet he held captive the attention of all about him.

He made no acknowledgement of our arrival, but his host being assembled, gently kicked his mount to walk on in painstaking slowness. All of his staff of generals, colonels, majors, and aides followed suit; including, I saw, General Hawkins, close at his side. As we formed a little column all our own, a little troop of fresh dragoons assumed positions at our front and rear, their carbines held aloft, each primed and loaded. Unflattering to their role, the countenances of our guardians were dark and uncertain, even sickly.

In perfect silence we rode away from the farmhouse, up to our infant fortifications, and between the little gap which stood between our central battery of artillery, where at least some men could busy themselves with cleaning the recently fired guns, and the ramparts. To proceed thus beyond the guns and into the open, upon the field whence I knew a devil had strode, was chilling. Every yard seemed to extend a mile on our slow walk, and much to his underlings' chagrin, it seemed our stoic commander had no desire to move quickly.

Still, not a sound came from the army as we passed, but every eye followed our steady advance. Even the light infantrymen upon the forward lines, I could only just see, frequently glanced furtively away from their front to observe us. Their anxieties were surely all the greater, being thus separated from their battalions with a devil between.

Our whole army stood hostage to a single corpse.

As we approached the subject of our interest, though I could not make out the gory pile from the tail end of the column, several of our horses began to act up and rightly refused to advance, even under the steadiest of hands and harshest of whips. Sparing no time for the animals' wisdom, Tomlinson at once dismounted. With nervous glances, his staff followed suit, handing off their reins to lower officers and men of our escort. Captain Russell, still at my side, bade me do the same before slipping from his saddle with ease. My own dismounting required the aid of two impatient dragoons.

The moment I met the ground, my pike was thrust back into my arms, and I was made to trot with the exasperated aide to catch up with the others. Emerging from the circle of grunting and uneasy horseflesh, at last I saw the gory scene but a few yards away.

Being then closer to hand, the vision of so much riven flesh grew more visceral, yet not, at first, in a manner disarming. Rather I came upon it almost detached from myself, and unfeeling, having long deadened to such grim spectacles as pooling blood and fragmented bone. That which lay before me was merely a finer stew than any I had witnessed before; an awful testament to the power of the artillery.

Conversely, most of the gentlemen held handkerchiefs fast to their faces in attempted safeguard against the raw meat's vile humours, and dared not stride too near it. General Hawkins could not conceal his disgust at the scene. While it was at first angering to view such distemper among those officers of such long and illustrious service, as I likewise drew nearer, so too was my own stoicism broken.

Though it remained only in crudely-ground heaps, still the flesh was *moving*. It shuddered and quivered in a rhythmic to-and-fro. Wherever some little piece of muscle sat, even devoid of limb, it convulsed with whatever connective tissue remained. One of the devil's legs, severely cut up but nonetheless retaining *some* semblance of a knee, weakly, yet rapidly and erratically, flexed itself over the blood-strewn earth. Its motions stirred up pooling chunks of gore as it steadily traced a little circle about itself.

"Good God..." From my side, Russell mumbled in disbelief. I heard someone stumble out from the crowd to be sick along the road.

Lord Tomlinson, alone, dared limp nearer the mess. With impatient snapping, he was attended by a hesitant aide, who stooped to help him kneel at its very edge. There the general contemplated all before him for some time. Extending his leathery hand - whether it shook from masked trepidation, or mere age, I knew not - to take up the remnants of a severed, though otherwise intact, finger.

Bringing the digit near to his face, it continued to contract and stretch in the devils' customary stunted, fanatical manner, despite being utterly drained of blood. Standing at his back, I saw no emotion from His Lordship, but could only suppose what strength of feeling he must have suppressed to retain such serenity. For my part, I could but lean upon my pike to keep upright. For all my weathering to the vile nature of our foe, I felt I might burst to weeping for the overwhelming nature of it all. I stood ill, abused, and dispossessed of hope.

Why had I not perished in Stowlham? How could I have *lived*, whilst so many good men suffered so? Could life itself, upon our tormented plane, be the punishment for my sins? I wondered whether the poor dragoon-turned-devil, scattered about the dead soil, retained some feeling of his state. There stands to me no more troubling prospect than the thought that, perhaps, he could.

"Well, Hawkins," spoke Tomlinson at last, "it would seem your man's summation was correct. They do not die."

With a flick of disgust, he threw the finger back into the churning pile, and gestured again to receive assistance in rising to his feet. General Hawkins came to his commander's side, then, and lowered his handkerchief just enough to address his superior with some dignity.

"Yes, sir. Yet they may be destroyed, all the same. I believe our plan sta-"

"And *all* of the dead are risen in like manner?"

"I, ah-" Even Hawkins, firebrand that he was, struggled to think clearly in the presence of such grotesquery, and fumbled over his words. "Well yes, sir, according t-"

"Then what of him?" His Lordship pointed beyond the gore to the *second* body. Not a dozen yards to our front lay the *other* dragoon, who had so valiantly attempted to save his comrade, and been so cruelly slain for his troubles. Even from a distance, one could see how his face had been viciously mangled. His once dashing features lay obscured beneath ribbons of flesh. A great quantity of blood pooled from his head where the merciful shot met his brain and killed him, one should hope, instantly. Alone and forsaken, he laid silent upon the field.

Silent, and *unmoving.*

I recalled how quickly the terrible convulsions seized Corporal White, and Richards; there had been no delay in their rising, nor in their attacks. Were the dragoon to rise again, he would have done it long ago.

Hawkins had no answer to the man's fate. Evidently, my recounting of events had been insufficient, though I at once knew the cause. Straightening myself to some semblance of dignity, I stepped forward to speak with a dry, wearily crackling voice over the assembled gentlemen.

"It wasn't a devil that got him, sir."

Every head snapped at once to me, the sergeant who spoke so plainly. I knew, however, that I had been brought along with the staff for a reason. Besides, I had long since been rendered dumb to the customary decorum of rank. Thus, I continued out of my turn.

"I believe the bodies only return should they be killed by one of the risen dead. Every one I have seen, does so at once. But of those men killed by our own fire, my lord, they would not..."

My words died slowly, yet their meaning was clear. I was enraptured, once again, with visions of the innocents caught up in Farwell's fire. Of Ensign Tell, pleading for the mercy I delivered. Ought I have smothered the poor woman, when I had the chance? To bring her an *unwanted* mercy, at the cost of my life? Her screaming from within the home, as I clambered out her window, still sang clear in my mind.

I did not notice Tomlinson's skeletal frame approach me, ere I was looking down into his eyes. A man of such authority, I had not realised how short of stature he was.

"By a Briton slain, a Briton he remains." The general murmured in a rare display, perhaps not of comfort, but of understanding. "It was a brother's mercy. What a strange and cruel world we have all awoken to."

He turned away from me, then, and made to rejoin our waiting horses. As our gaggle trailed after him, he raised his voice again.

"Should we survive the coming struggle, sergeant, I shall have you commissioned upon my own expense. Yet for the present we have other business to attend."

So we quit the field and its bloody mess, returning to our lines. The officers at once scattered to enact the many orders which Tomlinson had issued on our slow walk back, whilst I was reunited with my regiment. A party of sergeants was then set out with shovels and tinder to scrape whatever gory remains they could find of the devil into one of the half-finished pits, whence they set it unceremoniously alight to at last complete its annihilation. Initially, the unenvied assemblage had protested so menial a duty, but on taking the field, they soon fathomed how disastrously such a sight might affect the men's morale. They were pledged to the strictest silence, although it was soon widely known that one of them had secreted a twitching finger into his pocket as some cruel entertainment. From there, word rapidly disseminated through the lines of just how literal the enemy's *unkillable* nature truly was.

To our *unrisen* comrade, some greater decorum was afforded. He was buried with honours by his regimental brethren. Of the corporal who shot him, I knew neither his feelings, nor those of his comrades; but I knew he would not be the last to deliver such foul salvation. Indeed, as many a survivor of our dreaded campaign would soon learn, military necessity breeds little comfort.

I spoke little with my comrades in the subsequent hours, nor was I much addressed. Precious little noise was to be tolerated, save that of certain fussier officers precisely adjusting the sizing of their sub-divisions, or of the occasional messenger bearing notes of nonsense between senior officers. Overall, the army had formed in much better order than in earlier alarms, and little adjustment was necessary before we stood so nicely as if we had been drawn up to parade. Nor did we receive orders to depart from our lines, but were permitted only to shift our ranks to the bottom of the embankments, to sit as we had stood. Though our encampment was but a quick walk away, we had our lunch beneath the narrow shadow of our tiny ramparts. If nothing else, it was a mercy to be brought away from staring at the freshly ensanguined field, and imagining how it might soon be drenched all the more. Some of the men attempted to entertain themselves with a game of knock-chops, but none were terribly enthused. Many more busied themselves, as is ever the soldier's lot, tending to their cleaning, blacking, or sewing. Few were able to sleep.

Our few sutlers, likewise, were soon at play to parade up-and-down to hawk food and drink to their captive consumers. It was through those civilians, to say nothing of the officers' attending cronies and wives, that the fiercest of rumours fanned across the ranks like flames atop a terrace. The non-commissioned officers attempted to regulate any idle gossip within their squads, but in spite of their efforts, it soon became clear what had befallen our poor scouts.

It seemed the devils, having thoroughly expunged Stowlham of all life, had degraded into a kind of collective, drunken stupor. Be it sight or sound, any hint of life would draw them in mad pursuit, though never with sufficient predatory wit to *seek* or *pursue*. Thus, any distant sound would set them to a new site, whence, finding no prey, they would but circuitously amble. Thus, as Wilkes had earlier guessed, the majority had slowly come to convene upon a number of central points, enticed by a collapsed building or the whimpering of a freshly-slaughtered dog.

On rare occasions, it seemed one might find itself isolated nearer the outskirts of town, and so spy one of our dragoons who had come too near. The cavalry, noting this, had quickly learned to flee in their own circuitous manner, thus leaving the creature dumbfounded after only a brief pursuit. The only real requirement, then, was that the scouting parties keep well alert, and active in their communication, to relay where they had encountered stragglers and how far they had gone.

Such obligations ought to have been simple enough for the mounted arm; yet over those few days of exceeding length, it seemed that several of our men had grown somewhat *cavalier* in the face of the enemy. They took too much confidence in their limited experience with the corpses, and, like the infantry, were heartened by the rising of our fortifications. Some men drew too near the town as a foolish mark of *courage* among their fellows, while others fancied that evading the devils' pursuit was but a trifling matter.

Thus, it was owing only to the most *minute* of miscommunications, for which little fault could be laid at the feet of any one figure, that our poor victim assumed his attacker had been lured in *one* direction, rather than *another*. Thinking himself secure, he brought his mount through some brush, to step near directly upon a corpse in accidental ambush! He was soon seized by the leg and thrown from his saddle, after which the devil set upon him and inflicted a terrible bite. He managed to throw off his attacker just long enough to be discovered and 'rescued' by a nearby comrade - the man so recently laid to rest. The incident's sole survivor, then, was the horse, and to the credit of its noble kind it dutifully reappeared before our lines to rejoin its regiment after feasting for several hours upon the grasses of some safer pasture.

Given the day's events, I presumed there would be no further *misjudgements* as to our foe's nature, or the likelihood of an injured crony's survival. All during this time, a great number of our officers had been summoned to the headquarters for a final, grand war-meeting, the likes of which I was not privy to, and lasted some time. Every man then knew that battle would soon be met.

We spent all that day, and the night, upon the lines. Even in that unseasonably warm summer, the air was chilled, and most of our men sat huddled in silence about little fires that dotted the landscape like a yellow-red pox. Many could not help but find themselves staring up the short, albeit looming, embankment and wondering what might lurk just beyond. I could not begin to conceive the depth of feeling which must have existed amongst the light infantrymen, who sat in similar stature upon their forward lines with nothing at all between them and distant Stowlham.

Under normal circumstances, any man might have leapt at the chance to bring the *Bobs* their dinner, but the call for a few volunteers to stretch their legs and depart the lines met with scant enthusiasm. Behind our half-finished defences, the men felt more secure against the encroaching darkness when around their fires, and surrounded by the living. The great, dark chasm between us and the forward posts held naught but the burnt remains of a devil at the bottom of a shallow, unfinished grave.

In light of this natural fear, and despite the presence of the forward posts, our sentries atop the ramparts and the taller bastions to our rear were doubled, and likewise relieved twice as often. Few men had the stomach to tarry long outside the glow of our little fires. There were false alarms on two occasions, with sudden calls that set us scurrying to fetch our arms. Having scrambled up the artificial hillside into our divisions, we then discovered that what some distant sentry had taken for a shambling corpse was, in the first instance, nothing more than a brief howl of wind, and in the other, a fat hedgehog trundling merrily through our abatis. To assuage the reader's fears, the sentry's panicked shot at the creature missed its mark. Few of us managed even a wink of sleep, and with the steady advent of dawn, so fled any hopes thereof.

Ere there was even light enough to see them, already the cavalry had commenced its grand formation. I was only broken from another idle stupor by the distant signalling of their bugle, and the curt commands of their officers alongside the snorting of horses, rudely roused from their slumbers. Then, as the prospect of a paltry breakfast befell the infantry, there came upon us a most magnificent sight.

The first of the cavalry column appeared from behind the bastion to our rear, and proceeded to the little sally-lane between our ramparts and an artillery battery. On and on the column stretched, with all their myriad-coloured coats, and shimmering lace that reflected our flickering fires in the dull morning light. What little dew there was had collected upon the tips of fur caps, and dripped steadily down the cold metal of helmets. The procession soon began passing by my place upon my battalion's right, and near to the line's opening, in absolute quiet. They rode as if in a funeral procession; a spectacle both beautiful and tragic.

We of the foot observed with wonderment and horror those brave souls who would madly forge out to *corral* the very unkillable foes which had so brutally abused two of their own. All was silent, save the snorting of horses and plodding of hooves. Many of the men about me removed their hats both in salute and mourning for those they suspected would not last the morning. For my part, shameful though it was, I could not find the will to stand. My eyes had burnt half raw from staring long into the flames before me.

"Brave horsemen! Noble knights, all!" The quiet was jarringly broken by a call from above. Startled, I looked about to see that my new company's lieutenant, Baker, had crested the ramparts and run to their very edge. From that vantage point above the defile, he hailed the passing column with a wave of his hat in the air.

"God bless you all, my friends! Strength to your arms! Speed to your mounts! Bless you all!" He carried on alone in swelling, desperately heroic tones, before turning to us melancholic foot soldiers. "Come on, my lads! Three cheers for the cavalry! Hip-hip!"

Our first *huzza* came pathetically from but a few, uneager men. Lieutenant Baker mocked our efforts as light-hearted as he could, and urged us again. Many voices thus joined in the second cheer, invigorated not by zeal, but in protest of fate itself. By the third, the call stretched further still, as more and more voices joined the choir. Nor did that cheer cease, but ascended into a continual roll. The men roared encouragement to their comrades-in-arms, and hatred for the evil that had been thrust upon them. Hats were thrown into the air and muskets waved wildly about. The great dam of our emotions had been ruptured by one Lieutenant's call.

Our officers, who had largely remained with us upon the lines, all competed to give the most flourishing of bowing salutes, whilst the Sergeants all saluted in deepest respect. So too were the brave horsemen emboldened to meet the excitement. They sat higher in their saddles, and raised up their swords and caps to swear their duty would be done, and their brothers avenged. Even the horses seemed to prance in greater anticipation for their duty, aroused to nobility by the alacritous spirit about them. All the better, for extraordinary exertion of body and soul would be demanded of man and beast alike that day.

The cavalry thus departing through the ramparts, the infantry raced up our works to continue waving them off. At this, at last, I found my will to rise and join my compatriots. Though I could not summon the voice to cheer, I removed my cocked hat in salute. I felt as a captain must, in watching his ship slip beneath the depths.

In the faint morning glow, I saw the hundreds-long line of cavalry crossing the lane through our pockmarked field. It was troubling that so few of the pits were then fully completed, but many sat only deep enough to *delay* the devils, rather than entrap them totally. Some sections seemed scarcely more than shallow ditches. At least the soil thus extracted had proven sufficient to build up our three great bastions, upon which the heaviest guns sat. All about their long protruding barrels, men of the artillery likewise waved and shouted. Theirs would be a hot work, before the day's end.

By the time the final tail passed through our forward works, being likewise cheered by the light infantry, the morning sun was quite near the horizon. We could faintly hear the cavalry's instruments as they were ordered from their column into lines, and the distant pounding of so many hooves as they rode off to the domain of the dead. As all sign of them slowly faded, so too did our cheers, and we were again left in silence. Only the gentle whistle of slow wind accompanied our grim thoughts. There remained nothing left but to choke down the remainder of our breakfast, go through a morning inspection, and wait.

Once the divisions had all assumed their final placing atop the ramparts, the other sergeants passed the time checking and re-checking that flints were properly fixed, and locks sparked well. Some words of encouragement and comfort were exchanged, and trivial matters of formality strictly held in the attempt to maintain some normalcy. It struck me hard, though I tried not to show it, to overhear the idle curse of a sergeant chastising a man for his carelessness in remedying a loose button on his waistcoat. I thought of Sergeant Percy, and my own such infraction upon the fateful day which felt so long ago. I thought of the fear flooding his eyes as I abandoned him in the alley.

I was only taken from this recollective stupor, the likes of which were becoming disturbingly frequent, by Captain Conway's appearing before me. He held a great stone jug in his hands, and offered its weight up to me. It had been morning but a few hours, then.

"Would you do the honour, sergeant?" Asked he. Perhaps it was his attempt to ingratiate me unto the men, who beheld me in so alien a manner?

"Very good, sir." Cold formality was all I could muster. Awkwardly I shouldered my pike and took up the heavy jug. Moving from man to man, they welcomed the rum ration as a break from idle standing. Yet as I went down the line, pouring a tot into each proffered tin cup, I found their faces hardly discernible as they downed the drinks in single, long pulls. Every countenance took on the appearance of a one I once knew.

First came Bennett, who accepted the drink with his toothy smile. As he brought it to his lips, his throat was suddenly transformed into a pulsing pit of hollow muscle. Only after the cup came back down was he healed, and Bennett's face, too, had vanished.

Then came Richards, who nodded in morose gratitude for the drink before his eyes burst to spray me with their fluids. In truth, it was nothing more than the old stranger choking some spittle on my face after his drink, a natural product of potent liquor so early in the morning.

I was a man in two worlds, and could only with difficulty discern some truth. Each fellow down the line continued thus in some foul recollection of a former comrade and their awful fate. How cruel it was of the Divine, to again make good so many of those vile visions, ere the day's end!

As I reached the end of the line, and made to pour along the centre rank, I was at last revisited by those ghosts most tragic to me. Captain Lawrence stood alongside the ranks, pale and cold, and stared at me with wide eyes and a chattering mouth. Half of his skull was gone, and pressed against his chest stood a mutilated woman, who hid her face in sorrow. Her gown had been torn, and was rendered stiff from so much dried blood.

"Die with dignity." Whispered she. Though her face was buried, I heard the woman's final words with perfect clarity. She repeated them over and over again, and they rose in Hellish furore with every utterance. "Die with dignity. Die with dignity! *Die with dignity!*"

"Sergeant!" Again, I was awoken with a fright. A corporal had shaken me free of the phantasmic vision, and had uprighted the jug which I had wantonly allowed to dribble onto the ground. The curse he muttered as I came-to was reasonable.

Looking back before me, Captain Lawrence had transformed into our dashing Lieutenant Baker, who cradled not a corpse, but his wife. I could not hear the words either spoke, but watched as he quietly stroked her hair between every private, comforting murmur. His kind eyes paid me no mind whatsoever.

Blinking my vision clear again, I could only apologise to the corporal and continue with my duties. I had to focus my every effort on stilling the violent trembling of my hands, and made sure not to look up at the faces of any yet-lingering ghosts. Nevertheless, I could feel their jealous stares piercing me from behind every tin cup.

Before long I finished doling out the rum, and took the little remainder of it for myself. It was not half sufficient for the task. I then returned to the right flank of Captain Conway's grand division.

I stood upon the very precipice of the ramparts then, with a great continuous line of redcoats upon my left and a battery of guns below me to the right. Beyond them rose again the ramparts, which continued for so far as I could see in the grand battle line. The artillery's thick gabions, and the brush of abatis in the ramparts' trenches, appeared almost insurmountable to the devils; yet between the two, the narrow defile lay open like a wound. It was necessary, of course, to allow the cavalry and light infantry to retreat safely, but gazing upon it I was left only with visions of the dead pouring through the gap. In the *rare chance* that the enemy ever reached our position, some mobile barricades of chevaux de frise had been prepared for such; but I could not believe them sufficient. Standing for so long upon them, I came to realise that our defences, earlier so comforting, were in fact woefully inadequate.

With nothing more to withstand the pains of idleness, I could but wait alone amidst the crowd. None of the other sergeants or my officers made attempts at idle conversation, and for that alone, I was glad. Our silence was broken only by the occasional cough, muttered prayer, or an aide trotting down the line to convey messages between the generals and battalion commanders, who likewise moved anxiously up and down the lines. Before long, our own commander summoned his regimental band to strike up some 'rousing' tones. Impressively outfitted though they were in the finest Turquerie, I hardly noticed the jingling johnny with its horde of serpents, oboes, and bassoons as they slow marched along our rear. My every sense was directed immediately to the front.

The low position of the sun showed the morning to still be young, though it felt as if many hours had elapsed, ere some sudden movement from the forward line aroused our attention at last. The light infantrymen had been told to prime and load. As one they instantly leapt into action, and assumed their various queer postures of standing, crouching, and laying on their arms to gain their best aim through the brush before them. Then, from down the empty lane, one of the few staff officers who had stood beyond the lines came racing on his horse towards us. He waved his hat about wildly in the air, shouting something as he went.

Before we could make out his words, their meaning was clear: *Prime and load!* The order spat at once from the lips of every man of authority, save myself. Thousands then brought their arms to their breasts, slapped the pouches upon their hips, and retrieved their cartridges. Endless ranks of papers were bitten, torn, and spat. Pans were primed and shut, as little barks of *'bout!* from the corporals bade every sub-division, in their time, to cast about their barrels, pour down the remaining powder, and seat the musket balls, at the bottom of every crumpled cartridge, at the firelocks' muzzles. The air then sang with sliding metal as ramrods were pulled, twirled about in the air, and rammed their charges home.

Within perhaps fifteen seconds, all the line stood ready with muskets held aloft. Many seemed to tremble in the air, not owing to their weight. The next command to *shoulder, arms!* failed to still the men's quivering. I, too, felt a cold sweat stinging the corners of my eyes and dampening the small of my back.

We then waited in silence no longer, but jumped in fear as the air cracked and thundered with the first artillery shot. From behind us, the greatest of our guns had opened up to cast a twenty-four pound ball of iron across the field. I could not see it, but fancied I could hear the *swoosh* as it soared overhead. A great cloud, denser and darker than those few tendrils backlit by the morning sun above, trailed in its wake to pierce the still air. It rolled far across my sight before steadily slowing, to linger long above us. I knew then that we would not be long in firing, ere becoming utterly blind to the foe.

"Oh, Lord." I could only just hear Captain Conway whispering to himself. "I trust in thee. Please, thou art my God. Save me for thy mercies' sake - *please*."

His prayer would go unanswered on that awful day.

Firing the "Iron Hail" upon the Devils.

Part the
SEVENTEENTH

wherein The Battle

of Stowlham begins.

The board was opened. One cannon shot was succeeded by another to echo across the field, as every bastion opened an intense fire. Where the heavy balls were landing, and to what effect, none save the gunnery officers with their glasses could possibly tell. Each gun crew worked in exceptional haste, with insufficient time to fire the battery's last barrel, ere the first was pricked, primed, and ready again. I was uncertain whether to find comfort in such alacrity, or alarm in its evident necessity. The rounds blasting overhead were a constant cacophony, with shouted orders to *advance cartridge!* or *ram!* occasionally puncturing the din. The lighter gun crews to my right were well encouraged by the activity of their fellows, and offered up three hearty cheers for them. All behind the line, officers rode back and forth on excitable horses, conducting all the business of an army on the eve of combat.

The heavy guns were not firing long before the first of our cavalry appeared just ahead of the forward line. Even from my considerable distance, and with my view being obscured by the light infantry positions, it was clear they were in distress. Their spacing was poor, and they were overly hasty in moving again into a column, to pass through the defences. They hardly even seemed to be in a line, but merely transitioned from one wide mob into a narrower set of clumps. The bugler at their head was sounding the same panicked notes, over and over again, whilst the first of them tore full-tilt through the forward defile.

It was only just wide enough for four horsemen to pass abreast, but in their panic, many more attempted to go through. Soon there appeared a regular jam, through which but a few men could guide their mounts, in a manner reminiscent of those fearful men I had seen back in Stowlham, trying to flee the old man's kitchen. All at once my fears were redoubled, for I realised something had gone terribly awry.

Several light infantrymen abandoned their firelocks and rushed to the lane, working to clear some of the abatis and widen the defile. Although some were nearly trampled for their efforts, they soon succeeded in liberating the mass of horseflesh, which quickly streamed through to the field with verve. Most of the dragoons immediately set to reforming with their troops once they had crossed, yet some made at once to scatter and flee down the lane for our main line. It was those most consumed by panic who had caused the earlier delays, and should they have been branded as cowards, I dreaded the inevitable order to fire upon them. Yet as they cleared the jumbling masses of mounted troops, I realised that, to a horse, they galloped on without riders! Many of the poor things were badly cut up, and not merely from the splintered remains of abatis which they dragged behind them like fragmented chariots.

Despite the panic of their retreat, the cavalry made quick work of retiring as the light infantry worked to further clear the path. As they did so, it seemed the lights gradually gained a better view of their foe. Musketry began to pepper irregularly down the bobs' line, with their officers twirling swords and blasting whistles as they directed men to their targets. It was apparent the enemy was but a few hundred yards away, and in far greater force than was anticipated. My panic grew.

What could have happened?

As the frightening unknown played upon every soldier's mind, we could only wait and watch. Through my mind raced a dozen frenzied, groundless assumptions, as becoming hard of breath I attempted to calculate how long it might take for the rotting horde to reach us. The first horses were just then passing through the defile on my right, and I could focus on nothing beyond my fear. Their grunts and squeals of injury, fear, and exhaustion were an awful accompaniment to the rising din of battle.

The artillery still rolled unending across the field, as a great wall of smoke pushed steadily forward and threatened to eclipse the sun entirely. The pace of their firing even accelerated, as the gunners loaded with little care for swabbing their bores. So, too, did the light troops rapidly obscure any prospect of glimpsing the enemy before them, as thick clouds of smoke erupted from their musketry to swirl about the abatis before them. It was a testament to the lights' aim that none of our cavalry were hit by their fire.

The great rush of cavalry had then slowed to a steady trickle, as the last stragglers, mainly non-commissioned officers with a few riderless mounts in tow, came through the forward defile. As the last of them cleared the way, the lights again sprung into action to seal the gap, not only with the original abatis but with some chevaux de frise assembled for that purpose.

It was a cruel irony to be horrified by the *lack* of wounded men amongst the cavalry. Many sustained slight tears to their breeches and faint splatters of blood upon their person, yet none seemed *profusely* hurt in a manner requiring immediate care. Indeed, there were plenty of *riderless horses*, but no *wounded riders*.

What had happened to them? I hardly desired to dwell upon the possible scenarios, nor had I long to entertain conjecture.

Their field clear, the lights fired in all the more earnest. Rather than relying on any traditional order, as engaging a mortal foe demands, each man simply loaded and fired in his own time. With such volume, however, each successive shot was less well aimed than the last. Not only were their targets increasingly obscured by smoke, but the marksmen themselves began to panic. Soon enough they ceased using their ramrods entirely, but merely poured their powder down the barrel, tore the ball free of its wadding, and dropped it down the barrel before seating it with a solid rap against the ground. No tap-loaded musket then sat long upon the shoulder ere its ball was loosed into the evidently rapidly oncoming opponents.

"It won't be long now, men!" I heard Lieutenant Baker bellow as he passed up and down his sub-division's line. He held watch over half of our grand division, with Captain Conway, just before me, in the overall command. "Stand fast, and all shall be well!" Just behind us, the band still progressed steadily up and down, and struck up the old tone, *Britons Strike Home!* To such martial stuff, however, I could pay no mind; nor could I heed the cavalry officers behind me, who blubbered out chaotic reports to waiting aides. Rather, I had eyes only for the front, where the light infantry had already started to retreat.

Whistle blasts pierced the peppering musketry, interspersed with nondescript shouting from their non-commissioned officers to retire. Those men still with shots to give offered them up to the yet-obscured foe, before sliding off their little posts and rushing in a great open-order column towards the lane whence the cavalry had come. With muskets at the trail, they moved with an even greater alacrity than usual; several even overtook their file-partners in the race to our main line. Though they had considerable distance to cover, not a man of them slowed for a moment, save for the officers, to observe their progression. Still they made a great show of blasting their whistles and twirling their swords, as if the alarm were not already thoroughly heeded!

By the time the light bobs reached some half-way across the field, the source of their dread finally revealed itself. Its appearance was at once met with a gasp of awe and horror that shook down our lines along with many a quiet prayer. For my own part, I scarcely had emotion left to give, though I could hardly breathe and my fingers burned from how tightly I gripped the butt of my pike. My eyes stung hard from sweat and strain as I gazed out upon them.

"My God." Captain Conway had recommenced his prayers. "My God, My God, My God." He convulsed as he whispered. Meanwhile, the lieutenant continued his more lively encouragements.

"Think of England! Of your homes!" He moved along the ranks, clapping men on the shoulders and punching at the air with his sword-hilt. All the while, he purposefully kept his back to the foe, as if to demonstrate his being unperturbed by their presence. "By God, we'll smash the bastards! Smash them all, and cast them to the darkest pit! Now, my lads, you shall prove yourselves for men!"

There was nothing of courage in the little, resultant cheer. As once but a single corpse held command over every man's mind, now appeared the great *Fleshtide*.

The first few corpses staggered roughly forward, and threw themselves into the abatis of the forward line as if it were not there at all. I could not see them in detail, but knew they had each been thoroughly riddled with gunfire. Some were lacking in limbs, yet nonetheless pushed with all their might into the thick brush. Had but a small mob of one or two hundred devils been corralled in, as was originally planned, they might never have surmounted even that little blockade. Yet within a blink, the first of their number doubled, then tripled, and suddenly what I knew to be *thousands* of corpses came to crash and press upon the little barricade. The entirety of our front was at once overwhelmed with the silent, grasping masses.

"Hold fast, men!" Our brigade commander, whom I could hear but spare no glance for, was riding up and down behind the ramparts. "Waste not your fire! Let the guns play upon them!"

Up on the bastions, the cannon were still answering that call, as my heartbeat skipped to mirror the cadence of their firing. The balls, though out of my sight, seemed to soar well above the abatis against which the corpses pressed. Were they striving to avoid the barrier, so as not to clear it for the enemy? Or could the ranks of the dead truly be *so deep*? I had no way of knowing from my post. Only one thing remained certain: The cavalry had *utterly failed.*

I would not long be consumed in such nightmarish wondering, however. As the last panting light infantrymen reached our lines, at once closing the defile behind them with chevaux de frise, the first of the corpses began to break through the front.

They first broke through the forward defile, easily casting aside the hurriedly-placed barricades by the sheer weight of their press. But a miniscule gap had to appear for the first bodies to fall forward into our killing field. At their rear, the heavy smoke of the lights' earlier fire still obscured the enemy's number, so that it seemed they were utterly without end. Rank after rank then poured and trampled atop the first to fall inwards, widening the gap all the further as they went. They were yet two-hundred yards afield from me, but seemed only an arm's reach away.

At last came the time for our lighter guns to join their greater brethren. As they had already been loaded, they needed only to send their balls down the range.

"Gun ready!" Came vitriolic roars from the gunners, both of anger and fear.

Across the whole of the front, our enemy was legion. Near the whole of Stowlham was upon us! Moderate though the market town was, to have all its thousands brought to bear upon a single field seemed utterly overwhelming to our tiny army. Our artillery would not stop them alone.

"Number one gun, *fire!*"

The first of the lighter pieces belched a long trail of sulphurous fumes, soon to join with the cloud above as its iron ball was thrown across the field. It was a sure hit.

How brutal it was, to see the shot tear through the churning wave of meat, rending flesh and bone ere it disappeared deep into the smoky pile of them! It slowed many of the devils, yet could not hope to stem the tide. Where one corpse stumbled, another soon overtook it, and the fortification's gap cleared all the wider. Soon enough, the entire road was flooded by a heavy advancing column.

The second gun had the same effect, as did all the others, which fired rapidly in sequence. Ever did the corpses come on in their usual style, a flailing tangle of limbs trampling one overtop the other, and heedless of the muzzles into which they hurried. Even as the smoke of the guns drifted lazily before us, I could yet see them, unceasing on their broken ankles and severed legs, and crawling through the sea of entrails blown out by every ball. Upon such a gruesome spectacle, even Lieutenant Baker could offer no words of encouragement, and so resumed his place in anticipation of our firing.

Greater and taller rose the mass of bodies piled against the forward abatis. Nothing could deter the animalistic zeal of the devils, spurred as they were by the thundering of our guns and the allure of our flesh. Still, we of the infantry had not received the order to fire; though the light infantry, having retired to the bastions, had recommenced their marksmanship to add their little flecks of lead to the flying iron.

Upon our right, through all the deafening din, there suddenly issued a loud *crack!* A well-timed volley of musketry had erupted from our furthest flank to mark that our battle, at last, had commenced in earnest.

Through all the murky air, made scorching from continual firing, I saw the devils were clearly in greater strength upon our right. In addition to their own steadily encroaching column, only just kept at bay by the gunners of *Torrent*, a far greater threat had come into play. So great a number of devils had piled against the forward abatis that, alongside beginning to *break through* it all, snapping twigs and uprooting stakes through their weight and abandon, they had also managed to clamber *overtop* one another. For every devil thus impaled or entangled upon the abatis, there was suddenly formed a writhing bridge of flesh, crossable for the others behind!

Thus slowly overcoming our defences, the great Fleshtide had begun throwing itself into our field, landing all atop one another on the other side! At first, the mass of them thrashed and wriggled in an appalling orgy of gore, before, one by one, they crawled and stumbled onto unsteady legs and began their charge. First they came in small drips, but quickly rose in intensity as the forward lines were washed away.

With the first of the enemy coming over, the infantry there wasted not a moment in commencing their firings. Thus I saw the musketry blaze all along the right flank, volley after volley, by grand divisions, into the unperturbed foe. Yet while every blast sent great swathes of smoke over the field, utterly obscuring the whole flank, still the gore which pelted the writhing mass did little to slow them.

I was not long in observing the plight of those distant soldiers, however, as the same terror was shortly unleashed upon the whole of the army.

"S-steady on, men!" Conway found his voice at last, though it carried a distinct quiver. "Keep faith, and we'll make it out!"

With those words came the sight all had dreaded. While the enemy's column before us had been somewhat contained by the concentrated fire of our full artillery, there suddenly came from overtop the abatis the first corpse. It dropped like a ponderous sack, and rolled down the short hillside. Then followed the Fleshtide.

Within a blink there were dropping, all along the line, countless devils. They flailed, rolled, and tripped atop one another in great piles before righting themselves, one by one, and rushing towards us like a blood-soaked flood. No words could adequately describe the guttural sickness which threatened to then overtake me. It was only by a miracle I did not faint upon the spot.

"Now, my lads! *Now!*" I heard the boom of our battalion commander's voice, heroic and broken. I could scarcely hear him as he raced down the ranks, ordering us to commence *firing by wings*.

"Very good, sir!" Replied the distant captain in command of our line's left. Then came muffled commands for the whole of his troops to *make ready!* Rapidly pounding drums drowned the shuffling of so many feet and cocking firelocks whilst our own, of the right wing, stood fast. *Present!* Along the line, I saw some two-hundred muskets drop all as one. *Fire!* The left wing blinked from existence as the whole of them were abruptly curtained behind the veil of smoke and fire. The *crack* of so many muskets was piercing sharp, and the volley well delivered. A great wall of lead was thrown against the foe, and all at once, the balls crashed violently into the growing heap of flesh and bone.

Our battalion was not alone in its efforts; the whole of the army had likewise commenced their firings as the devils washed over the forwardmost lines. The great exsanguination had begun.

Chests were burst apart, tendons were severed, and loosed shards of bone cut into those surrounding every blast. To miss so vast an *expanding* target, at even so fair a distance, was nigh impossible. None could invoke discomfort in the *un-Christlike* action of firing upon a living man.

Still, the great exhibition of violence did little to stay the corpses, as unceasingly they crawled out from the pile to rush upon us; nor did it discourage the others which continued to hurl themselves over the rapidly disintegrating abatis. The Fleshtide only grew, as the visage of each devil was rendered all the more frightening by our injury to them.

"*Recover!*" Cried the distant officer and all his underlings the very moment the volley had loosed. Meanwhile, as our leftmost wing proceeded to reload, did Captain Conway spring to action for the right.

"*Make ready!*"

With a flourish of his blade, his nervous command was joined by the drums behind each sub-division. The sergeants and corporals, located all through the line, echoed the order heartily. For my part, still a useless supernumerary, I merely observed the ranks flowing through their places. The front-rank men sank to their knees, cocking their muskets as they dropped, while the centre and rear ranks turned sharp upon their heels, hoisting their pieces aloft.

"*Present!*"

Down the muzzles came, as drums pounded and leaders

roared. Each was perfectly on a level, as its bearer closed his left eye to gaze down his sight, picking out a target once his countryman. Every soldier sweated profusely. Many even noticeably trembled; yet every soul knew his duty, and dared not shirk from it. Their orders were coming too quickly, however, for firing by wings; the left had not yet returned their rammers. The captain's nerves were already showing.

There was but a second of stillness. Two hundred silent prayers, and the foulest swears.

"*Fire!*"

Instantly the triggers were pulled. Again the air quaked, as flints struck steel, pans ignited, and flame shot through their touchholes to set off the vile charges within each barrel. With a sizzling *crack* that set my ears to ringing, each musket lunged forcefully back into the shoulder of its wielder, and the balls soared out to the slaughter. The whole of us were at once engulfed even more thoroughly than before by fumes, so that I could little ascertain the impact of our volley.

"*Recover!*" Conway's voice choked through the haze. "*Prime and load!*"

Again the commands were echoed, and the drums pounded overtop those of the left wing, who were hurriedly concluding their own loading. Below and to my right, as upon the bastions behind, the great and small guns of the artillery continually lobbed shot after shot, whilst the light troops fired continuously in their independent fashion. All of this simultaneous tumult lent the atmosphere a distinct, fiery spirit of alacrity. *So this*, I recall thinking through my sickness, *was battle!* How overwhelming, how perversely *invigorating* and *horrifying* it was, that terrible art of war! Standing transfixed as I was in morbid observation, and nearly faint from fear and fume alike, I found I was intoxicated by it all.

"Well done, lads!" Through my mad reverie, I heard Lieutenant Baker call from beyond the acrid mist. "Get those muzzles up, and we'll send the buggers all to Hell!"

The left wing was then readying to fire their second volley. Behind us, the senior officers rode wildly to and fro upon shrill horses with orders and reports. My eyes watered from the sting of burnt powder, as the scent of decaying meat steadily came to assail us. More orders were shouted, and *so many drums* beat the men's every step as they sprinted through their firings. My ears rang from the relentless thundering of the cannon. I could have screamed, but somehow, against it all, stood fast to my pike.

Our lads upon the right having loaded, the left then fired their second volley. It was more ragged than the first, and to equal ill effect. So on and on did our line continue, as did all of the other battalions of foot, casting thousands of little lead balls down the range so they might pierce and embed themselves into the wickedness of Hell made flesh. Yet as I looked on, still the Fleshtide rolled forth. It crawled, limped, and otherwise struggled with all the swiftness that necrotic muscle would permit. Any one devil, being liberated of a limb or thrown back by the blow of numerous shots, was at once trod underfoot and rolled over by its companions. Thus it seemed the whole of their front assumed a rolling attitude, becoming a literal *wave* of meat bespecked with outstretched arms and biting teeth. Into this swell, we uselessly poured our fire.

It was not long before that wave grew more even-fronted, as greater and greater numbers of the foe came up. By then, our artillery was compelled to expand its field of fire, directing their efforts to wherever the enemy stood thickest. Despite all their extraordinary weariness and heat, still the gunners did not slow, but cast off their coats to work the guns all the harder. Still were great heaps of corpses ploughed down by every shot, but for all our efforts, ever did the Fleshtide advance.

Eventually it came time for the first of the ditches to serve its purpose. The furthest of the devils, unheeding of the ground beneath them as their unblinking eyes fixed firmly upon our smoke-obscured line, tumbled headlong into it as they came. They could not erect themselves within the graves, but disappeared from view, as yet more corpses fell atop them. Initially the pits seemed to have a great effect, capturing all the devils' Forlorn Hope, save those along the road. Not even their fingertips could stretch overtop the ledges as they stifled one another. Many of our men could not resist offering up a hearty cheer, for it seemed in that moment that our plan would succeed, and the foe bested by their own stupidity.

Alas, their enthusiasm was short-lived. As the greater number of devils within the mighty Fleshtide gained their footing and intensified their speed, so, too, was our firing ever slowed from the fouling within our barrels and the weariness gripping our limbs. We stood utterly becalmed by the duplicitous winds, as each volley obscured our vision further to prevent the men from taking proper aim. All while the first pits, which had earlier seemed so impassably deep, were fast becoming filled. Indeed, it seemed that in reality precious few corpses were required to fill the gap, before yet denser portions of the horde came crawling and trampling overtop the pulsating masses. As before, the flesh of their comrades had constructed a writhing bridge over which to cross!

Still the end of the great mob was invisible to us, and the forward line of abatis seemed to our eyes as a hill of all flesh, its original form only occasionally revealed by the mighty blow of a twenty-four pound ball. Though none were cognisant of it at the time, such shots served more to open up our former defences, and permit even *greater* flows of the undead, than they did to destroy them.

Upon such a sight, the men's cheering, swearing, and praying ceased, and they loaded ever-more desperately. A change of tactics was then decided upon, and new orders came down the line, being called by staff officers galloping down the line and attempting to maintain their coolness.

Firing by sub-divisions became our new means, and Captain Conway's dying voice was blessedly given some reprieve as his command concerns shrunk to the fifty or so men before him. From then, as any single group gave fire, so too did the one alongside them prepare to do the same. Thus, the whole of our line erupted into smaller bursts constituting a more rapid fire, and even greater accumulations of smoke.

"Steady on, lads!" The non-commissioned officers urged

the men through their harried action. "Mind yourselves! Cast 'bout as one! Mind your corporals!"

To preserve a semblance of unity among the men through their loading was a challenge. As they were in three ranks, they increasingly jostled one another as they rushed to ram their charges home. Many, I saw, could only with difficulty keep their eyes to the task at hand. Great quantities of powder were spilled from trembling fingers, and cheeks were stained black when men bit too low on their cartridges. One lad's hair was badly singed from an over-primed pan erupting too near to him.

Why were we bothering to fire in volleys at all? The enemy should certainly never have run for fear of them! How stupid, how arrogant, were we in our preparations. As if one might ever, truly prepare for such horrors!

Still I stood queerly transfixed, as if detached from myself in a dream. The sounds all about me seemed muffled then, and I could little fix my eyes upon any one figure. I saw countless opportunities where a *proper* sergeant might have provided some direction to the poor soldiers, so overtaken with their fear. In one place, a man was hurriedly knapping a new edge for his flint, which had gone dull at the worst time. In another, a soldier had unknowingly misfired, and made to double-charge his piece. I stood as if in Bedlam, and was frozen for it.

Commands exploded with spittle from every sub-divisional commander's lips, overlapping one another to join those of the Royal Artillery in a desperate, discordant choir.

Ready!

Recover!

Advance cartridge!

'Sent!

Prime and load!

Fire!

Prick and prime!

Fire! Fire! Fire!

Through it all, the Fleshtide came. The first line of ditches was then totally obscured beneath them, and within moments, they overtook the second line as well. All I saw through the great swirling clouds was exploding flesh and spraying blood. I leaned firmly upon my pike, then planted in the ground, lest I should fall down the ramparts into the waiting abatis below. I could smell naught but sulphur and urine and rot. I could taste *blood.*

"Independent firing, by files!" The new command came roaring from what seemed a half-dozen bellowing mouths, over and over again. "Fire by files! Fire by files!"

What had been a hasty, yet nonetheless orderly mode of shooting then descended into a most total form of chaos. From the regular rush of single volleys, now came a continuous screaming of musketry, as each file relied solely upon themselves to take their shots. What little window there had been for the gunsmoke to spread thin was then utterly lost. The sun above had long been lost beyond the great blanket.

The devils, by then, had surmounted the third row of ditches, which were shallower than those preceding and more easily bested. It seemed their pace only intensified, the nearer they came, for each consecutive layer of holes sat shallower than the last. Our decision to engage the enemy, it seemed, had been made too much in haste, while our enemy was more numerous than any had imagined. Still the fiends were clustered in greatest density along the road, and so as they neared, so too did our lighter guns change their mode of fire.

"Now for the canister! And the grape!" I heard a Royal Artillery officer, standing nobly atop one of his gabions so as to assess the enemy's disposition. He never once lowered his glass as he shouted to his men. "Give them the iron hail, *by God!*"

Those words elicited from the gunners a mightier roar than even the cannon might offer, as the charges were brought up and loaded with a furious haste. Their crews no longer minded the battery's sequence, and as each gun was prepared, its barrel was rolled up and at once belched forth a great cone of whizzing musket balls and smaller shot. These collided into a protruding clump of the dead with gruesome effect, churning up blood-red mud and casting limbs asunder, as corpses were sliced through like wet paper. A sizeable number of bodies were thus rendered to little more than heaps of quivering meat. Under no precept, moral or divine, should so horrendous a sight be pleasing to witness; yet this first indication of effective slaughter elicited a rapturous cheer from our men, pushed already beyond their physical and mental limits. Despite this temporary exhilaration, of course, still the foe came on as the slow were overtaken by the quick in their great, rolling tide.

By then, the ghoulish host's tail could at last be seen, as but a few isolated stragglers came trickling through the forward lines. Still, their numbers appeared insurmountable. They had passed beyond the fourth row of ditches, and left in their wake every pit filled with churning bodies. Many of them were indeed too shallow, allowing some corpses to find their way free of them. There stood but one final row, then, and it the most pathetic of all. I realised, with a slow dawning dread, that the devils would reach our line with two or even three of their number for each living soldier atop the ramparts.

Individual corpses could be seen more clearly then, as through the smoke there rushed farmers and craftsmen, their wives, and even children. Upon the occasional red coat, I tried not to look, lest it convey a soul familiar to me. Blessedly, no single visage was long visible, for with every blink came fresh bursts of blood, brains, and bone which obscured the lot. Few of them could be taken for former humanity, by that point.

With a start, I realised that, through the din of battle, a sound of woeful familiarity had returned to oppress my soul. Over all the shouting and gunfire, snaking its way through the sheer noisiness, I could hear *it.*

The *chattering!*

With their every injured step the noise grew, as teeth worked furiously in gross, mad anticipation of so much flesh.

Fingers snapped and feet slipped clumsily over the soil, long since made slick with entrails. Even as they twisted and turned so erratically in their rush, their eyes never once left those they had hungrily pinned. Not a few, I sensed, had fixed upon *me* for their target, and I felt my skin all prickle and burn. Every tiny, half-healed toothmark dotting my body seemed to cry out, as if yearning for its inflictor to complete what they had started.

"Keep it up, lads!" Baker was yelling still from the firing lines, all its order broke down into pure independence. "Give 'em the hot stuff! Pour it into them!"

Some men wept and trembled as they fired, others screamed with a righteous rage as they peeled off one shot after another into the unceasing foe. Many merely stood and loaded in rhythmic, detached silence. It was as if they were simply on parade, moving through their Exercise like so many automata, and fearfully resigned to whatever the Fates had spun for them. Most were hardly aiming by then, for the foe had come so close, and had pressed themselves into so thick a mark as to be impossible to miss. The greater mass of corpses could not have been more than a few dozen yards away.

Then, from amidst them all, one particularly large body suddenly emerged. One of its arms was nigh on detached, flailing wildly about its side, and it limped heavily on a stumped leg. Its foot had likely been taken off by a rolling roundshot. Yet it had gained something of a stride, and came on more directly, and at greater pace, than the others of its ilk. Half of its jaw had been blown asunder, and having been practically carved open, it was largely bereft of innards.

I found myself transfixed by that particularly mangled abomination. Before long it was nearly upon our trench, and thus incurred a significant degree of our fire. First I saw it take a ball in the shoulder, which blasted a great glob of flesh from its back, and obliged it to stumble pathetically. Another shot came then to its head, scattering its skull and painting the faces of the devils nearest. With a popped eye and gushing brains, still it lumbered forward. The third ball took off its kneecap and, at last, the devil collapsed forward upon the earth, where it was yet vulnerable to more shots, which crashed violently into its pulpy back.

Yet through all my disgust and fear, there came suddenly a clarity of action. Through revelation I had been restored to my self, as I saw precisely what was happening. The men had become transfixed by the nearest creatures, and their refusal to lay still even as they were forced to the ground by so much intensity of fire. Yet for all the attention they paid those nearest, singular bodies, they neglected the greater tide yet bearing down upon them.

"No!" Cried I. Against all inevitability, I at last took to my role of sergeant, lifting my pike to try and knock up the men's aim, away from the fallen devil. "The runners! Shoot at the runners!"

Even had I the time to alter our firing, there stood no utility to it. For just behind that first devil came two more, and upon their heels, the great tide of hundreds still. They trampled over the larger devil, and in their silent rage crashed headlong into the long spikes and thorny brush comprising the abatis of our trench. Their grasping arms were then but feet away, as we finally came face to face with the dead. Amidst their panicked firing the men screamed and cried out for God's alien mercy, and for a moment, all order was lost. All our preparations, all our mighty defences, and all our artillery had failed us.

The enemy had reached our lines, and piled before us in force. Our great nightmare had been realised.

Defending the Ramparts, at Great Cost.

Part the
EIGHTEETH

wherein the devils

break upon the ramparts.

The firſt devil was little thwarted by the stake which impaled it. As the jagged spar burst from its broken back, still the corpse pushed itself down the length in spite of its severed spine. Not once did it avert its gaze from us, as ball after ball futilely dashed its flesh. So too did its countless allies come crashing through our works, their eyes pinned to our men rapt with horror.

How woefully late it was to realise our stupidity in sharpening each stake to a point! For rather than halting the foe altogether, they offered no more than a minor delay. Our only salvation, then, was in the thorny mesh of our abatis, which served more effectively to entangle the devils as they cast themselves amidst it with abandon. Still, for every body thus absorbed, there arose a new bridge over which its comrades might clumsily clamber. The initial trickle of bodies was rapidly thickening, as the great Fleshtide itself drew nigh.

Our men's fire rang terribly true, with the foe mere feet beneath their muzzles. Skull after skull exploded before us, as still the senseless corpses pushed up on their former course. It would not be long ere the trench utterly brimmed with the vile, quivering remnants of once-life.

Many men had erupted into a series of fearful war-cries, so as to overpower their urge to scream. Any veteran of a nobler campaign might boast of the British soldier's disciplined silence upon the field of battle, and how only a single great *huzza* was exclaimed before crashing into the backs of so many Frogs or Doodles. Yet on that day, such discipline was exhibited by the dead alone, whose only song was the mad clicking of their teeth and tramping of broken legs.

Coupled with our extraordinary volume of fire, the height and steepness of our ramparts served to keep the foe at bay much longer than the forward positions. Most of our men had long since forgone the use of their rammers, though the requisite loss of force to their shots were of but minor concern, given the closeness of our range. Before us the foe disintegrated with ease; yet for every devilish body part thus shot apart and scattered amidst the dry brush, still a half-dozen more came on to assume its place. Ever onwards the tide rolled, and soon enough, less and less of our trench and its abatis was at all discernible beneath the mass of shaking flesh. As one fired into them, it soon became impossible to determine which devil their shot would meet.

Cries of "*keep them back!*" and "*push them down!*" fast became our watchwords between so much heathenish swearing as the first broken, necrotic fingers soon began snaking their way over the top of the ramparts. Once we had assumed our relative height to be insurmountable, but it was fast being dwarfed by rising piles of muscle, sinew, skin, and bone. Like Romans crossing over their own *testudo*, the corpses were thus becoming their own siegeworks.

With nary an order given, our front rank rose to stand before the foe, and throw them whence they came. So commenced the brutal employment of bayonets and musket-butts, of bashing heels and cutting swords, and, for myself and the other sergeants, of pikes. One man might spear an oncoming corpse through the neck, ere his file partner would shatter its teeth with his clubbed musket. As the devil thus staggered and tripped back over the shuddering mass, so would its flesh further burst from the quick firing of the rear rank man. Terrified though I was, still I kept my footing, and soon lost count of the teeth I dashed in with the rough heel of my pike. Through the awful din I could not hear the screaming which escaped me as I did so. There was nothing of catharsis in my actions, but only terror. My limbs grew weaker with every thrust, while the Fleshtide came unending.

I was not alone in harbouring such anxiety, for in addition to the wearying effect of such harsh and continuous exertion, so, too, was our foe's true nature at last on intimate display. No longer were the men firing upon a distant, non-descript mass of alien horror, but they loosed their shots and cracked their muskets between the eyes of *once-countrymen*. In one place, I saw an old shepherd, mangled beyond recognisability, being harshly beaten by a boy-soldier who was so young that he could have been the devil's son. Elsewhere, a young maid, already deprived of her throat, met with a well-shot ball which at once hollowed her face. She stumbled back then to be utterly subsumed by the crawling masses. I once forced the heel of my pike through the weak jaw of a mere *child*, who seemed scarce big enough, in his life, to even speak. The little devil had wormed its way betwixt surrounding bodies to grasp for my heels.

In the terrible struggle, there was little time to dwell upon any one morbid observation, yet these bloody visions have nonetheless imprinted firm within my memory; nor might even the great, degenerate *Mars* have endured such disturbing scenes without incurring some deep affliction of the spirit!

Yet through all the horrors, Captain Conway and Lieutenant Baker held firm rein over their sub-divisions. Keeping the non-commissioned officers upon our posts, they sped up and down the lines to direct the men's efforts wherever the foe seemed strongest. The captain seemed to have gleaned comfort from his prayers, as he repeatedly assured the men that God was with us all. Disregarding any risk to himself, he seized upon a devil which had clambered up to assume something of a standing position before our ranks, and with three hearty, breaking strikes of his sword-hilt, spun it quickly about and threw it against another oncomer!

"Keep faith, lads!" He cried fervent prayers between every

blow. "The thousands shall fall at thy side! Nor shall our Lord suffer the pestilence to walk! *Keep faith!*"

These mighty invocations, however, could not alone cease the tide, nor save the gentleman from his fate. There came unnoticed another half-destroyed corpse, sliding through the piled gore to reach over the lip of our ramparts. There it took firm hold around the Captain's ankle, and its pull soon uprooted him to crash hard upon the ground. The mutilated thing, its legs ripped away and innards trailing in its wake, immediately latched upon Conway's legs to try and chew through his thick gaiters.

"Captain!" One brave soldier dropped his firelock to rush to the aid of his kicking officer, trying to wrest him away. Another speared the assailant in its back, firing his musket as he did so. Their efforts were quickly disrupted, however, as the first devil was soon joined by two others, and they piled atop Conway to pull and bite at whatever they might reach in their terrible tug-of-war. Like Spartans for their Leonidas, man after man broke his ranks to bash at the corpses, and pull at their beloved leader.

"Get them off him! Save the captain!" Cried the soldiers, yet every man clapped on was soon redoubled by the ever greater heap of bodies, which clambered atop one another in frenzy as they gained the ramparts. Captain Conway gave a blood-curdling scream as the first teeth found report beneath his waistcoat. The attempts to save him began to founder, as one would-be rescuer found himself also seized upon! His leg being likewise taken hold of, he soon lost himself, and fell down into the heap. The Fleshtide had become an undulating sea in which he was drowned, as his wretched pleas were stifled under mounds of the frenetic undead. One of his cronies pleaded desperately for aid in rescuing him, yet there was nothing for it; already we could see the results of his being torn apart. If nothing else, the man's terrible end provided the devils with some little distraction from us atop the defences. Otherwise, there was little to stem their slow gain of ground.

On and on the musketry poured into the mass, and the compact soil was doused with vile fluids to render our footing more precarious than ever. Before long a second man slipped upon some brains; a third was snatched about the tails of his coat. For every man likewise hauled down into the trench, many a comrade would throw himself into harm's way to seek his rescue. Yet the barbarities of war were little sympathetic to such nobility, as instead their efforts were met only with further bloodshed. Gradually our ranks were disintegrating. Some few were blessed by the mercifully well-aimed musket shot of a brother, though many more were subjected to the agony of every awful bite, ere their suffering was ended.

I listened in horror to these terrible effects, as poor Captain Conway, feeling every bite, was slowly bled. No man dared visit mercy unto their superior, but focused all of their rapidly depleting energies on combatting his devourers. Through their great struggle, then, there suddenly came a moment when the valiant cries of *"fend them off!"* transformed into a plaintive *"get him away!"* I knew then that the pious gentleman had given up his ghost at last, to serve a new master in death.

Still I found myself little able to concentrate on anything save the unrelenting waves of devilry just before me. Nor could any man long be attentive to the general state of our forces, as our world was ensnared by swirling white smoke and red fire on all sides. Thick as the sulphurous mist was, there mingled among it also thick clouds of black, and soon the stench of burning flesh, to which I had become so disturbingly accustomed, joined with that of ammonial panic and sick. Somewhere down the line, I realised, the abatis must have caught fire. Whether that development would aid or hinder our efforts, I could not know.

Nor did I know how long we stood thus engaged, with every man bashing and shooting into the growing mess of meat and bone before him. Continually it seemed the Fleshtide would seize upon some unfortunate soul and, from the delay in his slaughter, came our opportunity to throw them back anew. We had become engulfed in a cruel, sacrificial stalemate, wherein we traded our blood for time; and as we spent that currency, ever did the Fleshtide come to resemble one singular, horrific entity composed merely of flaring limbs and biting teeth. Indeed, while the sheer *mass* of the devils had first served their ascent of our defences, steadily it began to detract from it, as the teeming horde became entangled upon itself.

In the throes of that chaos, there came a moment that I very nearly knocked Lieutenant Baker, who had since assumed command of our whole grand division, straight into the enemy's midst! He had appeared suddenly through the dense fog of war to grab hold of me, pulling me away from my bashing upon the rampart's edge.

The once-lively officer had a mad glint in his bloodshot eyes, and his face was stained by the acrid air. Through the cacophony of screaming, firing, the thumping of blood in my ears, and the teeming hive of ravenous teeth before us, I could not understand the words he shouted to me. When he spun me about with a wild gesture to the artillery, however, I at once caught his meaning.

Chaos had broken upon the battery. The brutality of the cannon's grape and canister shot had kept the foe longer at bay, and disrupted their mass to a more significant degree, but still the fiends had reached the guns' very muzzles. Through the small openings in their barrier of stacked gabions stretched dozens of grasping, broken limbs. Corpses seared their flesh upon the heated bronze of smoking gun barrels, and as the pieces recoiled from their fire, so, too, did thick layers of peeled skin come with them. As they were then loaded, the cannon were again pushed through the tiny gaps, pressing against the rotting torsos, and thence fired. Every resultant cone of double-canister cleared a disgustingly mighty swathe of flesh, yet still were the gaps hastily re-filled while the guns were loaded once more.

In those moments of relative quiet, as one piece or another was being loaded, numerous devils would find themselves dropping overtop the gabions, just as they were our abatis. Wherever possible these stragglers were then promptly apprehended by a slew of artillerists, and even pulled *back,* away from the working of the guns, to be crudely hacked into pieces with shovels and hammers. For every subsequent delay in the firings, however, increasing numbers of devils were finding such chances to worm through the gunports, and over the gabion wall. Ere I took heed of it all, the artillery's firing had slowed to a crawl. Indeed, most of the gun crews had resorted to their carbines as they tried to bash away those elements of the horde outside of their firing arc.

The worst vision came, however, not from the battery itself but the narrow defile which stood between it, and us of the infantry. For the devils were piled almost as deep upon the chevaux de frise as they were upon our ramparts, and had already nearly thrown it aside through their weight, as they had before. A little gap had appeared, and corpses thronged through it, widening the wound with every fall. One of the guns, in anticipation of the greater Fleshtide breaking through, was at once wheeled out onto the narrow road. Yet, to fire its double-load of grapeshot and canister would not only bring slaughter to the foe, but destroy the remaining chevaux de frise. Thus the defence came to rely upon a thin line of carbine, shovel, and rammer wielders, for so long as they could hold the line.

"The defile!" I only just heard Lieutenant Baker's shout, "Get some men firing into the defile!"

He did not tarry to see his orders effected, but again hastened down the line to survey the other side of his command. At last, I had no choice but to finally make good on my ill-appointed rank. I was surprised, on attempting a step, to find my legs nearly giving out beneath me. I realised I could scarcely feel them, but there stood no time to worry for my wits, as I forced myself shakily onwards towards some of the rearmost men. Our ranks had, by then, largely fractured. Still, I quickly gained the attention of a half-dozen with a sharp rap on their backs with the blood-soaked end of my pike.

"The defile!" I tried to bark the command as authoritatively as I might, through the hoarseness of my voice. "With me, to the defile!"

My order was evidently effective, as the group followed after me along the works, so quickly as I dared against the crowds, in Indian file. I formed my little command into a ragged line at the ramparts' end, facing to the right in enfilade. The thick smoke and heat of battle were so potent that even the end of the battery before us was fully obscured. The rapid flashing of distant guns and the chilling screams of men were the only indication that we were not alone in our struggle.

My men immediately levelled their pieces and took up firing into the mass below them, which threatened at any moment to turn our flank. The strength of our musketry was of little consequence to them.

The devils continued to press the defences further and further back, as the valiant souls of the Royal Artillery struggled to keep them at bay, without being pulled into the gnawing rows of teeth. Yet all our efforts were for naught, as at last, a large portion of the hastily tied chevaux de frise violently tore apart and collapsed. All at once the built-up wave fell forward atop itself, ever reaching and biting as it went.

"Retire!" One of the Royal Artillery officers screamed unnecessarily. "Go! Behind the gun!"

One man, being near the spill, was caught out by the tide. His compatriots could offer him no charity, but rushed for the gun whilst he was overwhelmed and torn asunder. Thus was joined another of countless martyrs in their brothers' cause, for by the corpses' teeming atop him in greedy bloodthirst, were others able to escape behind the gun. His cone being cleared, the gun captain at once shoved linstock to match, and the gun was fired.

The full blast of double-loaded grape and canister erupted from the barrel with so great a *boom* that my wits were, for a moment, wholly scattered, amidst the harsh ringing which assailed my ears. Again I could little see through the swirling river of thick white fog, though the shot's gruesome results were at once apparent. Still, the delay thus bought was short lived. Through the ocean of seizing limbs and shuddering torsos stumbled in those devils from without the cone of fire, which had been so effectively absorbed by the Fleshtide's forwardmost numbers. The gun having spent its rage, it seemed that nothing remained to stand before them.

Yet as my hearing slowly returned to me, I was awestruck to hear not only the sustained, panicked firing of my troops; for there came a signal from beyond the veil of my sight. The pounding of many drums, and the trilling of fifes. The latter was generally a useless instrument in most martial affairs, but in that instance, represented an extraordinary indication of what was to come. I turned to look behind the artillery, and saw them steadily emerging amidst all the storm of black and white smoke like an unending line of titans before the blaring of the bastion's guns above. First appeared the glinting of their bayonets, poised high in the air above tight, smart rows of ruffling black fur. They came on at the *march march* to within a dozen yards beyond the artillery, whence, after a long shout from their officers, they halted and dressed in a single motion.

"Grenadiers!" A high-pitched cry sang out within the ranks, which in all the haze seemed to extend forever beyond the gun battery. "*Present!*"

The pounding of their drums struck my soul. The artillerymen began to drop or flee, as the two-ranked grenadiers all lowered their firelocks in unison. The first corpses were again gaining headway through the many holes in the line, and the command came.

"*Fire!*"

The firelocks spat as one in a mighty *crack!* All had aimed true. The frontmost ranks of the Fleshtide, which had become *far* less compact owing to the artillery's fire, was made to stagger and collapse atop one another from the volley's weight. Yet glorious though the display was, it would only *delay* their advance. From my vantage point, I could only just see where the undead horde ended, while still stragglers came on to join the press. For all the slaughter the artillery had wrought, still an extraordinary number remained. Yet our lines had been breached, and the guns had been abandoned! Upon recovering from that volley, surely, I thought, the tide of them would completely overwhelm the poor grenadiers.

What came next horrified me utterly.

"*Charge your, bayonets!*" The shrill cry of their officer came, and silently the grenadiers readied themselves for madness.

"No! *No, you idiots!*" The chastisement choked from my lips, as terror and awe had worked to seal up my throat. I waved my hat about in desperation. There was nothing for it. The grenadiers' next order was a long, ferocious call to *charge!* So with a great *huzza!* rushed on the giants! They met the devils as they fell over the gabions, and stumbled back to their feet within the defile. Surely, I thought, with the inevitable demise of the grenadiers would come the collapse of our flank, and end of us all.

I now admit, with only the heaviest regret, that had my legs possessed the strength to carry me, I likely would have fled for my life upon the spot. If nothing else, I imagined that dying by a corporal's bullet in my back was preferable to the alternative offered by our foes. I found myself rooted to the spot, however, and near collapsing beneath my own weight. The troops I had '*led*' were totally oblivious to my state, caught up as they were with loading, firing, and knocking aside clambering devils.

In a wondrously fateful moment, however, my fears proved unfounded. With a zeal unrivalled by any other in our nation's long and storied history, those brave grenadiers smashed into the undead host. Where so many before had been overpowered and torn asunder, here it was the *dead* who found themselves fast swarmed by the *living!* For within the narrow confines of the defile, and being caught up by so much debris, the devils' narrow frontage had already been thoroughly cut up and their order disrupted. Wherever the fiends were in force, their numbers served more as an impediment, as the desecrated bodies became entangled amidst the limbs and intestines of one another, and the Fleshtide was unable to regain its earlier momentum. This contrasted with the grenadiers who stood fresh, and ready for the fray.

The heavy troops broke into half-platoons as they went, to isolate and destroy pockets of the enemy before they might regain themselves in full. Half of the men would stick the remains of their quarries fast with bayonets, forcing them to the ground. Then, their file partners would commence the gruesome work in knocking out teeth, snapping arms, and hobbling legs.

In this procedure, I realised, the grenadiers were not alone! Following closely behind, then, came up quite a novel force. These were the army's pioniers, who retained the tools of their trade in lieu of musketry, as well as a mighty body of our civilian volunteers, being equally armed! Even a number of farriers from the cavalry stood within that great, irregular line.

Thus, like mad Viking berserkers moreso than British soldiers, these men came with axes, picks, shovels, hangers, and every manner of crude spear one might imagine. They did not shirk from their grisly task, but at once joined the brave grenadiers in *dismembering* the devils! I observed one pionier give a great cry, as he heaved up his axe, to bring it squarely upon the head of an oncoming devil. It was split to the breast as though it were firewood. Another man, seemingly a mere farmer, wielded his pick like a bill hook, and dropped it about a creature's neck to thwart its pouncing upon an artilleryman, who in turn spun about to bash its teeth with a spiking hammer.

Many of our men suffered severe cuts and bites in this action, of course, but nowhere could the dead gain their attritional advantage. Any soldier set upon by the foe was at once joined by a great many of his fellows, and restored safely to his footing, while the encroacher was cut into all the more ferociously.

To my utter amazement, through courage and numbers, this queer breed of heavy brigade fast assumed command of the situation! Indeed, even the largest portion of the foe was being held at bay! With a roaring cheer, the blue-coats soon clapped back on their guns. Bringing up yet more rounds of canister and grape, they thought to conclude their earlier business. Even as the heavy infantry fought all about them, the gunners ran their guns back out of the ports, and, thence pressed against the thick Tide, again were able to fire.

Massive swathes continued to be cut through the enemy's

lines, further clearing the ground and coating all the scene with thick red globs. Every shot thus offered more time for our men to recover themselves and prepare for the next onrush, while the enemy only broke apart all the further. Even for the gun within the defile, it was soon taken up and pushed right unto the melee's edge, where a great wall of soldiers and polearmed civilians alike stood against the tangled Fleshtide.

"Clear the way! Fire!" With another cheer, all those corpses which had filled in the mouth of the defile were again cleared. Our men all became coated in the gun's vile effects, while spears of shattered bone flew out to join with the iron hail in cutting through the foe

There was no shortage of hot work to be done, and the guns were loaded and fired as quickly as possible. Between every shot, the grenadiers and their fellows would step up to fire, stab, and bash at any foes then appearing, whether through the gaps in the gabion walls, or in the defile itself.

Thus, against every odd, the oozing gap in our line was plugged! With every well-placed musket shot, every swing of an axe, and every blast of the iron hail, the Fleshtide found itself more thoroughly disrupted and disintegrated. Beyond the gabions and along the lane, enormous heaps of devilish flesh soon laid useless, mercilessly shredded to so many pieces.

The army had avoided disaster, but our battle was not yet won. Along the line of our ramparts, whence I stood, a different image was to be had. There, our forces were still embroiled in struggle, and growing severely wearied from continuously hammering and batting at a rush which seemed only to grow. In some places, the devils had gained a foothold, and so they stood atop the ramparts in substantial numbers, kept from raking down the lines only by the points of bayonets. Wherever one devil claimed a place atop the works, so it was followed by another, as they scaled their fascines of flesh.

Our men continued to slip and fall in the rising mire of gore, only to be pulled into the trench and swarmed upon. Bandsmen ran ammunition and water to the men as quickly as they could, whilst our drummers had abandoned their signals, turning instead to their little swords in aid of the effort. The air still teemed with the shrieks of men and the booms of musketry and cannon fire.

We might have collapsed entirely, were it not for the grenadiers' fellow flankers. For to our rear there suddenly sounded, like horns about Jericho, a great whistle blast. Unbeknownst to me, the light infantrymen had been ordered down from the bastion, and from the smoke they dashed like mad bloodhounds; not merely with bayonets and clubbed muskets, but many a shovel from atop the bastion, and even mallets and spiking hammers *'liberated'* from the heavy artillery!

There must have numbered many an old Indian fighter among them, for on their rush up to the embankment there resounded savage war-hoops; and like savages, the bobs crashed upon the daemonic foe with ferocity, to throw them back into the trench before us. At once our beleaguered fighters found themselves restored to full vigour, and redoubled their efforts. Our fire intensified, and where the enemy had gained a foothold, soon they were being outflanked and forced back again.

"Come on, sergeant!" Called an officer of the lights to me, with sabre in hand and a mad smirk on his lips. He rushed past me to swipe into the clambering, tangled masses along the ramparts. "Show them what for!"

I knew not how to feel in that moment, so utterly alien to me was the prospect of victory. Though I could hardly see past those men immediately about me, I could tell that the devils remaining upon the field itself were ever lessening, while those upon our lines were either so badly injured as to be incapable of meaningful movement, or were fast becoming so! With the arrival of our fresh troops, all their advantage atop us in fear and exhaustion had gone!

I could take no *joy* in the moment, but in a dark sense of righteous *fury*, I too found myself restored. My vision and sense had returned, and again I could recognise the world about me. So tightening my grip around my pike, and lifting my head, I strode the few steps to the front anew. Alongside my brothers, I recommenced the day's foul work, cracking into devil after devil to miserably haul itself too near. In the absence of such crawlers, I turned my polearm about to sink it into the heaps, further severing tendons and splitting bones in the process.

In that final moment of macabre glory, I heard, through my vicious cries, yet a *third* instrument joined to the beautiful song of slaughter: a *bugle*!

"The cavalry!" Called a fellow down the line. "Mind the cavalry!"

From the left, there suddenly came a great column of our horse, rushing down the field along our lines! Regulars charged with yeomen and volunteers alike in myriad uniforms and armament. Wherever a straggler came to join the ever-weakening Fleshtide against our lines, it was soon crushed beneath many dozens and hundreds of hard-pounding hooves. Sabres flashed and carbines fired into the backs of the Tide. Not a few corpses, suddenly befuddled by the appearance of life at their rear, attempted to extricate themselves from that Tide and strike at the cavalry. Yet the force and density of horseflesh was too great for their individual efforts, and the devils found themselves easily thrown aside, and likewise ground into pulpy messes underhoof.

The great pack before us was thus lessened even further, and it was with ever-greater ease that the nearest corpses were thrown back into the trench. As the whole of them were further deconstructed, fresher bodies, having been totally buried beneath their swarming compatriots prior, were suddenly exposed to our full fire and unable to right themselves for an assault. Great cheering erupted from among our ranks, as we again gained the height over our helpless opponents. Not even I could help but join in that elation.

Before the artillery, our situation was more promising still, for the guns had so thoroughly destroyed the foe that only a very few stragglers remained. Again the guns ceased their fire on the horsemen's appearance, and the grenadiers and auxiliaries set about finishing the job of hacking the enemy to ribbons. The cavalry likewise made quick work of the few bodies beyond the infantry's reach. Naturally, however, the work of the guns had not *yet* concluded.

"Worm out those rounds!" I heard their exhausted commander cry out joyfully, wiping his blackened face with a rag. "Load them with roundshot! Bring up the roundshot!"

Two of the guns were quickly loaded, and with a mighty escort of axe-men and grenadiers accompanying them, the artillerists took up their towlines. Thus, knocking aside any twitching limbs or torsos which remained yet in their path, were the guns rolled out into the very field itself!

As the cavalry passed our line, the little cannon were wheeled into place with great alacrity, to face in enfilade down the trench. Only the occasional straggling corpse had taken notice of their movement, and they were quickly dispatched. At once, the artillery's intention was evident. With a shuddering sigh I withdrew my pike, and took a step backwards. My hands trembled as I rose them to cover my ears. So too was I joined by many of my comrades.

"Number one gun! *Fire!*"

The cannon belched forth its vile charge. The iron ball cut down the trench, slicing bodies clear in two as it went before planting itself firmly into the jellied mess.

"Number two! *Fire!*"

The second round produced like effect, cleaving through the wretched, pitiful masses like a great scythe. Never before could any man have felt such relief, or cheered in such euphoria to be thus doused with splashing blood. It was a horrendous sight, and beautiful.

As the cavalry came to a distant about-wheel to again ride through the few stragglers, and the artillery repeated its artistry down the trench, we of the infantry had little to do but shoot occasionally into the pit whenever some more robust devil appeared. Somewhere in the midst of this, I sank to my knees, and though my eyes had long since grown numb to tears, I felt the great pull of weeping on my heart. It was a great labour to catch my breath; nor was I alone in being so affected.

Our business, I thought, had been concluded most miraculously. Looking all about me, I saw not a single man whose face was not thickly coated in *guts and black powder.* Yet, as the terrible fog of war began steadily to lift about us, I realised with terror that still the din of war was sounding.

To our left, and all the way down to the river where General Hawkins' Brigade stood, the hideous imagery of Hell vanquished only repeated. Many sections of the line had evidently been more cruelly used up than ourselves, but still, the conflict there was rapidly coming to its conclusion. Upon the army's right flank, however, a different and more terrible scenario had manifested.

Just beyond the farmhouse upon our centre, still the field lay utterly obscured by smoke and fire. There continued the roar of artillery, and the great guns of our central bastion had been turned upon a parallel line of fire. The rightmost bastion was totally beclouded, and invisible beyond the peppering red tails of gunfire. Musketry rattled incessantly to accompany a chorus of so much pain; nor were all these terrible signs constrained to the field before our works, but extended *behind* the fortifications.

I could already see many men from Hawkins' Brigade being formed up beneath the ramparts; the fellows hardly had time to collect themselves, ere they were dashed off for further action. Our own brigade commander then appeared, and speeding down the lines of his battalions, waved wildly as he shouted orders.

The Battle of Stowlham was far from over.

The Collapse of the Right Flank.

Part the

NINETEENTH

wherein the right flank collapſes.

"Sergeants! Reform this line!" Lieutenant Baker's voice, rough and ragged, reached my ears before I saw him emerge from the crowd, clutching his bloodied arm. Still, it seemed he embraced his sad promotion to our commanding officer. "Count off the men, all of them, into a single sub-division. Inspect their arms, and for the love of *God*, take some water, all of you! I suspect we won't be here long."

The other officers of our battalion, and those of the grenadiers and light infantry, likewise began to bring their survivors together. It seemed two of our sergeants had been lost in the struggle, and so again I was made to earn my post. Though I found my wits frozen in confusion and dread at the prospect of re-entering the fray, the same was true of most of the men, who were gripped by a stunned sheepishness. The greatest challenge I faced, then, was merely in securing the men's attention. Many were simply staring, wide-eyed and aimless, into the pit before them; others refused to look upon it, instead wearily cradling their heads and breathing heavily. What remained of the Fleshtide below us shook and convulsed as if it were a great pit of worms festering about an open tomb. Its stench blended awfully with the sulphurous powder and acidic bile.

I found I could not calm my shaking hands, which had worsened to become of significant debilitation. Even my attempt to handle my canteen was a struggle, though the splash of water upon my face was certainly not unwelcome. I was compelled to grip my pike exceedingly firmly, and with both hands, in order to keep them under some measure of control. Once more, I was not alone in my grievance, as many a man turned to his fellow for assistance in such menial tasks as reaching his water, or tallying the cartridges in his pouch. Our ammunition was all but depleted, of course, and we had no opportunity to scavenge our fallen, as they lay strewn below. Their eyes, loosely set in broken faces, seemed to study our every move in disdain and *scorn*.

The colonel's bandsmen were busy rushing cartridges and newly filled canteens to us, and were assisted in the task by civilian volunteers. Many of the women and children were at once eager to return to us, and assist in such efforts, but they were frightened away from the pits of slaughter with warning shouts. Some particularly stubborn women were even forced back to the camp by threat of the bayonet, for the men could not abide their proximity to the grisly spectacle.

"Oh God!" I heard a man crying as I passed through our newly-forming ranks. "I cannot see! W-why can't I *see?*"

The man had collapsed amid his comrades, and by his appearance, he spoke truly. One of our corporals was at his side, and, in an effort to calm him, slowly poured water over his face. It ran down his cheeks in pure black; just as the baptismal waters of that little church in Stowlham had down mine. This cleansing of the poor wretch's filth was ineffective at restoring his vision; still, not a man questioned the veracity of his claim. Regrettably, however, there stood no time to bring our casualty to the surgeon - if the surgeon remained at all - for upon being formed, our summons arrived at once.

Having received his own orders, our colonel soon appeared. Though in contrast to his men he was unbesmirched by blood and grime, still the lordly gentleman was haggard in his saddle. His hair was matted with sweat, and there was a perceptible pain in his voice as he trotted below the ramparts.

"Look at you all! *Look at you*, my brave boys! How *wonderfully* you have stood!"

Other officers of the general staff rode to-and-fro behind him, noticeably panicked, as reports were carried up and down the line. Their anxiety alone made it clear our situation was dire. Our colonel was fighting to keep back his tears, and one could barely hear his shouting over the mess of other voices, drums, whistles, and bugles that sounded as battalion by battalion all our forces were countermarched, at speed, unto the right flank.

"I am so sorry," the colonel continued, "but I must ask more of you! General Tomlinson has called upon us! Our countrymen stand against the tide, and they *bleed*, gentlemen! They wonder, shall they bleed alone?"

He gave a great flourish of his sword towards the distant flank, as the column of General Hawkins' men rushed behind him. Many of our men offered a hearty, guttural cheer in spite of all their weariness and trepidation. They cheered out of hatred of the foe, and the intoxication of slaughter, just as much from the desire to save their countrymen. I laboured to catch my breath and master my shaking, which only intensified with the colonels' every word. I had thought myself safe, for a time! I had dared to dream that victory had been won, and even that I had earned an ill-deserved salvation. Now I was again to be cast into the fire. I could but wonder at the Divine's cruelty in justice, and came near to screaming in madness whilst the others cheered in glory.

"Then march, my brave soldiers! March, and show the host of Hell what Britons are made of!" Concluding his militant speech, the colonel spun his horse about, which reared in a melodramatic display of heroism.

The whole of our battalion, save those men too wounded to even walk, promptly dashed down the rear of the embankment. Many moved with such haste that the corporals and other sergeants had to censure them, and restore the line's dressing, as we formed beneath the works. Under Lieutenant Baker's command, then, the remnants of the late Captain Conway's old grand division were wheeled to the left. In a dazed surprise, I found my legs somehow complying to the motion. Subsequently, we became the head of our battalion's column, and commenced at once our *quick march* along the line. Before us proceeded the great battery of artillery, which had likewise wheeled out their guns, and before them, the heavy, composite brigade of grenadiers and their axe-wielding counterparts. The light infantry had long since departed us, by then, upon some orders of their own.

Lieutenant Baker marched before me then, ignoring a painful limp as best he could, while the colonel and his staff trotted to our head. From the brief glimpse I managed of his face, our commander bore an anxiety even worse than his earlier, teary speech had betrayed. While atop his horse he had a clearer view of the fate which waited ahead of us, we on foot could hardly see beyond the men to our immediate front. We could only hear the world into which we marched; filled with isolated and desperate firings, the panicked calls of martial instruments, and so much screaming - not merely of men, but of horses. *So* many horses, I realised, that the cavalry must have been caught out.

These sounds only intensified as we marched on, and I saw that all our ramparts had been reduced to skeletal guards of militia and walking wounded. They presided in uneasy watch over the shivering pit before them, occasionally firing into it or stabbing at a solitary climber. It seemed that Tomlinson, wherever he was, was hurling every battalion available to him straight into the maw of slaughter. Yet to what effect?

New orders came from the front, as the aide de camp Captain Russell galloped from officer to officer, shouting complex manoeuvres so rapidly, they would have been indiscernible to any save the acutest of military minds. As the officer vanished behind us to continue his rounds, I noted his horse was different from the one he had earlier ridden, and one of his arms had gone limp.

"Grenadiers!" The same shrill cry pealed out from ahead. "At the half step! March!"

The heavy troops at once reduced their pace to a curt shuffle, their shoes creating an audible *tramp-tramp-tramp*ing as they went. On receiving orders of their own shortly thereafter, the artillery hastened to reposition their guns towards the right of the grenadiers.

"Battalion!" Our colonel looked back over his shoulder and roared, his fears only somewhat dwarfed by the grim necessity of action. "From column, into line! To the right oblique, *march march!*"

Many an unwitting groan and grunt was elicited as we limping, wearied, and injured troops redoubled our pace, advancing upon an angle. Any concerns for keeping step had long since been discarded, as it was everything the men could do to keep a semblance of their dress. Still, on I went with them, cursing my every footfall in the process. *How*, I pondered, could I possibly repeat the same folly which had so frequently and indiscriminately brought about such untold suffering? Not merely my own, but that of so many others! Had the right flank truly gone, as all seemed to indicate, then how might we scattered remnants hold any hope of victory? Why were we not in flight down the roads, so fast as our legs might carry us? I could scarcely fathom the answer, but knew that I deserved no less than the full measure of whatever lay before me; I could not again abandon those better men beside me, who raged against fate and died upon their feet. I feared my end, but would do nothing to escape it. Still I know not whether I exhibited the noblest of courage, or the most degenerative of cowardice, in that contradictory position.

Thus we charged past the little farmstead, which *had* been the army's centre, and made to form upon the right of the grenadiers and the artillery. On reaching our place, we too went to the half step, as the remainder of our battalion came up into line.

As we thus formed our front, at last we bore witness to the nightmarish scenes before us. In such a moment, a sergeant of quality might have offered some comfort to his men, but I could little conceive of any such rousing words. Rather I came again to near total collapse, and stumbled as the wind was stolen from me. Indeed, all the line seemed to recoil at the revelation, but still on we went.

The right flank had gone. From the desecrated ramparts to our left, and stretching for more than a hundred yards towards the not-so-distant camp, the area was naught but bloody slush. At the centre, our most distant bastion stood like Vesuvius coated in flowing, thick smoke. There hundreds of men held in a final stand, as a great horde tried futilely to scale its muddy slopes.

Most men, however, stood with no such elevated vantage. Across the field, they stood in small clusters of several dozen each, all back-to-back, with bayonets thrust outwards as gradually they succumbed to the hundreds of devils surrounding. In one spot stood the desecrated remnants of a line, its mud-coated Colours standing limp and forgotten, stabbed into the earth, at its centre. Indeed, many sets of Colours laid throughout the field, tattered and crushed under innumerable heels and only recognisable in little splashes of yellow, white, or blue scattered amidst sickeningly omnipresent red. The ensigns, who had once proudly carried them to their end, having tragically forsaken their sacred charges upon their necrotic rebirths.

Indeed, many of the corpses racing and staggering across the field, spoiled for their choice of slaughter, wore regimentals. Cavalry and foot, great officers and lowly private soldiers - all were joined with the undead foe to bite and claw at their former comrades and cronies with mindless abandon.

Some way off to our right, General Hawkins' Brigade had formed at a perpendicular angle to our own, while to their right, still more troops came. They included the larger portion of civilians and militia, as well as a strong contingent of sailors and marines, to accompany the walking wounded and other survivors of the slaughter which lay before us. To a man they proved an extraordinary credit to their nation, as they advanced to seal the gaps of our lines, and once again confront the foe which had earlier done them so much harm. Their hearts stood stalwart and resolute, where those of lesser men would have long faltered.

Above our heads, the heavy guns of the centre bastion still fired into the chaos, and heavy balls irregularly landed wherever the foe stood most thickly concentrated. This necessity served to make the scene even more grisly, as, whether known to the artillerists or not, the balls cut through many a noble last stand, de-limbing the living and dead alike; nor were they long alone in committing the sin of *fratricide*.

As we came to a ragged halt, perhaps no more than seventy yards from the slaughter, sizable swathes of devils were already aware of our presence. Our only consolation was that they descended upon us not as a mighty Fleshtide, but only in irregular clumps after their prior slaughters had concluded.

"Battalion! *Ready!*"

No time was wasted in dressing the ranks, nor in offering warning to those living souls still positioned across our front. To our left and right, other units had already begun to fire.

" *'Sent!*"

My mouth worked, yet I could not echo the command. I saw nothing but a lone drummer, scarcely more than a child, screaming horrifically amidst a sea of bodies; the drum at his side was caked in bloody muck. A former officer was in the process of ripping out his throat.

" *Fire!*"

Our line erupted in a ragged volley, joining the fire of those about us. The artillery, also, had unleashed a mighty wave of canister and grape through the crowds before us. The command to *load* was barely audible, but not a man required it. A great many corpses were aware of us then, and there would be but a moment before they were all upon us. I knew not whether we had delivered some mercy to the poor drummer, as the field had again become obscured to us for all the smoke of our massive volley.

The change then to independent firing required no orders, for the men loaded and shot their muskets as quickly as they were able. There stood no time for such niceties as *coordination* or even *aiming*, nor could any man manage to fire more than twice, ere the creatures were already crashing into our ranks.

The first of them tore through the smoke at a running pace, falling into every step astonishingly quickly, as the larger portion of its stomach dragged behind it. With its full weight, it crashed into the waiting bayonets of three men upon our front rank, who stood with their muskets braced far ahead of them, as they had been instructed.

"Stand fast!" Called Lieutenant Baker as the men struggled beneath the press. The other ranks immediately pummeled the corpse's face with their musket butts, and stabbed its arms with their bayonets. "Stand, damn you, stand!"

The one devil was soon joined by many others, each streaming out of the mist to forcefully collide with our line. Through the rattle of musketry and my own clouding eyes, I could not see far beyond me, but could only level my pike in transfixed terror as I waited for the first of them to appear before me. There lay to my right a great gap, at least two men wide, between myself and the next sub-division. They, too, were being rapidly overtaken. Even the waking nightmare of Stowlham had never paralysed me so, as I could but stand and wait for the unseen terror. I only caught a fleeting glimpse of the artillerymen as they took up their guns and ran with all haste to our rear. Whether they merely fled in good order, or had been ordered back to the second line, I could not know.

I was more conscious than ever of the blood thumping in my ears and pumping through my veins, as again I felt my bowels go watery from anticipation. All about me came shrill screaming and deafening firing, whilst across the line corpses continued piling deep against bayonets. Though I cannot say how I thus stood, there eventually came an abrupt, telltale *bump* as a devil impaled itself upon my polearm. The startling motion threw me aback somewhat, and I planted the butt of the pike in the soil beneath my feet. I could hardly see the pale and bloody creature that reached for me, as I emitted a scream like that of a child.

"Keep ranks! *By God*, I'll shoot you myself!" To my side I saw a corporal catching hold of a young soldier who sought to run. A fist collided with the boy's face, and he was thrown back into the ranks. He had already dropped his Bess on his flight; he was defenceless against the devil that crashed into him, setting them both to the ground.

Already our ranks had begun to contort to the verge of breaking. It took but one man's falling, whether from the pressing of the horde or from a crawling devil's bite, for a gap to open through which the greater tide could flow. Every fellow then slaughtered promptly arose as one of the enemy, and so ensured our demise.

I did not see it coming, but another body suddenly slammed into my right side and sent me falling into the ranks of my comrades, dropping my pike as I went. Whether it was a devil or a living man, merely tripped up himself, I did not know. I found myself suddenly laying between rows of heavy shoes, which trampled all upon my body and face as finally the ranks gave way to flee. Another body landed hard atop me, and I could feel the sharp pierce of teeth along my leg and on my hand, some even peeling at the thin skin upon my scalp, as my hat had been thrown aside. Again there came a heavy weight from above, and then I could see nothing. I could hardly breathe, and, struggling to open my mouth, it filled at once with coppery blood. I became torturously aware of the flesh below my eye being fiercely pulled back, and scratched by a cold, long nail.

I had been isolated from all the world, with only my excruciating pain, and a prayer it might soon cease; and thus had so many of my brothers, abandoned in the shadowy corners of desecrated Stowlham, met their ends. As I laid beneath the vile heap, through my panic came the thought that, perhaps, my long-deserved fate had finally been won.

My physical pains had steadily begun to wane, and I imagined myself in a prologue to the great *nothingness* of death, when through the fading layers of my remaining awareness, I was arrested by an immovable fear of the eternal torment that must surely await. Through all that had come to pass, and even as my *mortal* pains became fully numb, still I found myself wanting upon the precipice. There was no peace in my acceptance of the end, but sorrow unimaginable. Perhaps I wailed there, pathetically pinned beneath my mangled, biting killers, or perhaps I lay in timid silence. I know not, for I could hear nothing.

The last sensation I *can* recall was a sudden, fierce *shudder* of some kind, which raked through all the flesh which lay about me. To accompany it came a fierce pain in my shoulder, as if a large shard of metal had swiftly punctured me, and which served to momentarily clear my dying mind of fog, and intensify my horror. In the shot's immediate wake came a second great shudder, which swept over me in an undulous wave. A series of sharp blows, like so many hammers upon my flesh, followed all about my body. The pain overrode my every thought, and it was only then that I was pulled from wretched sensation.

My final thought was that I had, at last, been detached from the mortal coil.

The Horrors of Victory.

Part the
TWENTIETH

wherein the author
is faved from the heap.

The world to which I awoke was dark and suffocating. It reeked of burning flesh, and though I could feel but little, my pain lingered as a reminder of what I had endured. I was, for a time, certain that I had perished, and been deemed wanting at my final judgement. My mind faded in and out of scant awareness as visions of past horrors played upon me. I might have sworn, for a time, that I sat in a crowded little pub in Wiltshire, listening to Bennett laugh over some story long forgotten. Then I was stood in ranks, listening to Captain Lawrence offer some news that left me frightened and confused. He was interrupted by the sharp *crack* of a lash upon poor John's back, and I wondered after the reason for my friend's abuse. I heard screaming, and weeping, and the clicking of teeth as I stood alone in an alley. A corpse was before me, bearing first the face of Sergeant Percy, then of Corporal White, and of Richards, and Bennett. It seemed to shift and sway endlessly in a horrible display of lost humanity. With a cry of rage and terror I thrust forward old Bess, suddenly manifested in my arms, just as the devil's face became that of John.

I gasped suddenly, as I felt the tip of the blade pierce my own side.

~ 313 ~

"Cor!" A voice exclaimed from high above me.

A small beam of light had appeared near my eye, penetrating the great heap of human meat atop me. My throat burned as I coughed, and I was unable to move my mouth away from whatever pliable gore sat just before it. In the throes of my pain, I knew then that I lived.

"What's that?" A second voice joined the first. It seemed at once harried and exhausted. "Did you find one?"

"I don't know." Replied the first. "I swear, one of 'em just made a noise!"

"What? They don't make any noise, they jus-"

"Hel..." I could barely whisper the word. Every dragging breath was a Herculean effort, and I felt near to fainting. Yet my effort prompted the men above me to quiet. So, I tried again.

"*Help...*" My second plea yielded a better result, as the second man fathomed my plight at once.

"Hell!" Exclaimed he. "You bleeding idiot, you've stuck a live one! Come on, help me with this!"

At once the great weight atop me lessened, as with a low *schlick*ing noise, pieces of mangled corpses were pulled and thrown from the pile. The little light before me thus burst into a great, blinding stream as the final chunk of leaky torso was hauled from me. Though it pained me to do so, I could breathe again.

"He *is* alive!" I heard someone exclaim in equal parts shock and disgust. "Go and fetch the sergeant! Quickly!"

As my eyes acclimated to the light I could just make out one soldier, presumably the one who had 'stuck' me, as he darted off, calling to his superior. The other man, who wore a cloth about his face in guard against foul humours, tossed aside his firelock to stoop down and pull me from the muck. With a loud grunt, he lifted me up about my shoulders and managed to wrench me slowly free. Through my ragged choking I could not help but wail, as the feeling in my leg then returned as an extraordinary pain, as if it were being pulled apart.

I was not alone in my shock, for as I cleared the pile of bodies, my rescuer suddenly fell aback with a cruel expletive. Summoning what meagre strength I yet retained, I rose my head and looked at my legs, where I found my gaze returned to me!

The head had been crudely half-severed, and dragged a useless portion of torso alongside itself. Its teeth were latched firm onto the flesh of my calf. My pain joined with the terrible sight to make me feel faint, though I had not the strength to attempt shaking it free.

After a moment of utter confusion, my rescuer again took up his firelock and, gesturing to several of his equally-horrified fellows, enlisted their aid in removing the '*impediment*'. With a firm-placed shoe upon what remained of the creature's scalp, and an innovative use of his bayonet, he soon gained some little leverage over it, as to pry me free. The half-devil was shoved aside, chomping against the bayonet all the while, until it was further *dismantled* by the liberal application of a musket butt. When at last the work was concluded, the man, wiping his brow, looked to me as if I were a great anomaly.

It was then that a sergeant arrived on the scene, and, had I possessed adequate cognisance for it, I should have been surprised to recognise him.

"Christ." Sergeant Morse loomed above me, studying my wretched state with disgust. Behind him, I saw all the sky was darkened by tall plumes of black. "You found him in the pile?"

"Yes, sergeant. Just now, I did." The soldier seemed unsure if he should be proud or frightened.

"Right. Go and tell the captain we found his...favourite. You two, cross your firelocks for a stretcher."

Soon enough, I felt capable hands grab all about me. Gentle though they tried to be in the operation, my vision again blurred with pain. I whimpered pitifully as they lifted and sat me, uneasily, atop the weapons. My world was spinning rapidly, and my stomach had succumbed to a woeful queasiness. Were it not for a man to my rear, keeping me upright, I would have toppled over. It was only as my senses began to settle, then, that I could blink through my condition and better comprehend my wretchedness. I believe I was in even greater disbelief at my survival than my discoverers were.

The hole in my side from the bayonet, which after cutting through so much rotting meat had pierced my coat and opened a small gutter in me, was nothing to the greater corruption then infesting my being. I looked with horror to my hands, and saw how the flesh on one had been stripped, as though sanded off, from its back. I could not move my black fingers, and knew not whether their hue was owing to blood loss, or to the utter thickness of cruor which coated me from the pile. On my other hand, I lacked a finger outright. My legs were even more distressing to look upon, so thoroughly mangled had one of them become. Shattered bone was exposed to the air, while the state of the muscle about it was so poor, that to see my foot still connected at all was a surprise. Judging by the expressions of the men with me, I was certain my face had suffered similar disfigurement. I found I was able to breathe only with substantial effort, and I even realised that I could see from only one eye. Nor were my injuries limited to those inflicted by the foe.

Upon my shoulder, where I had earlier sensed some kind of impact, there was a messily large hole torn both in my coat and in the flesh beneath it. It was not the sort of injury to be made by the teeth of a witless corpse, but was instead from a ball. Whether by musketry or canister shot, I knew not, but were it a mere few inches to the side, it would surely have burst my skull. Across my body and in my clothes stood evidence of more shots having broken upon me; some had made a significant mess of my flesh, while others had merely skipped along my coat in a manner hardly perceptible. Had providence seen fit to nudge any one ball ever so slightly, I should certainly have perished.

It was only then that I realised *how* I had been spared my deserved fate, and I wondered if it might be possible for Providence to be denied its intent; for of all the flesh under which I had earlier lain, a sizeable portion of it had been *calm.* Indeed, within the little hollow from whence I had been extracted, two men laid *perfectly* placed so as to shield me from the worst of the fire. Were it not for their presence, I surely would have been slaughtered by either the writhing devils just behind them, or the heavy gunfire that had broken and slowed within their bodies.

Again, the preservation of my foul being had been secured by the unwitting sacrifices of better men. I could avert my eyes from their empty faces only with difficulty, and to this day, they remain branded in my sight alongside all my former comrades. As ill as I had felt before, my uneasiness at such a revelation was redoubled, and a terrible, weeping moan of the deepest melancholy escaped my lips. I lacked even the strength to cry.

So, too, did I then understand what transpired after my departure from the battle. In its heat, I had not noticed the forces that came up to our rear. Perhaps they were the light infantry, or some dragoons, alongside the artillery. On the collapse of our line, they had evidently unleashed their full fury upon our former place. Indeed, I would later learn how *little* they had waited before opening fire on us; nor were they the only men, on that awful day, to offer what has since been hailed by the pamphleteers as *The King's Mercy.* Exceedingly few, if any, could depart the battlefield of Stowlham with both their life and their honour intact, or with their mind untouched. Should any person claim otherwise, I brand them a *liar* of the cruellest sort.

With my place atop the crossed arms secured, my carriers then bore me across the *'field of glory'.* They were slow going, owing less to my precarious state than to the fear I might at any moment succumb and turn against them. I realised that the man behind me was not meant to offer me comfort, as he kept me upright by means of a ported musket laid across my back, but for the security of his fellows. Should my head have even *dipped* too low, I knew I would at once be pushed from my little 'palanquin' and dismembered. Of course, I could not blame them for such a precaution, though I questioned how I might have been treated if I had not worn the finer scarlet of of a sergeant, or earned so unfortunate a title as '*Captain Penn's favourite*'.

As I surveyed the ground about me through bouts of irregular consciousness, I wondered whether many private men, likewise badly wounded, had simply been skewered to save the effort, and risk, of their care.

Indeed, a scene of Boschian immolation unfolded all around me, the likes of which might never be comprehended save by those unfortunate enough to have borne it witness.

My eyes were first drawn to the great plumes of black smoke, and the massive piles of wriggling flesh beneath them. Teams of men hauled *wheelbarrows* laden with meat to the pyres. Others, stripped of their coats, shovelled them into the inferno. Within the towering flames limbs still grasped desperately as they curled like dead insects; their flexing muscles melted, and their eyes, which peered ever unblinking out at the labourers, oozed like boils.

The men were not alone in their efforts, as I saw also many women carrying gore-soaked abatis and tinder to keep the piles burning strong. Evidently, the men's former sentimentality for the gentler sex had since evaporated, given the service's newfound exigency. Just as before in Stowlham, great heaps of ash rained from the sky to singe the cloths each worker wore tightly about the face. No one dared look upon the fires as they worked, owing to the severe heat, horror, and shame.

Supplying the great pyres was an extraordinary exercise in crude butchery. All across the field lay pieces of devils, many still crawling. They were set upon by roving teams of musketmen, pioniers, and the brave men of our civilian corps. With firelocks and bayonets, swords and axes, picks and shovels, they bashed and beat the yet-reaching devils into finer pulps before they were shovelled unceremoniously into the wheelbarrows. Here, too, the women of our army did not baulk from their duty. They solemnly assisted the men with whatever crude weapon they could procure. As they had not exerted themselves in the battle, they frequently proved *more* capable of wielding the axes and shovels, with which they split apart the bodies.

Beyond the ramparts, though I could scarcely see it through the right flank's defiles, an even more *vigorous* butchery carried on. Many of the devils within the trenches had been buried beneath their fallen comrades, so that entire platoons stood ready to fire as remains were shovelled away. Then there were the many pits, all down the field, wherein so many devils had tumbled. Ranks of men stood to either side of those ready-made graves, firing volley after volley into their depths. Some creative artillerists had even managed to direct their cannon into them.

As our senior officers coordinated these terrible efforts, they likewise seemed to grapple with retaining their sanity, let alone to preserve some modicum of decorum. With handkerchiefs pressed tightly to their faces, they directed the wheelbarrows to one pyre or the next, and arranged the separation of the devils from the innocents. Through all the madness and confusion, I noticed that precious few of those noble generals, colonels, and majors were mounted.

Most horses, it seemed, were unwilling to approach the field where so many of their kind lay gored and twitching. Not only did the subsequent lack of wagons make even harder the army's labours, but the presence of so much half-risen horseflesh was also a unique difficulty. While those particular bodies were unable to rise, and thus posed little *threat*, their sheer weight made their dismemberment and hauling away both a difficult and heartbreaking task. Not a few cavalrymen were sat upon their knees, so near to the horses as they dared, and clutching an axe or shovel. They wept profusely as they summoned the necessary courage to proceed with the tiresome dismemberment of their old friends.

Indeed, for all the army, such was the most tragic part of their gruesome work; for while hacking up the remains of strangers was affecting enough, the majority of flesh upon that, the rightmost portion of the line, bore instead the faces of comrades and cronies. Men and women alike shuddered in equal sorrow and disgust whilst they worked, and seemed frequently incapable of carrying on unless they regularly detached, for a time, and buried their faces into a compassionate shoulder. The chaplains of our various regiments hurried to and fro, attempting to offer up prayers for the dead. They were overwhelmed and confused about how best to do so. The bodies were so thoroughly rent, that little remained over which to pray save featureless heaps. One bleary-eyed chaplain's hand *bled* with how tightly he clutched his crucifix. He stood, transfixed, a short distance from a wailing widow who embraced the meagre remains of a soldier. Her clothing was stained with his blood, as she held tight the headless, quivering torso and screamed her throat raw. How she had identified her former lover, I could not begin to guess.

Perhaps it most aptly speaks to the nature of the Hellscape, that its most *normal* scene was what is usually a battle's most tragic. For of all the deceased, there laid many largely intact, and *unmoving* in their death. As these glorious dead were discovered, they were arranged in a long, singular line some ways distant from the field. They would be buried there away from the others, so that they might be granted a measure of dignity. I shuddered as I realised how near I had come to joining their number, while some darker part of me *yearned* to do so still.

"Oh, praise God!" There came a sudden and unusual outcry of joy from my side, and clenching my jaw through my pain, I turned my head to see old Captain Penn running towards me as quickly as his weary, yet miraculously unscathed, limbs could carry him. "How happy I am to see you alive, old boy!"

He moved first to take my hand, but retracted it on seeing the state of my injury. Instead, he urged my bearers to make greater haste.

"Worry not," he tried to impart some comfort, sounding more to me like a *peer* than a superior, "for I shall see you with a surgeon the *moment* we arrive. I'll ensure that old Tomlinson makes good on his promise, too, eh?"

I was neither able nor willing to reply. Penn walked with a smile across his weathered face, perhaps to offer me some consolation, however minute. His optimism was queer, even *unnatural,* in such environs. In the mire of my feeling, and through my mounting pains, I felt a hatred for my patron rise in my breast. How could he be so at *ease?* How could he yet stand, so unmarred, so healthy, so very *alive,* and not loathe himself for it? My hatefulness owed more to envy, than righteousness.

"It's an awful business, this." He sighed. "But we must count our blessings. No battle is without its cost, and ours was one well paid. After all, 'tis better to weep in victory than in defeat. Oh, dear boy, how happy I am to see you alive!"

Still, I could not return the sentiment. To paint all that had transpired as a *'victory'* was sickeningly discomfiting to me. Nothing beyond Penn's own infuriating optimism felt anything at all like the triumphalist glory I had long ago envisioned, for that word. Had I known this feeling of *victory* in happier times, I should never have sought it.

We eventually came to the field hospital, where every indication of battle was on brutal display. Amid collapsed tentage and blood-covered wagons, atop which men had evidently clambered in their final stands, stood the converted old barn. It had stood strong through the battle, but became a horrific place all its own in the aftermath.

Men and women sprinted in every direction with buckets of bloody water and rags, as our wounded poured in from the front. Casualties were sprawled about in various states of injury in long lines down the structure's side, and sitting against short-cut tree stumps where a pretty copse of trees had once stood. Given the battle's scale, it seemed there were too few of them. The surgeons nonetheless had plenty to attend, as evidenced by the miserable pleas and wails which echoed through the barn's wide-open doors.

Within, despite all I have previously described, I bore witness to the *most* affecting and distressing of sights. Alongside the customary post-battle bustle of a military hospital, there was *another* presence. The seamen and marines of HMS *Torrent,* I saw, had been designated the most unhappy task on that unhappy day, nor did the *necessity* of it lessen its *woe.*

It was first made apparent to me when I saw several of the

sailors hastily hauling a man out of the hospital doors. The poor fellow had lost an arm, was utterly delirious from a substantial loss of blood, and had evidently been deemed by the surgeon as unlikely to survive. Under normal circumstances, such a man might be given whatever comfort was feasible to see him off with dignity to his end. Yet now, considering the new risk any wounded presented upon their deaths, no such luxuries were to be had. His expiring body was dragged behind the barn, and mere seconds thereafter, a pistol shot pierced the rank air. I soon realised this shot was not the only one, either. All around the camp, and in the surrounding fields, echoed frequent such '*mercies*', all loosed into persons deemed hopeless. Indeed, I later learned that most of these unfortunate men would never even *see* a surgeon, before some *boatswain's mate*, or some-such nonsensical rank, decided they were not worth the risk.

Where precisely stood the line between succumbing to a devil's injury, or to the blade of a surgeon, it seemed few were patient enough to determine.

I realised, then, that the rows of amassed wounded sat not of their own volition, but under the guard of stern-faced marines. They were men well accustomed to dealing with *mutiny*, and to enforcing the absolute will even of tyrant sea captains. Unpleased as they were with their task, they gave no indication of shirking, should one of the wounded attempt to flee. They would instead wait, upon threat of being shot, for the attentions of either a surgeon...or the 'cleanup crews'. Given the severe bruising on one fellow's face, it seemed one of the wounded had already tried to argue the case.

I was once more certain that, had I not worn a sergeant's uniform and been with Captain Penn, I would certainly have shared the same ignoble fate.

"Please, no...*please, God, no, please...*" As I was carried into the barn, we passed by two hard-faced seamen dragging another man. His face was so thoroughly bashed and marred, and his open wounds from bites and musketry so severe, that no question of his death remained. His whimpered pleas were scarcely audible, as his mouth had been torn asunder, and he had clearly been administered a copious quantity of either liquor or laudanum to try and ease his mind before the end. It had not done the trick, for still he was painfully awake, and all his fears remained. He implored his executioners and his God for mercy. Neither abided him.

"Don't worry, lad, I'm with you." Whispered Captain Penn to me as we entered the hospital. From my earlier disdain of the man, I found myself swelling to a desperate adoration. Just as was the man we had passed, I was petrified. "I'm with you."

Within stood much the same horror as without. Along the walls and in the stalls were rows of cots, the likes of which John had once rested upon. Near every one was occupied, and the moment a bed was taken, so, too, did some seamen employ their unique art and tie thick ropes across the patient's chest and legs. Marines and naval officers patrolled between the hospital lanes like *reapers*, armed with loaded sea-service muskets and pistols, frequently getting in the way of nurses as they did so. The moment a surgeon lost faith in his abilities, he had only to make a brief gesture, and his charge was at once carried off outside.

Otherwise, those elements more familiar to hardened veterans were likewise on display in their full, terrible 'glory'. Surgeons resembled butchers, with blood splattered about their aprons and drenching their arms to the elbow, as they dug deep into writhing, wailing bodies with the vicious tools of their trade. Amputated limbs were promptly tossed into piles, and for one odd moment, I was surprised to see that they were all quite still. So accustomed to abnormality had my mind become, that I found the *natural* state of them to be *unnatural!*

"Ho, there! I have a sergeant here, needing your attention!" Penn approached a surgeon who had finished extracting a ball from a subaltern upon his table. The young gentleman's face had gone pale, and he sweated profusely, but through his terrible surgery he had retained his full awareness. As the surgeon concluded sewing up his wound, he even made to depart the table without any aid from a nurse, so desperate he was to demonstrate his good health.

The surgeon cast me, and my leg, but a brief glance.

"No." He was blunt, but men of his profession are rarely afforded the luxury of sentimentality. It was a miracle that I was not seized upon on the spot by the sailors. Indeed, I may have been, were it not for Captain Penn and my bearers.

"This man is-" Penn began, before being fiercely interrupted by the surgeon.

"He is too far gone already! I have another *officer* to attend. Now get out of my way!"

Yet Captain Penn, in a rare exhibition of intensity, was not to be overruled.

"This man is the sole survivor of Stowlham!" His exclamation was verging on frantic. "He has the favour of General Tomlinson himself, and is to be *commissioned* upon His Lordship's *own expense*! I come to you under his *direct* authority; you *will* see to this man, damn you!"

The lie was an exceptional stretch of Penn's authority. I later learned, however, that the officer in question was but triflingly hurt, hardly even warranting the surgeon's attention. Thus, the surgeon not daring to risk the approbation of the general, offered a low grumble of assent. The first patient being cleared, and still carried off to be tied down despite his weak-voiced protest, I was laid upon the already-bloody table.

My removal from the crude seat of crossed muskets brought me a searing pain, and for a brief moment, I lost all sense of my surroundings. I blinked hard, and found myself lying flat, with the surgeon and Penn just above me. The three soldiers, still captive to the gruesome duty of my care, pressed me hard upon the table. Penn said something to me, but I could not hear him, and soon felt the tourniquet being tightened about my leg. Then a strip of thin leather was shoved between my teeth; I had no time to comprehend the horror of my next experience, ere it cut into me.

The force of my bite could have shattered my teeth, as the circular blade sliced deftly about my leg. I screamed through the leather and involuntarily writhed up against my holders.

Captain Penn continued speaking, but I could think of naught save the torturous pain, which was many measures worse than even the devils' sharpest teeth. My skin being sliced in a perfect circle, the surgeon tarried not a moment before heaving it back, so that he would have surplus to later sew shut. Had I harboured any doubts as to my earlier longing for death, they vanished in that moment. For a brief moment, I forgot even my guilt and melancholia. Such an ironic mercy, however, was not long to last. Just before I slipped again out of awareness, and the saw cut into my bone, I opened my blurred eyes to see their visages before me.

Captain Lawrence loomed where once Penn had stood, pale of flesh and impossibly wide-eyed. Lieutenant Farwell and Ensign Tell stood at his elbows, their skin torn and their uniforms smeared with gore. Corporal White was behind them. Then Richards, and Bennett, and all the others of my old company. The unnamed woman stood amidst the crowd, and behind them all, in the corner where I had watched him perish, John lingered silent and forgotten.

The spirits did not urge me to faith. They did not proffer comfort, or call to me, but beheld me with vile, disgusted contempt. I wailed for them all before slipping once more from the world.

The Author, upon the End of the Vile Campaign.

Part the
TWENTY-FIRST

wherein the author's narrative concludes.

It was the erratic pacing of a fly across my face that bore me again to unwelcome cognisance. I could not disturb its patrol, for I found that my body and all my limbs were tightly bound to one of the cots by a series of ropes and thick belts. I could but choke on stagnant air, hot with humanity, as I gasped for breath through the taut bandages covering my face and neck.

For some time I lay in silence, stunned by the Divine's cruelty in suffering me to live. From the corner of my eye, I saw other men similarly bound upon cots and tables, or fixed to the soil by means of tent-stakes. Little groups of sentries moved solemnly between us, their lamps glowing vividly in the dark as they passed them over our faces. Every pained squint or low moan seemed to relieve the guards, though not every casualty provided such.

On several occasions there would come a commotion from somewhere in the barn. A sentry would utter a sudden profanity, or yelp in surprise. These disruptions were always accompanied by a far more harrowing sound: the rapid, desperate *clicking* of teeth.

The first time this occurred, I was at once consumed by panic, and futilely wrested against my binds. I was not alone,

~ 327 ~

and could hear men all about the room crying for help and attempting to liberate themselves. Then came the sudden, thunderous report of a pistol shot, as dusty chips of wood rained down upon us.

"Silence!" A voice roared, and was sharply obeyed. There was a fleeting moment of quiet, save for the risen man's bound and chattering jaw. Then followed the same, gravelly voice. "Mr Willows, to your duty." The tramping of feet then preceded the low, wet thudding of axes and cutlasses sinking into flesh. After this first incident, the men remained silent.

Thus proceeded the *dispatching* of any man whom the Fates, in all their foul methods, had deemed lost to the devils 'teeth, rather than to a surgeon's sawblade. Throughout that awful first night, though he was not visible to me, I listened to the man beside me. Through all his weeping, his prayers were scarce perceptible.

Still, not all that transpired during my gradual recovery was so cruel. As the morning light dimly encroached through the wooden slats, our nurses returned with water and soothing words. They roamed between us in the dark, for always were the great doors of the barn kept sealed tight, with the heaviest guard just outside, lest circumstances should too quickly '*turn*' within. Despite their best efforts to disguise it, there was a palpable fear behind the pity in the kindly women's eyes. The ladle which one lowered to my lips trembled terribly, even as my meagre, choking sips of its contents betrayed my status among the living. The nurses were succeeded, then, by the surgeons and their mates, who inspected our injuries and sometimes loosened the binds of those men whose conditions had improved. I was thus restored to some movement, being gradually shifted into a sitting position so my bandaging could be replaced. Yet in spite of the *physical* relief this afforded me, there was little comfort to be found from what I saw of myself.

The absence of my leg did not surprise me. Nor could I find it in my dead spirit to be alarmed when the bandage covering my injured eye was removed, and I found it blind to the candle the surgeon's mate held close to it. The round stump at the end of my wrist, however, I had less expected. I could have *sworn* I had tapped my blackened fingers against my side in the night. One might consider it fortunate that my other hand remained, though less one finger, and an even greater fortune still that the surgeon found no obvious signs of infection as he sniffed and prodded at my wounds. Nonetheless, I was informed that I would carry some remnants of a ball in my side for the rest of my days.

"Should ever *Aesculapius* have blessed a patient," the bleary-eyed surgeon had muttered, almost in *annoyance*, as he replaced the bandage protecting my dead eye, "it must be you." His words were accentuated by another distant pistol shot, as if to emphasise my 'luck'. He swore at me as I flinched at the shot, forcing him to make an adjustment.

Any *'blessings'* notwithstanding, my binds were then replaced, though not so severely as before. I was fed a small breakfast of navy-style burgoo by another nurse, which aided mightily in restoring my health. I even managed a brief slumber, ere the naval detachment 'guarding' us was relieved by men of the cavalry. Thus was I reunited at last with my old comrade, Sergeant Wilkes, who had preserved through it all. A few tiny puncture wounds on his hand, in a distinct round pattern, seemed the worst that he'd endured in his country's cause. *Physically*, at the least.

Despite the cruelties which his duty that day demanded, he was kind enough to sit by me for some time. He ensured I received sufficient care from the nurses, and informed me of the events which had transpired outside.

"General Tomlinson is marched off with most of the army. He intends to bombard whatever remains of it, before marching in. The artillerymen counted the bodies up as best they could, and say there won't be more than a hundred of the *things* left inside. They're probably all caught up in debris, anyways. Seems like half the men will go in with torches and axes, rather than firelocks."

"You've been left behind, then?" Even in my woeful condition, my voice was surprisingly clear. I was unsure what to make of the news. I felt myself rather numb to the world, as if I were merely observing myself and Wilkes from a distance. As he considered my query, I watched the old dragoon's face scrunch.

"Not just for...*this.*" He gestured crudely about the barn as he explained. "Tomlinson ordered all the civilians to disband, but many of them haven't gone far."

The sergeant sighed and rubbed at his temples before he proceeded. He seemed more exhausted than I had ever seen him, even more so than when we had escaped Stowlham.

"Christ, but there are a lot of *sick wretches* in the world. I'd never have thought so many would be keen to pick at the remains of their own countrymen." His disgust, even anger, was almost frightening in its severity. "The students are the worst. They always come in the night, and conspire to distract us. They dive into the charnel pits looking for any finger still moving, or a beating heart to poke at. I almost shot one last night, but some up-jumped cornet stopped me. Went off on some nonsense about 'enough blood being spilt'. Damned idiot. There's too many out there for us to keep away, without making any *examples.* We still haven't finished burning the bodies, and all the pissing pyres are too large! Whenever the fires die, we shovel off the top layers, and the rest underneath is still red raw and moving. Meanwhile, we've only a tenth of the men as we had yesterday. Even the bleeding officers are stealing away with 'treasures', and we can't well *do anythi-*"

He caught himself before his voice could rise further. His face had gone red. While he was not alone in his feeling, it was unwise to express qualms about his officers so publicly. His next words, then, were uttered so quietly that I was unsure if he intended them to be heard even by myself. Nonetheless, they have remained with me in a most harrowing manner.

"Bastards, *all of them.* They don't know what they're dealing with..."

In the following days, my strength was steadily renewed. This was in spite of the decay which yet surrounded me, and the yet darker state of my mind. I found I was largely unable to sleep, for soon after Wilkes departed my side, there commenced the continuous thunder roll of artillery from distant Stowlham. One could only hope that no refugees were still huddled within the town's burnt carcass, and moreover, that no concealed horde would leap from its shadows and lay further waste upon the troops. I was kept awake not by the noise of the guns, but by my fear they might *abruptly cease.* I wondered, too, after Captain Penn and his men, and how they might fare in the town.

Others in my condition were less fortunate than myself. Several inevitably perished in the night, though a lessening fraction were thence hatefully restored. Eventually, circumstances were deemed sufficiently 'controlled' that the great doors of the barn were at last opened. The onrush of new air, though it was dusty and dry, was a blissful respite, as it swept away so much foulness. Later that very day, my binds were loosened for the final time, and I was granted my liberty.

As I departed the hospital, I again found myself to be a stranger. The few men who moved about the field appeared to me hollow, and humourless. None bore the elation of victory, but seemed nearly drowned beneath the affecting and unceasing nature of their newly required labours; nor did it seem that shovelling piles of gore, and turning over the pyres, was half so demanding upon their souls as keeping guard over the badly wounded. As slowly and awkwardly I limped away with the crooked rod I had been given for a cane, I tried not to heed the great stockpile of wood and hay beside the barn, to be laid across it at a moment's notice should the need arise, nor the two cannon which waited, double-loaded, before its entrance.

After my departure, I passed a brief time aimlessly wandering about the remains of the camp. I had no billets, and in my condition, no expectation of returning to my regiment. The charnel field burned still, and its keepers had gone black from ash and smoke.

Eventually, a new stranger found me, introducing himself as an aide of General Tomlinson. He made no effort to hide his dismissive disgust as he brought me before a small group of the remaining, overworked officers. Thence was his Lordship's promise to me fulfilled, as I was made to sign my mark and offer my oath, being transformed from a lowly soldier to a *gentleman officer* forevermore. I would never take up my Colours, being an invalid, but was just as soon discharged on half-pay. Then, being given a bit of money to secure my passage home, I was sent away from the army to live out my remaining days as I might.

Of that remainder, there is near nothing of interest, or necessity, to account.

Captain Penn, for all my censures of him, proved himself a dear friend in support of my cause. This was most beneficial in his reference, and his patronage, in securing me permanent billets. Indeed, owing to his incessant generosity, there should stand a significant sum of monies to my name. This sum, and indeed *all* my few worldly possessions, to speak plainly, are owed to *him* and *no others.* I fear my extraordinary debt to the gentleman, both financial and otherwise, may never be repaid. He was the sole man to bear me some comfort in the many dark days since Stowlham, and I may but hope for his success on the trials currently endured by our army in Flanders. I shall never meet him again. So, too, for Sergeant Wilkes, who likewise is still in service abroad.

It is likewise to Captain Penn that I owe my recent connection with the printer, Mr Klemmer, who has so generously agreed to print my narrative in full, and with all my little *'sketches'*, for those few subscribers who may deem it of interest.

Indeed, it seems that regardless of our macabre little dalliance, since aptly termed *The Corpse War of* 1793, the ancient heads of Europe yet contest with each other over evidently deeper considerations. For while the dead may have risen in Norfolk, no longer do they roam; but the *French,* having murdered their King, still desecrate all that is holy and march across the Continent with greater alacrity and unity of cause than any mere devil might exhibit. Nor do the British mob derive such pleasure from the murder of their cursedly risen countrymen, and the discomfiting *theological* implications thereof, as they do from our army's more joyous and heroic exploits at the likes of *Famars* and *Valenciennes.* Already, I see my war becoming supplanted in history, save among those most esoteric of natural philosophers. Of the inevitable stream of accounts from the fields of Stowlham, all save the most grossly aggrandising and trifling of them have promptly been dismissed as naught but *useless melancholia*.

As for my own narrative, I harbour little hope of any grand market sweep, nor of it much aiding those learned gentlemen who so incessantly pen letters to me regarding the nature of the risen dead. For such commercial and metaphysical matters alike, I have sparse concern. Rather, I am assured by Mr Klemmer that all my narrative's humble profits shall be directed to the many shamefully impoverished veterans, widows, and orphans of Stowlham, who have been otherwise so forsaken by our '*proud nation*'.

So, too, have I attempted to enumerate all I have seen, heard, and felt in unrepentant detail, though I fear myself frequently wanting in the task of conveying the truly afflictive nature of *The Corpse War*. I do so not to excuse my own cowardices, but to *justify*, and further *glorify*, the greater deeds of my comrades and my friends. They deserved better than to perish alone, afraid, and forgotten. It is in their cause that I have penned this, my crude testament. For myself, I lay no claim to glory.

Thus shall my narrative conclude, upon one final note of suffering.

Of all the horrors I have experienced, still none are so affecting as the spectacle of my own body. I am a corpse yet living, and have entered into grim brotherhood with the devils of my nightmares. My nose is gone, and I have lost an eye, whilst scars riddle my unshaven face. Even with the aid of my cane, I cannot but stumble, haphazard and slow, and frequently awake to find myself fallen to the floor. I regularly attract the curious attention of children, who challenge one another to peer through my window and gaze upon the *creature* that has taken residence on their street. Should ever I turn their way, they flee with shrieks of fear.

The surgeon who declared me blessed, then, was *wrong*. Some vile infection has taken root within me, body and soul. It festers in the stump of my leg, and in my wrist, and slowly contorts my flesh into mottled, stinking rot. I have found myself shivering in the heat, and the clattering of my own teeth has cast me into fits. Consequently I keep always an overlarge fire in my chambers to ward away this sensation, though I should sweat through my shirt and occasionally choke upon its smoke.

I am unable to eat, save the most minute pieces of bread, for my stomach disagrees with anything greater. No longer do I desire meat, for I have learned the scent of cooked humanity. The bottle, then, has alone preserved my cruel existence with sufficient time to tell my tale. So, too, with each passing day do I find myself less able to sleep. Whatever rest I win is invaded at once by visions of snapping devilspawn, and the wroth of spirits. I awake to their screaming, and my own alike, and always I feel their ichorous fluids filling my throat. It mingles with the taste of my own, as I often find myself biting my knuckles so hard as to draw blood.

I have lingered too long upon the mortal coil. Not a day passes in which the words of Captain Lawrence do not echo through my mind. At last I understand his final lesson, and have ascertained my duty. No longer do I fear my end, and I shall go to my punishment as a soldier. Yet my final watchwords derive not from any martial calling.

With what little I possess, I intend to *die with dignity*.

Thou haſt laid me in the loweſt pit:
in a place of darkneſs, and in the deep.

FINIS.

Thank You for Reading

Thank you for reading *The Corpse War of 1793,* my debut novel. I hope that you enjoyed this tale of historical horror, and perhaps even learned something of military life in the eighteenth century.

If so, please consider leaving a rating or review wherever you purchased your copy, or via a site like Goodreads or The StoryGraph. Reviews are extraordinarily helpful for introducing independent works like this to new readers.

About the Author

Brandon Fisichella is a public historian, author, reenactor, and presenter who brings the lived experiences of military history to life. His research is grounded in the memoirs and journals of common soldiers, and aims to represent their world as they would have seen it.

As the director of The Native Oak, he has produced hundreds of video lectures on topics ranging from the long eighteenth century to the world wars, and serves as editor of the book series *Something Like Philosophy: A Symposium of Military Privation and Suffering*. His focus on the harsh realities of warfare and its daily privations informs his fiction and grounds its horror.

Through his commitment to authenticity and respect for the past, he hopes to encourage readers to explore primary sources and better understand the extraordinary stories of ordinary people throughout history.

www.ingramcontent.com/pod-product-compliance
Lightning Source LLC
Chambersburg PA
CBHW031206310726
48969CB00001B/238